Natural Law

Joey W. Hill

NATURAL LAW
An Ellora's Cave Publication, March 2005

Ellora's Cave Publishing, Inc.
1337 Commerce Drive Suite #13
Stow, Ohio 44224

ISBN #1419951653

Other available formats: ISBN MS Reader (LIT), Adobe (PDF), Rocketbook (RB), Mobipocket (PRC) & HTML

Edited by: *Sheri Ross Carucci*
Cover art by: Regina Brytowski

Warning:

The following material contains graphic sexual content meant for mature readers. *Natural Law* has been rated *E-rotic* by a minimum of three independent reviewers.

Ellora's Cave Publishing offers three levels of Romantica™ reading entertainment: S (S-ensuous), E (E-rotic), and X (X-treme).

S-e*nsuous* love scenes are explicit and leave nothing to the imagination.

E-*rotic* love scenes are explicit, leave nothing to the imagination, and are high in volume per the overall word count. In addition, some E-rated titles might contain fantasy material that some readers find objectionable, such as bondage, submission, same sex encounters, forced seductions, etc. E-rated titles are the most graphic titles we carry; it is common, for instance, for an author to use words such as "fucking", "cock", "pussy", etc., within their work of literature.

X-*treme* titles differ from E-rated titles only in plot premise and storyline execution. Unlike E-rated titles, stories designated with the letter X tend to contain controversial subject matter not for the faint of heart.

Also by Joey W. Hill:

Holding the Cards

Making Her Dreams Come True

Enchained

If Wishes Were Horses

Snow Angel

Forgotten Wishes

Virtual Reality

Natural Law

Chapter 1

"It's your first night flying solo. Stay in your comfort zone."

Violet heard Tyler's parting words clearly in her head, but no other part of her was listening as she watched the most beautiful man she'd ever seen make his way through The Zone's Tuesday night crowd.

She chose the adjective deliberately. Handsome or sexy conveyed surface appeal. Beautiful addressed the whole package, inside and out.

This man was big. Over six feet, the broadness in his shoulders was enough to accelerate her heartrate. He was pure male animal. No matter what soap, deodorant or cologne he used, he wouldn't be able to obliterate the scent. He was powerful, a predator, but what made him absolutely irresistible to her, overriding her common sense, was that he was a sexual submissive. An alpha wolf who chose the role of beta in the bedroom, but only for the right woman.

The more seasoned Doms hadn't seen him yet. Thank God that Marguerite, a Mistress who never had a regular partner, preferring to pick up her choice of sub for the night from those available on the floor, had already paired off and was playing in the rentable rooms visible through the club's glass floor. It was one of the perks of The Zone, being able to see down into all the playrooms, unless a darkening screen had been engaged by a particular group of occupants.

Violet preferred smooth, clean-shaven men. Usually. This man had coarse, dark hair on his forearms and soft curls on his head, in a style cut short at the nape. He was mid-forties gray, but his hair had refused to blend, so his mane of white, black and silver invited her touch. She wanted to grip it, tug that firm mouth down to her lips, or better, hold his head between her thighs and see how clever those lips could be.

Violet crossed her legs, and took a sip of her drink. Though every instinct screamed at her to go stake out her territory before some other Dom saw him, she held her seat. Patience was often rewarded, and she'd rather suffer disappointment in anonymity if he was there to meet someone.

He had a straight blade of a nose, and a rugged face. His beard and moustache again upset her familiar preferences, but they were well-groomed. The beard was low on his jaw, just a line of gray and black that followed that strong line to meet the clipped sideburn in front of his ear. She couldn't tell the color of his irises, but if they were gray, she was a goner. The dark length of his eyebrows were straight slashes, perfectly following the shallow curve of his almond shaped eyes, giving an impression of conscious strength, someone dangerous to push.

A lot of subs used the locker rooms to change into role-playing clothing before taking the floor, a clear advertisement of their availability for play, but he wore street clothes, well-fitted jeans and a crisp white shirt tucked into them. The rolled-up sleeves revealed those furred, strong forearms and a pair of beautifully tooled silver cuffs on his wrists. The onyx inlay and scrollwork made them pass as an attractive accessory, but she knew what they were, had zoomed in on them like a hawk from a thousand feet in the sky locating a well-anticipated meal. They broadcast his status as a submissive here in The Zone, one of Tampa's most upscale and private fetish clubs for practitioners of the Dom/sub lifestyle.

Two hundred plus pounds of powerful male desiring to be at the beck and call of a Mistress. Or a Master. She forced herself to consider that, to squelch the scream of denial and disappointment in the possibility. To her, he seemed a little too rugged for the sleek beefed-up types the male Doms preferred. Those muscles were put to some type of active use, versus being sculpted in a gym just for show.

Fuck it. She was going to go for it. She could imagine Tyler shaking his head at her, nursing her singed ego when her male fantasy set her back on her heels, but her pulse was pounding and her hands were damp. This was the one.

She rose from her seat and went hunting.

* * * * *

Mac Nighthorse intended to stake out a good place to do some observation of The Zone's evening crowd, but the scenario under his feet caught his attention. Through the glass floor, in a room appointed like a medieval torture chamber, a girl stripped down to nothing but a silver chain mesh chastity belt had been tied to a rack. Her Dom flogged her, snapping the end of a short braided whip across her stiffened nipples and leaving red marks on the inside of her thighs with pinpoint accuracy. The chastity belt prevented stimulation of the area it covered, but of course that meant that the build to orgasm had been slow and excruciating. Mac had lucked out on timing and got to see the Master's work rewarded.

The girl shuddered, her mouth open on a silent scream of pleasure under soundproof glass. Through the duration of her surrender, her Dom kept up the strike count. Her response, caught by the candlelight illumination of the chamber, glistened down her thighs through the silver chain leg openings of the chastity belt. Moving to her side, her Master released her arms and let her hold him at last, stroking her hair, his face lit with pleasure and devotion.

That expression absorbed Mac, held him there a few moments more than he anticipated. When at last he turned toward his original destination, a quiet corner in the shadows, he found his way unexpectedly and deliberately blocked.

The obstacle had spike-heeled boots that followed her legs like a second skin, so they were as feminine and delicate as the dress she wore. Whereas most Doms preferred black and leather for the strong message they conveyed, this woman had chosen a dress of hunter green velvet. The décolletage was an elegant, low-slung drape that revealed the tops of her breasts and the lace along the edges of the dark green satin bra cups sewn into the dress. The skirt hugged round hips and flared out in a little garnish of slashes just below mid-thigh, giving him a glimpse of the lace tops of her silken thigh-highs beneath the boots.

He had to stop at her face much sooner than he anticipated. She was a woodland fairy, a pixie. With the heels, the top of her head reached his shoulder. She wore a simple silver cross around her neck, and a pair of earrings that were a fall of silver stars. Silver glitter sparkled on her skin over her breasts and sternum.

The raven black hair falling to her waist was not hers, but a beautiful wig that did great things for her small oval face, her skin looking like cream in his coffee in the morning, liquid and smooth. He'd bet those lavender eyes were contacts, but her beauty couldn't be disguised. Whatever her hair and eye color, she was a knockout. Her lips were liquid red and full, just the way he liked them.

The smell of lavender clung to her, with an underpinning of vanilla, and his nose was interested in having him take a tasty bite, even if the rest of his body was being sternly admonished by his mind to stay in check.

She was so delicate, it was hard to believe she was a Dom. But it resonated off her. A less-experienced sub wouldn't know, but he did, from the direct way she met his eyes, assessing him in a manner so potent he found himself fighting the urge to please her by casting his gaze down.

"I have a room below," she said, and it wasn't a request. "I want you down there." She pointed through the glass and he saw the room provisioned like a horse stall, complete with cross ties, bridle bit gags and other equine accoutrements modified for human sexual play.

"I'm nobody's pony, sweetheart," he said, and made to move past her.

"I'm not looking for a pony," she returned. "And I don't recall giving you a choice about it, slave."

She was green. It was obvious from the shift of her eyes, the pulse pounding high in her throat. He could smell her nerves. He bared his teeth in a smile.

"Make me, sugar."

"What does that mean?" Confusion and irritation crossed her features.

"It means I don't go down easy." He flicked an impudent finger under her chin and delighted in watching her eyes narrow in anger. Oh, yeah, she had it in her. His cock stirred, like a dog catching the scent of something interesting crossing his yard. "You've got to prove you can tame me."

He gestured to a table where a young man with an open face sat, bare-chested and in tight pants. "Go practice on Billy over there. He's friendly and eager to please."

"I don't want a cocker spaniel." The pixie reached up, caught her long-nailed fingers in the open collar of his shirt, dug into his flesh. She jerked, bringing him down a few inches, not because he wasn't strong enough to pull back, but because she made it clear she'd take a piece of him with the fabric if he didn't.

At the same moment, he felt the hard length of the riding crop she carried thrust home between the crease of his thigh and the heavy weight of his testicles. She exerted a pressure that was uncomfortable, not painful, but the motion definitely caught his attention.

The violet eyes and black wig hid her true looks, but not the satisfied set of that sinful mouth. The tip of her tongue came out to wet her lips.

"I want the pit bull, the one who runs his yard." Her crop hand slid down to grasp him firmly by the balls, still keeping the prop in the equation so he felt the insistent shove of the weapon as well as the curled clutch of her fingers against his hardening cock. "Get your ass downstairs into that room. And I want this shirt off."

Her eyes were inches from his. The noise in the room faded away and lavender took over his senses. A vibration rippled his nerves, sending a shudder through his body before he could prevent it. She felt it under her touch, he could tell from the surprised triumph in her expression. Her grip eased, her fingertips brushing a light caress over his nipple.

Mac reached up, closed his hand around a wrist as slender and delicate against his strength as blown glass, and he was the one that was shaking.

She could push his limits, despite her inexperience. But that wasn't why he was here.

"You honor me with your attention," he said quietly, meeting her gaze and then lowering his own, following etiquette to convey his respect that she'd won the point. "But I can't attend you tonight, much as I'm already regretting it."

He shifted his grip to her hand, lifted it to his lips, still not raising his lids, not daring to do so. Damn, how had the little minx gotten under his guard? He usually preferred a much more physically intimidating Dom.

Of course, his preferences didn't always dictate his choices. Tonight, despite his best intentions, they were trying to do so.

With the right amount of time, she was one of those who would be a true Mistress, able to break a man down physically and emotionally under her will. He'd already surmised that she chose a sub for more than just the packaging and what that packaging could do for her. Mac wasn't looking for a Mistress who dug that deep. It said something though, that he'd caught her eye. He guessed her to be in her late twenties, early thirties—very early—

but her level glance was an unsettling match for his own maturity.

He brushed his lips over that soft skin, felt the glossy surface of her nails press into his palm, and he didn't want to let go. But he did.

"A good evening to you, Mistress," he murmured. He stepped backward several steps, again observing etiquette, and did not turn his back on her until he was at a respectful distance.

* * * * *

Good Christ, what was that? Violet felt like she'd been hit in the solar plexus with a head butt. Fire slithered over and around her arm, radiating from where his lips had pressed to her knuckles, that moustache tickling her skin. Her fingertips, which had given him that intimate caress inside his shirt, along a nipple that had hardened instantly beneath her touch, were vibrating with need.

She had witnessed interactions between high-powered subs like this one and absolute Masters like Tyler. She had felt weak-kneed watching them, aching for a taste of that supreme Nirvana, a one-on-one interaction where the will of Master and desire of sub melded into an explosive energy of its own, a magical synergy captivating them as well as those watching them.

That power had rolled between her and this sub. She'd seen it in the shift of his eyes, the shudder of that magnificent body. Well, perhaps she'd leave him alone for a few minutes. Or maybe she'd find someone to demonstrate to him just what he was missing.

* * * * *

Mac sat down at the sanctuary of the shadowed corner table. Unfortunately, it placed him directly over the room she had indicated. In a moment, he'd move, but he wanted to regroup and refocus before he made an ass of himself.

"Lord Almighty," he muttered. His eyes couldn't help searching out his pixie in the crowd, and now he got an eyeful of the back of her dress, what there was of it. The lack of fabric showed off the curve of her shoulder blades, a mole just on the inside of one that he'd like to kiss, working his way up to a neck so slender he thought one of his hands could almost encircle it.

Two thin straps of green crisscrossed just below the shoulder blades, and then there was the unimpeded bare slope of skin, all the way down to the dimples above her ass where the low waistband deprived him of viewing more. She was wearing a silver waist chain, and there was a tiny tattoo just above the left side of her hip. From here, squinting, he'd guess it was a tiny lavender flower.

She paused, bending to adjust the fit of one boot. She was in the shadows, but because of his position and the dim light of the wall sconce, he alone got a clear view as that skirt inched up and up, stopping just shy of where he'd be able to see the crotch of the panties she wore, if any.

Oh, that's good, Nighthorse. Really torture yourself.

She straightened, and then looked over her shoulder at him, her eyes sending a "fuck you" challenge that he felt straight to his testicles. He'd bet he could eat that little pussy until she screamed and spoke in tongues. It wasn't a far leap to imagine her crooking her finger at him, pushing his head down there to smell lavender and woman, the musk of a wet, soft cunt with a flavor of vanilla.

"You keep staring at her like that, hon, we're going to have to get the fire hose before the building goes up in flames."

Mac started and focused on the amused face of the waitress now standing at his table, her hip cocked. The discreet gold name tag pinned on her red corset read "Mariah".

"Is she a regular?"

Mariah's lips lifted in a smile. "Something, isn't she? Violet's been mentoring with one of our stronger Doms for about six months, and she came with friends as a voyeur for awhile before that. She knows about everyone in the place now. I won't swear to it, but I think tonight's her first time on her own. You're a bit out of her league, hon, but I suspect not for long. You go easy on her if you're interested, hear? We protect our regulars."

It was a direct warning and one Mac appreciated. He was the newcomer in The Zone tonight, a welcome but unknown quantity, and she'd just informed him that looks wouldn't get him anything but a boot up the ass if he got out of line. She'd delivered it with smooth, inoffensive professionalism and a sexy smile that didn't dilute the message a bit. He didn't mind, because the message meant he'd be looked after too, if he needed it. The Zone had trained their staff well.

In a Dom/sub fetish club, that attitude from management was worth the price of admission, and the intense screening process. The Zone had a hefty membership fee to go with the in-depth background checks. They went to great lengths to protect the identities and wellbeing of the upper middle class and wealthy clientele which could afford and demanded their extra care.

"You got it."

She nodded, gave his wrist a brief caress before she straightened, went to get his drink. Her latex pants, laced up the back, couldn't help but draw his eyes to her great ass and the accessibility of it. He wasn't surprised by the outfit, because clubs often had wait staff employees equally willing to earn money on the side by being someone's rented sub or Dom for the night, where there were no emotional strings that the dating pool hazarded.

Yes, The Zone went the extra mile and then some to anticipate the needs of patrons and protect their privacy. It was a dangerous, ballsy venue for a murderer to cruise for victims, but one had. Not just once, but twice. The person he was looking for was smart, arrogant, and had money. And she was a woman. His gut told him that, even if the evidence collected thus far didn't yet support it.

His gut also told him that she liked the pickings on these grounds and would keep coming back. Particularly if she believed no one had made the connection, that the obsessively discreet nature of The Zone's yuppie clientele had obliterated her tracks.

But one homicide detective had made the connection. Mac just wished he had figured it out when he'd stood over the first body, instead of the second. But then, he hadn't known the first victim personally.

The thought brought back the intensely uncomfortable memory of the meeting he had arranged with his sergeant earlier in the week, the meeting that had led to his presence here tonight, and the much more pleasant chance encounter with a woodland fairy with violet eyes.

Chapter 2

"I've got a meeting with the captain at ten, Mac." Sergeant Darla Rowe took a seat behind her desk and lifted a brow as one of her top people closed her door before taking a seat before her. She straightened, put her hands on her desk, one folded over the other. "What's on your mind, Detective?"

"We found a second body last night," Mac said, forcing himself to sit back in the chair and ignore the painful knot low in his belly. The dead kid he'd just stood over had had a much worse day than he was having, no matter how bad his sergeant's reaction was going to be.

He'd been working in her squad over two years, and he trusted her. She had a level head, an unfathomable patience for bureaucrats, but no tolerance for bullshit, and she was loyal and fair to her people. He was counting heavily on fair, but he was venturing into territory where fair was often drowned by moral reaction.

"Same MO. Mid to late twenties, male. Worked as a stockbroker. Good WASP background, church-goer. He was dressed in a leather thong, dog collar, cuffed spread-eagle to his four-poster bed, dildo up his ass, begging your pardon. Bullet in the base of his skull."

"Detective Ramsey said she thought that the murderer may resent the victim's social standing, might be trying to humiliate them." Rowe nodded. "Have we been able to keep a lid on the press?"

"No leaks on the way the vic was found. We've told them it appears to be a sex crime, bullet to the head, but that's all." Mac lifted a shoulder. "Connie has good instincts, but we're still waiting for the official psych profile, and it doesn't mesh to me. If the perp was trying to humiliate them publicly, I'd think she'd have sent pictures to the paper by now."

"She?"

"Nail scorings on the victim's back suggest it, but they were done with gloves on. We're doing DNA checks. In both cases a caller has contacted one of the parents, told them that they have to come right away because there's an emergency at the victim's home. I think she's revealing the truth about the victim, perhaps re-enacting a similar trauma that happened to her, or something she wants to reveal about herself but never has gotten the chance or the guts to do it. Just amateur analysis, granted, but it smells right."

Darla's eyes narrowed. "'Revealing the truth'?"

"Yes, ma'am. Both men frequented a fetish club called The Zone in Tampa. I had a uniform go down there today, talk to the manager, confirm their memberships with a warrant to pull their specific records. They were very cooperative as soon as they understood their members could be in danger. They'll be a helpful ally. I think our murderess is a practicing sexual Dominant, a Mistress, and she's choosing her victims from The Zone, even if she's not playing with them there. Granted, two victims doesn't establish a definite pattern—"

Rowe sat back, her brows lifted. "But it does give us some lead on her preferred trawling grounds. Excellent work, Detective. Who called the families?"

"A man, both times. Called from a pay phone, but it's suspected from the speech patterns described by the parents that the caller was a drifter or homeless person the perp paid to make the call. Different men, based on the voices described. We're casing the local liquor and convenience stores near the booths to which we traced the calls to see if the store employees remember a homeless person coming in and dropping an unusual amount of money for a bottle of booze in the past forty-eight hours. However, both calls were made from the worst areas of Tampa, so it's likely they've rabbited and we can take our pick of a few thousand drifters."

"So how did you make The Zone connection? Business card for The Zone in their wallets?"

Mac hesitated. "No, ma'am. Both victims were extremely circumspect about their lifestyles. That gels with the reputation of The Zone. The club even provides lockers there for members to keep their paraphernalia, so it's not kept in the home. They don't give out member ID cards. They put your social security number on file and when you come, you enter it into the entry key pad. That's how you get in." He shifted. "I've done a little research."

Sergeant Darla Rowe had seen Mac Nighthorse come out of situations that would give nightmares to the most grizzled veteran. He'd started his career in undercover work, proving himself so adept at deep cover and maintaining the integrity of his personality in that high stress area that they'd kept him in it for over five years. When he'd advanced into public field work, he had quickly obtained his Detective rating, working cases 24/7 to solve murders, armed robberies, kidnappings. She'd listened to wire taps of him breaking up volatile drug deals. A few months ago, he had taken down a Tampa serial killer one-on-one in the cramped quarters of the sewer system when the killer had gone to ground there with an AK-47. Mac had been disarmed, his arm broken during the fight, yet had brought the killer down with nothing but determination and a healthy dose of fury. He didn't freeze, and he wasn't cocky. He was so steady the other guys called him The Oak, not just because of his size, but because of that unflappable demeanor, no matter the circumstances.

At the moment, she was watching the wooden arm of her visitor chair grow slick with nervous sweat from his palm.

"What's on your mind here, Mac?" she asked, pointedly glancing at the damp surface.

He stared at it, then leaned forward and clasped both hands loosely between his splayed knees. It emphasized his broad shoulders, the long columns of his thighs. As usual, Darla sternly forced her gaze off the nice shape of his groin outlined by the dress slacks. Since she was happily married, it was aesthetic appreciation only, but it wasn't exactly professional to be caught eyeing the crotch of one of her detectives. She had often wondered why Mac didn't have a woman in his life, but suddenly she got the feeling she was about to find out why.

"To find her, we're going to need to send someone undercover into The Zone. She's picking up submissives—that's the terminology—and winning their trust, so she's likely already working her next target."

"So we pull in an undercover team."

He shook his head. "That won't work, Sarge. This isn't a seedy adult club where the criminals mix with the thrill seekers. The activity at The Zone is legal, and the clientele is high dollar. This is about sexual gratification, not perversion." He raked a hand through his hair. "It's not the same as the criminal side. To most people in the vanilla world it looks that way, but it's the difference between a murder and a natural death. One is coercion. The other one's about natural law. A cop who doesn't understand that would stand out so clearly he might as well wear his badge pinned on his chest."

Darla sat back. "I'm going to repeat my question, Mac. Why don't you tell me what's going on between the lines here?"

He nodded, looked down at his big hands, laced them together, then he raised his face so he could meet her expression square on. Those silver eyes could freeze a criminal in his tracks or pry the truth out of the most devious snitch. Right now, they looked like they were facing the prospect of a prostate exam with Andre the Giant donning the latex gloves.

"I know those types of clubs, Sarge. I've been part of the D/s scene since I was in my late twenties. I know the language and the people. The Zone isn't my usual haunt. It's out of my income bracket." A light smile touched his lips. "But every club has a certain percentage of new blood running through it, guests of members, prospective members, people who try it out for a couple of months."

"I see." She tapped two fingers on the desk, a meditative gesture that the men and women of her squad recognized as a sign that she was mulling things over in her head. "And if you're made as a cop? You're a little well-established to be doing undercover work again."

"It might not rouse suspicion, particularly if it's obvious I'm part of the scene. A cop who plays in those waters would have as much interest in concealing his or her profession as any of the well-heeled clientele. On the floor, most use assumed or first names only. The rule is, if you happen to see someone you know on the street, you either pretend you don't know them, or that you met them at a mainstream place, like a bar. That's how I made the connection. I recognized the second victim. He's been at my usual club before, several times, but I knew The Zone was his preferred digs."

He sat back, sliding into the familiarity of the case, trying to ignore that his sergeant's gaze was as intense as a dentist's drill.

"Robert Myers was a submissive. High-powered, but amiable. Enjoyed having a woman dominate him with soft bondage techniques, but he could accommodate a higher level. I don't know if that figures into the MO or if there's some other aspect of the two men that was the attraction. The psych profile may help me figure that part out. I'm expecting that in a couple of days. Neither of them would have let his dick overrule good sense. Again, begging your pardon, ma'am. They would have spent some time with the murderess before taking her into their homes, or they would have already known her in the scene."

"Do you have someone on the inside you can use as your initial connection to the place?"

"Not at this point, but I should be able to pick up someone. It's not unusual to connect with someone there for play. Sometimes it sticks for a few days, sometimes just for the night, but by then you get to be a known face."

"How will you bring in your backup?"

He shook his head. "I won't be able to do that in this scenario. Unless they're part of the lifestyle, they would be made as fast as a cop trying to pass himself off as a dope addict. I figure I could keep Consuela—Detective Ramsey—informed of my itinerary and whereabouts through the usual call-in set up."

"You going in as a Dominant or a submissive?"

Mac blinked. "A sub. Makes more sense that way."

"I'm not seeing anyone buying you as someone's whipping boy, Mac. Not with your size and presence."

She watched him lace and unlace his fingers again, lean forward, and felt the shock run down to her toes at the truth she saw in his pained expression.

"It's best I go in under my own preference."

"Well, I'll be damned," she said at last.

Mac surged up from his chair, moved to the corner, restless and establishing some distance. He despised himself for it, but this was likely the most uncomfortable conversation he'd ever had in his life.

Everyone in the D/s lifestyle knew how the vanilla world viewed bondage. Few looked beneath the cheesy porn site depictions to discover the emotions that drove one of the most intense forms of sexual interaction there was. That was why it wasn't revealed or discussed. For most, the concealment came not from shame, but from the simple understanding that it was, in fact, beyond most people's comprehension, like a choice of religion or lifemate.

"You know I'm a good cop, and I've served the squad well. This is my personal life, and as much as you don't want to be hearing this, I sure as hell don't want to be saying it. But those two kids were picked up and are dead because someone in that lifestyle picked them. I'd be breaking my oath to protect and serve if I didn't do what I can, use what I am to help them."

"Sit down, Detective."

Mac clenched his jaw, sat, and deliberately put his hands back on the chair arms.

"Just be quiet and let me think a moment, if you don't mind."

He nodded. He'd lost his mind. Why hadn't he made up a story, a civilian friend who could take him into the scene? He had likely just blown away the rest of his career. But he hadn't made the decision hastily, had given it a great deal of thought since he had stood over Myers's body. If he got into trouble, he needed a fully informed backup, which also meant keeping the sergeant in the loop. He didn't want to think about having to go through this again with Connie, but it would have to be done.

Darla took a paper from her desk, picked up her pen and scribbled on it. Mac leaned forward as she extended it across the desk. He took the paper, looked at it, then at her, confusion on his face.

"That's my pager and cell phone, Mac. You'll use me as your call-in backup. I assume most of your more risky work will be at nightclub hours, so we'll work out a check-in and reporting schedule. I don't get a code on my pager during the arranged times, I send a team looking for you."

He wouldn't have to reveal his secret to his peers. The pain throbbing in his gut eased to a mild case of indigestion.

"I'm still not sure we shouldn't send in an undercover officer."

"It's like I said—"

She shook her head, holding up a hand. "No, I understand. Your logic is sound, but you're vulnerable. You're going into a situation that's personal to you, which means someone can fuck with your head." A slight smile crossed her lips. "Begging your pardon."

"No one else can do it but an insider," he replied, not denying her concern. "This murderer, whoever she is, she'll know. It's the kind of thinking you pick up on from each other, and she'll know someone who's faking it, who isn't true. Look, people not in this lifestyle don't understand it. It's that simple. Some level of resentment, condescension or outright revulsion would come through."

"I trust your judgment. I just want you to be very careful. You hear me? You're one of my best. I don't want to lose you."

Sergeant Darla Rowe didn't dispense compliments liberally. If they brought in Tampa's leading crime lord or busted open a chain of chop shops, the most they'd expect from her would be, "Good job, Detectives. Be sure to have your report on my desk in the morning." Complimenting them with her actions, not words, she busted her ass for them, as long as they were busting their asses for the people of Tampa. Nevertheless, she had chosen this moment to tell him bluntly how she valued him.

Mac had no words for how her response or her direct, steady gaze made him feel, so he rose as he would at the conclusion of any normal briefing. "Yes, ma'am."

A smile flirted around his sergeant's lips.

"What?" he asked, surprised to see her color rise.

Darla gave a little laugh, waved a hand. "I guess I'll just have to live with the images that come into my brain now when you say that." At his blank look, she repeated his words. " 'Yes, ma'am'."

He stared at her in shock, but her tone and countenance were open, honest and teasing, like any cop ribbing another. Familiar ground. Relief flooded his chest like a hot shower at the end of a particularly harrowing collar. He was alive, he'd survived, and he'd done the right thing.

He grinned, albeit cautiously. "Thanks, Sergeant."

"No, no. Don't thank me yet." She rose, retrieved her keys and purse. "After my meeting with the captain, you're taking me out to lunch, Nighthorse. " Now her expression was serious, his boss again.

"We'll pick a place cops don't go, but if I'm going to be your backup, I need to know the language and the scene, so I know what's normal and not. Otherwise, I might send squad cars screaming in after you for the wrong reasons, or worse, ignore something I shouldn't and you end up dead."

"Sarge…" He slid his hands into his slacks. She came around the desk, stood before him. A sturdy, well-dressed woman with an elegant carriage, Darla Rowe had poise and class written all over her, and it came through now.

"Mac," she said firmly. "It's not prurient curiosity. If you'd brought Detective Ramsey in, you would have briefed her in detail. What we talk about stays with me, unless I need it to save your life."

"Or to bring down the perp," he said.

"As I said, you're a good cop." When he opened the door for her, she startled him by raking an appraising gaze over him that damn near caused him to blush. "Of course, some of it *is* prurient curiosity. If there are any outfits you want to model for me so I can better understand—"

Mac choked on a laugh, wished it was appropriate to give her a rib-crushing hug. He suspected she'd knee him in the balls if he tried.

"Now, Sergeant, I think that qualifies as sexual harassment."

"In your dreams, Detective."

Chapter 3

So here he was. He wasn't the murderess's target profile, so it would be unproductive to position himself as bait. Obvious white collar professionals, Rodriguez and Myers also were pretty-boy types of slim build. Hooking up for a few casual nights with a well-connected Dom or two, those who could identify all the Mistress players in The Zone, that would help him to start narrowing down a suspect list.

"Ah, hell."

"Problem, hon?"

The waitress put his drink down on the coaster.

"Yeah, you could say that."

Violet had brushed off his suggestion of the accommodating Billy, and was now in dialogue with a tall, handsome blond with Norse looks and interested blue eyes.

The waitress followed his glance. "Fair's fair, love. You passed her up. Can't be jealous now."

"It's not that." Though he ruefully admitted it could be, because he found he didn't like watching her with someone else at all. What was it about her? She cocked a hip, and the shift of that backside beneath the snug skirt distracted him so that he almost let the waitress get away.

"Hey." He caught her wrist. "The guy she's talking with isn't a regular, is he?"

"I think he's here on a guest membership like you, hon."

"He's bad news. His name is Jonathan Powell, and he was a regular at True Blue. You can call down there. He's a vicious bottom. Likes to play with his Mistress's heads and screw them up. They revoked his membership."

Mariah considered Powell. "I'll tell the manager right away, have him give them a ring. If your story checks out, we'll invite him to leave."

"Good." He rose and she intercepted him, placing a hand on his chest. "Hon, you let us take care of this, okay?"

Mac looked past her, watched Jonathan reach out, touch Violet's waist lightly, just a brush of contact as he spoke to her with properly downcast eyes and deferential expression. His blood temperature ratcheted up about twenty degrees.

"She's green, and there's her pride to think of," he said casually. "I think I can coax her away from him without making a scene, and that will make it easier for your staff to get him out of here before he tries to latch onto someone else."

Mariah studied him with a dubious expression. "Okay, big guy," she relented, stepping out of the way. "But you behave, mind? Doesn't matter what your intentions are, you spill blood in The Zone and you're out. Period. No exceptions."

"Got it. Breaking and gouging okay. Just no blood."

He gave her a wink and moved away, but she watched him a moment, undecided. She wasn't fooled by his charm. Something dangerous was brewing around that one. There was a misconception, sometimes even among new staff, that male subs were shy, non-aggressive wimps who wanted a woman to beat on them. The high-powered ones could be as possessive as any alpha Dom, and though she thought his story would likely check out, he was too focused on little Violet. Green or not, she'd caught his attention.

"Good for you, girl," Mariah murmured. "He's going to be a handful and a half."

She noted how his eyes never left the figure of the pretty Dom in the black wig, the hunger as his gaze covered her naked arms, the nearly bare back in the tight dress she wore. Mariah made a mental note to hang around a bit after shift. If Violet got this hunk of prime real estate downstairs naked, she'd like to see it. Even across a crowded club, the heat between the two of them was enough that she felt it. She'd like to see how it stoked in the furnace of one of the playrooms.

* * * * *

Violet didn't really like Jonathan Powell. He was handsome enough, and smooth, but her mind was on the man who'd just blown her off. It would have been one thing if he'd been cutting. She could have called him an asshole in her mind and nursed her stinging pride with someone like the affable Billy, who had looked after her longingly as she went by his table.

But he'd been so courteous about it, so perfect, and all that had done was raise her desire to have him at her mercy to a level that had all her glands on high alert. She went for Powell because she could tell he was on par with the object of her desire. She wanted her interaction within sight of his table, had made sure he'd been looking when she did that little move with her boot. If she did get him in restraints, she was going to make him beg. It went beyond pride. She had a good sense of humor about her overdeveloped competitive spirit, but this was way more. This was an instant, overpowering craving that had swept over her the moment she saw him and decided she had to have him.

She felt him behind her before he even spoke, knew from the energy pressing against her shoulders that it was him. And because of the frost that abruptly hardened Jonathan Powell's gaze, bringing out a coldness one didn't often see a sub display before a Dom. Definitely a competitor, then. She'd chosen correctly. Her blood heated.

His fingers slid up her spine, starting at the lowest exposed point of her back, which was just barely above the soft dip between her buttocks, and trailed upward, stopping as a light touch between her shoulder blades.

"Mistress," he said softly in her ear. She didn't look at him, tilted her head away. A cold gesture in appearance, but it made the whisper of his breath flow down the side of her neck.

"I believe the lady was already engaged," Powell said. He was trying to remain within the rules of the house, but Violet clearly saw the rage simmering below the surface. He had been strongly interested in her overtures.

Did she want someone who blew her off one minute and was accommodating the next, or someone like Jonathan, who had been interested from the moment she stepped up to him?

And who had given her the creepy crawlies the first time he touched her waist. But that wasn't the point.

"I didn't give you permission to touch me," she said, still not looking at the object of her true interest. But she was not looking at Jonathan, either.

"No, Mistress." His voice drew back, as did his touch, and her skin screamed in protest. His voice lowered to a sensual murmur. "Forgive me."

She turned on her booted heel, effectively dismissing Jonathan for the moment, but she knew he wouldn't move until he was sure he had been relinquished. A good sub would not insult a Mistress by walking away until he had leave to do so.

The big man before her now was just as overwhelming to her senses as he had been ten minutes ago, his scent in her nostrils, flaring them with his heat. The wide expanse of his chest filled her vision, the soft neatly trimmed hair along his strong jaw and those firm lips inviting touch.

"Forgiveness has to be earned," she stated. "So what are you going to do to earn it?"

"Whatever Mistress demands."

Jonathan took a step forward, pressing himself against Violet's back, latching his hand onto her waist. "I think it's time you back off, Mac."

Mac thought how pleasurable it would be to seize that wrist and break the finger bones one by one while Powell screamed for mercy. He glanced at Violet's startled face. Even in a secure environment, it was unsettling to be a woman weighing less than a hundred and twenty pounds caught between two men with the potential for violence emanating off of them.

"I think you've made a mistake, Jonathan," Mac said coldly. "Most Mistresses don't take kindly to being topped by a sub. She's not that green."

Violet closed her hand over Jonathan's at her waist. Mac had a moment of trepidation, then her fingers curled in his well-manicured ones, twisted, and put his hand roughly from her.

"You're making me uncomfortable, and I'm not interested any more." She glanced at Jonathan. "You can leave."

The blond Norse god gave her a disdainful look. "I'd rather have someone who knows what she's doing anyway, rather than a little girl playing dress up. Little bitch cunt."

"Son of a—" Mac started forward, but Violet lifted a hand so her knuckles slapped against his chest. He could have easily gone past her. Though Jonathan was beating a retreat, it wouldn't have been a bad idea to make sure he scampered all the way out to the parking lot. But there was another reason Mac didn't do that.

He swallowed. She'd got him. There'd been an unmistakable order behind her quelling gesture, and his body had instinctively reacted to her wish, voiced or unvoiced. The nerves quivered under his skin, recognizing it, and he forced himself to keep his voice rough, afraid of showing that to her.

"You should let me follow him and put his pretty face under a Bridgestone."

She cocked her head, and there was so little space between them he ached with the need to touch her. "I think it's time you let *me* decide what should and shouldn't be done. Don't you?"

He stared at her. He was here on an assignment, but his assignment required that he be an active player. For that he needed a partner, a well-connected one. She'd been here awhile and had made a lot of friends, if the waitress was right. The only problem was the one his sergeant had pointed out. Even though he ruled her out as his suspect because she was too inexperienced, she could definitely play with his head, distract him. He had enjoyed the company and demands of Mistresses, but she was a different animal from those he'd been with before. It was a fine line to walk.

He'd take it one night at a time. After all, he might blow it with her tonight and have to hook up with someone else. His gut clenched at the thought. He wanted this one. He wanted her.

"Yes, Mistress," he said.

Chapter 4

She didn't know what to make of him. Tyler had counseled her to keep it light and easy her first night on her own, and here she was, in the deep end of the pool.

He followed her to the lower level, to the door of the room she'd reserved, a room with polished wood paneling and carved rafter beams, the trappings of a stable for a prize thoroughbred. The large stall area was mounted with a variety of stainless steel polished rings to cross tie at different heights and distances. On a sawhorse made of finished maple with antique hinges, a saddle had been mounted. Bridles, tethers, crops and buggy whips hung on a wall rack, as well as a few things she'd requested provisioned as extras that one wouldn't normally find in a barn. "Stand there," she pointed to the middle of the floor outside the stall and went to a control panel in the wall. "I'd like privacy for our first time together," she said, watching his face.

No flicker of disappointment, or of relief. Based on his unassuming mode of dress, she suspected her prize was not an exhibitionist. However, that wasn't to say he wouldn't be turned on by being displayed at his Mistress's command. He might be the type of sub that got turned on by whatever turned his Mistress on. Taking a deep breath with her back turned to him to calm her reaction to the thought, she still felt his intensity like hands running over her neck and shoulders, her bare back, the curves of her ass, the delicate skin of her inner thighs. She could imagine the press of his lips in those places, chaste, light kisses where his mouth would quiver with the restrained desire to open wide and devour her, one taste at a time.

Some subs—she liked to think of them as bottoms—didn't care who the Mistress was, as long as she delivered the gratification the sub sought. But the subs for whom the desires of a specific Mistress *were* the gratification, those subs sought to serve in whatever manner commanded. Some were instinctively protective as well, as if they were reincarnations of palace guards for ancient queens. She thought of the look on Mac's face when Powell had insulted her. The nasty comment had delivered a blow to her ego, but Mac's reaction had kept it fully inflated.

She engaged the darkening feature of the ceiling glass so the club visitors could not watch them. She knew the staff security could still monitor them through the discreetly placed mirrors, but no one else would be privy to this evening's entertainment.

"Mac. That's your name?"

"Yes, Mistress. If it pleases you."

"I'm having a hard time finding anything about you that doesn't please me, Mac. What's your given name?"

He hesitated, those silver-gray eyes shifting. "Mackenzie."

"Mackenzie. I like that." She stayed at the wall, watching him, making no attempt to move closer. The air was getting still and warm.

"Take off your shirt, Mackenzie. And next time you come into this club to meet me, you'll take it off at the door."

Mac slipped the buttons of the shirt. Violet watched him, studying the lowered eyes. He was not trembling or hurried, but somehow she felt an explosive tension coming off of him. If she had to bet, she'd say that she made him nervous. Very nervous, but he was very, very good at not showing it.

Why someone like him was nervous about someone like her, she didn't know, but she knew D/s went deep into the psyche of each individual, with often unpredictable reactions.

She wouldn't let herself fill with doubt or fear of not doing the right thing, or let Jonathan's mockery come through and unbalance her. Mackenzie might just be showing kindness with his attentiveness, but even so, she was going to make him wish for another night, and then another.

Like any art form, if she focused on performance, end results or audience reaction, she'd lose the edge, pull herself out of the spiritual undercurrents driving the sensual process. Nature would take them to the right destination, though she enjoyed having the freedom to play with the right amounts of water, sustenance and light to make Nature's beauty thrust its way eagerly out of the ground.

He removed the shirt from his shoulders and she drew in a breath. Speaking of Nature's beauty. He was as beautiful as she had expected. A furred and powerful chest, with that same silver, white and black pelt he had thick on his skull. Sleek muscle, curves and angles that meshed in perfect imperfection. A couple of scars. The hair narrowed down to its delightful indicator point on his flat belly and disappeared into his black jeans, which she noted had a tighter fit now, due to his erection straining the denim. She made an effort to keep her face impassive, not lick her lips and dance for joy as she wanted to do.

Choosing a soft-bristled grooming brush from the wall, she moved toward him at last. One step, two steps. Her booted heels were loud in the silence between them. He kept his eyes down as she approached, circled behind him and laid a palm on his bare back between his shoulder blades.

"Someone trained you well," she said, noticing his hands stayed loose, undefensive at his sides. His skin was smooth and hot beneath her touch, but she resisted the urge to tighten her grip. Whether he was advanced level or not, he was a beginner with her as his Mistress, and she knew the importance of establishing the ground rules.

Plus, she wanted to take it slow, savor these very first touches the way a first kiss was supposed to be savored. One never knew if that first kiss might be the first kiss with a soulmate, such that everything done with him after that point would be the ultimate choice of a lifetime.

Violet lifted the brush, slid it over his skin, watched the bristles bend and mold over the muscles in his shoulders, his shoulder blades, his back. The bristles were soft, but still worthy of being called a brush, so they made faint trails in his skin, stimulating it.

"So what's your safe word, Mackenzie?" she asked, passing her hand down the same trail, using her nails a bit.

"I don't use one. If I can't take it, I don't deserve you."

Violet stopped. "That's a pretty high risk to take, Mac, with someone you don't know." It genuinely concerned her, for he obviously came to these clubs on his own, and he was not a regular at The Zone.

"Nevertheless." He kept his gaze on the floor. "I serve my Mistress's pleasure, whatever that pleasure might be. I don't have one, and I don't want one."

"I'll set the rules, Mackenzie. What if I make you watch me while another man fucks me?"

He stiffened and she smiled, rubbing her brush down the other shoulder. His skin was getting damp. "That would bother you, then?"

"Only because I know I could do anything he did for you, better."

Violet pressed her lips together against another smile, even as she felt her knees quake. She'd no doubt he could. His voice alone, the shift from sensual deference to impudence, was making her wet.

"Arrogant slave." She laid down the brush, chose another, this one with stiffer bristles. "I'll bet those jeans are getting very uncomfortable."

"Shall I take them off?"

"Not yet. I like to see your cock straining against them for me. I'm not ready to let you be comfortable."

She loved the feel of his skin beneath her palms, his heated stillness. When she caressed his nape with her long nails, he bent his head forward, making it easier for her to stroke him there.

A breath drew in his muscles, his buttocks tightening in a very appealing manner as she returned to her brushing, increasing the pressure of her strokes with the stiffer brush, raking his skin, bringing the blood to the surface to sensitize him further. She alternated across, varied from light to hard, so his skin would not get numb to the stimulation. His breathing grew labored. Though she wanted to do so, she didn't have to look to know his arousal was increasing.

"You seem to be getting a bit fractious," she murmured. "Follow me."

Putting down the brush on a ledge of the stall partition, she lifted two tethers of soft nylon from where they draped over the doors. Turning so she could see him come toward her, she suppressed a shudder of reaction at the sight of that muscled body, lightly perspiring with nerves and heat, the silver eyes, intent with desire. The awkwardness of his gait drew her attention down to his cock, now clearly outlined against the front panel of his jeans.

"If you could do anything you wanted to do right now, Mackenzie, what would it be?"

The path of his eyes coursed down the front of the velvet dress, but he took another step closer, so close she felt his hand brush her hip. Felt his fingertips take the liberty of caressing the lace top of her thigh-high, seeking to trace the bare skin just above it, below her dress's short hem.

"I'd kneel at your feet and eat your pussy until you came in my mouth, your hands clutched in my hair, nails digging into my skin. I'd listen to you scream my name. Mistress."

His fingers inched higher, his eyes gauging the rise in her pulse rate, which she felt beating against her throat as clearly as she knew he could see it.

"You need to learn some manners." She caught his wrist in a firm grip.

The tether was similar to the nylon ropes found in a horse barn, only this one had a cuff at the end of it. She fitted it around his wrist. "Turn outward so your back is facing the back of the stall, and put both arms behind you, crossing your forearms."

His fingers flexed as she laced the cuffs on his wrists securely, making sure he had blood flow, but tight enough that he could feel the restraint, send the message to his mind that it was the first step toward the total domination she intended to exercise over him tonight. As she did the lacing and checked the pressure, her knuckles were brushing the ass hugged by the denim. It was too tempting. She allowed herself to free one hand, close it over the curve of one buttock, grip it hard, enjoy the feel of it flexing tensely under her touch. The fingers of his cuffed hand reached, found her other hand wrapped in the loose end of the tether, and he caressed her palm, seeking a grip.

She drew out of his reach, wrapped the slack of the ropes around her fingers and tugged him further into the stall. He turned his head, meeting her gaze as she moved him, her palm sliding around to press against his stomach just above his waistband to guide him backwards. There was no escaping the mental comparison of leading a stallion within proximity of a mare, his eyes dangerous and intent on hers.

Steady, girl. He's big and strong, and he knows what he's doing, but you can handle him. You know what he needs, even before he does. That's what a good Mistress did. Break him down to the core, so he was open to her, both finding ultimate completion in a total connection of the mind with the body.

Tyler's words, but her pounding heart had a different name for it, which went beyond words to pure feeling.

For a Mistress like her, it wasn't about getting off. She knew true Doms were artists who used a variety of methods to break subs down to the bone and drive them to a level of fulfillment they never could have experienced with their emotional and physical shields in place. For such a Master or Mistress, the stimulation came from that successful breakdown of a sub, so that he was completely linked with the Dom's desires. At its heart, that was what she hungered for, getting the sub she wanted to willingly surrender all to her, more than he even knew he had to offer. She wanted to tame the stallion that could not be tamed.

"I didn't give you permission to meet my gaze," she said. "Face forward and eyes down."

Mackenzie held her eyes one more moment than was appropriate, then shifted his attention to the floor. His bare, broad back faced her, the smooth taper to the firm waist just screaming for her touch.

She threaded the loose ends of the tethers through a ring above her head on the stall wall and drew the ropes tight, drawing his shoulders back and up so that she crossed his arms as close to the elbows as she could, a just short-of-uncomfortable posture that got his attention. It bent his body slightly forward, which she could tell he didn't like, for it put him off balance. He was going to be a lot more off balance when she was done.

It was an effective method of restraint, because with his arms crossed nearer to the elbows than the wrists and pulled up at that uncomfortable angle to his shoulders, he could not move back. The lack of slack kept him from moving forward.

"I want you uncomfortable, but not in pain," she said, testing the ropes, drifting her hand across his back. "You'll tell me if you begin to hurt. Answer me."

"Yes, Mistress," he said roughly.

"Good." She moved around to his front, stepped back five paces and then simply stood a moment, enjoying him.

"You've got a beautiful chest," she noted. "Those incredible shoulders, the cords of muscle at the neck. Long thighs, impressive cock."

Standing in the shadow of his body with her spike heels, she was a bit taller than she wanted to be. She bent over, her back to him, to lift the hem of her short skirt and take down the back zipper of the first boot, well aware that he was seeing her thighs all the way past the top of the thigh-high. The posture revealed the elongated almond shape of her pussy in the green satin thong, the base of her ass cheeks.

The rings clanked as he tested how much slack he had, and she hid a smile when he came up just short, as she knew he would. She unzipped the other boot, stepped out of them and kicked them out of her way, turning before he could get the bright idea to try to use his legs to rub a knee up the seam of her thighs. She wouldn't put it past him to be so brash.

Taking up the brush with stiffer bristles again, she ran it down the center of his chest, tugging the bristles through the curly hair there, down the abdomen, tickling the waistband of his jeans, her fingers playing in the area between denim and hard muscle. She placed the brush at the juncture of his shoulder and neck area, and this time brought the brush down over the nipple. The area drew taut immediately, and she felt his muscles clench against the pain as the hard bristles scraped over the sensitive skin. She alternated as she had before, going down one side, then the other, letting her fingers trail behind so the harsh scratch was followed by the soft caress of her fingertips, soothing him.

It also allowed her to note the increased rise and fall of his chest, the thunderous pounding of his heart beneath her palm, the instinctive moistening of his lips, the shift of his body to relieve the pressure between his thighs.

"Be still," she commanded. "Keep your eyes down."

His lids flickered. "But I like looking at you, Mistress."

She ran a hand along his jaw, the smoothly clipped line of his beard, wondering how it would feel against her most erogenous areas. "I'm glad to hear it, but I'll decide when. Are there things you're not comfortable doing that I should know about?"

"With respect, same answer as before, Mistress. I'll do all you ask of me, or I'm not worthy to be your slave." His gaze briefly flicked up to hers, then quickly back down before she could chastise him. "You choosing me to serve you, bring you to the highest level of pleasure, those are my only desires."

It was so close to what she wanted to find in a lover, she barely managed to control the shiver of reaction that went through her vitals at his words. She knew of subs who would let a Dom do anything to them. Most clubs revoked their memberships once they found them, because the wrong Dom would push them past physical and emotional endurance, and could cause them serious physical harm. But Mac didn't strike her as that type. He had limits in there somewhere; he had just somehow managed to keep Mistresses from running up against them. The strength of her concern surprised her, as did the wave of protectiveness that barbed her words.

"That's stupid, Mackenzie. If I have you gagged and decide to ram a railroad spike up your ass, it's going to be a little hard for you to change your mind."

"I trust you'll do what's best for me, Mistress. Whatever you feel is appropriate."

A good kick in the ass for being that unsafe. However, she suspected now was not the time for a lecture. Maybe if they spent more time together.

Whoa, hold on, girl. This might be just a one-night flirtation for him. She knew subs who played 100% in the dungeon, but once they walked out, they didn't look back. They had no plans to pick out curtains with their Mistresses. Ever.

"Well, I'm giving you a safe word. Water. You ask for water, I ease off."

"I'll die of thirst first."

This time he met her gaze square on, and she felt the impact of it to her toes. He didn't just look at her; he ravished her. She'd always thought it was a cheesy word, but the way his attention moved over her, dragging her into him, making her weak, made her picture Victorian heroines swooning in a lover's eager arms. Ravished was exactly the right term for it.

"You've been a sub for a lot of women, haven't you, Mackenzie? No, I don't want an answer to that." She placed a finger on his mouth, held it firm there for only a moment, so he'd get the message, but she wouldn't be putting her knuckles within prolonged proximity of those clever lips. "But I don't think you've ever had a true Mistress. You're still setting the rules, holding up the shields. Let's start by removing some. The rest of your clothes first."

That surprised him, she could tell. He hadn't expected her to move that quickly, and truth be told, she had not intended to do so.

"Your shoes," she said coolly. "Toe them off. You don't expect me to remove your shoes."

"No, Mistress." He awkwardly managed it, using the leverage of the tethers binding him, grunting a little at the increased pain on straining tendons.

"And the socks."

He stepped on the toes of his thin dress socks, worked them off his feet. More bare skin. She was eager for all of it, but she kept the pace slow, teasing, as she approached him. As she stepped directly in front of him, she saw the angle would give him an excellent view of her cleavage. *There* was an incentive to keep his eyes lowered, she thought with satisfaction.

Violet forced her fingers not to tremble as she reached for the button of his jeans. She deliberately let her touch slide over the hard length of him, nearly groaned at the steel heat she felt. "I hope you're not one of those who can't hold back," she observed. "You're pretty hard now. I'm not sure you've got the stamina for what I have in mind."

Mac brushed a smoldering glance over the top of her breasts. "You're hard to resist, Mistress, but I think I can please you."

The taunt was there. Oh, he had pride. She delighted in it. She firmed her lips. "We'll see," she said indifferently.

She slipped the button, took the zipper down. Slow. She was hyper-cognizant of his breath on her neck, the tension of his body, the muscles pulled back to restrain his movements. She reached in, slid her hand beneath the waistband of his dark underwear, leaving the jeans open in front but otherwise unadjusted, and closed her hand around him.

He made a noise, a catching of his breath, but she had closed her eyes, inhaling him through all her senses. The powerful organ in her hand, pulsing against her palm, the wetness at the tip like a tiny kiss against her wrist. She was aware, even if he was not, that he had moved impossibly further against his restraints, straining toward her, toward her grip.

She had small fingers, and she used them to good advantage now, sliding them down his length, finding the base where the curve of his testicles began, her fingers tangling in the soft hair on them. Then back up, caressing him, stroking him, easing her grip, tightening it.

"Violet…" he said. Her head lifted, tilting at an angle because they were so close now, her thigh pressed against his, her lips no more than a finger span apart from his just above her. He had cut himself shaving this morning, she noticed, just a tiny nick on his neck.

"Don't move," she said. "Not an inch." She rose up on her toes, placed her lips there, sucking on the closed cut gently, kissing him. Her grip on his cock tightened as she did, and his body quivered against hers, holding back, when she could tell all he wanted to do was disobey.

Violet took her lips away.

"Don't hurt yourself like that again. I'll have to shave you," she warned. "I expect you to take care of what's mine." She dug her nails into him, just a bit, and he flinched, but did not twitch under her tight grasp.

"What do you want, Mac?"

"Whatever my Mistress wants."

She tightened her grip. "Don't patronize me. Tell me what you want."

"To make you come."

"Try again." She worked her hands beneath his waistband, took the jeans and underwear down to his thighs, freeing his cock and giving her an unimpeded view of his bare, muscular ass. She ran her nails over it, scoring him lightly, then reclaimed his cock, starting a slow rub, up and down his thick, long length.

"Mackenzie," she measured her tones, matching them to her strokes. "I'm going to make you come in my hand, and it's going to be very messy and displeasing to me, if you don't stop the bullshit and tell the truth."

He shifted. She might not have caught it, except her knee was pressed against his leg and she felt it, that subtle attempt to change the effectiveness of her strokes with the angle of his body so he could sustain himself, resist her pressure.

She made the same minor adjustment, followed him, and brought her thumb into action, stroking the tight vein beneath the base of the head.

"Violet, stop."

"I'm sorry, Mac. That's not the safe word. You'd die of thirst, remember? But you don't have to die of thirst. Just ask for water."

In a movement so quick she couldn't follow it, he dipped his head and fastened his teeth on her throat. "Why waste it, sugar?" he muttered around his grip. "It could be jetting into you, or I could be attending to your pleasure, eating out your pretty cunt."

His jaw had the strength of a pit bull in truth, and Violet felt a moment of panic when she could not immediately jerk back.

Making her decision, she hoped it wouldn't bring security into the room. She swung her head and smacked it against his cheekbone. He let her go with an oath and she tried to focus, because she had hit one of the harder bits of his head with a softer one of hers. Barring that, she'd been forced to put some power behind it. She was proud that her hand did not pause in its motion, working him even more intently. Despite the pain she knew she'd caused him, his body was responding to her demand, focusing on the pleasurable goal happening below his waist.

He tried to twist away, but with his shoulders drawn up, he was limited in how fast he could move, and she stayed with him easily, sensing victory in her hand.

"You'll come for me now, Mackenzie. Spurt yourself into my fingers like a teenager unable to control his hard-on. I can feel it coming. Let go."

She pulled a kerchief from the top of her stocking, just under the lace, and hooded him with it as his body began to buck. His seed thickened the vein beneath her fingertips. As a warm trickle of blood slid down her neck where he had bitten her, her own reaction wet her thighs.

His body lunged forward, the ring bolts clanging harshly against the pull of the tethers. He snarled, his semen shooting forth into the doubled square of cloth. Some of it jetted past the cover, dampening her wrist, and the potent, erotic smell spurred her desire. Violet couldn't take her attention from his face, watching the battle of a powerful man against his own body, against the emotional vulnerability she had pressed on and forced from him through the uncontrolled physical release.

The orgasm was fast and intense, and left him shuddering, the wide chest expanding to take in air. "Whoa, there," Violet leaned her body into his to give him some support. He was double her weight in muscle, but the leaning worked, and gave her the excuse to hold him in her arms. She liked the way he felt there, and caressed the line of his back just above his waist, the firm, damp skin. She gave herself a moment, because she liked it so much, then she made herself do what she had to do.

She released him abruptly. She folded the kerchief over and dropped it on the chair seat. Moving behind him, she loosened one wrist cuff enough that he could free himself. "We're done," she said.

"What?" he straightened.

"You can get yourself loose from there."

"But, Violet, what—"

She stopped him with a level look. "You look me up when you want a Mistress, Mac. Instead of someone to jerk you off or someone you can jerk around. I'm not interested."

"What the hell game are you playing?" he said, his brows drawing over his eyes in a way she was certain would intimidate the hell out of most people. She merely arched one of her own.

"I'd ask the same of you, if I cared. You're good, Mackenzie. You're very, very good. You'd make almost any Mistress within these walls think you're playing the game the way it should be played. A little rebelliousness mixed with the charm, the subservience. If I'd wanted a trained pony, I'd have gone to the circus."

"I don't know what you're talking about."

"Of course you don't." She turned away, picked up her boots and the kerchief. One step toward the door. Two steps. Three. Brisk, no dragging, her intention obvious.

"Wait." She stopped at the door, but did not turn. She just waited.

"Don't leave. Tell me what I'm doing wrong."

She closed her eyes to compose herself, to conceal the quick surge of triumph and lust that the rough, angry confusion in his voice roused in her. There was more to him than met the eye, as she had suspected.

Rotating on her heel, she faced him, sweeping his delectable body with an expression that did not reveal a trace of how she felt looking at him standing there, the jeans and underwear shoved down to his thighs, his chest bare, the wrists still held in restraints. "That's part of what you're doing wrong. You're so worried about right and wrong. You're trying to control the situation, Mackenzie. Who controls this situation?"

"You."

She laughed. "You're saying what I want to hear, not what you believe. You, what?"

"You, Mistress."

She took a step forward.

"Let me tell you what I expect, Mackenzie. I'm not a dabbler. I'm not a casual one-night trawler. I'm looking for a solid bond, a total commitment. I don't expect to find it in every man I bring to these rooms. In fact, I don't expect to find it in most of them, but I choose men interested in finding out. Once I find it, I don't expect to take it outside this club right away, but it's what I intend when I do. I want to be some lucky man's Mistress, and you're just wasting my time if you're going to hide." She stepped up to him, until that large body was just over her again, the fury and desire in his eyes cloaking her aroused body in heat. "I want to flay off every inch of your shields, your emotional skin, so I see and know everything you are, every part you hide from the rest of the world. I'm fully capable of it."

"I don't know…if I can let you. Get that close."

A sigh broke free, and now she did soften, cupping her hand under his jaw with gentle fingers. "Bingo. That's who I'm looking for. The man who tells me what's happening in his head, what I'm doing to him. Who trusts me, or is at least willing to try. The man who can completely let go to pure sensation and feeling. That's it, Mackenzie. That's what I want. You want to run from that, you can. Just don't waste my time with your act if you're only here for the turn-on."

"I've got to think about it."

"So think." She turned away from him, though moving back toward the door felt like moving through deep sand, all the muscles of her body screaming in protest. "I'll come back here tomorrow between nine and eleven. If you want me, you'll be in this room, stripped. Nothing on. You put on one of the cock harnesses, tether yourself to that ring in the floor, the minimum amount of slack necessary between it and your cock. Your knees will be spread as wide as you can get them, your hands laced on the back of your head. You stay straight upright in that position until I decide to come down here."

She looked over her shoulder, stifled a groan of need as she saw his cock hardening again at her words. "Can you hold a position that long, Mackenzie? How badly do you want to have a Mistress worth having, rather than a playmate?"

Chapter 5

He wanted to run, to turn his back on The Zone and pretend, at least for twenty-four hours, that it and Violet didn't exist. That the shameful moments had not existed.

But he made himself stay, made himself talk to other club members, find out more about his fiery little Dom. Everyone knew Violet. She went to many of the outside private parties, where D/s couples got together in their latest pairings. Several times a week, she played at The Zone.

She was perfect.

She also terrified him, and he didn't know why. Why was she different? He'd had Mistresses do all manner of things to him. He'd tolerated it, and most of it turned him on. She had overwhelmed him, shot him up and over a pinnacle with her clever fingers before he'd even had a chance to catch a breath. Her sultry voice teased his mind, the faint smell of lavender still on his body from where she had pressed against him.

He didn't go home. He went to the office. Nodding briefly to the dispatch officer, he went back to his desk, switching on the lamp. There were several new reports on his desk. Psych profile, forensics for the last victim, the latter not telling him more than he already knew. He knew the method of restraint, how a bullet tore through flesh. The profile was disappointing, a generic analysis.

It is possible the subject was traumatized by a sexual betrayal or rejection, and has had to pretend the betrayal or rejection does not exist, therefore leading to suppression of an enormous anger... By calling the parent, the person they perceive as responsible for their pain, they are likely punishing the authority figure.

He didn't blame the Psych department. Likely very accurate, it was a standard evaluation of motivation for crimes of sexual violence. Most serial killers weren't terribly original in that area, just in their methods of expressing that pain. It was her way of killing that would lead him to her.

His gut told him the frustrating truth; that he only had one piece of the jumbo brand 10,000 piece puzzle. There was something odd about this murderess, a secret she hadn't yet revealed with her actions. He lifted the list of regular Doms provided by The Zone in exchange for a confidentiality agreement. They hadn't forced the issue of a warrant. Connie had been visibly impressed when she relayed the manager's message to Mac: "If our people are getting hurt, we want to protect them. If that gets someone's nose out of joint, their snit isn't worth someone's life."

Because of that, he didn't regret the personal funds he'd chosen to invest in The Zone guest membership, rather than requisitioning a reimbursement. He'd even consider going for a full membership, if it weren't for Violet being there. What was it about her that made his gut clench in anxiety, even as his cock jumped up like a dog waiting for a treat?

He ran his hand over his face to the side of his neck and froze at the thump of his pulse in his jugular. So caught up in what she was doing to him, he hadn't even registered until now the blood staining her neck when she left him. Jesus. He had bitten her. He'd never used his strength against a Mistress, though the throbbing bruise on his cheekbone told him she'd handled him all right. No fear in that one. A porcelain doll with a core of iron.

The thought made him smile, but it worried him for her, that she was too green to know when she should back off. But had she needed to back off from him? Or had she done exactly what she should?

Would he go tomorrow night? Of course he'd go, he was on assignment. But the question was, would he go to that room, wait for her, accept her as his Mistress for another night?

Mac picked up the photo of Jesse Rodriguez, a twenty-three year old accountant, stared into his dead eyes. Yeah. Yeah, he would go to The Zone tomorrow night, because Jesse was never going to get to enjoy the anxiety and anticipation again. He had died because he'd taken the risk with someone who had killed him, and that offended Mac deeply, on a personal level he felt too raw to explore.

In the computer reports Consuela had run for him, he saw that there were no related crimes in all fifty-one states for the past two years. It looked like his murderess had just started her killing spree. They needed to find her soon. Six weeks between her two victims meant she was a fast learner. She'd found a release for the pain she nursed inside. The hunger would keep growing, and she would go after whatever would ease the craving.

Just like him. He muttered an oath and slapped the file shut. Violet was not the murderess, but she obviously had the power to destroy him. He'd go to The Zone, but not to her. There would be other, less distracting

Mistresses with whom he could hook up and mingle, watch the play beneath the floor. He'd follow that strategy. See if he could start zeroing in on a killer that he was certain was already stalking her next kill.

*****

Violet had a hard time sleeping, and found it even more difficult to focus on doing her job throughout the next day. Her body ached with unsatisfied desire, but the idea of relieving it with a toy after she'd left Mac had left her cold. She wanted to build her own anticipation as well as his, though she knew it was entirely possible she'd pushed too hard and he wouldn't be there. Or worse, he'd be there and not in that room. A flat rejection.

No. She stood in front of her bathroom mirror, pulled her hair from her face, pinned it up so the curls just brushed the nape of her neck, and tucked the black wig over it. Not a rejection. If he shunned her, she would think of it as a retreat. She'd unsettled him, knocked a sizable dent in that arrogant attitude of his. Was he man enough to admit it and come back to her?

She certainly wanted him to do so.

The phone rang and she picked it up as she leaned forward to apply her eyeliner.

"So, did you take my advice?"

She grimaced. "You have spies everywhere, Tyler, so don't pretend you don't already know how last night went."

He chuckled. "Oh, I know you picked up a prime target, but word is you engaged the privacy screen, so no one but those who won't be bribed know how it went. I do have reports that you came out alone. Mistress Marguerite reported that he came out a quarter of an hour later, looking like he'd had the carpet of his world yanked out from under him. Was that a good or bad thing?"

"I won't know until tonight, if he shows up again."

"Your boy socialized a bit after you left."

"Did he?"

There was a significant pause, and Violet cursed mentally.

"There was definitely a jealous note to that, maybe even a tad possessive. He got under your skin."

"I got under his more."

Tyler laughed, dropping all the slyness from his tone. Violet couldn't help but smile at her own reflection in the mirror.

"Fuck you, Tyler."

"Anytime, darling, but it would be like two tigers. We'd rip each other to shreds. So you liked this one, then. All those months playing with me, you don't find anything more than casual playmates. Your first night out on your own, you find one you want to keep. "

"Just a virgin reaction to her first solo scene."

"Spoken like a crude cynic, and not like the sweet Violet I know. Don't get worried, kitten. Let it happen."

"I have to worry, Tyler." She put down her mascara and leaned against the counter, rubbing a finger over her forehead. "I can't take risks. I'm already daydreaming about taking him places, for heaven's sake."

"Well how about something safe to ease the craving? My plantation house, this weekend. I'm inviting four lady Doms, including yourself, for an overnight of play with the sub of their choice. I'll have Mark and Stacey from The

Zone staff there to be chefs and domestic help, and to join in if we need some free agents. You can take a side trip to Lilesville, use that gift certificate your friend Sarah gave you. To decorate him, or yourself. Or expand your toy chest."

"I wasn't ever going to use that, Tyler. It's for five hundred dollars. It feels like a bribe."

"Her new husband gave it to you because, thanks to you, he gets to sleep with Sarah every night for the rest of his life. I've seen Sarah. He should have given you ten times that much."

"Pig. I'll think about it. And he's got to want to go, anyhow. Will you bring Leila?"

"Absolutely. In fact, I think this is the perfect weekend to break her into the joys of interactive play. Maybe we'll see how far we can push your boy."

"You'll need to take it easy on him, Tyler. He comes off tough as nails, but if you find the way in, he can be hurt."

"We all can, love. We all can."

*****

She didn't look to see if the ceiling darkening feature had been engaged or not for her room. She went to the changing room. It was nearly ten-thirty. If he had obeyed and prepared himself for her as she had told him to, he'd been on his knees for almost an hour and a half.

Shedding her overcoat, she put it in a locker. Tonight she'd worn a dress she'd picked up in the Asian district. The blue satin with a touch of Lycra to cling to her curves had side slits in the form-fitting skirt and a pattern of black dragons with delicate long whiskers and sharp curving talons done in black and silver embroidery thread. A stiff line of ribbon sewn at the base of the bodice lifted and underlined her breasts. Her heels were black satin with braid trim, and she wore sapphires at her ears. No underwear beneath the dress, just a pale blue satin garter belt to hook the sheer hose. The deep vee of the neckline revealed the path of the silver nipple chain across her sternum, strung with sapphire and black beads to weight the pink tips, keeping them stiff and pushing against the snug fit of the bodice.

It was her most sensual dress, and she was uncomfortably aware of how deliberately she'd chosen it from the closet. If he was here, but spurned her attentions, she was going to make damn sure he regretted the choice.

Closing the locker, she took a deep breath. *Let it happen.*

She took the stairs down to the lower level, comfortable in the high heels, and moved into the carpeted entry hallway, lit with candelabras.

The hallways of the playrooms felt like her private world. Calm settled over her shoulders, and she soaked it in. Painted with an ornate tapestry of images, the vaulted ceilings offered equal visions of pleasure and pain, silhouettes of bodies, the gleaming curves of exposed skin, a ready hand or brushing of lips. Nearly two hundred scenes painted along the arched hallway interlocked into a mural, a masterpiece created exclusively for The Zone by a famous artist patron who chose to remain anonymous.

She went to the door of the room she had reserved, keyed in the access code, then hesitated, hand on the latch. It was cowardly, but she needed another moment before she faced the potential of an empty room, the slap in the face it represented. In that moment, she knew that more than pride was involved. With that thought came the realization that, if he *was* in the room, she was risking her heart, a far more dangerous sacrifice than her pride.

"Two nights in a row. He must be worth it."

Masters at taking arousal to the cutting edge of pain and then pushing their sub a little bit past that, Tamara and Kiera were twins, Mistresses who chose to work exclusively as a team. A unique commodity, even in the fetish world.

When Tyler had first introduced Violet to T&K, he had told her, albeit under his breath, "Most subs don't know whether to beg for more or run screaming after spending ten minutes with them."

Tonight they were dressed in white latex mini-dresses. Tamara's had a high neck and long sleeves, whereas Kiera's had a neckline plunging almost to her waist in an imitation of the Marilyn Monroe classic. Tall, elegant black women with dark hair streaked with deep red highlights, their lips and fingertips were painted in the liquid red they favored, perhaps to remind subs of the blood they were willing to draw in the name of pleasure.

"Are you going to Tyler's this weekend?" Tamara asked, turning a cane through her long, elegant fingers like a baton. In her other hand she held a group of electrode pads.

"Tell us yes, flower girl," Kiera chimed in, "and tell us you're bringing that sweet baby waiting in the stable for you."

"To share," Tamara added, a gleam in her eye.

With Herculean effort, Violet suppressed the urge to pump a victory fist. Her emotions surged through her, making her want to spin like a top.

"Maybe."

Kiera ran a caressing nail with a lethal metal tip down Violet's forearm. "Well, if you do, we hope you'll consider letting us play with him a bit. It would be fun, and you could test how he obeys you when you're in a generous mood."

"Ease up, girls." Marguerite joined them. She had her sub on a leash and he was following her on all fours, naked of course, the leash attached to a collar with metal spikes that turned inward, pricking his skin. When he sat back on his heels at her command, to display himself for the pleasure of the other Mistresses, Violet saw a strap ran from the collar down to a restraint of a similar make at the base of his cock. The spikes pressed into his scrotum, a state that could get much worse if Marguerite chose to yank.

However, Violet knew Marguerite was rarely cruel, though she made her slaves submit to many things, like this, that made them vulnerable to the possibility of much greater pain. She could establish a level of trust with her one-night subs that many Mistresses could not achieve in months with a regular partner. Violet suspected it had to do with the absolute command that poured off of her, like the aura of an all-powerful Goddess. The long blond hair was almost pure white and tied back on her shoulders, the clear blue eyes as direct and penetrating as that of a Saxon deity.

Marguerite, while friendly with all of them, did not encourage camaraderie. She was soft-spoken and helpful, would welcome observers to her sessions with a sub, but there was much about her clearly posted with "do not trespass" signs. She came to The Zone once or twice a week. No more, no less, staying exactly two hours. Picked out a sub, a different one every time, and for those two hours used him in a way that apparently helped her deal with whatever darkness lay within her. Whoever or whatever she was outside The Zone walls, Violet expected it was a very different person than who she was within them.

"It would be fun for you to watch as well." Kiera was still making sly suggestions.

Violet pulled her attention away from the attractive slave on the floor, with his stiff cock in its cruel restraint and his eyes directed toward the floor. Marguerite caressed his hair with tenderness, her expression quiet, tranquil.

In contrast, Violet wasn't sure if "fun" or "tranquil" would describe the way the twins operated. While watching the two of them work was undeniably a visual orgasm, Violet preferred her mastery in the area of emotions, not the realm of pain. She had seen T&K take a sub to the limit of both and beyond. It was disturbing, and yet so potent it felt like witnessing a sacred ceremony. Or a session in a Baghdad torture chamber.

She realized suddenly that, if they knew he was in the room, then he had left the ceiling screen open. He had not done anything to protect himself, a message that he was leaving himself open to her desires. She nodded to the others, closed her hand on the doorknob, took another steadying breath. She'd kept him, and herself, waiting long enough.

"Enjoy, flower girl," Tamara's chuckle caressed her spine as Violet turned the latch and stepped into the room.

* * * * *

Mac kept his head lowered as the door opened, but it was difficult, particularly when that lavender and vanilla scent wafted into the room, tightening his cock in the harness instantly, painfully increasing it with every step she made across the wood floor. She was wearing a dress again. He could hear the rustle of the soft fabric, and he saw the shadow cast by the light, but she wasn't close enough to show him what shoes were making that crisp tap against the slick finished wood.

His back and legs ached from maintaining the straight-up kneeling position; her punishment, he was sure, for his behavior last night. He hadn't moved an inch, had left the ceiling clear so anyone she asked could tell her, so she'd see he could take anything she could dish out. His shoulders throbbed from keeping his hands laced behind his head for the entire time.

The whir of gears and a flicker of shadows told him she was closing the screen, making it just the two of them again. He stifled the sense of relief.

"You've done well. I'm pleased. You may lower your hands to the floor, knuckles flat on the wood, please."

Her voice, soft velvet, told him she was indeed pleased with him, and his heart tipped in his chest, ridiculously. She was coming back toward him. Tap. Tap. Pause.

"Keep your head down."

He obeyed, but his muscles trembled with the effort as her small hand reached down, came into the field of his view and grasped his cock in firm, gentle fingers. Through the openings of the harness, her skin touched his, and his cock jerked, responded, leaked a drop of semen onto the delicate pulse point of her wrist.

"My apologies, Mistress," he said.

"For what?" Her hand released him, rose, lifted his chin.

He had seen many beautiful women. After thinking about her for nearly twenty-four hours, waiting for her on his knees over ninety minutes and then, the longest time of all, these few moments she had been in the room, letting him hear her body move but not permitting him sight of it, he expected he had exaggerated the appealing quality of her features and form.

If anything, he decided he had not done her justice.

He supposed there was some standard for beauty that model agencies used, somewhat the same way dog breeders did it. Legs must be this length, proportion of torso to arms must be this, nose this shape, eyes this color. He was sure she might not meet all those standards. But her lips were a deep, wet burgundy, and those violet eyes beneath slim brows and the mass of upswept raven curls held him, affected him so that he knew he would have waited on his knees for her until he lost all feeling in his limbs.

"For dripping on you, Mistress."

She was bending forward, for if she had squatted, he would have been taller than she was. The bodice was snug enough that it did not gape, but the low neckline showed him she was wearing jewelry to stimulate her breasts. He saw the shape of her nipples pressed against the tight fabric and wished he could see how lovely they looked, enclosed in the silver rings which he was sure would match the beaded chain strung between them.

Her face came closer. Just as his lips anticipated the brush of hers, she turned her head away and licked delicately at her wrist, tasting the drop he had left there. He could see the pulse in her neck beating in time with the rapid pulse in her wrist, felt his blood heat further knowing she was aroused.

"You exercise control when I tell you to do so. If you hold back when I haven't commanded you to hold back, it's as much an insult to me as ignoring a direct order. Now, where was I?"

Her touch slid away from his face, caressing it before she curled those clever fingers around the full length of his erect cock again.

"You are nicely equipped. I like that," she purred. "But that big cock of yours may cause you problems in serving me as I wish tonight."

"I won't let it," he said, meeting her gaze, so close to his. Her lips seemed even closer, and he thought he might lose all control and kiss her in a moment, just to suck on those lips and see if they tasted like a perfectly ripe plum, as they appeared to.

"We'll see. But first, I need you to tell me the rule I imposed last night."

Mac tightened his jaw, averted his glance. "Mistress will not need—"

"It is not Mistress's needs the rule serves, but her desire to protect her possession. Don't fuck with me, Mac, or we're back to where we were last night, and I walk out of here."

His attention shot back to her and he cursed himself for the involuntary protest his expression conveyed. Even though he knew she'd seen his moment of alarm, of need, he made himself go deadpan. He didn't want her more than ten feet from him. Hell, he might tackle her bodily to keep her here with him, where he could just have the bliss of smelling her, aroused woman with lavender and vanilla highlights.

"If I'm thirsty, I should let you know."

She considered him, and the silence stretched out between them. It wasn't enough, he knew it wasn't, but damn it, he didn't need it. He wouldn't break. He couldn't.

"For tonight, that will do. But I know you can do better. What surprises me is, I don't think you know that. No one's ever broken you, Mac."

Damn right. He couldn't keep it out of his eyes, so he lowered them, but knew she'd seen them flare.

Instead of getting aggressive with him, as he expected, her gentle touch stroked his hair, caressed the nape of his tense and screaming neck, disarming him.

"You deny yourself the pleasure of surrender. I suppose I'm just going to have to force you to see what you're missing."

After that cryptic remark, she backed from him two steps. She lifted her foot from the floor and placed the point of her heel against the muscle between his shoulder and pectoral, used him as a stool to bend forward and adjust the garter fastening at the top of her stocking.

Mac lifted his hand without permission, but it was an automatic gesture to curl his arm over her leg just above her knee to steady her so she didn't fall. She appeared to have perfect balance, but it certainly gave him the excuse to feel the texture of the sheer hose and the hint of smooth skin beneath. The heel dug into his flesh as she shifted her weight forward, but the discomfort only heightened his body's response in that odd way that certain levels of pain could do.

A small frown line puckered her brow, made him want to kiss it. "This pair of hose has a tendency to roll, but I do like the color of them," she murmured, then flashed him a small smile. She straightened, lifting her foot clear of him, not dragging it down his skin. The motion gave him a quick glimpse into the shadows beneath the skirt, a fleeting image of the pale petals of her pussy just beyond the silk of the stocking and the garter. She wasn't wearing any underwear, and the brief exposure brought the scent of her arousal to him. He wanted to seize that leg, bring it back to his shoulder, bring both of them to his shoulders. He'd scoot her forward with both hands gripping her soft cheeks and hold her waist to make her ride his face, work his mouth up between her thighs until he reached the heaven he had just seen.

He knew he could, knew he was ten times stronger than the little pixie, but he also knew what happened in these rooms wasn't about physical strength, not always.

She did not tell him to lower his gaze again, so he had the full pleasure of watching her walk across the room, the shift of an ass he now knew was buck naked beneath that skirt. It had to be a stretch material, because otherwise she had to be sewn into that dress. But it was classy, the dragon pattern across the blue, the soft flutter of ribbons as she moved. She knew how to tease a man to insanity and yet keep him back at the same time. Like a goddess. A tiny fairy goddess.

She brought a wooden chair over to face him, the kind a stable hand might tip back against the wall to draw on a length of straw and catch a nap, but this one was not old and scratched. Like all the accoutrements of this room, it was a finished, expensive dark wood, a valuable antique.

"Not your usual barn chair," he observed.

"Because this isn't a barn," she said. "It's a suite for thoroughbreds to be petted and pampered by their Mistresses or Masters. Or disciplined as needed."

She set the chair less than two feet from where she had him kneeling, tethered by his cock.

"Let's take care of those hands now." Violet moved around him, touched another control, and he heard the eyebolt in the ceiling engage, lowering itself on a wire. He didn't look up, he knew better than that. This was the challenge, every time. He had learned not to show the fear, but it was there, nipping at his vitals. He'd gotten to the point he could be anyone's sub, allow any woman he chose to play Mistress to him. *To* him, but not *over* him. The similarity of the thought to what she had expressed to him last night struck him, raised his trepidation.

"Lift your wrists above your head," she said. "And put your hands through the cuffs."

Mac obeyed, his heart thundering in his chest. She pressed another control. The cuffs tightened, with a hydraulic control like the powering of a blood pressure cuff. She stepped forward, her knees brushing his back, and tested the fit. She'd got it right on the first try. He couldn't get loose, but the blood still circulated, pumping with a vengeance.

"I'm going to take you up, now," she said. "You tell me if you get thirsty, Mac."

"It won't happen, Mistress."

"I'll remind you of that when either your arms are dislocated or your cock gets ripped off."

"You won't let that happen, Mistress. You have plans for the latter, at least."

"Yes. Yes, I do." Her tone was slightly amused, in a way that made him somewhat ashamed of the desperate attempt at charm, though he didn't know where the shame came from.

"Spread your knees for me, Mackenzie. I need them about three feet apart."

He moved his legs apart, feeling the cock harness strap that ran between his legs lift and divide his balls. A moment later he felt the straps of the ankle restraints bolted onto a slide rack on the floor tighten on his flesh. She added a second set of restraints to his calves just above the knees and tied them to rings in the floor parallel to the outside of his legs, leaving just a touch of slack. He didn't have long to wait to find out why.

The gears whirred, and the cable above him began to retract, taking his arms up higher and drawing his upper body into a straight, stretched line. He'd obeyed her orders and made sure he was back far enough from the ring in the floor that there was little slack in the tether between his cock and the harness, so when she anchored his legs to the floor and began to raise him up, the line between cock and floor became even tighter. His knees left the floor a half inch, pressing against the knee restraints, and he grunted despite himself.

The switch locked him into position, and she came around and ran her hand over his scrotum and bound cock, testing the tension of the line between the harness and the floor. It was taut enough to cause him apprehension, but not painful. With his ankles spread and shackled to the floor behind him, his body suspended in the air by the ceiling cable, his calves bound and his cock tethered to the strap pulled taut to the eyebolt in the floor, he was counterweighted on all sides. Gravity would not twist or pull him in any direction that could injure him. However, the position itself was excruciating and left him vulnerable. There was a knot of tension low in his gut that he had not experienced since his first time being trussed by a Mistress. He was also hard as steel and getting harder, his desperate lust and the emotions she was somehow driving in him giving him one of the most enormous hard-ons he'd ever had. In odd contrast, she was methodical, tender in the way she touched him, her fingers brushing his naked body lightly as she passed him, fondling his shoulder, his throat. He tried to nip her fingers as she passed, but she just smiled at him and went back to her chair.

She sat down like a lady at tea, crossing one ankle over the other, folding her hands in her lap. She took a long moment studying him, erect and suffering.

"I know making you sit there and do nothing while I look at you may not do much for you," she observed. "Men aren't very psychological when it comes to stimulation. Suggest the erotic to a woman in a voice rough with passion, or on the written page, and she'll become wet. But a man needs visuals." She uncrossed her ankles, and inched up her skirt with a finger following the line of her thigh, tracing the garter. She put the middle finger of her other hand to her mouth, wetting it. He followed that finger as if it were the last crust of bread for a starving man. Her knees spread wider, displaying those soft pink cunt lips again. With barely a hesitation, she slid the wet finger deep inside herself, up to the last knuckle, and he heard the sucking sound of her eager pussy, soaked already, taking her in and craving more. Craving something he would kill to give to her.

She drew in a deep, shuddering breath, her gaze still on him. "Now what are you thinking, Mac?"

He stared at that finger, wet his lips as it came out and went back in. "How much I want to fuck you."

"How crude, Mackenzie. Where's that polish? Your control? The charm you wield so easily?" Two of her other fingers got involved, started rubbing her clit. Her hips lifted, accommodating her, starting to move in sinuous circles, building with her reaction.

"I think I might just keep doing this until I come. Would you like that?"

"No, Mistress."

"No?" She arched a brow. "You don't want me to feel pleasure?"

"I want to give it to you, Mistress." He bit back a groan as her finger came out, glistening with her juices. He could smell her strongly now, in his nose, in all his senses, coursing through him like the effects of an illegal street drug. Mac struggled to summon a rational thought. "I can give you far more pleasure, Mistress. With any part of me you desire."

He'd rip someone limb from limb just to win the right to put his smallest finger inside her, feel that heat and silk clamp down on him. He gasped as the harness buckle bit into his cock, ruthlessly pinching the engorged flesh between the stiff strap and the metal.

"Mackenzie—" Her sharp eyes went from his face to his cock. "Ask."

"Let me make you come, Mistress."

Her pretty jaw flexed. "Stubborn son of a bitch. Ask."

He shook his head. His Mistress stood, withdrawing her hand from herself and straightening her skirt with a quick shimmy of her hips. She raised her fingers high, brought them to his eager mouth. He latched onto them without hesitation, drawing them in, sucking her taste off them and making sure he made it enjoyable for her too. Taking care to slide his tongue smoothly along the line of her knuckles, the tender web of skin connecting her fingers, rather than slobbering over them like a Saint Bernard, the way he wanted to do.

"Ask," she said in precise, angry tones. "And I will let you make me come with your tongue, let you bury your face in my pussy and eat your fill."

As bribes went, it was the best he'd ever been offered, but there was more at stake than that, a wall he didn't dare go over. The pain was lessening the size of his erection. Not much with her scent so close, her taste in his mouth, but enough to give him some focus.

"Please, Mistress, let me bring you pleasure." He met her look, aware that his own was defiant, challenging, but there didn't seem to be anything else he could do. The fear was pumping too hard behind it. It was the last defense he had.

Violet moved across the room from him, to the wall. She chose a braided crop and threaded it through her fingers, her back to him. She put it down, chose a cat with metal tips. She shook it out, testing its weight on her arm, nodded to herself.

Mac waited, his breath clogging in his throat, thick with the fury of a cornered, dangerous animal and the lust of a powerful man. He wanted loose. He wanted to bend her over the chair, take her ass with hard thrusts that would have her screaming for mercy and more. He didn't want her beating him.

Violet turned, walked back to him. She left the cat on the chair, squatted, unsnapped the leash holding his cock tethered in its harness to the floor, giving him some relief. Then she moved around him, removed the ankle shackles, lowered the taut line holding his wrists above his head, loosened the cuffs on his calves.

"Free your hands."

If she was thinking of walking out on him again, she'd have been smarter to leave him bound. Knowing he wasn't thinking rationally, but unable to help the violent bent of his feelings, Mac nevertheless remembered to stay where he was, though he wanted to struggle to his feet and seize her. His cock ached like fire, screamed for release on a couple of different levels. His back, shoulders and thigh muscles had hours of tension in them, and yet he was sure sinking into her body would make all of that go away.

She stepped away from him, in front of him, four steps past the chair. She kept her back to him and he watched, stunned, as she shrugged the clinging material off her shoulders. With the black wig in an upswept style, it exposed her nape, emphasizing the beauty of her bare upper torso, the sweeping line of her shoulders, arms and back. Her back was smooth and golden, the spine a shallow valley drawing his eyes down to the beginning rise of her buttocks, visible because she pushed the dress low on her hips. He saw that tiny mole on the inside of her shoulder blade.

"Mackenzie?" She tilted her head so he could see her profile just above her right shoulder.

"Y-yes, Mistress?" He cleared his throat. Why had he thought she was green? Because she didn't have much experience? He had forgotten the wisdom that all subs knew, that great Mistresses were born, not made, and the really great ones relied as much on intuition as training to do what needed to be done.

Most Mistresses had respected his boundaries, would have good-naturedly moved past the sticky point of his pride and gone onto something they both found pleasurable. Not this one. She wasn't here for recreation. She wanted to crawl into his soul, or rather make him crawl into hers. Hadn't she as much as told him that?

"Mackenzie?"

He froze. He'd done the unthinkable. "I'm sorry, Mistress. Can you repeat that?"

Her lips curved, but he wouldn't have called the expression a smile.

"I said, pick up the cat, and lash me with it. Ten strikes."

Chapter 6

This time he bit down on his tongue before he asked her to repeat the question. He had heard her clearly enough, but shock made him want her to rewind, play it once more.

"I'm waiting."

"Mistress. I can't."

"Did I or did I not just give you a direct command?" Her tone sharpened.

"But I'll hurt you. Forget it. I won't hurt you." He felt his loins tighten along with his heart as she turned her body several degrees, showing him the curve of one bare breast. The silver ring of the nipple chain glittered in the light. A small tassel of sapphires and silver beads hung from it, beneath the stiff peak.

"Then I'll show mercy, and reduce the count. You will strike me once, and put all your strength behind it, or this will be the last time you'll ever see me. You'll leave this club and never come back to it. Do it."

She turned away from him again, folding her arms at her waist in front of her.

Mac closed his hand on the handle of the cat o'nine. Nine lash ends, all tied in knots with a fringe of tiny pewter tassels, a variation of the cat some favored here at The Zone. He'd been lashed before by Mistresses, but had never done it himself.

"Put your back into it," she said quietly. "Like an overhand throw."

"Mistress—"

"Mackenzie. Do as I tell you." Soft words, but with steel underneath.

She would leave and he would never see her again. Did she get off on being whipped? He'd not heard of a Dominant who did, though many did it as training for themselves to learn how it felt, how to do it without hurting their subs in irreparable ways.

"Just do it, and it will be over. Three seconds. Now," she snapped.

Mac jerked forward, and put his strength behind the strike, though everything in him told him not to do it.

He had misjudged her height. The lashings struck her shoulder in a sparkling fan and then curled over, the metal tips slapping her front sharply, so that he felt the tug of her flesh as he reflexively jerked back.

He knew the signs of pain, heard it in the cry she bit off, the indrawn breath through her teeth, the tightening of her shoulders and buttocks beneath the dress.

He dropped the flail and lunged forward, catching her by the shoulders and turning her around. "Ah, Jesus."

The metal tips had bitten into the soft upper curve of her right breast, leaving tiny tracks of welts, nearly half of which were welling up blood. But the ones that horrified him most had struck and drawn blood on the areola of that beautiful mauve nipple.

"Violet, what the hell were you thinking? Fucking Christ, I've never flogged anyone in my life. I didn't know—"

She reached up, put her hands around his neck, and brought his mouth down to her lips.

He was quivering with fury at her, and she played havoc with his senses, bringing softness and sex into the equation. His hands slid to her bare waist, brought her closer, groaning as her thighs pressed against his still-harnessed cock. Due to the circumstances, it had lost some of its power, but her moist lips drove it back to painful rigidity almost instantly. She was in his arms, her body all his, and she was as small and delicate and precious as she looked. But even though she trembled with the pain he had caused, he felt the strength she possessed beneath it all.

He gladly would have stood forever with her there, his tongue stroking hers, his hands holding her waist, itching to go lower, grip that round, beautiful ass and squeeze her, hold her tight against his cock, make her feel his need, his desire to possess and be possessed all at once.

She pushed him back a little and he sucked in a breath. "I could break your stubborn little neck," he growled.

"I could say the same for your big thick one." She touched it with her fingertips. "The way you feel at this moment? *That's* how you make me feel when you let me hurt you. I can take care of you, cherish you, and not consider you weak." Her gaze was hard, at odds to the softness of the mouth and body he had just sampled. "I know you're a strong man, Mackenzie. Everything about you fairly screams it. But you're vulnerable to me, no matter how hard you play a game to try and pretend you're not. You won't play games here. This place isn't about games. It's about getting past the games."

She reached down, unbuckled the harness. Mac stifled a groan of relief and winced as she gently peeled back the straps. He was torn between lust and pain as she traced the deep red marks ringing him.

"You're tearing me into pieces, sugar."

"And I'll know how to put them together," she returned. "But now I hurt, and I want you to make it better."

She rebuckled the harness, restricting his cock again, though one notch looser than before. Before he could orient himself to the surprise of that move, she put pressure on his shoulder, and he understood what she wanted next. Mac dropped to one knee, putting his face level with the damage he had inflicted on that pretty areola, marked with a purple welt and swelling for all the wrong reasons. He placed his lips over it gently, with no sucking pressure, and simply laved her, like a wolf giving succor to his mate's wounds, offering soft caresses with his tongue. His hands at her waist gripped flesh, the softness of her dress, his thumbs sliding across the hip bones he knew were bare of panties beneath the skirt.

Violet closed her eyes and he felt her relax in his grip, let him take over, take care of her. Emotion swelled in him, surpassing even his physical reaction. He moved from one welt to another, tenderly offering his mouth to soothe her needs, and her quivering lessened. It told him that the marks had to hurt like a son of a bitch, even now.

"You should get those tended," he said at last, staying on his knees before her. "With something topical."

Violet ran her fingers through his hair, brushed it from his temple, slowly, meditatively, as if she were calming him as much as herself. "I think it's time to give you some attention," she said.

"I don't deserve it. You should let me take care of your needs."

It felt uncomfortable to be at the center of her focus, particularly after she'd so ruthlessly and efficiently stripped away a couple of his outer layers. He had more, but that wasn't the point. On the first night, he had told himself that she was not the type of Mistress he typically sought. His body didn't give a rat's ass. His surly subconscious was fast losing control of the situation.

"I was cruel to you, to make you sit here so long waiting for me," she said.

"You were punishing me, as I deserved."

"Yes. Yes I was." There was a smile in her voice. "But I also know how to be kind."

She moved away from him to a cabinet. Mac watched the movements of her hands as they withdrew a bottle. She had a light dusting of freckles on her bare shoulders, like a person who spent time in the sun on a job, not a tanning bed. What did his slim pixie do when she wasn't here?

Whoa, boy. He almost winced at the horse reference. It was dangerous to start thinking about what a Mistress did outside club walls. Here is where their relationship belonged, especially since he was here for another reason.

* * * * *

Violet turned. He was quick, but she could tell he'd been watching her, studying her in a way she could feel in her bones, deeper than the surface, seeking what she was, who she was. That was what she'd said she wanted, wasn't it? A man who was not a one-nighter, but could go further with her. When the need to sexually dominate a man figured prominently in one's search for a lover, the relationship pretty much had to start within a club like this. Otherwise, she could find herself neck-deep in a relationship with a man who had no interest in that, and then how would she handle it? Yes, he might be everything outside the bedroom she wanted, but he would be missing the one key ingredient, the one it had taken her several failed relationships and a couple of therapists to find out she had to have.

Of course, that hadn't been the therapist's diagnosis. According to him, her need to serve as a Mistress was a product of a past she must overcome to enjoy a normal, healthy sexual relationship. He'd also been free with the prescription pad, pushing a list of mood drugs on her to "moderate" her behavior. She wished she could have strapped him to a rack and modified his behavior, with a very different mind-altering experience.

Sometimes, you just were what you were. Unfortunately, this was one of those things that only those who felt it would understand. Tyler had helped her see that, understand and embrace it, integrate it safely into her life. She knew that it would be difficult and tremendously dangerous to translate a relationship outside these walls. If it always had to stay here, she had thought she could live with that. Until now.

She wasn't quite prepared to say that Mac was Mr. Forever, of course, but she could say that she had experienced a stronger reaction to him in twenty-four hours than any man she'd ever met, in or out of the clubs. It hadn't been anything he'd said or done, exactly, but something emanating off of him that had hit her hard the moment she looked at him, something that interacted with her own energy and compelled them to this moment. Thrilling and terrifying all at once.

She pointed to an upholstered bench of heavy wood, about three feet in length, that was equipped with a variety of restraining straps. "I want you on your stomach on this." At his wary look, she raised the bottle. "I want to rub this into your back."

The bench was long enough that when he complied, it accommodated the length of his torso from the top of his head to his pelvis. He moved carefully, and she noted the relaxing of his features when he took the pressure off his legs and back. It told her the effort it had taken him to maintain the position she'd ordered. It also told her he hadn't cheated, which did wondrous things to her stomach and all the tingling parts of her.

"Be still," she ordered, and buckled a strap around his waist. She also utilized the ones provided on the front legs of the bench to hold his wrists, effectively binding him to the bench and in this prone position. His knees were on the floor, and she had him lift slightly so she could slide a folded fleece blanket beneath them, ensuring his comfort, and strapped his ankles down to the floor bolts provided for that purpose.

Being restrained had tensed up that powerful back, but she pretended not to notice and ignored the question in his expression. Instead, she poured some of the liquid from the bottle into her hands and worked it in her palms, lubricating them and her fingers. "This is going to go on warm," she said, "And then it gets warmer. Not painful. It's a liniment that should ease muscle strain."

"Mistress does not need to see to my comfort," he protested again. "I am here for her pleasure."

"Taking care of you gives me great pleasure," she assured him, laying her hands on the broad rack of his shoulders. *Oh, yes. Great pleasure.* She curved her fingers over them, rubbed, circling her thumbs.

He forgot to suppress a grunt and she smiled. "Tell me something about yourself, Mackenzie."

"I like pasta." He cleared his throat. "Alfredo sauces in particular."

Violet shook her head. "You just can't put a sock in that smartass streak, can you? But you'd taste good, flavored with a cream sauce." She spread the liniment lower, working behind the shoulder blades. God, he was built like a linebacker, only leaner and tougher. "How'd you acquire this body of yours? It's not just from a gym. You do something else."

"Yes, Mistress." His arms relaxed further, and she kneaded some more, loving the fact that she was giving him pleasure, easing his pain. "I do cross-country, survival course competitions. Military camps, things like that."

She watched the ridges of his torso take on a gleam, kept a peripheral sensor on how much he was relaxing beneath her touch. Picking up the bottle, she worked more oil into her hands, then poured a thin stream of the viscous fluid down the valley of his spine. It headed toward the seam of his muscular buttocks, where she knew it would seep in and lubricate him. She saw a tremor go through him, sensed that he knew where her mind was headed.

"It doesn't surprise me to hear that. You like to test yourself. That's what you've used your Mistresses for. They're just an extension of your workout, testing your skills to resist weakness." She kept her tone neutral, but he stiffened up under her touch.

"No. It's not like that."

"This is like going to the gym for you, Mac," she continued, ignoring the protest. "Go to the gym, do twenty reps, go to the D/s hangout, get jerked off by some accommodating Mistress. You're not invested. You're high-power, so high-power you've never been topped. Because nobody sees those shields you maintain in such a charming way. Nobody has tried to go beyond using that beautiful body of yours and reveal what's underneath. I'm going to make you beg."

"I don't beg. I serve."

"Well, it serves me to have you beg. You won't use me or survive me, Mackenzie." She rose so she stood at his shoulder, where his face was turned toward her, his mouth inches from her thighs. Shrugging out of the dress, she let it fall all the way to her ankles, leaving her in just the hose, heels and nipple chain. Violet stayed there a moment, watching his silver eyes course from her ankles to her face and back again, and appreciating that he looked at all of her, not just her breasts or the pussy so close to his face. She leaned forward, whispered in his ear, staying out of range of his mouth.

"When I'm done with you, you'll belong to me. Heart, cock and soul."

She straddled his hips in an economical move, slid her oily hands down to massage his sides, feel the expansive rib cage, the stretched muscle over them, and back up to those shoulders that suggested he was descended from Atlas. As she ran her hands down him again, she leaned forward and pressed her body up against his naked back, spreading the oil with her breasts, their hardened tips and the slender nipple chain dragging across his slick skin. His cheeks clenched beneath her spread legs, and she bent her knees, running her pussy down along the crease of his ass, kept sliding down so she took the oil from his bare back to his buttocks, moving in slow circular movements to grease those powerful haunches, her now oily thighs rubbing his from her astride position.

She came back up, but didn't put her full weight on him, just enough to get the job done and let him feel a hint of her, the press of her thighs around his hips, the slide of her pussy over his spine, the soft give of her breasts caressing his shoulder blades.

"The nice thing about this is that the oil of my cunt is being rubbed into your skin with the liniment," she murmured, enjoying being astride her steed, feeling his power bunched and coiled between her legs, knowing his cock had to be stiff against his belly, and pressing against the restraints of the harness again. She ran her touch down behind her, one hand sliding down the channel of his buttocks, fingering the strap that ran behind his scrotum, holding the contraption in place. The muscles rippled beneath her and she heard him exhale as she fingered the soft skin, probably the only soft place on him. She cupped his sac, spreading the heated oil, and he groaned as the heat and stroke of her fingers took effect.

"You like that, hmm?" She slipped off his back and took her hands down his thighs, down the muscles she had abused by purposefully keeping him waiting. She followed one column with both hands, stroking the long length to the knee and back up again, finding a crevice between testicles and leg, and working oil in there before dropping her touch to cozen him again, kneading the thigh muscles, earning another sound of appreciation and desire.

"Do you make good pasta, Mackenzie?" She switched to the other leg, appreciating the gleam of his body, the polish effect of the lubricant. She lifted one hand from her task and drew a nail down his lower back, between his cheeks, playing lightly around the opening there. His buttocks tightened, capturing her motion.

"Please don't make me come that way, Mistress."

"You said please. That's progress. Why not? Tell me why."

"Because..." She almost heard his teeth grind as she probed, tested the tight ring of the opening. "...I'd rather bring you pleasure."

"We already discussed this, Mackenzie. Your pleasure is my pleasure. And you'd rather not make yourself vulnerable. That's the issue. What will you do, now that I have you tied on this bench? You can fight me, make it tougher on yourself." Her other hand reached up between his legs, circled his restrained cock. "Of course, I'm not sure that's possible."

He made a noise of futile protest as she eased her fingers into him, deep inside, the lubricant making it easy to slide into that heat. She was soaked instantly by his clenched reaction on her fingers, the power of lust and fear quivering through him. "But why don't you try honesty for once? Or you can spend the rest of the night scrubbing this room after I make you get yourself off with no condom."

"It makes me feel like some prepubescent geek fucking a wet dream."

"But aren't I a wet dream, Mackenzie?" She made her voice a silky purr.

Violet stood, straddled him again, keeping her fingers in him, her arm stretched behind her, testing that bundle of nerve endings that in a man was almost as sensitive as a woman's clit. She leaned forward, rubbing her breasts against his slick back again. Whispered in his ear, caught the lobe in her teeth. "Aren't I?"

"Sugar, you are the wet dream of all wet dreams," he growled, turning his head to rub against her. When she pressed her lips to his cheek bone, he lowered his head like a proud stallion in truth so she could touch his brow with her kiss.

"So what's wrong with that, Mackenzie?" she said, turning backwards on him, her bare buttocks and pussy at the base of his neck, her thighs along the lengths of his arms. She worked her fingers deeper into his ass, wriggled. "Ah, there we are."

"No." His breath bellowed out, fighting her, fighting the inevitable.

"No, what, Mac? My God, you are sexy." She sank her teeth into his ass, tightened her legs on his body as he jerked, bucked. Held close by the wrist and ankle manacles, he could not dislodge her.

"No. Just no." Panic was real in his voice now, but she heard the hoarseness of lust as well. "I don't want to lose control. Mistress, please..."

"You say 'no' and 'please', but still you're not thirsty."

"Goddamn you," he hissed. With a quick movement of her spiked heel, she slid a nearby pail under the bench. She tilted the edge of the container to get it under his long, erect cock, enclosing it on all sides where it was suspended in its cage of straps just at the end of the bench.

"You finally gave me a truthful answer, Mac," she said softly, watching his buttocks clench and push, then pull against her as she ruthlessly fucked him with her fingers, brought her other hand around to feel the tightening of his balls. She loosed the harness at the base of his cock a notch, enough to let him go where she wanted him to go. "But you're going to lose control with me. As often as I wish it. Let go now, spill your seed into that pail, or I swear I will find the biggest strap-on on that wall and fuck you blind with it before you get a single taste of my pussy."

He didn't growl or snarl this time. What came out was more of an enraged and frustrated roar. His knees lifted as much as they could, slammed back into the floor as his body heaved and rocked and gave up the fight, shooting jets of semen into the bucket even with the restriction of the harness, which she knew would prolong it, make it even more excruciatingly pleasurable.

"That's it, baby," she crooned. "Show me how much you want to fuck me." She couldn't tell where the wetness of her pussy ended and the oil of his back began, but she didn't care. She rubbed both over him, marking him, working her body with the delightful plunging rhythm of his.

He fought against the inevitable so hard that the strain of the powerful muscles was art in motion. She enjoyed it, every convulsion and tightening, every grunt and moan. When his head dropped forward on the bench at last, resting on his arm, she slowly withdrew her fingers, teasing him as she went so he shuddered even more. She freed his arms, but bade him keep still with a hand to his back as she picked up a towel and lifted herself off him.

Violet took a moment or two to clean herself, conscious of his eyes upon her. She kept her expression cool and indifferent, the picture of control, until she squatted and lifted his head with her hand.

His much larger hand seized her wrist, dragged her forward and his mouth fastened over hers. Not gentle, not practiced, just raw, brutal strength and desire. She felt his teeth as much as his tongue, felt his frustration, fury and lust all there, felt her bones melt under his strength.

She could have yanked away, punished him for his roughness and breach of etiquette, but she knew that was what he wanted. He wanted her to act like an enraged Mistress. Punish him, not because that got him off, but because it would establish emotional distance, the familiar territory where he was comfortable.

So instead, she raised her other hand, stroked the side of his face, balancing his brutality with gentleness. She stroked his hair around to the back of his neck, loving touches that were an equal answer to his violence, until his kiss eased into a groan of need that pulled her heart into her throat.

She put a finger between their mouths, separating them, then brought her lips back to his still ones with a feather soft touch, tasting him. A cinnamon flavor, wrapped in the surrounding smell of his aftershave, the scent of sex and sweat underneath that. She loved the way a well-groomed man smelled after sex, a mixture of the civilized and the primal, both offerings of respect to her. One scent indicating his desire to groom himself for her pleasure, the other indicating that he had exercised his desire for her. Trailing her lips down his cheek, she brushed his shoulder, then she lowered her hand, unbuckled his cock harness, rubbed her thumb over the deep red impression where the point of the buckle had dug into him earlier. "Idiot," she murmured, stroking him there. He was soft, spent in her hand, but she could feel the little twitches, see the flare of his nostrils as she fondled him, all indications of how quickly he could be roused again. He had a fast recovery time. Good. He would need it. Because she wasn't done with the lesson.

She rebuckled his wrists to keep him still as she rubbed the towel over him, cleaning him up. He said nothing, and she did not draw him out. She could tell a thousand thoughts were chasing themselves through his head, and the foremost might be that he'd had enough, that this was more than he wanted to give. Well, he was here now. She had him for tonight. She cleaned him with wet towelettes, which were left in every room for the patron's hygiene needs. She wiped him down; head, shaft, scrotum. He roused under her touch, but still he said nothing, and her nerves were starting to vibrate with anxiety, even as her fingers itched to continue slowly stroking that cock, which was rising to life again.

She had her head bent close to his, drying the oil from his back with the towel, when she felt his lips brush her cheekbone. Suppressing the urge to turn her face to him and devour him in joy at the simple victory, she kept quietly to her task, let him nuzzle her, nibble her neck.

"Mistress, let me go, let me make you come," he whispered against her ear.

She closed her eyes as his nibble on the lobe dropped, became an open mouthed, strong pull on her throat.

"No. You can't trust a new pet off the leash until you're sure he'll obey your commands. You're a new pet, Mackenzie. My new pet. So you'll be on the short leash until I'm sure that stubborn head and big cock of yours both understand who their Mistress is. It's too soon." She pulled back from him, stood to establish distance, and for the added psychological benefit of standing over him, which she knew would piss him off. "I'm going to go home." She met his gaze squarely, her eyes impassive, though there was a spring of tension in her lower belly, just looking at him lying there naked before her. "I'm going to put a vibrator in my pussy and imagine it's your cock."

His jaw tightened, but he kept his voice controlled, at odds with the flash in his eyes. "Take me home. Let me do it for you instead."

She shook her head. A grim smile touched her lips. "I suspect I'll have to come a dozen times before I'll be calm enough to sleep."

"Then don't do it. I'll be worth the wait."

"Nice try. I should give your ass a good beating, trying to give orders to a Mistress." She gave his face a light swat with her nails, was not surprised a bit when his eyes shot fire at her.

"No, Mackenzie," she said, her lips thinning into a straight line. "You don't want to fuck me for the right reasons. You just want to erode my control, make me lose my senses so I'll go easier on you next time. But I'm keeping the reins. I'm not giving up a bit of it, and I'm going to keep pushing you until I have all of you, not just the cock you're so free with. It's time you start realizing that having a Mistress means everything is hers, as I said before. Your heart, your mind, your soul and your body. Cock, ass, whatever I want of you is what you give me, and if you can't get that through your thick skull, it's going to get way rougher before it gets easier."

"You're the one making this harder," he said, with a look in his eyes she was beginning to anticipate. "You're a cock tease."

Violet tossed the towel to the side.

"You know, you get mean when you get scared, Mackenzie, but you're not going to drive me off. You want some punishment? You got it. I can be the bitch of your dreams, *sugar*, but I can also be so much more. If you'll stop being such a chicken-hearted bastard, you'll find that out."

She went to her bag of personal belongings and withdrew something she hadn't anticipated using tonight. Something that made his eyes go dark with apprehension. "You're not putting that in me."

"Really? Of course not. Not if you say the words. And you know the words, Mac. Are you ready to use them?" At his fury-laden silence, she nodded, went behind him. She placed a hand on his backside, fingered him despite his futile attempts to jerk his ass away from her touch. "Still well-lubricated. Well, then."

He bucked up and she neatly reached under him, caught his balls and twisted, just enough to freeze him in place as he realized to move further would cause him excruciating pain. She slid the plug all the way in, to the flared wide tip. He had a tighter ass than she'd expected, which suggested his tension and that he did not do anal play often. She stood, took the remote and programmed it, then set it down on her chair, putting it just out of his reach.

"Now I've programmed that for three twenty-minute sessions," she said, meeting his enraged glance as she turned it on. The twitch that went through his body, the jump in his cock, told her she had seated the plug right where she should. "It will build, get stronger and stronger, then go back to a low speed, then build again. I suspect it will make you come each time." She nudged the pail under his stiffening cock again. "As regular as milking a bull for sperm. I'll ask the staff to come release you at the end of an hour."

His head snapped up. "You're not staying to watch?"

"No, I'm not. They will." She hit the ceiling switch and the darkening feature reversed. It would be a full house. Even with the soundproofing, she sensed all eyes would be riveted on the handsome male specimen below, left bound and being jerked off for their entertainment.

"Violet, don't do this." His face was wild, desperate, and she saw his legs trembling, already starting to feel the effects of the vibrating plug. Sweat was shining on his brow, those magnificent muscles glowing.

She continued as if he had not spoken. "At the half-hour point, I'll send Mariah down to give you water. She'll force feed it to you if necessary. I won't have you dehydrated. At the one hour mark, she'll come and release you, and you can clean up after yourself and go home. If you've never held a plug this long, be sure and wash yourself out with this." She put a bottle of salve next to the remote. "It will soothe the tissues, so you'll be ready for Friday."

"Friday," he said, staring at her.

She hadn't intended to extend the invitation, or at least that's what she'd told herself, but now she knew she'd planned to take him from the very beginning. She was nuts. She could barely control him. If he were free now, he'd have her slammed down on her back in an instant. The thought made her thighs tremble.

"Friday," she repeated firmly. "There's a group of female Doms from The Zone who are bringing their current slaves to a weekend place on the Gulf that belongs to a friend of mine. I want to bring you. You don't have to go," she added. "If it's too soon for you to go off site, I'll understand, and we can keep playing here." She softened her tone, stepped forward, and dared to get close enough to twist his hair in her fingers. He licked her wrist, bit down on her palm, the jerky movements of a man being pushed to climax and fighting to hold back.

She hesitated, then plunged forward, ignoring all sense, caution. She focused only on those beautiful eyes, so angry and needy, all at once. "If you've still got the guts, meet me out in front of The Zone, at four o'clock."

"It's too soon for you," he said, surprising her. "You don't know me well enough. You should be more cautious about going off alone with strange men."

She squatted, met his burning gaze, and felt his fingers strain against his bindings, whisper at her ankles to caress her. "I can handle you, Mackenzie. Now, you think about tonight and what you did to deserve this punishment, and maybe you won't have to go through it again in front of four Doms this weekend, but I suspect you will. You're just that goddamned stubborn. Bring that plug with you Friday. If you're a good boy, I'll just put it back in my bag."

Her lips twisted at the expression on his face, one step away from murder. "I'll be thinking of you when I'm in bed tonight," she murmured. "Making myself come with the fingers touching you right now." She pressed her lips to his, the briefest of contacts, before she drew back, taking her ankles out of his reach, and stepped toward the door.

"Mistress…Violet…son of a—don't do this."

"Good night, Mackenzie." She glanced up. "Looks like a large crowd tonight. I think they're going to enjoy the show."

Chapter 7

Five times. God, her knees were too weak to get her out of the car and take her into her house. She'd stayed, stuck to the shadows alone with her glass of wine, and watched over him as the hour passed. No way would she ever leave his care to someone else, unsupervised, but he hadn't needed to know that. The plug had brought him to orgasm five times, a tremendous response rate, and she had sent Mariah down with water for him at two twenty minute intervals instead of only once. He'd mesmerized the club crowd, positively stolen the show of the other open rooms. Who could resist watching a powerful man, a gladiator restrained, sexually stimulated to climax again and again? The build up of the sensations until he could not help himself, until he had to let his ass plunge and clench as if he were thrusting into a woman, the broad shoulders flexing, back muscles rippling, the head pressed down hard against his chest, refusing the natural desire to throw it back and let them see his face. On the fourth time, he had ten minutes left to go and she didn't believe he could go again, not without full collapse.

The body was the locked gate to the soul. Break the body, and the soul would have to defend itself. She wanted that vulnerability, wanted to show him what gift that truly relenting to a Mistress would bring him. She believed she'd done the right thing, but then the fifth climax took him and his body merely shuddered through it, a man too tired to resist the inevitable. When Mariah released him, he simply lay down on the floor. She felt eyes look toward her, felt judgments being weighed as to what she'd done.

She wanted to be down there helping him, but with a grim smile through the tears welling in her eyes, she watched him shrug off Mariah's help, snarl away the two male attendants she'd sent down. He snapped at them like a pit bull in truth, struggled to the room controls on his own and darkened the ceiling, shutting them all out. But not her. She could feel his exhausted heart pounding in her own chest, feel his trembling muscles in her own thighs. This was either battle or courtship, or both, and though the ultimate outcome was uncertain, she knew she had won this battle. At least she thought she had, unless he didn't show Friday. Then she would have lost the war.

Her body actually shook with pent-up desire all the way through the drive home. When she walked up her stairs and let herself into the house, she felt as weak as a person with the aftermath of the flu.

She chose a hot bath as her release, wanting its comfort and the sensual, bone-deep pleasure and tranquility it offered. Her emotions were too wrung out to seek her toys. Toys sought for non-playful reasons simply heightened stronger, more painful yearnings. She had no desire for release except through means of the man she had just left.

Violet had taught herself to accept that someone with her proclivities would likely always have relationships only within the confines of a place like The Zone. Two sessions with Mac, and she wanted more. She wanted it all again. Despite his easy invitation, she knew it would actually shock Tyler to the bone that she'd invited her new slave to do something outside the club area so soon, invited him to get to know her life, because she wanted to know his.

You're setting yourself up for such a hard fall, baby. But she'd done it, so she'd ride the horse until it tossed her, and hope she hadn't gotten a mean bronc that would trample her or toss her into a wall.

She decided on lavender bubbles with a touch of aloe and left her clothes in the bedroom, sinking down into the water with a blissful sigh.

When the phone rang, she reached over, hit the speaker button on the unit next to the tub.

"Hello, Tyler."

"Checking caller ID again?"

"No, I just knew it was you. You know, stalking is illegal."

"But spying isn't. Within reason. You okay?"

She closed her eyes. "Complicated question. I'll take the next one. Better yet, no questions. You talk, keep me awake so I don't drown."

"I thought I smelled bubble bath. Need someone to come scrub your back, darling?"

"You offering?"

"I would, but you'd just be imagining I was that poor bastard you wrung out dry. The consensus is you are one scary bitch."

"He's goading me, Tyler. He wants me to test him with the macho stuff, the floggings and pain. That's easy for him, way too easy. I want the stuff that gets under the skin and makes him vulnerable. He always falls in with Mistresses that want his cock."

"You want him."

She paused. "Yes. Yes, I do. I don't want anything less. If he won't give me that, I don't want him. So how long do I keep trying?"

"As long as he keeps showing up, I say he's interested in giving that to you. That's the way the really difficult subs can be. They don't know that's what they want, but their subconscious does, so they keep coming back for it. In the meantime, you're getting very popular. A couple of subs have practically begged me for an introduction." Another pause. "Violet? Any interest?"

"No," she admitted. "I just want him. I'm bringing him this weekend. If he shows on Friday."

A startled stillness on the other end of the phone. Violet waited, watching bubbles run down her thigh when she placed her foot on the rim of the tub.

Tyler's voice was soft when he spoke, reminding her why she considered him one of her closest friends. "If he doesn't, he's nuts. You're doing great."

"Am I? Or am I pushing too hard? I remember all the things I've learned and seen, but when I'm in there, something else takes over. Gut, or instinct."

"You've always trusted your instincts, Violet. It makes you good in the vanilla world, and it makes you the kind of Mistress no sub can refuse in this world. It's an art form. How often have you heard a writer or painter say 'something just takes over'? Maybe there's a Domination muse."

She snorted with laughter, sending a paw of bubbles across the tub. "Idiot."

"An idiot who cares a lot about you. I think it's good you're bringing this guy. If you're falling this hard, this fast, I want to check him out."

"That may even be part of why I'm bringing him. To get an objective opinion."

"Fair enough. Get out of the tub before you fall asleep. Now, while I'm on the phone. Just remember, Vi, my objective opinion isn't going to matter two damns if it turns out you're already gone on him."

"Yeah, but you'll be able to say 'I told you so' when he stomps my heart into little pieces."

"That's what I love about you. Always looking on the positive side. Night, Vi."

"Night, Tyler."

* * * * *

Mac stared at his ceiling and listened to the clock tick. The case file for the S&M Killer, as she'd been dubbed, was scattered at the end of the bed, the crime scene photos fanned out on the floor. He'd tacked several key pictures to the ceiling just below the skylight window, angling the neck of the bedside table lamp up so he could spotlight every detail.

Serial killers sometimes liked to take trophies, leave a mark. For this killer, it was how she left her victims. Both cuffed on the floor by the footboard of the bed. Arms spread and manacled to the top railings, ankles to the posts, so her victim was pulled out to an uncomfortable angle. His point of gravity was forward, hanging by the weight of his arms because his legs were spread out too wide for him to keep his balance under stimulation and there wasn't enough slack to let him be on his knees. She'd climbed up on the bed behind him, leaving her knee prints in the spread, and shot out the back of his head with a hollow point. She hadn't wanted to look in his eyes in that last moment. Why?

Maybe she didn't want him to see it coming. Maybe she didn't want him to suffer. Perhaps she was killing some part of herself, and didn't want to see him as a separate identity. Both victims had suffered a light flogging, had reached climax shortly before the kill. She'd given them pleasure before death. She wasn't interested in torture, not yet. But if she kept doing it, and everything indicated she would, that would change. She was all-powerful, had him at her whim. Why not push the boundaries, see what it felt like to push past where he was willing to go, if it was the same rush to push past his pain threshold as it was to take his life?

Mac had tracked killers long enough to know that eventually the blood lust had a dark power of its own that took over. Its only blessing was that it dulled the wits of the sharpest murderer. But he'd rather not wait until this one reached that point.

She'd already chosen her next victim, he was sure of that. She would be in the process of winning his trust, working toward this ultimate goal. The ultimate surrender.

He blinked. He'd covered this ground for an hour now. After he'd slept for six solid hours. When he'd gotten home, he'd had no choice. He had abandoned pride, fallen across the bed and let exhaustion take him where it wanted to go while his body built back up a reserve. His lips twisted.

He'd made the decision to seek out another Mistress, one less distracting. That resolve lasted for about an hour as he did some mingling, checking out a few leads he'd identified from the previous night, following up on some promising conversations. Then, right at the time she had dictated, he had turned his feet toward the downstairs area. He'd stopped at the top of the stairs, managed to fight with himself for a good solid minute before he went down, straight to the room she'd reserved, and done as she'd told him to do. And he knew without a doubt he'd be outside The Zone on Friday, waiting for her.

He'd done it for the case, because he hadn't found another Mistress that suited his purposes as well as Violet. However, he knew he had done it for a hell of a lot of other reasons besides, reasons that had nothing to do with the case at all.

She had drained him. He had almost cracked, almost begged her not to leave him that way, a performing act for the others of the club. But he had managed. Mostly. She disturbed him, deep down, the things she said, the way she was making him feel. She made him furious, but not in a way that made him want to turn his back on her. He wanted to show the little minx she might be tough, but he was tougher. That he could please her beyond her wildest dreams, if he could just figure out what the hell it was she wanted, and why he felt like he couldn't stay away from her. Even though he'd never been so apprehensive under a Mistress's hand as he was with her.

He wasn't in control with her. That was it. Mac forced himself to face it, face that there might be some truth to what she'd been telling him about his previous Mistresses. She saw through bullshit, and she wasn't hesitating to reach right through it to curl her little fingers tight around his balls. He didn't know what she'd ask next. What if she wanted something that he couldn't handle, that would break him down completely? He could turn away now, before that happened, but everything in him strained toward her, as if she were a drug in truth. He was afraid he wouldn't refuse her anything.

* * * * *

Violet wished she'd had more time to unwind after work. She'd run over shift, and it had been a hellacious day with an overabundance of assholes. She had planned on a long bath so she could come to The Zone in the right frame of mind, but had only had time for a quick shower. She cursed herself for not deciding to go up to Tyler's on Saturday, so she would have had Friday to prepare herself. The plain and simple truth was she'd been too eager to see Mac again to wait.

But there were other ways to regroup. She pulled into the convenience store parking lot across from The Zone and sat there a moment, just gazing across the street at the front entranceway of the club from her screened position.

He was there. He stood, waiting for her, talking to Richard, the front doorman for The Zone.

Just seeing him there made her feel like a sailboat catching an evening wind. Certain parts tightening up, others loosening as the sails strained forward eagerly with the wind. The captain relaxed at the helm, knowing she could ride this tack for awhile, just enjoying the beauty of what lay before her. Leave the cares of land far behind.

The last two times she'd left him, he'd been pretty much naked. But even seeing him in clothes—the black jeans he seemed to favor and a blue dress shirt with sleeves rolled up to just below his elbows—made her instantly, noticeably wet. The way he stood, leaning against a column of the entranceway, arms crossed over his chest. He smiled at something Richard said, and she let out a soft gasp as her pussy vibrated in response. Maybe she should have used one of her toys this week. She'd gone from work stress mode to high arousal mode with barely a pause in between. She knew what those silky curls on his head felt like now, twining over her fingers, and she wanted to be touching them. Black, silver and white. He would smell good, as he had the past two times; soap, a touch of aftershave or cologne, and heat. That heat had its own scent. If they could extract an oil from it, they'd have an aromatherapy candle any woman would want.

The sun had not yet set, and so he wore sunglasses, which just drew attention to his mouth, the strong jaw, the smooth beard. She wanted to see his eyes.

He turned his head and though he shouldn't have even noticed her, his attention slid into the parking lot of the convenience store, found her and her car in a matter of several seconds. He said something to Richard. The other man grinned, offered an appropriate male gesture of farewell. Then Mac was walking toward her.

She couldn't help smiling at him as he crossed the street, and she kept smiling, an easy thing to do, until he stopped at her open car window, leaned in. He took in her casual appearance, a snug pair of blue jeans and deep hunter green placket shirt. "You look like you have a secret." He touched his finger lightly under her chin.

"I do, Mackenzie. You're it. Take off the sunglasses."

And because it pleased her to do it, the moment he complied, she curled her fingers in the open neck of his shirt, brought him in for a kiss, a touching of lips that she deepened, or maybe he did. Their tongues tangled, and she felt the heat of it rush up from her toes to the point of fusion, energizing every part of her, erasing any weariness or stress she'd carried from the mundane world. His hand came up, cradled her face, his fingertips in her hair in a romantic, protective gesture she liked very much. When she broke the kiss, she was smiling still.

"I missed you," she said, and his eyes crinkled in an attractive way, returning her grin. They were looking at each other like a pair of foolish teenagers, and though she knew she should be appalled, she wasn't. She was just...happy. Excited.

When she lifted her leg over the gear shift and moved into the passenger seat, she could tell she'd surprised him. "I want you to drive. If you can handle a stick."

He laughed then, and it coated her like melted chocolate, a warm sound. She wondered if he had any idea how deeply sexual a creature he was. Not the prettiest or most handsome man she'd ever seen, but beautiful and sexual in the way predators were. Mesmerizing.

He opened the door and slid one leg in, ducking his head to take the pilot's seat of the black Stealth. He gave her a sidelong glance, and she leaned over, reached down between his legs and released the seat lever so it eased back, making room for his longer frame. Taking her hand back over his leg, she caressed his thigh with her palm, enjoying the feel of the hard body beneath the denim.

"Talk about a ticket magnet," he observed, familiarizing himself with the controls and readjusting the mirrors.

"I have a Fraternal Order of Police sticker," she informed him, poker-faced. "I give regularly."

"Mmm-hmmm. I'm sure that stops them from pulling your ass over."

She grinned, reached over and took the sunglasses from the open collar of his shirt where he had hooked them, put them back on his face. "Just shut up and drive. Take I-75 to state road 48. It's not the most direct route, but it will be less traffic."

When Mac glanced over a moment later, she had taken a brush out of her purse and removed the wig. He missed a gear and winced at the resulting complaint from the engine. Fortunately, a stop light caught them at the next major intersection so he could turn and look at her without risking both their lives.

Short, sassy auburn hair curled wildly around her face and stopped just above her shoulders, enhancing the impression of a forest fairy he'd had when he first saw her. She looked toward him with that big, beautiful violet gaze, and he felt his heart skip a beat and stumble, just as he'd made the engine do. "What color are your eyes?"

She rummaged in her purse again, withdrew a lens case. She pulled the contacts from her eyes, put the case away, then blinked at him with irises that were a soft blue like the Caribbean, so close to the lavender of the contacts he suspected they were more enhancement than a different color.

"The light, Mackenzie," she said gently.

He jerked his attention back to the road when the guy behind them blared his horn. He missed another gear accelerating. She raised a brow. "Are you sure you've driven straight gear before?"

He chuckled. "Sugar, last time I drove one, there were a lot less distractions. You've got to give me a moment to catch up."

She smiled, and he could tell his reaction pleased her. "So, what do you drive?"

"I've got a pickup for hauling and a bike for everything else. A Honda VTX."

She frowned. "Motorcycles are very unsafe."

He shot her a pointed glance. "And I suppose you got this thing so you could drive Miss Daisy around?"

She relented. "A motorcycle, hmm? Those long legs with all that power between them." She ran her nail down his thigh and his cock tightened against the crotch of his jeans. "Will you take me for a ride sometime?"

He grinned. "Sure."

"Will you let me drive?"

"You got a bike license?"

"No."

"Then, no."

"Oh, that's just an excuse. You just don't want me handling your wheels."

He looked her up and down. "You can handle anything you want of mine, sugar, but when we get to the bike, that's in the same territory as marriage."

"Have you ever been married?"

Violet knew the answer, even before he shook his head. Not her slave. She was sure he'd never let a woman get that close. And it made her woman's heart wonder why, though she suspected she already knew a large part of the reason.

"Want to explain that?"

"I can't." His gaze shifted, and his voice was quiet, telling her he wasn't avoiding the question. "It has to do with some things I just can't talk about."

"Ever?" She reached out, touched his face so he would look her way.

"Not yet," he said.

"An honest answer, so I can live with that. "

They drove in companionable silence for some time, and she enjoyed watching the capable way he navigated the car through Tampa's traffic to the interstate, the way he shifted gears, the movement of his long legs as he maneuvered the brake and clutch. Actually, she thought she could make a pastime out of just watching him. He was aware of her intent stare, she could tell, but he handled it well, his sub training kicking in so that he did not try to make conversation. That would have intruded upon her obvious, deliberate perusal and been considered rude.

Nevertheless, her scrutiny aroused him. She could tell by the flicker of his eyes, the press of his lips, the occasional swallow that moved the muscles of his throat. It wasn't until they merged into the interstate that she relented and broke the silence.

"Would you like to turn on some music?"

"Sure."

She opened the console, held up a handful of CD's for his inspection.

"Smashmouth? Matchbox 20? Avr…Avril Lavig…Ay-ya-ya-ya."

"Avril Lavigne," she said, narrowing her eyes at him.

"Well, thank God." He plucked out one of the choices. "At least you have a Credence Clearwater Revival tape."

"I'm sure my father probably left that in here."

"Brat."

"Old fogey."

She considered him as he put in the CD, the teasing look in his eyes doing amazing things to her pulse rate. "How old are you, Mac?"

"Depends on the day."

"Mackenzie."

He glanced at her, relented. "Forty-three. You?"

"I turned eighteen a month ago, I swear."

He let out a low whistle. "Well, you're out of luck then, sugar, because I only date high school girls." He lifted her hand, pressed an open-mouthed kiss on her knuckles that shivered through her. "I'd guess twenty-seven."

"Would it make you happy, me being that much younger than you?"

"You make me happy just being near me, sugar. But if I'm right, it would scare the shit out of me."

She smiled. "I'm thirty-two. And I know what scares the shit out of you, Mac." She leaned forward, pressed her lips to his neck. "It's not my age."

Chapter 8

They stopped at a general store in one of the picturesque fishing towns. She bought cheese, blackberry preserves, a fresh tomato and a couple baguettes to go with the bottle of wine she had in the car already. He got her a fountain vanilla coke and himself a Dr. Pepper. As they pulled back onto the rural route that would take them to Tyler's secluded home on the Gulf, he reached over and took her hand. He just held it, a simple, sweet gesture that tugged on her heartstrings as she watched his long fingers completely surround hers, the way his index finger stroked her knuckles idly as they talked and rode.

She had him pull off at a roadside picnic area to eat their snack. The location overlooked a breathtaking view of a small man-made lake that fed into the marsh areas. Maples had been planted in the protected area, and they were starting to experience some fall color, which added to the scenic view. "Could you eat?" she asked.

He grinned. "I'm six four and two hundred twenty pounds of muscle, sugar. I can eat."

"Braggart. Mess with me, and I won't share dessert." She produced a small bag of M&M's.

"I hope you brought six more of those."

Bypassing the picnic table, she went further down the slope to the water. He helped her spread out the blanket she'd brought and then took an edge while she laid out their lunch, handing him the cheese, baguette and knife.

"Can you cut off a few pieces for a sandwich? How many do you want?"

As they ate in easy silence, she took the time to study him. The way he ate, like a man, with whole hearty bites she knew would have him finished and eyeing her sandwich in no time. He had manners, though, using a napkin liberally and chewing with his mouth closed. Things like that were important, as was the way he wore his clothes. He wasn't a fashion plate, but his shirt was ironed and the jeans were not faded or ripped. It mattered to him how he presented himself, and she liked that. She reached out, stroked a hand through his hair, enjoying the feel of the curls, the way they ringed her knuckles like a baby's. Touching his cheekbone, she traced it as he chewed, feeling the movement of the muscle in his jaw, the wonder of him. Smoothed a finger over the trim moustache, stroked the beard line. As he had when she looked at him in the car, he sat quietly beneath her touch, not interrupting her pleasure with an interactive response. It stirred the deep primal part of her, the way he understood so instinctively how to be a submissive and please his Mistress. She knew he sensed the rousing of the Dominant in her, for his chewing slowed, his fingers curling on the napkin on his knee, adding to the heat of the stillness increasing between them. She liked that part, feeling the weight of anticipation unfurl in her lower belly and seeing he was aware of it, wary.

"What do you like, Mackenzie?" she asked softly.

Those silver eyes rose. "I like you."

His eyes were serious, his lips firm so that she wanted to take a bite out of them. "I meant, what do you like to do? Hobbies, passions? Other than the things you do at The Zone."

And how long had he done that? How many women had he called Mistress before her? It mattered, but it wasn't right to ask it, not yet.

"You mean, other than you?" He caressed her knee, laid a kiss on it, nuzzled, worked his way up her denim-clad thigh, nibbling so she felt the press of his teeth. She accommodated him, shifting to part her legs slightly for a moment, then tugged on his hair.

"Enough," she reproved, though she knew her voice was a bit breathy. "Hobbies, Mac."

"Tall ships," he said. "I like putting together models. I read old sea stories, the really old ones you only find in junk shops or at library sales, things written by the sailors themselves in the eighteenth or nineteenth centuries. And cooking. I like cooking."

"Did you ever go on one? A tall ship?"

"Sure. There are trips you can take in the reproductions, where you sign on as crew and work a couple weeks. It isn't exactly like the good old days. They make you wear harnesses when you're working out on a yard a hundred feet above deck."

"Well, it would be such a mess to clean up otherwise. Do you have your own boat?"

"A little McKee craft I take out on the weekends. I'll take you out sometime. In fact, I'd really like to take you."

A shadow crossed his expression and she frowned. "You okay?"

"Yeah. I'm getting lost in you too fast, I think." He looked startled that he'd spoken so bluntly to her. "I mean...I didn't mean..."

"No, that's fine." She shook her head. "I like when you tell me straight out what's in your heart." *And I like the fact that you're feeling out of control.* "Motorcycles, tall ships…you *are* an adrenaline junkie, Mackenzie." Knowing what she knew about him, she expected nothing less. But there was at least one question to which she didn't know the answer, and she'd ask it before she lost her nerve.

"Are you involved with someone? I know you said you haven't been married, but—"

He flicked a glance at her. "What kind of guy do you think I am?"

She lifted a shoulder. "It's not unusual for a man to visit the club scene alone, especially if his girlfriend isn't into it. Double life sort of thing. I know some married guys at The Zone whose spouses know about it, even give them their blessing, because they feel like it keeps the craving under control. Like a limited indulgence in drugs to keep it from becoming a destructive addiction. Or obsession."

He didn't smile. "Hey." His hand covered hers on the blanket and she raised wary eyes to his steady ones. "I'm all yours, sugar. Okay?"

"Okay." Relief spread through her and became warmth when he kept hold of her hand and lay back on his elbows. She twisted her fingers over his, spread them both out, played idle finger games with him for a few minutes in silence as he studied her. The air grew charged between them, and she pressed her lips together. "Me, either," she relented. "I'm not involved, or married."

"Good. I don't share."

It was a provocative statement, delivered with a tone and a direct stare that was far from submissive. She was bemused at the reaction of her own body, a jump in response at the possessive statement that tightened her nipples against the soft lining of her bra.

"Me either." She gave it back to him with a hard, penetrating look to let him know he was dancing on the line. "Not unless I order it, and I'm there to watch."

He inclined his head. His move. "I... There's no command of yours I'll refuse, but... I'm not much into men. The whole ass-fucking thing..."

"Has a woman ever done it to you?"

He sat up, linked his hands over his knees, and her sharp eyes noted the defensive posture. "Just some finger stuff or plugs, like you did."

"No Mistress ever—"

"Most found that they were wasting a perfectly good cock that they could use for their own pleasure."

Defensive, definitely. Almost surly. She saw him bite it back, try for a smile to smooth it over.

"You're a submissive afraid to let go of control, afraid to have your most vulnerable areas investigated." She studied him, let him squirm a bit under her intent regard. "You tell a Mistress she can do anything to you, no safe words, no boundaries, but then you con her into doing only what keeps to the edges of your comfort zone."

"I prefer the word 'charm'."

"I call it like I see it." She took a bite of bread. "And you should know better than to argue with me about it at this point. Tell me why you're a sub, Mac. Why not be a Dominant? You obviously bleed alpha. What's driving you to submit to a woman sexually? Open up."

He opened his mouth, took the offering from her fingers, lightly nibbling one fingertip, then caught it in his mouth between his teeth. He did not let go when she exerted gentle pressure, and she narrowed her eyes as his hand lifted, circled her wrist, held her captive to run his tongue along her sensitive knuckles, nibble on the pads of her fingers. Instead of resisting, she relaxed, waited until she had his attention to lift a disinterested brow.

"You know, horses sometimes do this," she said. "Catch your hand in their mouth when they're playing, not realizing they can hurt you. Or at least people say that. But I think horses know exactly how strong and tough they are." She took her free hand, ran it along his jaw line. "I think they know they can take your fingers off, and they're reminding you that, no matter how often you ride them, what saddle or bridle you put on them, they're stronger, and can take you down in a moment." She slid her touch under his chin, squeezed his jaw with her fingers, exerting the bite of her nails until he got the message and eased up. "But those beautiful, magnificent creatures bow to our will. They serve us only if they trust that they're better off with the reins in our hands." She cocked her head. "Only if they believe without a doubt we're worthy of being in control."

He let go with his mouth and she removed her fingers, but he did not relinquish her wrist.

"I'd like to make love to you. Here. Now."

She swallowed, closed her fingers into a fist. "I don't think I'm ready to let you do that, Mackenzie. You don't trust me enough."

He shook his head. "It's to prove you can trust me."

For it to be as good as it should be, it had to be a two-way street. He didn't understand that. Still, the idea of lying in the late afternoon sun, a touch of fall nipping in the air, with him inside of her… it was a difficult image to resist, particularly with his fingers playing over hers, his silver eyes marking every response of her body.

She could imagine how it would look to a hawk flying overhead, the two of them entwined. Mac's thighs and buttocks tightening and releasing as he slid in, drew out, the slow strokes she would demand, that would drive her to the edge, fulfilled. His smell, his arms wrapped around her, his lips against her neck.

He was closer now, his mouth only a breath from hers, his hand sliding to her waist, drawing her closer, drawing her down against him. She cupped a hand to the side of his head, met his tongue just inside his lips, then he drew her in, opening his mouth to devour hers, his arms closing around her, holding her secure, letting out a groan of pure pleasure she felt rumble in his chest, pressed against her aching breasts.

His hand closed over the tight denim covering one ass cheek , and used the hold to shift her over so she was lying on him, one of his thighs pressed up between her legs, sending a ripple of erotic pleasure shivering up through her lower stomach and chest, tightening her nipples against his hard body. His hand kneaded her ass, stroked the crease of thigh, two fingers sliding down the curve of her buttocks, in between her legs, curling under the intersection of stitched seams so the heel of his hand was against the base of her ass. His fingers hooked over her clit at the crotch of the jeans, pressing on her, kneading her like a cat, making her shudder, her breath coming faster.

"Let me put my cock in you," he murmured, kissing her neck, nuzzling, biting.

Her grip on reality was slipping away. He was entirely too potent, his hands sure, knowledgeable, knowing exactly how to drive sense and control away, coaxing her into compliance. His arm pressed against her buttocks, and she felt the metal of the onyx and silver wrist cuffs he had worn.

With an oath, she slapped her hands against his chest and shoved off him, rolling to her side, coming to her feet in a crouch, putting a good four feet between them.

"This is bullshit," she said, really angry with him.

He sat up. His color was high and his erection tremendous, distending the front of his jeans and making her wish she wasn't so sure of what she knew, or that she could forget it and just take what he was offering to relieve the throbbing want in her pussy.

"What's bullshit?" he asked. "What the hell are you talking about?"

"Don't take that tone with me," she warned. "You won't charm or con me, Mackenzie. I told you. When we make love, it will be because that's what you want and I want, not because you want a change in conversational topic, and you figure a good fuck will distract me. I'm not easily distracted, not when it's important. I asked you why you play the sub side of the fence. I expect an answer."

And this was important. Maybe too important. She wanted to slap him for making things this difficult, but his recalcitrance also turned her on, there was no denying that. He looked very appealing to her, leaning there tensely on one elbow.

"I don't know," he said at last, irritation in his tone. "I… Why is it women want to analyze? I just…do. When I'm with a woman, it's the way I feel. You're not complaining, are you? So why does it matter?"

Because you matter. Because the answer to the question is important to you, but you're afraid to answer it.

"I want you to stand up and unfasten your jeans, take them down with your underwear to your knees. I want to see you. And take those damn wrist cuffs off. Some other woman gave them to you, so I don't want to see them. You're mine, Mackenzie, and I don't share you, not even with memories."

He hadn't expected that, or the gear change, she could tell. She watched him process it, glance around them, and she softened, leaned forward, laid a hand on his jaw. "We'll hear a car if someone pulls up. We'll have a few minutes before we see them. That's why I came down here. You can trust me to protect your privacy, Mac."

He nodded. His gaze still held anger and frustration, but he obeyed, rising to his feet. He took off the cuffs first, dropped them to the blanket. Violet lowered herself to one hip, watching him intently as he took his hand to the button of his jeans and worked it loose with those large, capable fingers. He lowered the zipper, then pushed the jeans down his hips with his underwear, freeing his cock so it stretched out in full magnificent rigid glory.

"Unbutton the shirt so it's not in my way," she ordered softly.

He obeyed, and she watched him become longer and harder, his body responding to her commands and her perusal. She touched her tongue, just the tip to her top lip, and his testicles contracted.

"Now." She lifted her lashes. "Lace your hands behind your head. And don't move them unless I tell you to do so. And you are not allowed to look down. Not even once."

"Yes, Mistress."

"I like it very much when you call me that." She slid over along the blanket, ran one finger along his length, felt his heat, the iron hardness of him, noted the drop of moisture gathering at the tip. She smoothed her knuckles down the side of his hip, the top of his thigh. "Two of the ladies that will be there tonight are twins. They work in tandem, and they like pain. They're good at administering it, and they like to share subs. How do you feel about me sharing you with them, Mackenzie?"

She watched his face, saw the shadow, saw it masked. "Whatever pleases Mistress."

"Hmmm. This does." She took up the white plastic spreading knife and spread some of the blackberry preserves on the top of his cock, just the length of the shaft behind the head. He drew in a breath as she covered him with her mouth, bringing his flesh and the tartness into it, circling the base of his cock with one small hand and squeezing firmly as she sucked and licked the condiment from him.

"Jesus Christ."

She smiled, drew back just enough to speak. "Keep your hands up there, Mackenzie. I want to play with you a bit. You're mine, aren't you? My plaything?"

"Yes, Mistress. God…yes."

She licked a long stroke down the underside to his scrotum, as if she were enjoying a lollipop. "Close your eyes. I want you to be totally focused on where I lick you next."

He obeyed, though the effort it cost him was visible.

She brought her hands around him, her palms caressing his thighs, his hips. They trembled with the strain of keeping completely still as she'd ordered, while she slid her lips up and down his impressive length. His fingers clenched behind his head, his biceps bunched in a way that made her want to rub oil all over his body again, polish those muscles to gleaming. In an ideal world, a Mistress could keep her slave stripped and oiled all the time, in public or out of it. She wouldn't mind the envious stares of other women, knowing she owned that erect cock, all that beauty and power at her command.

Well, if she could ever get him to stop being so damn stubborn, it would all be at her command. Glancing up to make sure his eyes were still closed, she reached into her purse. She ran the base of her tongue along the ridge of his engorged head as she did so, and made the adjustments she needed with the bottle of lubricant.

She took her hands up his thighs, caressing his hips and curled around those muscular buttocks. He jerked at the cold touch of the new plug, his muscles starting to tighten, but she had already inserted the head of it and used his movement to thrust it past the relaxed muscle before it could clench up. It was a smaller plug, but large enough to be noticeable to the wearer.

"Violet," he made a strangled noise. "Not again."

"Eyes closed, Mackenzie, and keep your hands up there."

She kissed the tip of him, licked the head gently once more, and then used her hold on his waist to stand up, letting his bare cock brush her jean-clad hip. She worked his underwear and jeans back up his legs, over his hips and delectable ass, buttoning and fastening the jeans so their snug fit and the tight hold of that powerful muscle would keep the plug in place. She had to maneuver the zipper carefully over his erection and put her hand in a couple of times to ensure it was tucked in properly. She felt his apprehension, saw the quiver of his arms as he restrained himself, fighting against instinct to relinquish himself to her hands.

"I won't use the remote," she said, taking her time buttoning his shirt, fondling his damp, heated skin. "Unless you pull that crap with me again. You can't charm your way out of things with me, Mackenzie, and you won't drive me away by being threatening and surly. You can choose to walk away, and that's it. A polite, courteous break of contract because two people no longer see the benefit of being with one another, as one or both feels they have nothing left to offer the other."

His hands were faster than she expected. Before she could blink, they were gripping her upper arms hard, and he'd lifted her to her toes. "I did want to make love to you," he snapped. "It wasn't bullshit. It wasn't a game."

"I'm glad to hear it. I told you before. To me, none of this is a game. Even when you try to play me, it's not a game." She stared up at him, used her elevated position to press her lips to his hard, angry mouth, nipping at him until they changed, yielded, opened. Abruptly he was consuming her, his arms sliding from their grip on her upper arms to clamp around her body, holding her against his taut, roused one. She played her fingers over his broad back, over his hips, clutched his ass and pressed on where the plug rested. Exerting stimulating pressure, and also making sure there was no visible indication he was wearing it. She didn't want to humiliate him, just enforce that he was hers.

"Violet," he groaned against her mouth, and it was hard for her to maintain a rational thought in his embrace. He was all-encompassing, the press of his torso an eclipse of heat that gathered her in, made her want to stay inside those strong arms, inside the span of his attention, for a few centuries. She stopped worrying and gripped the muscles of his wide back, clutched shirt and skin and surrendered to her own ferocity. Meeting his mouth with tongue and teeth just as furiously, her body quickened at every touch of his. His large hands dropped to squeeze, knead her buttocks, as possessive of her as she was of him.

It was insane. She'd never been so mad for anyone in her life. She wanted to eat him alive. She pulled away to suck in air. "Are you sure you don't wear some type of pheromone cologne?"

His grin was quick, feral, as distracted as a wolf taking a moment to acknowledge his joy in the hunt before the charge, the lunge to take a throat. Hers, in this case, his lips pressing on the vulnerable artery, biting the mark he'd left on her, this time nursing it, offering her an apology with his gesture even as his tongue flicked fire around it. She arched her throat and as she did it, turned her body, so her upper thigh was pressed against his prominent cock. His hand cupped her left breast, stroking, molding it, her nipple sliding between his index and middle fingers to squeeze with an intensity that was ruthless in its determination. He moved his thigh and it was between her legs, rubbing, setting off screaming nerves everywhere.

"Come for me," he whispered roughly. "For God's sake, give me something."

It was a savage whispered plea. It came from the place inside him she desperately wanted to make open to her, so when she heard it, she wanted to reward him for that, and give to him.

As if her internal decision to grant his wish slammed down a lever, her response gushed forth, flooding her blood stream, tensing her muscles in that perverse way a physical release did, as if it was pulling energy from the body as quickly as a drawstring, taking the elasticity from every muscle and tendon.

She played the game so well that she did not permit herself orgasm often, so when she came it was hard, shattering. In this case, she could not say whether she had permitted it or he had won her surrender with his whispered words, his strong hands, his overwhelming determination to claim something of her, make her his Mistress.

For she knew that the Mistress was as much the possession of the slave, even if Mac did not know it yet. As a result, it was not without a little fear that she felt the waves come crashing down on her.

The full shock of it hit her pussy at once. Even under her clothes she felt the spasms clench her against the pressure of his leg, and she clung to him, breathing fast, soft breathy moans, a shaking that swept through her limbs and made him hold her tighter. He pressed his lips to the soft skin by the corner of her eye and stayed there, working his leg against her, letting her writhe on it until her body weakened, the drawstring released, all the muscles going loose and quivering.

Holding her close, he held her up. His erection was an iron bar against her hip, and she was pleased he was that way, knew he would suffer from wanting her until she gave him leave to release himself in the way she designated. She also knew he would use all the considerable reserves of his personality to try and make her agree to the way he wanted to do it. Deep inside her, while fucking her pussy.

She was looking forward to the challenge, all the more because she wasn't sure what the outcome would be.

Chapter 9

"So did you have any questions you want answered, before we get there?"

It was only a thirty-minute drive to Tyler's from the picnic site, but Violet made good use of the time. She posed the question while she ran her fingers up and down his thigh, wandering frequently over to the curve of his testicles, making him keep his legs open to provide her access. She knew the plug teased him, and she added to it. As a result, he stayed fully, uncomfortably erect all the way to the turn-off to Tyler's private access road.

"If it pleases my Mistress..." He cleared his throat, but did not completely succeed in removing the hoarse need from it. "Who'll be there this weekend? I'm new to The Zone, so I'm not as familiar with the players."

"Tyler's about your age, and was my mentor. He's an erotic film producer. Not porn, not Triple X stuff. He does European erotica and Red Shoe Diary type things. A couple collaborations with Zalman King, but he feels like ZK gets too artsy, loses the erotic connection sometimes. I met Tyler at a party, and he was the one who helped me figure out what I liked from a man sexually, why I was dissatisfied so much. We hit it off right away, and later he told me that sometimes Doms just sense one another, the same sense that lets them identify a sub at twenty paces." She pinched him lightly and he bit back a grunt of frustrated desire. Violet smiled. "At the time, I had urges, but I thought there was something wrong with me. He helped me understand about D/s, introduced me to places like The Zone. Discretion is very important to me, in the job I do, so he helped me learn to keep the two lives separate."

Mac glanced over at her. "But you don't want to keep them separate."

She studied the horizon, appreciating how intuitive he was, but not wanting him to see he could read her that easily. "I wish they didn't have to be kept separate. One of the rules is to keep play in The Zone, not take it out of those places." She curled her hand under his inner thigh, increasing her grip, letting him feel the possessive need in her touch. "He also told me that once you understand the rules, then you can break them.

"I told you some about the twins already, Tamara and Kiera, T&K. They're more than Mistresses. They're pure Doms, through and through." She sharpened her tone to be sure she had his full attention. "They brook no disobedience of any kind, from any slave. You might want to keep that in mind, with your reluctance to use safe words. I may not always be in the room to protect you this weekend."

His gaze snapped from the road to her briefly. "So while I'm there…they can…"

"If I tell them they can. Unless my slave wishes to tell me about any boundaries he has in that regard."

Mac was silent for a few moments. Violet waited.

"No, Mistress. Your pleasure is my pleasure, as I've said before." His tone was low, pained. The need to reassure him gripped at her heart, but she squelched it. He had to learn he could trust her. She continued, as if the tension in the car had not just increased threefold.

"The third Mistress is Lisbeth."

"Lisbeth?"

"She's not a Zone regular, but she's a friend of Tyler's. Her favorite haunt is a place called—"

"True Blue."

Violet's brows lifted and he shrugged. Uncomfortably, she noted. "She was my first Mistress. The one who started off my training, gave me the cuffs, when I 'graduated', as she put it."

"Oh." Violet digested that, glanced at his face. "Is that going to be a problem?"

"You tell me."

Which meant maybe yes, but he wasn't going to tell her anything he perceived she didn't want to hear, anything that made him appear vulnerable.

"No problem for me, then." She decided to play along, and watched the muscle in his cheek jump with tension.

Tyler's drive ran several miles off the main road through a forest of live oaks and long leaf pines before it reached his restored antebellum plantation house. Violet put her hand back on Mac's cock as he drove through the winding curves, working the gear shift, and her blood stirred as he automatically parted his thighs wider, accommodating her. She hummed casually to herself, registering his tension, his every involuntary shift that showed the plug was combining with her stimulation to tease him to a higher level of arousal. She suspected his apprehension served as an additional catalyst, for his cock was enormous beneath her touch. He didn't know what to expect, how much he would be tested this weekend, how much she intended to enjoy him.

Since he didn't seem disposed to ask any more questions, she kept up her idle stroking, squeezing and pinching as she desired in the charged silence, until it was broken by his breath rasping in his throat. He made a somewhat less than smooth turn into Tyler's circular driveway before the house and brought the car to a stop behind a silver Jag marked with the T&K license plate.

"Violet, I can't go in there like this."

She arched a brow. "Are you refusing me?"

"Are you commanding me to meet your friends with a hard-on this size?"

She stretched up, kissed his cheek, moved back, nibbled his ear. "Yes, slave. I am. You're about to meet four very powerful and experienced Doms. I'm a baby to them, and I want to impress them." She laid her hand back on his crotch and squeezed again, earning an indrawn breath. "This is very impressive."

"Is that what this torture is about?" He sounded caught between irritation and amusement.

"No. But I think it makes you more comfortable to think so." She rubbed her hand over him again, one hard sure stroke this time that made his hips lift to her touch before he could stop himself. He caught her wrist and they froze, looking at each other. His eyes glittered, his jaw held tense in obstinacy. She made her face blank, unreadable.

"Let go of me, Mackenzie. Now."

He drew a deep breath, closed his eyes, and she squelched the desire to reach out, stroke his temple. Instead, she passed her thumb over the head of his cock, startlingly prominent through the denim. It was a lighter touch this time, but there, emphasizing that her interest and pleasure was to keep him visibly, painfully aroused. "Get out of the car."

It took another humming ten seconds of tension, but he reached for the door, opened it with a muttered oath that made her hide a smile.

She was anxious, too, but she made sure she covered it. She didn't know how this weekend would go. It would test the strength of the bond growing between them, a bond that seemed deeper than expected at this juncture. Understanding a couple of the reasons for it in a way she knew he did not yet, she hoped that this weekend would enhance it, not shatter it. She'd no doubt they were going to go into some uncomfortable territory. That was the nature of mixing a D/s sexual relationship with the things of the outside world. She was willing to take the risks, even knowing the stakes were growing higher every moment she was around him and her desire to claim him, keep him, grew.

"We observe certain etiquettes while we're here," she said. "When you're with me, you follow me, a pace behind." Mac dropped back a pace, and she nodded, didn't break stride. "Don't meet any Dom's gaze directly unless instructed to do so. You obey my commands, and if you have any questions, you ask permission before you ask them. Finally," she glanced back at him, "subs are required to be unclothed for the duration, only wearing what toys and jewelry their Master or Mistress deems is appropriate."

She registered his jerk of surprise just as Tyler opened the door, before she could knock. *Here goes, girl. Don't blow it.*

"Right on time." Tyler smiled down at her. In his mid-forties like Mac, he had the look of a relaxed pro golfer.

Tanned and with a lean muscularity, he kept his dark hair touched with gray trimmed close, so that the immediate focus was on his deep-set brown eyes, prominent nose, and curved, firm lips. He had a universal appeal; Violet had yet to see the person Tyler couldn't make feel at ease when he chose to do so.

"Tyler, this is Mac."

Tyler glanced over her shoulder. "Mac. Welcome to my home. I'm sure Violet explained the rules to you. Lower your gaze."

She also knew he could turn that warmth into instant coolness, as he did now. Used to a Mistress beating the hell out of him for infractions, and playing one-on-one, Mac was going to be stressed by a group, co-ed dynamic like this. Being a sub was a lot more than that, though Violet couldn't blame any Mistress for wanting to keep him all to herself.

Tyler had ratcheted up her slave's tension with the immediate gauntlet. Assessing him as a Dom was one thing, and part of what was expected this weekend. But as he studied Mac thoroughly, lingering deliberately on the prominent erection so that Mac was sure to feel the regard, he was clearly evaluating her choice in a protective, fraternal way that had a unique flavor with the Dom angle thrown in. Mac, an obvious mundane world alpha, was being compelled to act as a submissive member of the pack to a male challenging his claim on her. She could almost see the rise of his hackles, but ultimately he obeyed. Somewhat. Interestingly, he cut his eyes over to her first, making it clear it was her will he was obeying, not Tyler's. Further, he averted his gaze, rather than lowered it.

Tyler's lips twisted, acknowledging the cut. "You've got your hands full with this one, Violet. Maybe a weekend with us will teach him some manners. When you enter the hallway, Mac, there is a changing room to your left. You'll leave all clothes and jewelry there, except for what your Mistress has instructed you to leave on. You will then come join us in the main dining room, where you will kneel by your Mistress's chair."

Violet laid one hand on Mac's forearm. His silver gaze flickered to that contact, and she felt the heat singe the fine hairs along her wrist. "Mackenzie," she said. "You may remove everything."

She thought to give him a break, to preserve his dignity somewhat, but she should have known Tyler's ears would catch the slight inflection.

"I thought he looked a little stirred up," Tyler chuckled. "Maybe you should use a larger size next time, Violet. He's still far too rebellious for a slave with his Mistress's will shoved up his ass."

She tightened her grip on Mac's arm as the muscles hardened beneath her touch. "Go undress," she ordered softly. "Now, Mackenzie."

Feeling a maelstrom of emotions vibrate off him like an impending explosion, she held her touch a moment longer, and then let go, turning her back on him. There was frustration, anger, and something else, the thing she was trying to rouse, the confusing jumble of feelings every sub fought at this stage of the game. A tug of war between will and desire, control, power and need that fucked up their minds. If the loss of control frightened them enough, they would do things to deliberately earn punishment, to test the will of the Mistress. Knowing Mac, Tyler had just ensured they were in for a lively evening.

He turned, offered his arm to Violet. "Let me show you to the table."

As they left Mac in the foyer and headed further into the house, Tyler's fingers tightened on hers. "Don't look back. You'll only whisk him away someplace where you can pet him and protect him and abandon your resolve to break him down. You wanted us to play it hard this weekend, to help you. This is step one."

"He's so obviously one-on-one," she swallowed. "I'm afraid this will tear something loose in him, Tyler."

"If it's his heart, it will make it all the easier for him to give it to you. Violet," Tyler took her by the shoulders now that they were out of Mac's sight, and put a restraining hand to her chin. "He's not damaged. He can say no, and the game immediately ends, no censure, no anything. He takes his place at the table and joins us as a neutral, a voyeur only."

"But I don't know if that's true. There's something that keeps him from saying no when he really wants to say no. I don't know what it is."

"Then you'll get to the bottom of it. You're in charge of him, sweetheart." He brushed a finger over her cheek. "You're really gone over him. It's cute. I've never seen Violet in love."

"I am not. Don't be a smart ass." She scowled and he grinned, though his eyes grew a shade more serious in contrast.

"I'm not. If he's good for you, I'm all for him. If not, I'm hiring a guy to kick his ass. Based on his size and that lethal look he has in his eyes for me, maybe several guys. Oh, speaking of lethal, did I tell you? I almost got Marguerite to accept an invitation to come this weekend."

"You're entirely too fascinated with her, Tyler."

"I can't help it. She's like a dark pool, and every writer knows the best stories lie beneath still waters."

"She'd have to pick a sub, and I don't think she takes anyone outside."

"I told her I usually have a couple Zone staff available for play as well as food service. She said she'd think about it and maybe be here next time. Come, you should meet my Leila."

Leila, it turned out, was the centerpiece of the large glass table in the formal dining room. A tawny-skinned woman with large dark eyes, she had a mass of flame red hair that had been fanned out like a rippling crimson scarf across the polished glass. The table was etched with an oval border of silver roses that framed her naked body. Her arms stretched out to either side of her, her palms supporting two plates at the five place settings. The position would require her to remain still while the two Doms at those seats ate their meals.

Her ankles rested on the very edge of the table, while her thighs had been spread wide apart so her pussy would be open to the head of the table. Leila's navel was pierced, and the loop there secured a chain that ran down to her clit where the matching piercing had been drawn taut, not painfully, but enough to make her feel the tug between the two pierced points.

"This is my Leila," Tyler said, stroking his hand down her flank and caressing a nipple, displayed full and stiff in pewter shields inset with uncut gems. "Leila, this is Mistress Violet."

"My pleasure, Mistress," Leila said, her voice strained, her eyes on the ceiling.

"Take your place, Violet. Any place you wish except the head of the table. I reserve the pleasure of that view. Leila has an incredibly responsive pussy. She gets wet if I simply tell her to do so."

"You're fortunate to have such a lovely, obedient slave," Violet murmured, overwhelmed to hushed response. In the presence of Tyler's Mastery, reverent tones always seemed most appropriate.

"And the perfect centerpiece. But we need candlelight."

The other Mistresses were assembled already. The twins had taken the plates Leila was desperately balancing, of course, and Lisbeth was at the foot of the table. Violet took a moment to meet the unreadable but not unfriendly gaze of the woman who had been Mac's first Mistress. She was older than Violet had expected, possibly early fifties, but a well-cared for fifty, with blonde hair pulled back in a sleek bun. Her expertly applied make-up accentuated a lush mouth, high cheek bones and vivid green eyes that had a powerful charisma emanating from them. None of it appeared to be the result of a surgeon's knife, as she had the bone structure of a woman who had enjoyed good looks all her life and obviously knew how to maintain them. She wore black slacks and a soft turtleneck that emphasized a pair of generous breasts. Her hand rested on the shoulder of a naked man, about the same age as herself and in impressive physical shape. He rested in submissive kneeling posture at the arm of her chair, his head bowed.

The twins had their sub on his hands and knees beneath the glass table. Violet could not determine his features, because his chin rested between Tamara's splayed thighs, his face buried, unmoving, in her crotch, as she had apparently commanded. His body and his shoulder-length streaked blond hair suggested the sleek lines of a thirty-something pretty boy, hung like a Texas longhorn, with a tight, slender ass that Kiera idly brushed with her heel, occasionally teasing his anus with the spike tip.

"Oh, Violet, you've outdone yourself," Tamara said admiringly.

Violet turned to see Mac standing at the door, his eyelids lowered, waiting for her to be seated. Seeing him through their eyes, her breath caught in her throat. The broad gleaming shoulders, furred chest, tapered hips. Long, powerful arms and thighs. Impressive cock. All completely exposed to their appreciation.

There was an arrogant set to his expression, despite his observation of the requirement not to meet the eyes of any Master or Mistress present, including her. He was still semi-erect, and as his eyes carefully coursed over Leila without the lids rising inappropriately, taking in her predicament and the submissive posture of the other men present, it grew even stiffer.

Violet took a seat to Tamara's right and gestured. "Come here, Mackenzie. Kneel by me."

"If that cock was mine, I'd keep it in a chastity belt when he was away from me," Tamara observed. "Keep that bad boy from misbehaving with his hand…or anyone else."

"I don't cheat on my Mistress," Mac said coldly, going to one knee at Violet's side. "In any way."

His words seemed to startle Lisbeth, Violet noted. The woman's eyes widened slightly, then she covered her surprise by lifting her wine to her lips.

"I think we need candlelight," Tyler interjected. "Mac, please remember not to speak unless spoken to. We will forgive two infractions, but the third will likely incur punishment from your Mistress." He picked up a tapered candle from the sidebar, flicked on his lighter. "David," he nodded toward the man at Lisbeth's feet. "With your Mistress's permission, please lower the lights." He passed an amused glance over T&K's young man under the table. "Since Collin is somewhat occupied at the moment."

At her murmured command, Lisbeth's sub rose and complied, so the illumination was limited to the light of the early evening coming through the bay window, creating shadows and a rose and gold hue over the room and all the people in it.

Tyler stepped to Leila's side, between Violet and his seat, and used the lighter to heat the base of the candle. Leila's brown eyes were on his hands, and she drew in a sharp breath as the hot wax dripped onto her stomach, over and around her navel. Her arms trembled at the initial moment of excruciating heat and then continued to quiver at the lingering, tingling sensation Violet knew it roused in the nervous system. When enough drops fell, Tyler seated the candle in the cooling puddle of wax he'd created, adhering it to her body. As the candle burned, it would drip more wax down its length, adding to the puddle, continuing to stimulate her skin with its heated touch.

"If the rest of you would oblige me, there is a candle and a lighter by each of your settings," he instructed. "Feel free to place the candle where you'd like."

Violet felt Mackenzie's attention on her as she stood to imitate Tyler's actions. She chose the shallow indentation between the hip bone and the navel for the short taper.

Leila tried to quell her movements, though her breath gasped out of her, and her arousal could be smelled plainly. Sweat stood out in a sheen on her shoulders, slicked her breasts. As Kiera dripped wax on her nipples, Leila cried out, her tongue caressing her own lips. She closed her eyes and turned her head this way and that, trying to hold the rest of her body still so as not to unseat the candles, but incapable of not moving.

"Last one," Tyler said softly.

"Master, I cannot bear it," Leila said plaintively. "I'll come, and shame you."

"You will not come, for you only come on my command," he reproved sternly. "Do you wish to please me?"

"More than anything."

"Then be still. And I will permit you to come if you must, but you cannot unseat Kiera and Tamara's plates, or any of the candles. That would be very rude and would displease me greatly."

"Yes, Master."

He flicked his lighter again, and Violet watched, mesmerized, as he positioned the taper just over her swollen and glistening clit. Mackenzie's hand stole around her ankle, caressing her, and she almost gasped as Leila did at the intense pleasure of his lightest touch, magnified by the visual stimulation Leila was providing.

"They are all entranced by you, love," Tyler said quietly. Leila screamed, a soft cry, as the first drop fell, but she did not move. She whimpered; soft, staccato noises of need as each drip came, slid around and over her. When she was coated, Tyler placed the base of the candle amidst the petals of her sex, just below the piercing, gently working it into place in the cooling wax so he stroked her clit, made her teeth grit in concentration.

Mackenzie's hand eased up Violet's calf, tickled the back of her knee, but he could go no further where her leg met the chair without the aggressive move of taking his fingers to the top of her thigh. Not surprisingly, he tried it, but she put her hand over his, staying him with a light touch, keeping her eyes on Leila though she was hyperaware of him there, so close beside her.

"I think we need to make sure you have something to focus on throughout dinner," Tyler commented, his voice catching, revealing how the response of his lover was affecting him. Leila's eyes widened as he produced a vibrator from inside a velvet cloth bag by his plate.

"Oh, Master, I'll come too hard."

"There's no such thing," Lisbeth observed. "The harder the better." She shifted her focus to Mac's bowed head. "And I'll bet he's hard as a rock now."

Harder than rock. Mac felt he could give diamond ore a challenge. Leila's soft gasps and moans, her struggle to hold her straining spread-eagle position without any visible straps or bindings, would have been riveting by themselves. But Violet's rapt attention and the fact those lovely thighs pressed together at the knees could not hide the unique smell of her own arousal, so close to his nose, were driving him crazy.

Leila began to come the moment the broad head of the dildo stretched her pussy lips, pushed carefully into the wetness below the candle's sensitive saddle and began to disappear. Her whole body shuddered hard, enough to make the glassware tremble on the table, but she did not move at first, only cried out repeatedly as her fluids ran down the pink sides of the vibrator where they could see, her labia rippling over its thick sides, milking it as a flush raced from her chest to her face.

"Oh, God," she murmured. "I can't. Master—"

In sync, Tamara and Kiera closed their grip on her arms from elbow to wrist and Tyler laid his hands on her thighs to steady her as the orgasm swept over her. Her body convulsed, tried to arch against them and dislodge the candles and upset her balance of the plates.

Violet closed her hand around the taper at Leila's hip and belly, holding it secure while the girl thrashed and her moan became a long, keening cry of release that vibrated the glass in the bay window, making it sparkle with the sun's fading light.

Mac's fingers crept up to her hip, his need and desire communicating itself through his touch, a desperate desire for relief.

Not yet. She was incredibly aroused herself, but he was going to earn her attention tonight. He was testing her still, she could tell, for his hand had made free to steal to her hip by caressing its way up her thigh while her hands were occupied, though she had prohibited him from going that route only a moment before.

"That's my girl," Tyler dropped a soft kiss on Leila's cheeks, her mouth, holding her jaw so she did not get too greedy with the kiss. Watching her was like seeing a woman parched with thirst try to take a swallow, when a sip was all that was permitted, a hummingbird pulling from a feeder.

"These Mistresses are so impressed with you," Tyler said. "I can hardly wait to take you to my bed tonight and fuck you until you scream for me again."

"Take me now, Master," Leila begged in a whisper. The Mistresses had retaken their seats, but Violet saw that, like her, every Dom at the table was hanging onto the hunger in that voice, absorbed in her want, responding to it.

Tyler smiled, the affectionate heat for her still raging in his eyes, in the arousal in his pants he did not bother to hide from this assembly, but he shook his head. "First, we eat, my love. We have guests. Don't be rude and make me punish you. To keep you remembering your place..." He made an adjustment on the vibrator. "We'll keep this on low setting, which will torment you without appeasement. That will be the job of my cock. We've games to play tonight, and I don't want to tire you out."

He took his seat and summoned the domestic staff for the meal to begin. Violet's salad was served by a familiar face. A six-foot tall twenty-something with brown hair like silk and the face of a cover model for formal wear, aesthetically from the same mold of the sub that Tamara and Kiera had brought tonight. Despite her preferences for a more rugged-looking man, Violet had played with Mark before, as he was an amiable and willing sub on The Zone staff, and he was undeniably easy on the eyes. Tonight he wore only a pair of tightly fitted trousers and a sheen of fragrant oil on his impressive muscles. He set the small salad down in the center of her plate and smiled at her.

"Let me know if you need anything else, Mistress Violet. We're here to serve." He ran a light finger down her arm playfully, but with a deferential sweep of his lashes, to apologize if she took it as an inappropriate gesture.

"Touch her again, and I'll break that fucking arm," Mac murmured, never lifting his head.

Mark froze. Conversation around the table stilled, for though the threat had been delivered in a low voice, Mac had enunciated clearly. As Violet suspected he had intended to do.

Never mind that his words, blatantly expressing his desire to be sole provider of her wants and needs, ran frissons of pleasure through her vitals. On more than one occasion, Tyler had pointed out to her that she was more of a one-on-one Mistress herself, which was another thing that she suspected had attracted her to Mac. Like called to like in the subconscious.

However, his words were a direct challenge she could not leave unanswered. She had known he would go too far, and he had done so early, bringing the issue to a head.

Proof of the point, he had raised his head and was now staring at her, hard, defiant, a clear "what are you going to do about it?" look. His position made it easy for her to follow through on her response. She slapped him across the face, using her full strength, careful to hit his jaw line instead of his eyes or the sensitive area of the ear. The strike was hard, strong, but not painful, and the psychological impact was effective. Shock was replaced by fury, and something else, something that wrenched at her heart. She masked her response to that and kept her tone cold. "It is not for you to say who touches me and who doesn't, Mackenzie."

"The hell it isn't."

She struck him again, opposite direction, using the back of her hand this time. "Put your lips to my foot, and ask for my forgiveness."

He stared at her, five charged seconds. The stillness at the table was palpable, the only sound Leila's ragged breathing as the vibrator continued to stimulate her with a soft hum. Tyler gestured for more wine, casually, though his eyes were as intent as the other Doms on the struggle, and the nuances of control and trust that were working furiously below its surface.

Her willful sub lowered his head at last, and his shoulders curved forward, his hips rising from his heels, giving Tamara a view of his backside that Violet envied. She waited as he went lower, lower, and then she felt the press of his mouth come to rest on the toe of her shoe. "I won't say I'm sorry," he said, his voice muffled. "I want to be the only one who gives you pleasure."

She couldn't think of anyone better equipped to do a lifetime of that for her, but he wasn't finished.

"And I *will* break his arm if he touches you again."

Unexpectedly, she felt herself stifling a smile at the sullen statement. She heard Tamara muffle a chuckle, and appreciated the other Dom's understanding of the situation. "Stay in that position," she demanded. "Spread your knees two feet apart, let Mistress Tamara see those oversized balls of yours that are always getting you into this kind of trouble with me."

He trembled, his hand now curled around the arch of her foot, but he obeyed. Tamara purred in approval. Violet shifted her attention to the Dom twin. "Mistress, will you do me the honor of paddling this arrogant slave's ass ten strokes to teach him manners?"

"With pleasure." Tamara rose, went to the sideboard where an array of floggers and paddles were assembled next to the makings of after dinner coffee. She chose a paddle of one-inch thick wood, nine inches long, with holes in it.

Violet had seen Tamara wield one like it before, knew that the splayed leg position was just to make the sub feel excessively vulnerable. Tamara would not come anywhere near the sensitive sac, but Mac would not know that. Violet laid her hand on his head, stroked his hair back with a deceptively light touch. "Proceed." She nodded to Tamara. Leila's breathing was getting louder, and the room was thick with sexual heat, every eye watching that muscular ass quivering in the air, waiting to take its punishment.

Whack! Wood paddles made a lot of noise and hurt like fire when wielded with strength. Tamara had a good arm. Mac let out a grunt, his fingers tightening on her shoe.

"Do you apologize?"

"Only for causing you distress, not for my actions."

"Again," she nodded. "Three strokes in succession."

Mac might have been under the impression he could handle a spanking from a woman's arm, but Violet suspected he was rethinking that as his shoulder pressed into her calf with the force of the next three strokes. His buttocks were already turning red.

Violet caught her fingers in his curls, a painful grip this time, keeping his mouth shoved to her shoe. "You will apologize, Mackenzie."

"I can't, Mistress. I want to be the only one who serves you."

"Perhaps you will, if you learn to submit to me. Stop fighting me, Mac." She nodded. "Four more."

This time, his fingers tightened on her before the blow came, and she felt his breath expel sharply against the flesh of her ankle on the second stroke. Violet worried that she had chosen the wrong number, that she'd underestimated Mac's ability to bear more pain than he should. Given the power Tamara was putting behind her strokes, he should have been screaming.

On the fourth, he let out a hiss. Violet ran a hand down the curve of his back, slick with perspiration. "Ask forgiveness, Mackenzie. You know you stepped across the line."

Tamara landed strike nine at that moment, when he was unprepared, and he bumped hard against her shins, catching onto them to keep from being thrown to the floor. His breath rasped hard, in time with the rapid rise and fall of his shoulders. Violet bit the inside of her cheek, to let her own pain pull her focus from his. "Mackenzie—"

"I ask your forgiveness, Mistress," he mumbled, his fingers going around her leg like a manacle, holding her hard, fast, communicating his physical strength at the same moment he capitulated to her emotional power over him. "I spoke out of turn, without your leave, and deserve to be punished. Please do not spare the final blow, and if you think I deserve ten more, I will submit to your pleasure."

Out of the corner of her eye, she saw Tyler's lip curl in grudging admiration. Kiera and Tamara looked as if they would have given Violet their Jag in exchange for a chance to have Mac in their dungeon for one night, testing his resolve against even higher levels of pain.

Fortunately, he was all hers. Stubborn, foolish, hard-headed jackass that he was.

"I think one more should be sufficient," she said, though she wanted to call an end to it now. "Mistress, if you please."

"My pleasure again, Mistress." Tamara ran her long nails down one curve of Mac's ass, digging into the angry red color, and he gasped. She pulled back and brought the paddle back into play, one loud hard smack to the contour of his buttocks, skillfully just above the joining point of his testicles so the sensation would sing down into them but not harm him.

"Sweet Christ," Mac muttered, though only Violet heard the whispered expletive. She wanted to soothe his pain, but that wouldn't drive the lesson home.

"Now sit up, put your ass against your heels so you feel the burn," she said. "We wish to proceed with our dinner." She caught his chin as he straightened, hauled him up the last few inches and was relieved to see the flash of temper in his eyes at her rough handling. "And if I wish to have Mark eat my pussy, and command you to sit there and watch, you'll hand him a towel to wipe his mouth after I come. Do you understand?"

He was bleeding where he had bitten his tongue. She rubbed her thumb at the corner of his mouth, gently taking the blood away. At the same time she forced her eyes to remain hard, unblinking, though tears threatened behind them. She sensed Tyler's tension just beyond them, but Mac wouldn't hurt her. She didn't know how she knew that, because her beautiful slave looked like he wanted to break her in half, but she knew.

"Answer me, Mackenzie," she said, in her softest, firmest tone.

"Yes, Mistress." He sounded like he was strangling on it.

"Yes, what?"

Kiera drew in a breath at her audacity. If she was pushing past the twins' boundaries, Violet knew she was in dangerous waters, indeed. But the rules be damned. She wanted him to surrender. To understand what serving a Mistress was, because she wanted him like she'd never wanted anything in her life. She wasn't backing down. He'd accept her hand as his Mistress completely, or she'd call the game over. She knew the treasure that awaited them both under all his fear and stubbornness, and she wasn't taking half.

Mac swallowed, showed his teeth. "If you command it, Mistress, I will hold a towel for Mark to wipe his mouth, after he eats your pussy." His gaze lifted to hers, and his silver eyes were torn between fury and an aching desire so strong it blasted straight into her heart. "Though I would beg my Mistress's permission to wipe her pussy first, for a sub should never attend to his needs, or that of another slave, before the needs of his Mistress."

Violet could not take her eyes from his. She mutely offered her hand, glad she only had to raise it a fraction before he seized it, pressed his mouth hard atop her knuckles. She didn't want the others to see the way she was trembling, but he felt it. His fingers tightened on hers, somehow conveying chagrin and reassurance at once, in that protective way of his that spread a warm balm over her frazzled nerves, making it all right. For the moment.

Through the gesture, she could feel that he regretted causing her the conflict, but she knew regret didn't translate into victory. She'd only breached one wall. Those that remained might be even more difficult. She was angrier with him than anyone she'd ever known.

Tyler was right. She was in love.

Chapter 10

After dinner, the Doms changed into their preferred swimwear and adjourned to the pool house, a beautiful glass structure that overlooked the water. Equipped with a pool table, wet bar and bookcase full of reading selections, the room invited diversion and indulgence. Comfortable wicker lounge furniture, set up in private groupings buffered by the artful placement of tropical plants, allowed group or one-on-one interaction equally.

During the meal, it was obvious that the displays by Leila and Mac had ratcheted up the sexual tension of all the guests to a higher level than Tyler had anticipated for this early in the evening. The lingering touches bestowed on the subs, the frequent wetting of lips and shifting of bodies, the distracted tone of the conversations. The heavy stillness of the air hovering around the table, though the palm frond ceiling fan was going at high speed. When Violet fed Mac his meal from her fingertips, she completely lost the thread of anything going on at the table.

Always a skillful host for his D/s parties, Tyler rerouted the nature of the tension by suggesting to the Mistresses that the slaves could play a game of water volleyball while they took their ease around the pool and watched.

David, Mac and Collin were typically competitive men, but Leila's charming enthusiasm and relative inexperience thrown into the mix kept the testosterone level down and the tone of the match appealingly playful.

Violet discovered there was no better game than water volleyball to display a body to its best advantage. She watched as appreciatively as the other Doms as naked torsos stretched and turned. Genitals were generously exposed as the men came out of the water to spike a shot over the net or jump up high to return a volley. The white heart shape of Leila's ass entertained and stimulated them all as she lunged, laughing, after the ball. Her breasts, heavy and wet, nipples tight with cold, could not help but keep the men semi-erect, even in the water. Violet enjoyed the beauty of every form displayed, but her eyes kept coming back to Mac, savoring each time he dropped beneath the surface to rewet his skull and came back up, water sluicing off his body, muscles rippling across his back as he pushed his hair off his forehead.

"He's extraordinary, isn't he?" Lisbeth sat down with her White Russian and chose a chocolate-covered strawberry from the silver tray left on the patio table between them. "It's something about him. Tarzan-like. He's not handsome. He's definitely not pretty. He's just primitive. Beautiful. Raw sex."

"Sounds like you miss him."

"Sometimes." The woman's green eyes were as pale frosted as her white hair, pulled back from her elegant features. "You don't like me, but you've refrained from cutting remarks about my age, which would be easy ground. I appreciate that, and as such, I want to tell you straight out I've no lingering designs on Mac. Mostly I enjoy breaking in the 'virgins', watching them discover their submissive nature, the awareness of what power and control really mean in sex. I like to watch them grow.

When Mac was ready, I cut him loose with no regrets. I introduced him to his nature and trained him. That was all."

"You did a piss-poor job with the training," Violet said bluntly. "He still hasn't accepted it. He plays with it, better than most subs fully embrace it, which is why so many Mistresses have let him get away with it. He hasn't let anyone break him down, move into his soul."

"Very astute. You get right to the point in a conversation, don't you? But you and I both know there's no way I would have accomplished that." Lisbeth reached over, touched Violet's hand in an affectionate gesture that surprised her. "You know the truth of it as much as I do. You're just worked up from dinner. He's a one-woman sub. And I don't mean he needs and prefers one-on-one play, though he surely does. I mean there's only one woman he's going to let be his true Mistress."

She leaned back in her chair, examined the tray to pick another strawberry. "When I look at Mac, I think of that perfect meal behind glass, accessible only if you know the combination to make the glass slide back. You can't shatter it to get to the meal. That will just ruin the feast." She paused.

Violet cocked her head, not saying anything. Part of her resented the woman's intimate exploration of Mac's mind. The smarter part of her knew she should hear the rest of it, and so her pride was relieved when Lisbeth continued without a visible sign of encouragement from her.

"He lets a woman hold the reins sexually, probably the only aspect of his life where he allows anyone to dominate him. However, the key is that he 'lets her'. His heart is that of a true sub, but no one's ever taught him that being a true sub means the only choice is surrender. I believe only one woman is going to be strong enough to do it, *the* woman. Though he barely knows it, he's waiting to possess and be possessed. He's following his instincts. As I said. Primitive. Raw. Animal."

Lisbeth made a humming noise of pleasure as she bit into the strawberry, the chocolate smearing across her upper lip so that her tongue came out, delicately brought the sweet into her mouth. David missed an easy return volley completely and she chuckled.

"I don't mind making you jealous," she said, flashing teeth at Violet. "Because what I got to sample of him *was* tasty. But from the sparks flying between you and him, I'd say you might want to try being that one woman."

Violet watched Mac laugh at something Leila said, engage in a brief splashing match with her, palm the ball and return to the back line to serve. "So how many do you think he's auditioned?"

Lisbeth cocked her head. "I'd ask why that matters, but to the woman who wants the role, I can imagine it would matter a great deal." She lifted a shoulder as Violet turned her gaze back to her. "Not as many as you might think. He's done a lot of playing in the dungeons, one-night type stuff, but since me, he's resisted becoming someone's regular playmate. He's so charming, he's managed to stay a free agent without offending or insulting. It's clear he's been looking for something he didn't even really know he was seeking. The more inexperienced Mistresses didn't get that, but it was pretty obvious to someone who's been in the game as long as I have. And to the person who might just be that lucky Mistress for him."

Violet raised a brow. "I haven't known him very long."

Lisbeth waved a dismissive hand. "Don't play games with another Dom. Do you know, in all the time we were together, he was never possessive with me? Never even used a possessive when he talked about me? Or any other Mistress I ever saw him with. But you, at dinner. 'My Mistress'. He said it, implied it, several times. He's never done that. Ever."

She had as much as she wanted to think about at the moment. Violet gave Lisbeth a courteous nod, rose. Mac's gaze was on her the minute she moved, and when she came forward, he stroked over. He caught onto the edge of the pool and crossed his arms on the concrete, curling them in a loose circle around her ankles.

"Hi," she said, squatting on her heels.

He smiled, a wary gesture that said dinner was not forgotten, but he reached up, traced his thumb over her lips and cheek. She let him, pressed her jaw into his hand, closed her eyes. It released the band of tension around her lungs, and she felt weightless. A moment later, she realized it wasn't an illusion of her mind. He had simply curled his arms around her coiled form and taken her into the heated water with him, scooped up against his body. She wound her arms around his neck, pressed her face into his throat, felt the pulse jumping there. He tipped back her chin, put wet lips over hers, and she let herself float, shifted so her legs were wrapped around his waist, feeling the strength of his hands pressed against her back, holding her curves, contained in a modest bathing suit, against his bare torso. The head of his cock bumped the crease of her buttocks.

"Take me back to the edge of the pool," she said, feeling both steadier and more messed up. She shouldn't be reacting to Lisbeth's familiarity with Mac, as it was obvious the woman was not a threat, but she wanted Mac to be hers, all hers. Though it was an irrational thought, she fervently wished she had been his first and last Mistress.

He took her to the side of the pool, lifted her out of the water and sat her back on the lip, her feet rubbing against his waist and rib cage as he stayed between her knees, watching her watching him. His silver eyes studied her face, jeweled with tiny beads of water. They coursed down her neck, over the tops of her breasts, visible in the scoop neck of the one piece, down, down. Further down. He began to sink, his knees bending to take him lower, his gaze staying level with her face, communicating what he wanted to do.

Though she could tell he was offering it out of hunger, and as a continuation of an apology for dinner, a way to make amends, she liked those reasons. Violet also liked the idea of having him serve her pussy in sight of his previous Mistress. A branding that, while outside the bounds of civilized behavior, loosened the tension within her further.

"Mistress, may I?" His mouth was even with her thighs, the breath tickling the sensitive skin.

"You may." She whispered it.

Mac's eyes flared hot, and he put his hands on her knees. Tanned, rough male palms against the white delicate inner thighs slid forward, nudging them further apart. She leaned back on her arms to accommodate him and he raised her legs onto his shoulders as he dropped lower into the water. Her heels floated, grazing his back.

She had imagined that he would be very, very good at this. With the first touch of his mouth on her, she knew she'd understated it. He didn't move the crotch of the swimsuit right away. He breathed on her, heating her, then put his mouth over the wet fabric, sucking the moisture of the pool off of it, through the fibers, creating pressure and suction on the flesh beneath that throbbed in response at the moment of first contact. The reaction rocketed through her body, tensing every muscle, digging her heels down in the water into his back.

No way was she going to be able to stay in an upright position. As if her mind was being read, hands closed over her upper arms. Mark held her, giving her back support. She guessed that Tyler was helping her test the lesson of dinner. True to Tyler's ironic sense of humor, Mark held a towel.

Mac's attention lifted. Remarkably, Violet watched Mark lower his gaze, acknowledging Mac's dominance over the situation.

"Only to give your Mistress ease as you pleasure her," he murmured.

Mac gave an imperceptible nod, settled back to what he was doing, tiny nibbles on her pussy, his hands stroking the inside of her thighs even as he held them open, countering that strange impulse to close them against the wave of pleasure screaming through her nerves. She had thought about how his well-groomed beard and moustache would feel against her inner thighs and pussy, and now she trembled at the additional overpowering sensations, the alternate rough and soft brush of the hair against her tender skin as he moved his head.

Violet lay back into the solid wall of Mark's chest as he sat down, his thighs on either side of her, his groin pressed nicely against her lower back, but her focus was all on the man working between her legs. His tongue, teeth and lips driving her to insanity, making her twist against the gentle but unshakable restraint of his hands holding her spread wide to his pleasuring.

She gasped when his finger slipped under the cotton crotch, pulled it aside, and he slid his tongue into her. A slow unfurling so she felt it push past the labia, sample the moist heat within, flicker so he tickled the inside channel, while the broader part of his tongue pushed up, rolled against her clit.

"Ah…" She couldn't get a breath. He was barely moving his mouth, and yet every slight altering of position was rocketing through her as if he were working her like a steam engine.

Through glazed eyes, she saw how they were affecting everyone else. Tyler had brought Leila out of the pool and onto her knees to serve him in a like fashion, a mirror image across the pool from Violet, only he sat in a chair and she knelt on a towel he'd folded and provided for the comfort of her knees. He stroked Leila's hair as he watched them, and Violet's attention drifted to the girl's pale buttocks, moving rhythmically with the bobbing of her head on his cock, her back to Violet. Leila's pussy glistened with a liquid heat that had nothing to do with the pool.

Lisbeth had made David sit next to her knee and watch both sets of oral play. She had commanded him to masturbate himself as he watched, though Violet heard her firm murmured command. "You will stroke yourself until I command you to stop, but you are not permitted to come, because I want to save all that lovely seed of yours for me."

Collin was back on all fours serving his two demanding Mistresses. They had rebound his cock in a tight harness, the back strap threaded through the gold ring pierced through his scrotum and attached to two leashes. Water still dripped off his body as they had him go back and forth, pulling aside the crotches of the matching black string bikinis so he could eat each pussy in turn while the unencumbered twin tugged idly at the piercing with her leash, giving him no relief. Both of the twins watched Violet and Mac intently with those liquid dark eyes. As Collin brought his mouth away from one cunt and took lips moist with one sister's arousal to the other, Violet wondered anew at the familial relationship between T&K.

Then any idle thought was blasted away as Mac set his teeth lightly to her clit, abruptly holding steady there. Just a bare increase of pressure as he smoothly thrust his tongue in and out of her, lapping her moisture up, until all she could see was a sparkling white haze that rose off the water, obliterating everything but the sense of immersion in sexual heat, of being surrounded by it, inhaling it. His hands tightened on her thighs even as she fought him, fought the reaction that seemed to be rushing down too hard, too strong.

"Come for me, Mistress," he muttered. "Please, God."

His actions became audible, a sucking, appreciative noise that did her in, as all her senses were impacted, hearing, feeling, seeing, his head working hard over her, his heated breath, the flex of his shoulders. Tyler's hand tightening on Leila's head, forcing her down harder on him. The rasp of David's breath, his panicked expression as he knew he was coming close and his apprehension that he couldn't stop. The smack as Kiera brought the leash into play, strapping the loose end smartly across Collin's tight ass. He obediently raised it higher as he had been trained to do, displaying the glint of the scrotum ring and asking for more as he kept up his rhythmic licking of her sister's cunt. Tamara's long-fingered hands gripped his head, her body rising up on the lounge chair, close to climax.

Violet beat her there. She arched back abruptly, Mark's strength increasing on her upper arms as she screamed, thrashing against the strength of two men strong enough to hold her still, let her feel every sensitive movement of Mac's lips as her pussy convulsed, rippled, contracted against him with the force of an orgasm so hard her vision grayed. Her heels kicked, splashed water, thumped hard against his back and still he held on, his mouth fucking her as she bucked, even as her pussy got so tight with her response that it was a screaming pleasure to feel the thrust of his tongue, over and over.

She came down with soft cries, like a runner gasping to catch her breath as she crossed the finish line. The orgasm spun away, its aftermath like that of a full body massage, leaving every muscle limp, her heart pounding against her chest like a hammer. He became still, his mouth sealed over her pussy, his tongue still deep within her, but not moving, as if knowing she couldn't bear any movement, even her own. Her involuntary twitches and quivers brought more soft whimpers from her lips. She put a trembling hand to his hair, curled her fingers into it, partly a caress, partly to just hold on, connect to him. Be one with him.

Mac lifted his head at the pressure of her fingers, and before she could give him an order not to take liberties, any order at all, he had moved up, sliding her legs off his shoulders, and crushed his mouth over hers, his hand cupped to the back of her head. Her hands fluttered helplessly to his shoulders as he devoured her, let her taste herself and his own raging hunger. She was distantly conscious of Mark, still pressed against her back, separated from Mac only by the width of her own body, but then he slid away discreetly, and there was only Mac, his arms coming around her to hold her up, hold her to him.

Fortunately, she had enough brain cells to stop her beloved slave when he tried to draw her back into the water.

"No," she murmured, pushing against his shoulder. He was more than strong enough to resist her, of course, but this was about strength of will, not his ability to bench press three times her weight. She knew that Mac's subconscious knew that, even if his conscious awareness didn't, for he stopped the moment she spoke. He did not let her go immediately, though, his body still and explosive as a lion before leaping for prey.

He reached between them, his gaze on her face, and pressed the towel to her vibrating pussy, absorbing the moisture there. Violet arched, her breath catching, her fingers digging into his shoulders. With some amusement, she wondered exactly when the towel had been transferred. Mac adjusted the crotch of her swimsuit back over her, his fingers brushing her still swollen clit, and then he stepped back, his fingers trailing down her calves and ankles, reluctant to break the connection. A moment later, he finished the formal retreat by deliberately lowering his glance from hers in an expression of deference. It tightened the emotion and need squeezing her chest to the point of pain.

"Dearest?"

Violet looked up, found Tyler above her, offering a hand, his touch on her shoulder a reassuring anchor. He looked a little flushed himself, suggesting Leila had served him well, but Violet thought he looked far more composed than she felt. But then, Leila didn't seem intent on smashing out the foundation blocks of Tyler's conception of life.

"Would you like to take a stroll in the garden, see my new orchids?"

Chapter 11

Translation: Get some breathing space before your brain cells explode?

Violet blessed Tyler's intuition and took his hand to let him help her to trembling legs.

Tyler glanced over her shoulder and Violet saw the two men's eyes lock, Mac daring the repercussions to briefly make the contact before he shifted his gaze, a grudging acknowledgement of the rules of the house.

"I'll take good care of her," Tyler promised, surprising Violet.

Mac made a bare movement of his head, but it was impossible to tell if it was acknowledgement or warning. Violet frowned. "Behave," she said. "Play nicely while I'm gone."

Lifting his lashes, he gave her a slow, easy grin that didn't dilute the intent passion in his eyes. Despite the wavering line of the blue water, she could see that he was ramrod stiff, with a circumference that made her catch her lip in her teeth to stifle a groan of desire.

"Hurry back, sugar."

She nodded, let a thought roll around in her mind, shifted her glance to Kiera and Tamara. "Keep him occupied."

All the way to the door, and through the glass as she stepped into the gardens, she felt his attention on her, his sudden apprehension. She didn't speak to Tyler until they made the first turn on the winding path, taking them out of sight of the pool occupants.

"Am I totally screwing up?" she demanded.

"Well, if you—"

"Oh, God, Tyler," she began to pace around a small clearing that provided a bench and a wishing fountain next to a bed of the exotic orchids he spent so much time cultivating. "I feel like he's ripping me apart from the inside. He's so damn stubborn. I've never met a sub like him. He wants to be a sub, but I have to fight him for every inch of control, and he's always testing me. Is he fucking with my head?"

"You're—"

"No, he's not," she said firmly. "I can feel he's not. He's just afraid. No one's ever pushed him hard enough, made him trust enough to really let go to a Mistress, and he's pushing back. But do I have the ability to do it? I'm *so* over my head here."

"*Violet.*" Tyler used a tone she rarely heard except when he was dealing with a rebellious sub or a primadonna actress. It brought her up short. He smiled at her look of shock. "Sorry, love, but you were going like a locomotive there. You love him."

She set her jaw, fought panic. "I've known him three days, Tyler. You don't love someone in three days."

"Of course you can fall in love in three days. Don't be stupid. After that it's just a matter of how hard you're willing to work to stay in love, to see if it becomes a forever, kids-and-mini-van type of thing." Tyler approached her, put his hands on her shoulders. "You're doing everything right. Do you hear what I'm saying? You're being tough, but you're showing your emotions, showing you care. The paddling was inspired. You showed you can be as mean as he can be, when it's warranted. That you expect him not just to act as a submissive, but to *be* one. Yes, it likely would take Mistresses of Kiera and Tamara's ilk to break him physically, but that isn't what D/s is about. Not for you. You've seen what's deep inside him, something no one else can see, and you know what it's going to take to get him to embrace it, better than he does himself."

"'I don't go down easy'," she recalled his words. "He said that, when we first met."

"Well, he went down on you easy enough," Tyler gave her a mischievous wink, forcing a smile out of her. "Violet, you wouldn't want someone who did. I think you better find out more about your boy's vanilla life, because I have a feeling your relationship is already exploding outside the confines of the dungeons."

She thought of the picnic, the drive, and knew he was right.

"He's killing me," she said, and he put his arms around her so she could put her forehead to his chest, close her eyes, breathe deeply. "He was bleeding, for Chrissake."

"Bleeding for you. A blood bond. Come on." He tipped up her chin, gave it a little squeeze. "Let me tell you about my new orchids that you just about trampled during your little tantrum. I'm going to have to move these inside soon. They were shipped here specially…"

* * * * *

By the time they walked back together, Violet was feeling more centered, more in control of her emotions, and therefore ready to take command of Mac again.

The pool area was empty, and Stacey, the other Zone help Tyler had hired for the weekend, was cleaning up wine glasses and cups. "Mistress Lisbeth took her slave to their bedroom 'for awhile', but said they'll be back for late night cocktails," she said, with a slight smile. "Mistresses T&K took Mac, Mark, Collin and Leila down to Master Tyler's playroom."

Violet felt a small twinge of alarm. "Did you give the twins leave to play with Leila?" She asked as they went through the house and down the staircase to Tyler's personal well-equipped dungeon.

"They've played with her before. They know her limits, and she'd tell them if they breached them. I've told her what my restrictions on her playing with others are, so she knows where the lines are, for me as well as her. Mac?"

"He says, 'Whatever will please my Mistress'." Violet rolled her eyes. "But he's an expert at using that charm of his to keep his ass out of trouble. I guess I shouldn't worry so much about him."

"Hmm." Tyler gave her an uncertain look. "I'm not sure even Lucifer's charm would have an effect on T&K."

Violet schooled her face to an impassive mask right before Tyler opened the door to the playroom, and she was glad she had taken a moment to do so.

Mac's feet were spread apart, ankles manacled and locked to bolts in the floor, his arms stretched so high over his head that his impressively massive rib cage tilted upward, his arm muscles straining. Surprisingly, the twins had also forced a ball gag into his mouth and buckled it tight around his head. Mark knelt at his feet, sucking Mac's cock with pure male intuition of how rough and strong the working of his mouth and the grip of his hand needed to be.

Leila knelt against the spanking bench, her breasts shelved attractively on the burgundy upholstered surface. She was faced in the direction where she could watch and be roused by Mac and Mark's tableau. Collin had been ordered to kneel to the side of the bench, his cheek lying just in front of Leila's breasts to suckle her nipples without interfering with the stimulating view. His arms were tied behind his back, and a chain ran from the locked cuffs, fastening him to the ring in his scrotum. Tamara and Kiera obviously preferred their sub immobilized much of the time.

Kiera glanced over at Violet and Tyler from where she lazed on the day lounger, massaging her sister's bare feet. Two pairs of spike heels were on the floor, giving Violet an odd impression of two women after a long day of work, kicking off their shoes and watching the best that cable had to offer.

"Well, I guess Mac wins this round," Tamara smiled. "I told him that if he could keep from coming until you arrived, I wouldn't put this enormous strap-on I have up his ass. It's a shame, because I was looking forward to trying out some of Kiera's wondrous oil on him." She lifted a vial from the table, shook it. "Coat a dildo with this, or better, shoot it in, and he won't be able to keep himself from coming. He'll spend a three-day load and won't be able to stop screaming for more." She lifted a brow. "It's great for humbling an overly proud sub, like yours. And he stays hard as a rock throughout, so you can get an endless variety of enjoyments from his suffering. What do you say, Vi? You want Kiera to go ahead and do him while you watch?"

Violet studied Mac's face. The muscles of his neck were contorted with the effort to hold back. Mark was paying him back in spades for the earlier threat, putting all his effort into relentlessly working him. Mac was huge, and she felt her pussy respond to the sight.

"Why the ball gag?"

"Oh, that." Tamara cocked her head at Mac, met his furious gaze. "He has a problem with the rule about not making eye contact, as you can see. And he got somewhat worked up, a bit rude in fact, when I decided to let Mark go down on that nice piece of meat of his. Didn't say no, though."

Violet shifted her glance to Mac, and this time he averted his glance with a sullen expression. Oh, he was worked up all right. She sauntered across the room, keeping her face an unreadable mask, and stopped just behind Mark. Ran a casual hand over his hair while she faced Mac. "Keep going," she murmured.

Mac hissed around the gag and Violet took a finger, wiped away the small area of saliva that had escaped the corner of his mouth, brought it to her own lips.

"What do you say, Mac? Are you thirsty?"

He gave a sharp shake of his head, but his eyes were asking for something else.

"No," she said softly. "I think the gag is a good idea. Because it means you have to listen, instead of thinking about how to con me. This is about what pleases me, Mackenzie. It pleases me to see you come, in whatever manner I desire. Does it please you to have another man sucking your cock?"

He shook his head violently, bucked to try to dislodge Mark. The other man just chuckled, held on and kept going.

"I didn't think so. But your cock doesn't care, does it?"

It wants you. It was in his countenance as strongly as a scream in her mind.

"I know it does. I like seeing your cock hard for me. It understands what you don't, that everything that's done to it is by *my* command, so it responds to every stimulus as if it's in my pussy. That's why it's hard now. For me. Because I asked Tamara and Kiera to keep it that way."

She pivoted on her heel, giving him her profile. "Mistress Tamara, I would like that strap-on, please, and I would like it coated with your sister's oil." She turned her head, met his eyes. "I'll do the honors. He's mine, and only I will fuck him. Ever."

She turned back, put a hand on Mark's shoulder, squeezed. Understanding, he released Mac, backed off, so Violet could stand before her captive, letting his erection's wet tip touch her thighs.

"Bring your head down to me," she said.

Mac bent his neck and she unbuckled the gag, sliding it carefully from his mouth and handing it to Mark to take away.

"Mistress, please don't." The emotion in his silver eyes suggested he was struggling between wanting to coerce her through anger, and beg her out of sheer desperation. His lust was roused by her Dominance, but his expression told her he was apprehensive of the act itself, the ultimate act for a submissive male in thrall to a

Mistress. An act she knew had never been forced upon him.

She ran her palm up his chest, played with the right taut nipple, scraping it with her nails, and felt his wetness graze the skin on her thigh, just beneath the crotch of the swimsuit. She brought herself up full against him, let him experience every curve. "Are you thirsty?"

He caught her lips in a kiss. "Only for you," he said, a panicked note to his voice she was sure he wished was not there. "I'm yours, Mistress. Yours to do with as you wish."

While he had seemed to regain his composure after dinner, regrouping enough to give her pleasure at the poolside, she had known it was all show. Dinner had stripped the veneer of his whole act. Frightened of how his body was reacting, of how helpless this whole weekend was making him feel, she suspected the foundation was starting to crumble, and dared to hope the message was getting through. That he was starting to turn to her for shelter from his emotional fears.

"Are you mine to do with as I wish?" She wanted to hear it again.

"Yes, Mistress."

She nipped the base of his throat, the ridge of his collar bone. "So if I want to slide a cock deep, deep into your beautiful ass, make you come the way Kiera described, then that would please you."

"If…if it pleases you. Yes." A tremor ran through his torso and she ran soothing hands down his arms.

"Tell me what's in your heart."

"You. Just you. I'll do anything you want me to do. Just…please. Just with you. Mistress," he added.

She pulled her head back, looked into his eyes. "Just with me. That's a boundary of yours, isn't it, Mackenzie? Tell me."

He pressed his forehead against hers, squeezed his eyes shut. "Yes," he muttered. "Just with you, Mistress. Please."

Violet touched her temple to his cheek briefly, then withdrew. Kiera was preparing the strap-on for her, a hard rubber cock about eight inches long. As Violet watched Mark roll a condom over Mac's engorged organ, Kiera and Tamara fitted her with the device, tightened the holding straps between her legs so the cock sprang proud and erect before her, like an impressive man's organ in truth. Mac's eyes never left it, or her. From the quivering in his body, she could surmise he was anxious. Afraid as well, but willing to endure both to please her. Well, she was hoping to make it worth the suffering to him.

Kiera knelt and lubricated her further, as if she were doing it to a man, with lingering, stroking detail. Mac, Mark, all the men in the room watched those clever caramel-colored fingers slide up and back on the shaft. Tamara put her back to Mac, blocking his view, and lowered her voice so only Violet could hear her.

"This here holds a reserve of oil." She tapped a small, almost imperceptible button on the joining mechanism at the base of the strap on. "When he's close, press here, and you'll jet into him like a man. That sets off the real firecracker show." She showed her teeth in a quick, feral smile. "The outside, the lubrication, just warms him up, makes him start to feel the loss of control that's coming."

She glanced over her shoulder, sent Mac a sultry smile, then turned back to Violet. "You've never seen anything like it, Vi," she whispered. "It burns like hell at first, but then, just when you think it's going to be excruciating, it does something to them."

"It won't hurt him, will it?"

"Only the burning, and believe me, it simply rouses the nerves to pain, like a spanking, and that's what makes the next reaction so intense. We always do the lubricant first, because you can tell in a few strokes if there will be a bad reaction and can pull out." She gestured with her head. "We keep a jug of distilled water with a pump behind Tyler's bar if we have to do a fast enema. Regardless, you'll want to do one on him later, clean out the oil." She shot Violet a wicked grin. "He's choice, Violet. Kiera and I would love to sink our teeth into him and eat him in small, tasty bites."

They weren't the only ones. Violet turned, now prepared, and walked toward Mac. Walking with a strap-on was an experience she always enjoyed. Moving with slow, sensual steps enhanced the sensation against her own pussy, and made the hard rubber cock move in a more lifelike manner with her body's movements. It made her feel powerful, eager to make Mac all hers by sliding those eight lubricated inches into his ass, consummate the bond between Mistress and male slave in a way that could not be denied.

Someone had set a short stool just behind him, and she thanked whoever it was for their foresight, her mind too muddled with lust to have calculated that the difference in their heights would require it for her to comfortably accommodate herself in him. The rigid line of his shoulders grew more so as she stepped up on it, her heeled sandals tapping on the wood surface.

Leila cried out. Across the room, Tyler stood behind her, had begun to smack her buttocks with a belt, leaving red stripes on her pert ass. The girl shuddered, stimulated already by the tableau going on before her as well as by Collin, still suckling on her tight full breasts, now squeezed and distended in a parallel bar restraint to make them more sensitive. The head of Collin's cock was so engorged it was nearly purple in its harness. Kiera was choosing a cane from the wall that Violet was sure she would employ to increase the fervency of Collin's efforts. Tamara perched on the couch, enjoying a full view of all groupings.

The dungeon had been laid out for this, so each Dom could see what the other was doing, use it to further drive the arousal of their own slave. Though Mac could not see Violet, he could obviously feel her coming, and he was positioned squarely across from Leila, giving him a panoramic view of her sensual distress.

It was dizzying, overwhelming, a synergy that was explosive and hot, just as it had been at the pool, this many people immersed in a symphony of sexual pleasure.

Violet was going to make sure that Mac would be the crescendo for them all.

She placed a hand on his shoulder, leaned forward to put her parted lips against his ear. "This is going to be a hard ride, Mackenzie," she whispered. "Everything that happens to you here is my will, for your pleasure and my own. I'm going to fuck you hard, and there's going to be nothing left for you to hold onto except me. I'm tearing everything away. From this moment forward, you'll always know who your Mistress is, who holds the bit in your teeth."

"Give it your best shot, sugar," he said, that spasmodic quiver rippling through his tense muscles. He was scared, she could tell. Scared that she was right.

She knew she was.

Violet put one hand to his waist, the other under his arm. He was too broad to reach all the way across his chest, so she raised her palm to cover his heart, her fingertips on his sternum. Lowering her other hand to guide the tip of the large cock in between his buttocks, she seated it against his anus with gentle, probing fingers.

As she did so, she pulled her body in closer to him, and the dildo eased in, meeting that initial resistance of the powerful sphincter muscle. Violet stopped, pressing light kisses to the base of his neck, short nibbles along the ridge of his shoulders, letting the oil Tamara had generously applied seep in, loosen up the passageway.

"Violet—" Her name came out of his throat in a harsh whisper.

"Sshhh..." She bit his neck gently, tightened her stomach muscles and eased slowly, inexorably inside him, taking her time, waiting a second after each forward movement. He drew in deep breaths, trying to calm down enough to accommodate her, and she stroked his chest, teased his nipple with her fingertips.

"Open up, baby," she urged. "Let me in."

As the muscle released, she slid deep within, all the way, feeling the tightness of his ass, her body flush against the back of his, her upper thighs pressing against his buttocks, absorbing their jerk of reaction.

She tightened her arm around his chest and waist so she held firm to him. Her other hand dropped, cupped his testicles, fondled the base of his sheathed cock as he groaned. She withdrew a small amount, went back in. Then did it again, just tiny, incremental movements to stroke the hypersensitive gland deep inside and to coat his passage with Kiera's special oil.

She was familiar with heated oils, expected a similar response to it as she'd seen subs demonstrate before. Her first indication something was different came from Mac's reaction. His breath sucked in deep, his body freezing in motion, as she continued to thrust and pull out.

"God…Mistress—" His voice was strangled. "Jesus…"

She felt the power of the repercussion roll through him, shudder up his thigh muscles, through his buttocks. As she reached down and gripped his cock, she found it had become hot iron in her hand, impossibly hard. He made a guttural sound of pleasure at her lightest touch.

"*No.*" When he turned his gaze, tried to see her, she saw the pure panic of a swimmer a hundred yards out in a riptide, realizing that he was about to be swept out and beyond help. Completely at the mercy of the elements, though in this case the overwhelming current was his own body's response.

"I'm here," she said firmly. "You're mine, Mackenzie, and there's nothing you can do but let go. I'm here."

His lip lifted in a snarl of pure rage and lust hopelessly mixed together, and the shudder became a convulsion. Abruptly she was riding a bronc in truth. She was glad Tamara had manacled his feet to the floor, because he began to buck, his body thrusting into the air wildly, furiously, hard rasping moans coming from his throat. The orgasm did not just shoot through his cock, but seized his whole body, bringing him to a violent pinnacle. His buttocks clenched down hard on her penetration, only the lubrication allowing her to slide in and out of that tight grasp, stroking him as his groans became a roar, his fingers digging into the chains above his head, his whole body straining forward in a half crescent that should have been physically impossible.

"Amazing," Tamara murmured. "I've never seen one come that fast from it."

Violet registered the comment, made her decision. It was a ruthless one. As he jerked, she released the reserve, shooting it into his ass, rocking forward on her toes, pumping into him like a man in truth, hard, strong thrusts, demanding surrender.

She held on as his movements became even more erratic. Stroking in, stroking out.

"Violet... Mistress...please...son of a bitch...shit..." He screamed her name, begging her, but she was relentless, because she could feel his walls crumbling before his body's reaction, like concrete giving way before a battering ram. An explosion of shields she knew he'd thought to be impenetrable, falling away in confused disarray. He lost all composure, became just a rutting beast who wanted to fuck her, fuck her ass *now* if she'd let him go. He snarled, informed her that he was going to plunge his cock in her pussy, ram into her until there was nothing but him, nothing but the two of them. He wanted to suck her tits, bite them, just suck on them, just serve her, pleasure her until her come gushed into his mouth, over and over...

Much of it was incoherent, and Violet's pussy trembled with every wild promise or threat. The cock was equipped with a clitoral stimulator at the top that pressed against the crotch of the swimsuit with every thrust, but she thought his words alone brought the orgasm roaring through her blood. As her own body's instincts took over, she fucked him even more pitilessly, greedily, wanting the sensation of the stimulator striking against her spasming clit with every powerful plunge. She cried out, the orgasm passing through her, washing everything away that did not matter, leaving clarity. His low-toned, viciously spat desires became something else. A rasping, hitching sound, a labored gasping that gripped her heart, pulled it right out of her chest and into his bound hands forever.

He had continued to come throughout her orgasm. When his body finally started to jerk less convulsively, she estimated nearly five minutes had passed since he first started to come. Now his body was doing what she could only liken to a dry heave, only with a much more pleasant purpose, humping the air, unable to control his response as long as she was thrusting the cock in and out of his ass. So she kept doing it, at a slow, tortuous pace, fascinated. He was making soft sobs, and she stroked his chest, his furred belly, the impressive quivering muscles, murmuring soothing words to him, even as she kept going.

The dry orgasms lasted fifteen minutes. Each time she thought he was settling down, he would arch, cry out, and again he would furiously fuck the air another several minutes. She was soaked in sweat and wanted it to go on forever, wanted to see him gripped helpless in the throes of the pleasure she had provided him.

"Time to pull out love," Tamara whispered in her ear. "I know you don't want to, but after this long, he'll be left with some terrible hemorrhoids if you keep it in him."

Violet slowly eased out, her hands slipping away, and Mac gasped at the sensation of the withdrawal. Tamara helped her remove the strap-on. "I've never seen anything like this," the twin admitted quietly. "It was...God, my knees are weak."

Violet caught her shoulder for support herself when the clitoral stimulator gave her one more stroke as it was pulled away, but like the orgasm itself, she thought her lack of strength had more to do with watching Mac's response than any direct physical stimulation to her own.

"It can continue like this for a good half hour more," Kiera told her. "For him, maybe longer. It's best to leave him chained through a couple more, to make sure they're getting less intense. I know you want to release him, but until the intensity lessens, he won't have any control, and he can hurt you without meaning to, the big bruiser. Besides which, we can all enjoy the show." She raised a brow. "And you might like to enjoy the benefit of a hard cock that won't go down for awhile."

When Violet came around to face him, Mac looked away, his shame plain. She bent, dragged the stool to his front, stepped back on it so they were eye level. Cupping his face in her hands, she began to kiss each tear away, tasting it, taking it into herself. By the time she was done, the weight of his head was resting in her hands. When his body abruptly tensed again, his eyes widening, she brought her hand down, gripped him. He rocked forward and his face contorted in the throes of an orgasm without seed. She felt the velvet steel of him thrust through her fingers, watched the muscles of his body strain, the manacles creak against his strength, enhanced by the power of the stimulant.

"Please, Mistress," he pleaded a moment later, in a broken voice. "Let me loose."

"We have to wait," she said softly. "For just a few minutes more. Besides, you're so beautiful to watch,

Mackenzie. Don't you realize it?" She made him turn his head to look, as much to distract him from his helpless state as to make him understand. "Kiera was going to cane Collin, but she couldn't. She and Tamara have done nothing but watch you. They're mesmerized.

"And look there. You see Tyler, fucking Leila on the spanking bench while Collin sucks on her nipples? Her pussy is dripping. I can smell it, and I know you can, big male animal that you are. She started coming the moment Tyler put his cock into her, and she's about to come again. He's kept her facing you the whole time. Watching you while he moves in and out of her, so slow, she's about to lose her mind."

She knew what she was doing, wasn't finished drawing out his response, hammering the lesson home. She felt her words have the desired effect and her lips curved in victory.

"Violet…Mistress…" The desperation had a hopeless quality, his body shaking violently. Good. He was realizing and perhaps accepting that none of his responses were under his control anymore. Exactly how she wanted him.

"See how she can't control herself, how she is completely a creature of sense, totally enslaved to Tyler's will? Like you." She guided Mackenzie's face back to them when the convulsive movements of his body made him drop his chin. "Look at Tyler's delight in her total submission, his rapt attention to her. Everyone is absorbed by the two of you, Mackenzie. Don't you understand? There is nothing that pleases a Master or Mistress more than that moment when we achieve this for our slave. A sphere of total devotion, all their senses focused on and meshed with their Master's desires, so that even a whispered word from me is like the stroke of a hand over your cock, or the thrust of it into my wet pussy." She slid her thighs over his hard heat, and the wetness of the crotch of her swimsuit pressed against the top of his cock. "You're mine, Mackenzie. Say it and mean it."

"I'm yours, Mistress. All yours." His voice was hoarse, his eyes fierce and wild.

Violet caught his lips in a kiss, digging her nails into the back of his neck, channelling her reaction into the drawing of his blood.

She'd helped work subs in this room before, as Kiera and Tamara had done for her, but this was the first time she'd felt this all-encompassing centering on a person she perceived as belonging to her. Interacting with him this way while they both drew from the energy of the others in the room brought to the moment an almost spiritual power that made every movement against his body dreamlike.

"I won't let you go." He rested his brow against hers, and the tears he could not stop were on her own cheeks. "Ever. Not ever."

You bet your ass. Just you try it, Mackenzie.

* * * * *

To his horror, on the heels of that admission, another climactic wave hit him. There was no rise or approach. Just as before, it exploded from his lower belly, swept his whole body, seizing his cock with the alarming sensation of coming without any bodily fluids to show for it.

Sanity snapped. He fought the manacles like a wolf in a leghold trap. It was irrational, a fight or flight response. He'd never run from anything in his life, so fight it was, though he didn't know what he was fighting so hard. The metal bit into him and he didn't care, he would rip the flesh from his bones to reclaim what had gone beyond his reach.

"Stop, stop. Mac, stop!" Her hands were on his face, his neck, holding him, soothing him, making him look at her. "Calm down. Take a deep breath. Take another. Listen to me. Calm down."

There was command in her voice, which caught his attention, but it was the fear that brought him back to himself. Fear for him. Blood was running down his arm. He made himself stop, his chest heaving like a bellows, sure the whites of his eyes were showing like a rabid animal's. But he kept his eyes on her, used her as his focus, made himself shut out everything around them.

His deep breaths turned into shudders. She brought his head down to touch her forehead once more, a meditative posture he discovered had a calming, soothing effect. She stroked his hair, once, twice, over and over.

"Ssshh…" To his shame, he realized his face was wet.

"I'm not crying." *Again.*

"Okay. I know. It's fine. Mackenzie, I need you to think about something."

"I don't seem to be doing anything at the moment." It came out thick, his chest weighted down by far more than the light touch of her hands.

"Always the charmer," she reproved gently. "Hush a moment, and listen. You remember how you couldn't answer me, when I asked why you thought you were submissive?"

"Yes."

"You couldn't charm your way out of that. *You didn't know.*" She touched her thumbs to his lips, her beautiful blue eyes very close to his face, so that he felt he had fallen into them, that swirling Caribbean color, touched by a dying sun and turned into violet. His Violet.

"I believe that you don't know, any more than I know why being your Mistress is so important to me. You need to accept that, that there isn't any explanation. Then you can let go of the reins. You have to give up control to me, Mackenzie, for no other reason than I command you to do so, and you want to do it. You're afraid, you're angry, it doesn't matter. You just have to do it. I'm here to catch you. All right?"

He stared into her eyes, only inches away from his, and fought past his fear to obey, to hear what she was saying.

When he was seven, he had stood at the top of the steepest hill in the neighborhood, alone, clutching his skateboard, scared to death but knowing he was going to do it. Just like he had known a handful of months ago that he was going to follow a man who craved only death into a dark hole and only one of them was going to come out alive. At this moment, he saw the truth.

In every terrifying moment of his life, *she* had been there. He had sensed her presence waiting, just beyond that next challenge, knowing he was following a path he didn't always understand but knew he must walk. Her voice, her touch, had been there. Calling him. For the hope of her, the dream of her, he had come to this moment.

Starting in undercover work and then becoming a homicide detective, he had worked as a cop for twenty years. He'd been at it long enough to have paid the price of his reputation, his soul immersed in situations so deep and darkly violent there was no way to stay untainted by them. They had been locked inside, and somewhere along the way his heart had become a dungeon, a place he no longer knew how to open to invite in the full gift of a woman's love. Or offer the same from himself.

But he didn't have to figure out how to open up that dungeon, because she had already found a way in. She stood with his darkness and violence, unafraid, the light of her soul a flashlight that could guide him through that labyrinth and keep him from losing his way. All the fears he had, of never having a complete relationship with a woman because he could not offer all he was to her, the light and the dark, dissolved in her arms.

She was wrong. He did know why his heart was submissive to her. And just like that seven-year-old child, and the forty-three year old cop, the soul of the man stood before her and knew what he was going to do, despite being more afraid than he'd ever been before.

"Mistress?"

"Yes, Mackenzie."

"I'm… very, very thirsty."

He closed his eyes as her arms wound around his shoulders, her cheek and hair touching his skin. Her breath left her in a long, soft expulsion, and he wished he could hold her.

He was terrified of his vulnerability to her, but she was right about that part. He would just have to be afraid, and give everything to her anyway, because she'd left him no choice.

She was his Mistress.

Chapter 12

Violet removed the stool, unbuckled the manacles. As he moved forward, she thought he was falling, and lunged forward to catch him, but he caught her hands, shook his head slightly, and continued to his knees. When he was there, his hand lightly at her hip to balance himself, he curled down, and pressed his lips against the side of her foot, just above her arch.

She laid her hand on his head, tears running down her face. Mac lifted his head, saw them. He straightened, still on his knees so his eyes were just below her face, and caught each on his thumb, wiping them away for her, pressing them to his lips like a gift.

Gradually, she became aware of the silence around them. A quick sweep of her attention around the room showed that the play with Leila and Collin had stopped. At some point, Lisbeth had joined them with David. Each person was still, watching the exchange with the solemn formality afforded to a religious rite. In this case, a sub's complete acceptance of his Mistress's sexual dominance over him.

Mac got to his feet. When his arms went around her, she stepped into his embrace, holding him, feeling the tension in his shaky muscles as he fought to stay on his feet.

"We're going to bed now," she said.

*****

When they reached the bedroom, a room done in a soft blue with a gauze-draped canopy bed and a balcony looking out over the water, she pressed him to a sitting position on the bed.

"You've served me well," she told Mac. "Now I'm going to tend to you. Stay here."

Overwhelmed, his body weak with an exhaustion unlike any he'd ever experienced, he watched her move around the bathroom like a pleasant dream. Testing the water in the Jacuzzi tub, setting out towels, soaps, shampoo.

When she was ready, she came to him. He opened his knees at her approach and she stepped between them as he'd hoped she would. She wrapped her arms around his shoulders as he clasped her around her waist and hips, feeling her breast pressed against his jaw, her buttock beneath the palm of his hand. She laid a kiss on the top of his head. "Come get into the tub, baby," she murmured. "I want to bathe you."

He managed to walk, but his muscles had never felt so liquid. "I feel like I could just ooze across the floor to the bathroom," he said with a short chuckle.

"I don't doubt it." She looped a companionable arm around his waist, guided his hand to her shoulder. "You *will* lean on me if you need to," she ordered.

She tensed slightly when she delivered the order. Mac recognized it for what it was. She was braced for his usual smart-ass attempt at a denial, cloaked in charm. Instead, he put a finger to her chin, guided her face so she looked up at him.

"I did," he said simply.

She raised her hand to his, cupped it. "So you did."

They made it into the bathroom, and he followed her guidance to step into the Jacuzzi and lower himself where the jets could massage his back and leg muscles. He groaned in sheer bliss.

He discovered she meant what she said, that she wanted to bathe him. Burying her fingers deep in his curls, she shampooed his hair, ran slippery hands over his slick shoulders and back. She washed his genitals, even made him lift up and turn, eased her fingers into him and washed there, soothing him with a soft murmur when he tensed.

"I got a little rough. I'm sorry, Mac."

"My Mistress never owes me an apology for getting pleasure from her slave. I should be doing all this for you."

She chuckled. "And how selfless of you to offer to wash my pussy and ass."

He grinned at her over his shoulder. "Don't forget about the breasts. That would be the worst chore of all."

She flicked soap suds at him. "Behave. Let me finish this. I probably need to do a very gentle enema on you or you're going to hurt like hell tomorrow. Tyler left one up here that has a balm in it to help. "

He shifted, uncomfortably. "I've never...I can do that."

She leaned over, putting her chin on the point of his shoulder, touching her lips to his ear. He pressed his temple to her head, so she spoke into his throat.

"You belong to me, Mackenzie. I want to wash it all away, every woman's touch from you, inside and out."

And she did. He submitted to all of it, every caress and probe of her fingers, every kiss brushed over his skin, every request to turn and bend, stand or sit, until finally she was done, and he had never felt so clean and cozened in his life. She bade him lie back in a tub of clean hot water, dissolved mineral salts in it for muscle pampering, and left the jets running on a low hum as she put away everything. Mac just watched her move around the bathroom, feeling as if he could do that for eternity, never needing to move again, as long as she stayed near enough to smell her scent, see her face.

At some point, he drifted off, for the next thing that came into his awareness was her touch, moving slowly up and down his arm, her fingers following the line of his muscles, wandering over his bicep to his shoulder, down the pectoral, the nipple, then back to the inside of his elbow, as she explored her possession. He felt the difference in her touch. He was hers now in truth, and she seemed content to take this quiet moment to touch him purely for her own pleasure. Almost as content as he was to have her do so.

He opened his eyes, saw she was kneeling on a folded towel next to the tub. The bathroom was illuminated only by candlelight now, pillar candles in artful groupings in the corner shelves of the room.

"Come join me...Mistress?" He ran a hand up her side, trailed it along the soft skin of her upper arm so his touch brushed the side of her breast. At her pointed look into the water, he lifted a shoulder. "My cock may not be ready for you yet, Mistress, but I can bring you pleasure in other ways." He lifted lashes wet with the steam of the room to show her the truth of his words in his eyes. "I'm yours to command."

Her gaze softened, a charming combination of desire and need that made him want to nip on her tender mouth. She stood up, untied her robe, let it fall. She pushed the swimsuit to the floor as well, leaving just her standing before him.

It was the first time he'd seen her completely nude, and the simplicity of the gift she offered, the shrugging of shoulders, the falling of the cloth to the floor around her small feet, brought tears to his eyes again, embarrassing him. But he blinked them back, didn't look away, looked while she stood patiently, giving him time to view every inch of her. The tight calves and smooth thighs, the swell of her hips. She kept her pussy cut close, just a fine line of down covering it. He wanted to run his knuckles over it and so he reached out of the tub, a lone arm more than long enough to reach his desire, but he stopped, just shy of making contact.

"May I touch you, Mistress?" he asked, in a voice husky with emotion.

"The way you're looking at me, if you don't, I may scream."

He touched his knuckles to her soft mound. Stroked it in the direction of her silky fur and found it as glossy and soft as a cat's pelt. He passed a thumb over her clit and she shuddered, though he kept his touch light, easy, just learning her shape. From her solemn look and the smile playing on her lips, he understood this was the gift he had earned. He had let go for her, and now he could have anything.

Everything about her was so small, and yet there was that resilience to her that he had sensed from the beginning. A resilience as tough as he was, maybe tougher. There was no arguing it, not after tonight. He outmatched her physically, but her emotional core could blast his own into shards. Had blasted it to shards.

He moved his touch up, splaying his palm out over her belly, his smallest finger and thumb grazing the opposing hip bones.

"Do you have any children?"

"No." Her voice was soft, like feathers falling on his face.

"Have you...do you want them?"

It was an intimate question, and when she did not immediately answer, his expression changed. "My apologies, Mistress. I was out of line to ask—"

"No," she covered his hand with her own. "Mackenzie, you can ask me anything." She knelt, so they were eye to eye. "There's room for any thought, any question, any desire. And the answer is yes, I want them." She touched his lips. "And when I'm sure I've found the man who wants me as much as I want him, I want marriage first." Her lips curved. "That's the old-fashioned way, you know. Marriage first, baby second."

"Mmmm. I knew you were an old-fashioned girl, from the first moment you shoved that crop against my balls." He grinned, reached up, curled his finger around a loose lock of hair, tugged until she came down and met his lips. He closed her in the circle of his arms and slid her into the water with him, nestling her body in between his thighs, her hip pressed to his genitals, her breasts on his chest. When the kiss broke, she fitted her head beneath his chin. She laid her hand over his heart and he watched her lashes fan her cheek as she closed her eyes and made a sound of pleasure.

"I would be content to stay this way forever."

"Thank God."

She laughed, a quiet sound that was just an extension of the caress she was making on his flesh with the idle movement of her fingers over the curve of his pectoral. "I have to admit, that was amazing. The way that oil worked. It pleased me tremendously." She tilted her face up to him. "You pleased me tremendously."

"I'm glad. I just hope..." He hesitated, ran his touch down her spine, made her shiver. "I'd like to ask that you never use it on me again."

"Why?" Her tone was neutral, giving him nothing of her thoughts, but her hand continued its movement, reassuring. Encouraging him to speak and share his mind with her.

"It's... I want to serve you because it gives you pleasure for me to do your bidding. Not because I'm a mindless beast."

She nodded. "All right. I won't."

"Just like that?" He could not keep the surprise from his voice. "But when I asked you to stop before..."

"Just that simple. You want me to know that your obedience comes from a total willingness to obey my desires. Because every part of you consciously craves to do so. That's why you asked, and so that makes the oil unnecessary, and unwelcome."

She reached down in the water, found his cock and closed her hand on it, stroking. He thought a miracle would be required to get him erect again tonight, but perhaps contact with her flesh was a miracle, for from the moment he had laid her down on his body he had started to become more stiff, just having her so close. At her grip, the blood pumped into it hard and fast, leaving his head so quickly he felt a bit dizzy. It stunned him that she was able to command his body to rise to her touch, despite it having done so countless times already in the same few hours.

"I want you to come for me again, Mackenzie."

"I don't know if I can, Mistress."

But if anyone can get me to do it, it would be you.

"We're going to go slow. Very, very slow." Her fingers teased him, lines up and down, a faint stroke beneath the head, a squeeze of her fingers that told him she knew exactly what she was doing. She shifted up, so her knee was on the bottom of the tub, her thigh pressed against the round curve of his testicles. It lifted her breasts to his mouth.

"Suck them," she commanded softly. "But put your hands on the rim of the tub on either side of you. You can only touch me with your mouth."

His lips closed over the nipple of the left breast, and he made a sound of pure hunger in the back of his throat. She tasted wet and hot, and he thought he could even taste the flavor of the blood pumping through those delicate blue veins just beneath her skin. He wanted to curl his hands around her breasts, squeeze them, distend them, feel their weight and shape change beneath his kneading, but he obeyed, suckling her urgently, lapping his tongue over the stiff tip, watching her lips part on soft croons of pleasure. Her hands gripped his shoulders, dug in as his cock kept rising, hard and long beneath the water, until it lay along her knee, straight up along the line of her thigh, pointing at what it wanted.

"Do the other one," she whispered.

He switched, making sure he took his time getting there, licking the deep crease between them caused by her forward gravity position. He nuzzled the crescent swell, the undercurve, knowing the sensitive nature of a woman's body, of this woman's body. He knew it because he felt her every minute response as if it was broadcast in his mind, a clear picture of what she desired. He fastened on the other nipple and made a greedy sucking noise, goading her with the sounds of his hunger toward where he hoped to God they were going. He had never wanted to be inside a woman's cunt more.

She hummed, sighed, made small noises in the back of her throat that became more urgent as he used the cleverness of his mouth to bring her nipples to painful turgid arousal. She shifted, taking her breasts from his mouth to reach over, flip open the elegant hinged top of a carved wooden box on top of the commode. Condoms. Tyler had thought of everything for his guests.

Like a water sprite caressing him, her hand found him again beneath the water. He fisted his hands on the rim of the tub, wanting so badly to touch her he felt like he had to crack the tile beneath his grip to balance the desire.

It was a different type of hunger. Two hours ago, it would have had a bright, needy edge. Now it was a deep-inside, gut-aching need, something that involved his heart as much as his loins.

As her fingers rolled the condom down on his cock, she followed right behind, her pussy sliding down his length, a tight, wet sheath so incredibly welcome that his hips surged up to impale her, unbalancing her with the force of his penetration. She caught onto his shoulders and cried out as the uncontrolled descent lodged him deep inside her small, tight glove.

"You okay?" He froze, torn between anxiety and a raging desire to keep thrusting, bounce her on his loins until the craving in his belly eased, though he suspected with Violet it would never ease.

"You're a lot to take at once," she gasped. "Give me a second."

"All the time you need." Though his arms were trembling, his thighs quivering with restrained power as she shifted, making some adjustments, torturing him. Teasing him. She rose up, sliding up his length, then lowered herself again, stroking him. "Stay still," she murmured. "This is too good to rush. You're too good to rush. I want to fuck you."

"I'm not going anywhere, sugar."

She smiled, kissed his mouth, held her lips there as her body rose and fell.

"Touch you," he muttered. "Let me touch you."

"Yes. God, yes."

His hands skimmed her arms, down the line of her ribs, his thumbs brushing the sides of her breasts before he settled at her waist, then lower, gripping her hips, taking her into a line of strong, deep strokes that could please them both, drive them both.

The balance of power shifted. It took a moment before it registered, that she'd stopped using the strength of her own muscles and was just hanging on. She had let him take the reins, to drive them both to the edge.

"You feel so good."

Inane words, no poetry, but it was all he could manage with need tearing at his insides. No woman had ever felt so good, and somehow he knew that no woman's pussy would ever feel as good, as right as Violet's. It was terrifying, the realization that he'd suddenly found everything that could mean home, without knowing how long he'd be welcome there.

Her lips were a distracted smile and he wanted to make her insane, wanted her to lose all control, now that she'd chosen to give him some of it. He wanted to do things that gave her no choice but abandon everything to him, let him pleasure her, take care of her, now and forever.

He tightened his hands on her hips, held her still so he could ever-so-gently close his mouth on her left nipple, run his tongue around it, pull on it with easy tugs that he knew would get exponentially more intense as he kept it up and held her still on his cock.

"Mac," she whispered.

Her plea was the music that the soul could hear at sunrise, if the mind was still enough to hear it. Completely wrapped up inside and all around her, he let the desperate rasp of her breath and the convulsive clutch of her fingers on his shoulders guide him as he kept up the suckling caress. He heard her cry his name, felt the glory of her pussy squeeze his cock, struggling to pull him deeper, to get him to thrust into her.

He eased his grip, and began to move her again, but making it more gentle. Slow, languorous strokes that widened her eyes, made her nipples tighten even further and her breasts swell before his eyes as he stoked her fires. Bringing wet heat to a boiling tempest around him, mirrored by the wake in the tub, matching the lapping noises he made now at her breast, he brought her close with one arm curled high on her back. His other arm banded her hips, unleashing his strength in ways that were devastatingly controlled, making her his with every long, heated stroke.

"Mac," she gasped again. "Please—"

"Let it build, sugar," he urged, his mouth tasting as much of her as he could, teeth nipping, drawing her in deep. He felt her contract on him, felt the shudder as she fought it. He went still, watching in wonder as she hovered on that precipice, keeping her there by not moving, not letting her move. It was like capturing a dolphin in mid-air, sleek and perfect, heartbreakingly beautiful. So alive that she seemed to give life to everything around her.

"Mac," she gasped. "Damn it. Now. Move now."

Her mouth was open, drawing in air, her face rigid with the intensity of her pleasure and focus, and so he let the moment go, let them both go, stroking hard into her. Her pussy clenched around him like the fists she clenched on his shoulders now, her nails digging into him, marking him as hers. He used his strength to serve her relentlessly, stroking deep and fast, proving his power and devotion to her, driving her higher.

"Mac…oh, God…" Reason left and the power of the climax took over, her body undulating on his, breasts quivering with each rise and fall of her torso, pale skin slick with water so that light flashed over her as she moved.

"Scream for me, Mistress," he urged.

Almost as the words left his lips, the cry burst from hers. Her eyes reflected that beautiful moment between ecstasy and panic, when everything became about one thing, every function of the body focused on experiencing and surviving a force that seemed too powerful to be survived.

Her hands scrabbled, found his hair and latched on, a painful tugging he relished. He knew by now that she liked to pull hair, bite and claw, his little Mistress, and she sank her tiny fangs into the top of his ear. He growled in response, then groaned, long and primal, as his cock did the impossible and gave up more seed to her than he thought he had left. He wished it were not hampered by the condom, wished he could make her feel the hot stream of his need, but it was the only mar on a moment of Paradise, like the imperfection on the perfection of an original Persian rug woven by the finest artists.

She rode him through her aftershocks, whispered to him, demanded that he make her keep feeling it, fuck her harder, and he did. Someone with great foresight had made sure the tub was installed inside a sunken tile area, with additional discreet drains to take away the water that now furled and rolled out of the Jacuzzi, drops sparkling in the candlelight.

She lost purchase on his shoulders and fell against him, letting him press his face into the valley of her sweet breasts, feel the quiver of her curves against him.

"Oh, God. Oh, darling. Darling, darling..." Her lips pulled into a smile against his face, and he turned his head to capture them, locked her tight in his arms, holding her so close he thought he could have wrapped his arms around her twice if it was anatomically possible.

Holding onto him with one hand for support, she lifted her upper body and the free hand to show him what she held in it. A silver, black and white ribbon of his hair was wrapped around her wet fingers. She made a rueful face. "Sorry."

He kissed her palm, closed her fingers over the strands. “They’re yours. Like every other piece of me you want. I’m all yours, Mistress.”

Chapter 13

"I want to take us a little off the beaten path on the way home," she told him. "Take the turnoff to Lilesville up here. I have a gift certificate to use and you're going to help me spend it."

"Nope. Female shopping is definitely a boundary. Way too cruel a punishment."

"Jerk." She punched his arm. "You'll like this. It's a sex shop."

She wouldn't give him further explanation, so when they pulled off the scenic rural route and drove up to the quaint rambling house that had been attractively landscaped for its purpose as a retail venue, Mac raised a brow at the *For Her* sign. "I've been conned. This is one of those women's boutiques."

"It's a woman's sensuality shop," she corrected. "*For Her* sells sexy things that turn women on, and the owner sells it in a way that women feel comfortable shopping for it. Erotic, not pornographic. I know him, Justin Herne. See, there he is now."

Mac saw the tall man come to the door, well-dressed in slacks and tailored shirt. He had a lean, muscular build and his brown hair was pulled back in a sleek tail, emphasizing the precise perfection of his features.

"And just how do you know him?"

She slanted him a mischievous glance. "He's something to look at, isn't he? He's my friend Sarah's husband. Newlyweds, in fact. I did Sarah a favor that helped bring them together. As a result, Justin gave me this very generous gift certificate." She pulled it from her purse, laid it in his hand. "Which I want you to go in and use."

Surprised, he glanced down at the five hundred dollar certificate. "Must have been some favor."

"A story I'll tell you on the trip home. I got all the intimate details, and I promise hearing them will get you hard as a rock." Her hand wandered over his leg and his cock stirred.

"What do you want me to buy, Mistress?"

Her fingers moved to the inside of his thigh. He shifted to accommodate her, so she could tease his testicles as she lifted her other hand in greeting to Justin. "Pick me out something you know I'd like. And no cheating. No asking Justin or another customer for help."

With that, she stepped out of the car, leaving him watching the distracting sway of her ass in the snug denim as she went to greet Justin. The man met her with a warm embrace, Mac noted, married or not. He decided it was time to get out of the car. A guy who owned a women's sex shop might have some different ideas about monogamy.

"Justin, Mac. Mac, Justin." Violet introduced them. "I'm going to go enjoy your garden, Justin, and Mac is going to decide what would please me." She caressed Mac's forearm. "He's learning to be very good at pleasing me."

Justin's dark eyes shifted to Mac. It was the first time any Mistress had publicly exerted her Dominance over him. Lust warred with discomfort, his body roused by her obvious claim stake even as he felt embarrassed to be revealed as such to another man outside the strict structure of a place like The Zone or Tyler's. But when he left the two of them chatting in the garden and stepped into Justin's shop, he realized Justin was already keyed in to the dynamics that ruled their type of erotic play.

Every item in the shop—lingerie, play toys, costumes, videos and erotic romances, even bath oils and soaps—were selected to further a woman's erotic fantasies, including some very classy and high-priced bondage toys and restraint devices.

Mac's lips twitched at a butt plug with a horse tail. With her equine fetish, she might like that, but he damn well wasn't picking it out for her. He'd let her discover that one on her own and then torture him with the threat of it. Which with her sadistic streak, he wouldn't put past her. He grinned at the thought. As he passed his fingers over a soft camisole, he remembered the texture of her skin beneath his, the arch of her throat, her cries as she came, the clutch of her fingers on his arms, his hips. The smell of her hair, her half-smile.

"It's hard to know what to get for a woman when you want to give her everything, isn't it?"

Justin had apparently stepped into the doorway while he was touching the garment, staring into space. Mac realized he had a tight, crushing grip on the soft fabric and he released the satin, making an awkward attempt to smooth it.

"It is," he agreed shortly.

"Do you want a suggestion?"

Mac opened his mouth, closed it, gave a shake of his head.

"She forbade you to ask for help."

That definitely pushed way past the threshold of his comfort zone, and made itself uncomfortably at home in the living room of his psyche. So he shrugged. He wouldn't lie, but he wouldn't, couldn't engage a man like Justin Herne on this issue. "I have to know what it is," he said. "That's the point."

Justin nodded. "I'll leave you to it, then," he said. He stepped forward, placed a brief hand on Mac's shoulder, met his eyes from an equal height. "Take care of her. She's very special to us."

As another customer came in, he turned away, and Mac watched him slip into the mode of the warm, professional shopkeeper. He shifted his gaze to the window and found his Mistress sitting on a bench amid the early autumn flowers of the courtyard garden, gazing into the sparkling ripples of a fountain. The sun was making her a bit sleepy, and she laid her head on her hand, turning sideways on the bench so she could watch the fountain and let her thoughts wander where they would. All she needed were wings and a sprinkling of dust across her cheeks and he'd easily imagine her as a garden fairy, alighting in this sensual, quiet place to dream dreams only fairies understood. Of butterfly princes, rides on the backs of swallows, or naps taken in the cradle of a blooming rose.

As the customer brushed past him with a murmured, "Excuse me," and a lingering, appreciative glance, he realized he'd been drifting himself, just standing there watching her for nearly ten minutes.

As if she sensed his attention, Violet's head rose, and she looked his way. She studied him with serious eyes, then lifted her hand, pressed her lips to her palm and blew a kiss.

Watching those delicate fingers, that moist mouth press against her skin, a warmth swept through him, as if she'd blown pixie dust to him in truth. He smiled, lifted a hand and turned to find something that would make his fairy queen happy.

*****

Violet opened her eyes at a feather light touch on her calf.

Mac sat on the ground next to the small bench, one leg crooked up, his fingers cupped over his knee while his other hand played lightly with her calf. The bench was small, but he could have sat with her. He hadn't. He had waited at her feet, patiently, for her to wake.

She feigned a casual stretch, aware of his eyes coursing over the tilt of her breasts as she did so. "I didn't mean to nod off on you," she said.

It was surprising to have to admit to herself that she was flustered as much as pleased by his devotion to her needs. It was one thing to have it in The Zone or at Tyler's, where the environment demanded and expected it. She knew she had thrown down the gauntlet when she had introduced him to Justin in the way she did. He had met the test, accepting her unspoken desire to have him embrace his submissive role in a semi-public manner with barely a hitch in his stride, and he'd stayed in it, as if he had taken her actions as an unspoken command to do so until she said otherwise. It was unsettling, but undeniably arousing.

She stroked his neck, ran her hand through the thick curls, grazed her knuckles down his jaw, across his upper lip, along the facial hair that was so soft in one direction, so marvelously not when his lips were moving between her legs. He turned his head, kissed her fingertips one by one as she offered each. His gaze never left hers, and her nipples tightened sweetly beneath her shirt, rising up for his attention.

"So what are you thinking, Mackenzie?" she asked quietly, stroking him.

"I'm thinking I'd like to sit on the bench, hold you in my lap while you sleep as long as you like."

"Mmm. What did you buy me?"

He turned to the decorative bag behind him, pulled it forward. Violet was conscious of his nervous tension as she reached in.

"I bought you two things. I was sure you'd like…at least one of them."

She lifted out the custom-made Italian ankle boots. Designed in hunter green velvet that would perfectly match the first dress she had worn with him, it had black ribbon lacings, the ends of the laces tipped in emerald beads. The elegant stem of the heel was three inches.

"There're also three extra sets of laces in there. You can do them up in a gold foil color for Christmas parties, and there's a brown with these smooth, earth-colored stone beads to tone it down, wear them with jeans. And then there's one set in a matching green lace. I chose the boots, but Justin pointed out the laces and the ways you could wear them. I don't think that's cheating, exactly."

She suppressed a chuckle. "I love them, Mac. They're beautiful. They're perfect." She set the boot aside, leaned down to kiss his firm mouth. "You're perfect."

His hand curled up behind her neck, holding her there, prolonging the embrace, and she had no objections. She couldn't think of a more wonderful moment, basking in the sun of a secluded garden, Mac's lips on hers, his touch on her body.

He pulled back slightly. "The other thing. If you don't like it...it may have been too forward, but you said I should get you something you would like..." He stopped, shook his head. "I should probably take it back."

"Not until I've seen it." She was curious as to what item Justin had in his shop that would be causing Mac such concern, and she reached back in the bag.

It was a hinged box of carved wood, the top engraving of a pair of whooping cranes. "This is beautiful, Mac. What were you so worried about?"

"Inside." He inclined his head. "The gift is inside. I just thought you'd like the box, so I bought that." He shifted. "I bought the boots for you, too. This...I thought you'd want to know it was bought with your money, so to speak."

"I know how much Justin's shoes cost. You spent too much already, and I told you to use the certificate," she scolded.

"I did. Inside the box." He placed a hand over hers on top of the lid. "But I can get you something else if you don't like it."

Curiosity fully roused, she released the clasp of the box and raised the lid when Mac reluctantly slid his hand away.

The silk-lined interior held two things. One was a key. The other was a man's silver bracelet. The Italian design of flat pewter links joined by smaller links would be an appealing look for a man who wasn't a runway model, but who knew how to dress well and attract a woman's eye.

"It locks," Mac said, as she looked down at it. "I used Lisbeth's gift at The Zone so Mistresses would know what I was...but they never really tied me to her. You hate it. I'm sorry, it was selfish, and presumptuous. I just—"

Violet laid the box to the side, reached down to take hold of his shoulders and dropped into his arms, unbalancing him with the unexpected move so he rolled back to take her weight. She ended up stretched full length on top of him on the garden path, her mouth fastened on his, hands fisted in his hair. He recovered quickly, his arms sliding around her back, tightening the embrace so every curve and valley of their bodies fit together, and he swallowed her soft murmur of pleasure with the contact.

Violet lifted her head from the kiss at last, though she thought she could have lain there forever, feeling the hard strong length of his body beneath her, tense with leashed passion.

"So you like it, then?"

She lifted a shoulder, affected a neutral look. "It'll do."

He grinned.

Violet lifted herself off him, and of course as soon as he recognized her intentions he helped, providing extra strength with his hands at her waist. She took the bench again, looked back into the box and fingered the smooth flat rectangular pieces, nearly an eighth of an inch thick, joined by the smaller square links, like an elegant masculine chain.

"How'd you know my shoe size?" she asked, her mind moving over a myriad of thoughts, desires, possibilities, trying to rope them in, struggling for rationality, caution.

"I noticed your shoes at Tyler's, lying on the floor this morning."

"Some men would notice the shoes. Most wouldn't notice the size."

"I'm not most men."

She flicked her lashes up at the arrogant tone, then saw the spark of humor in his eyes, not quite covering his concern at her sudden quiet. It warmed her, his attempt to draw her away from darkness. She wasn't surprised he knew her shoe size at all, when he was so accomplished at picking up so many of her mood shifts.

As if he read her thoughts, he put his hand against her calf. "I notice everything about you, sugar."

"I'm beginning to see that."

And the realization was opening up her heart further to him, so that the vulnerable organ was all but lying at his feet, ready for him to pick it up and cradle it in those large hands. Or crush it with his formidable strength, enhanced tenfold by the fact that every third heartbeat in her chest seemed to be caused by him. When a slow smile transformed his expression, it jumped and accelerated, making her revise that. Probably every other damn beat.

Well, she wasn't a coward.

Violet closed the box, laid her hands over it, resisting the urge to grip it possessively, the way she wanted to do with him. But relationships didn't work that way, not D/s or vanilla, or any kind in between.

"I want to put this on your wrist more than anything, Mac," she said. "But I need to wait."

His eyes sobered and she looked down at the box beneath her hands. "There's something I want you to know about me first, and then..." She looked up, met his gaze. "If you don't regret choosing this as my gift, I'll put it on your wrist, and call you mine in truth."

"All right. Tell me."

She shook her head. "When we get home. I want to tell you when you have some space to think about it. For now, I want you to come up here and hold me like you said, and if I drop off for three hours and your legs fall off from lack of circulation, you'll have no one to blame but yourself."

He shifted uncomfortably. "Violet, there are things about me...we don't have to know everything right away to be all right with something like this." He nodded to the box.

"Yes. Yes, we do." She tapped the surface with its carved wooden cranes. "I take this very seriously, Mac, and I think you knew exactly how seriously I would take it, which makes it all the more special to me. I can't give it without you knowing the one thing about me that may make you decide not to pursue our relationship further."

"Sugar, there's nothing in the world that could do that."

She smiled. "There's that charmer again, but I can see you chewing on what it is I'm going to tell you. Come up here."

He looked as if he would try to persuade her further, but apparently came to the correct conclusion that she was not going to be deterred from her plan. Rising to his knees, he slid his arms beneath her thighs and behind her back and stood, lifting her at the same time. He turned, brought them back into the bench with her cradled securely against him, her legs bent up, held securely in his arms so she was limp and comfortable and immediately at peace, almost as if by giving herself into his arms she had entered the quiet sanctuary of a church. She scooted around to nest herself down, and the erection beneath her immediately drove out any thoughts of institutionalized religion.

"I seem to have a rather sizeable lump in my bed, but I don't think I want it removed," she observed.

"Good thing," he returned dryly. "With you sitting on it, the only chance it has of going away is if it's whacked off."

"Would you ask for water before I did that?"

He chuckled. "At the top of my lungs."

"Progress."

But she saw the shadows in his eyes and reached up to touch his face. "What I tell you *will* matter, Mac," she said softly. "I don't know if it will be for good or ill, but it will matter."

He didn't say anything this time, just held her closer. She shut her eyes, forcing herself not to push the moment, but to savor it, seeing as today might be the last she could enjoy him. The truth could set you free, but sometimes freedom was the last thing a person could want.

"What was that?" he asked.

She cleared her throat. "I said, what's that old adage about setting something free?"

He tipped up her chin. "If you love something, set it free. If it comes back to you, it's yours. If it doesn't—"

He paused, and a chuckle bubbled out of her at the same moment a devilish smile crossed his face. They finished it together.

"—hunt it down and kill it."

*****

She left him at the club, with several lingering kisses. First in the car, and then through her window after he got out, until his back ached and his heart felt like it would explode. Then there were ten minutes of standing there, their hands linked and resting on the base of the open window, while they simply considered each other. No, that was too adult, and he was too honest not to call it what it was. They gazed at each other with no attention to anything else in the world. What was best, he felt no need to pull away. She was the Mistress. She would say when it was time to leave. All he had to do was stand there, drink in every aspect of her, enjoy the feel of her small-boned hand within the clasp of his, and wish time would just linger there as long as they wanted it to do so.

"Well," she said at last. "I guess I better go. Work tomorrow."

"Yeah." Taking a chance, he tightened his grasp, unable to help himself, and bent down one last time, seizing her lips in a kiss that was undisguised, hungry, greedy, conveying all he felt and wanted from her. His other hand found its way to the side of her face, her neck, tightened so he felt her pulse rage beneath his touch.

When he lifted his head, she was holding onto his wrist, her nails pressing into his flesh. He was scored by her in a dozen places on his back and upper torso, and he gladly would have let her take every bit of his skin off if it would please her.

"Be careful in this death trap," he said. "When can I see you again?"

Though she flashed a reckless smile at his warning, her eyes were serious as she considered the question. He knew, with a tightening in his gut, that she was about to tell him whatever it was she felt was so important that she wouldn't fully offer the gift he'd selected until he'd heard it.

Reaching into her purse, she took out a business card case. She held it without opening it for a moment, tapping it on the steering wheel. Then, her decision apparently made, she removed a card, wrote on the back of it.

"I want you to come to my house for dinner, Wednesday night. Can you cook, really?"

"Yes."

She raised a brow. "Just yes? No qualifications, like 'I can only cook burgers or toss salads'?"

He braced both hands on the window and squatted down so they were eye level. "I attended three semesters of cooking school. I can cook you anything you'd like to eat, sugar, and give you a chocolate dessert that will melt in your mouth."

A delighted, sinful smile crossed her face and she tangled her fingers in the chest hair visible in the open collar of his shirt. "How about I make you so hot *you* melt it? Then I can lick it off every last inch of you."

He caught her lips in another quick kiss and didn't flinch when she bit, capturing his tongue and teasing it with her own. When she broke the kiss, her cheeks were flushed and violet eyes bright, for she'd donned her concealments before they were in sight of the club. He loved knowing their true color, knowing that the lavender was an enhancement of the glowing iris that was already there.

Her gaze flicked down. "I want you to wear something obscenely tight," she said. "No underwear, so be careful of what's mine when you're getting yourself zipped into them. I want you shaved, close." The direction of her glance indicated what part of his anatomy she was referencing. "Your shirt and shoes go off at the door. I plan to sit on the counter and fully enjoy watching you cook."

He lifted a brow. "I'll do all that, and bring groceries. Do you have a fully stocked kitchen?"

"Mackenzie, I have everything you need."

She pressed the card in his hand, but he saw the hesitation before she did it. All those who took D/s play into the sanctuary of their homes had to weigh the choice very carefully, for a lot of reasons. No one was in a better position to know that than him, given the case he was working now. But he did not want to see worry in her eyes. He took the card she offered, but kept his attention on her face. "You can trust me, Violet."

"I know that," she said.

"It's not going to make a difference, whatever it is."

"Yes, it will. I just… No, don't look at it yet. Not until I drive away. I just want you to know, if you change your mind and decide not to come—"

"Violet." He started to look at the card, her insistence be damned, because the fear in her eyes alarmed him, but she closed her hand over his palm, hiding it.

"—I will understand," she said firmly. "But if you do come, I'll want to talk about what you're really doing at The Zone, and if I can help. I don't have to ask if what we have is real or not. This weekend answered that. Maybe we can use that to help you, Officer. Or is it Detective?"

If she'd told him she was an alien on a mission to investigate the sexual nature of the human population, he would have been less knocked off his feet. At his expression, she managed a smile that was strained around the edges and stroked a quick hand down his chest, caressing him through the open collar of his shirt again. "Doesn't change my terms for how you dress that night. Hope to see you Wednesday. I'll be thinking of you."

She was gone a full minute, the Stealth merging into traffic with practiced ease, before he thought to look down at the card in his hand. He blinked. Felt the rug she'd just pulled out from under him rear back and slap him hard on his ass.

"Son of a bitch."

Chapter 14

He wasn't going to come. Why had she been so stupid? It was too soon.

No, it wouldn't have mattered. It would have been that much harder to accept in a week, two weeks, particularly if they continued on at the same level of intensity. She'd suggested dinner as a way to ease up, of sorts. Take them out of the realm of the dungeon or a home like Tyler's, which were geared specifically toward D/s play. This was about how they got along when it wasn't whips and chains, at least not totally. They'd tested those waters on the way to and from Tyler's and she'd found them to her liking. She wanted more of everything when it came to Mac Nighthorse.

Yes, it was better to get it out in the open now. Despite what she had told him, it might have been an act on his part, and she'd just been part of whatever his undercover assignment had been at The Zone.

"Violet," she muttered. "Don't start doubting yourself now. You know that's bullshit. Nobody is that good at undercover."

But he *had* been on the job in The Zone, and she'd known it the moment she had seen him for the first time. As clearly as she'd known he was a genuine sexual submissive, the most unexpected combination she'd ever encountered in her life.

But it was five after. Submissives, particularly those like Mac, were not late. Ever. Not for their Mistress.

She moved to the window again, cursing herself, and saw a black Dodge Ram pickup pull into her driveway, Mac at the wheel.

She hastily stepped back so he wouldn't see her there, but she stayed in the shadow next to the lace curtain panel to watch him get out of the truck, reach into the back area to retrieve the groceries, and turn to come up her walkway.

"My, oh my," she murmured.

She suspected the jeans were new, or he didn't wear them often. They were stretch denim and clung to every muscular curve of his lower body, his ass and long thighs, outlining the heavy bulge of his cock and testicles, creasing in all the right places as he walked. He wore something easy to remove, a heavy weight black cotton T-shirt.

Violet hoped old Mrs. Zerbrowsky wasn't looking out her window or she'd have to call 911 to have the widow's pacemaker jumpstarted. Her own heart was doing a triple-time beat up against the base of her throat, but it wasn't all due to his appearance, though it by itself screamed sex on demand. Her demand.

It had as much to do with the intent focus of his eyes, and the dozen lavender roses he carried in one arm. They were wrapped in a matching velvet cloth and tied with a ribbon. In the opposite arm he carried three bags of groceries.

He hadn't just showed. With the flowers, he'd made it clear that he'd showed because he wanted to do so.

Violet moved to the foyer. Outside the range of the window, she allowed herself a little spin on the hardwood floor, then composed herself at the door and opened it.

"Hi," she said.

She'd worn a soft knit dress in a deep blue hue that etched out her curves in detail, since she'd chosen not to wear a bra or panties. She was barefoot, because she wanted to enhance a casual atmosphere, but as she opened the door, it reminded her forcibly how much taller he was.

Those silver eyes covered every inch of her, and when they rested on her face at last, it was all she could do not to seize him by the shirtfront and kiss him the way she wanted to do. Because she knew the rewards for waiting, she reined herself in. Also, though he had chosen to be here, there were things they needed to talk about.

"Mistress," he said softly, extending the roses.

She took them and he stepped over the doorway at her gesture. She closed the door with a quiet snick that locked them together in intimate solitude. Mac set the groceries down on the bench of her antique hallway tree. Crossing his arms over his abdomen in order to grasp his shirt, he pulled it from the waistband and lifted it over his head, baring his upper body as she had ordered.

The naked hip she glimpsed when he stretched told her that he had followed her every demand, and there was nothing under those form-fitting jeans but him. The movement brought the light smell of his aftershave to her, just a touch of cologne, and the musk of the male animal beneath it.

Mac laid the shirt aside, neatly folding it over the arm of the tree, toed off his shoes and placed them beneath the seat.

"I missed you," he said, his dark lashes fanning his cheeks as he lowered his gaze. "I'd like to honor you, Mistress. Show my devotion to you."

Violet swallowed. "Very well," she whispered.

He knelt, one knee then the other. As he had that night at the supper table, he bent, but now he offered the deference to her as a gift, those broad bare shoulders flexing to take him low enough so that his lips touched her sensitive instep. She didn't expect him to be completely well-behaved, and she wasn't disappointed. His tongue traced the arch, and she drew in a breath, the sensation from his mouth tightening every nerve ending between the point of contact and her pussy.

Moisture flooded her so instantly that she couldn't control it. Her response trickled down her thigh to her knee. It worked its way over the shell of her knee cap, forced by gravitational pull to the inside so it ran down her calf, as if eager to race to where his lips pressed against her skin.

She knew when it reached his mouth, for he abruptly went still. Then his lips moved slightly, taking in her taste. He licked it away, began to trace the path of her pussy's invitation up her ankle. The heavy, soft knit dress covered his head, settling on his shoulders as he followed the track, sucking the dew gently from her skin even as more came down her thigh. Like a hot spring from deep within the womb of the earth, her pussy was eager to offer its honey to his mouth, but only one drop at a time, wanting to tease. He was above her knee now, his beard brushing her thighs, the hair on his head tickling her clit. Her thighs were too close together to allow him access to the deep channel between them, but he wasn't deterred. Violet moaned as he reached the top of her thigh, his head completely covered by the skirt. She watched his skull turn, jolted and cried out as his lips touched her clit, the tip of his tongue and his moustache making a tiny tickling movement against her, like the quivering of a light bulb filament.

Unbelievably, she came. Suddenly, explosively, a climax of vibration rather than convulsion, shuddering up through the balls of her feet to arrow hard and fast through her cunt. The flowers dropped from her grasp, rolled down his back in their soft wrapping and to the floor, scattering several lavender petals across his calves. Her response gushed forth between her thighs, and he made a soft growl of pleasure but did not move his mouth or tongue from giving butterfly kisses to that tiny jewel of spasming flesh. The moment she started to come, his arms lifted, went around her hips and thighs, a double band to anchor her, keep her steady. Perversely it kept her legs sealed together, so it only doubled the force of the quivering sensation on the clitoral point of contact, especially when she struggled against the inexorable force of his strength.

When she finally could breathe, he was carrying her weight, her toes not even on the floor as she clung to his shoulders, his mouth pressed against her clit, at last unmoving.

"I think you missed me, too," her slave murmured, his face still obscured by her skirt. The movement of his lips, the soft abrasion of his moustache against her made her whimper, a quiet cry. She reached down, cupped his chin, felt his hot moist breath through the fabric, a little ragged.

His act of devotion had been the perfect one to catapult her over the edge, a physical and emotional stimulus she could not resist, sweeping any control away.

She could say it was partially the culmination of several days of intense sexual frustration, and partially him, but it was all him. She had denied herself any satisfaction, only wanting it from Mac.

"Put me down," she said, her voice unsteady, and he obeyed, setting her on her feet as if she were porcelain. Violet stepped back, uncovered those beautiful bare shoulders, the tousled head, the face rigid with his own suppressed desires. She bent, kissed him gently on the lips, let him clasp her trembling hands as she tasted herself on his lips. "Come make me dinner," she said.

* * * * *

Violet had never appreciated the erotic art of cooking until she watched a man she desired as much as Mackenzie do it. The capable way his large hands sliced the fresh vegetables after carefully washing them, sliding his fingers into every crevice to gently remove any dirt, leaving the glistening color of the green zucchini and yellow squash unmarred. The firm, human flesh-like covering of the ripe tomatoes responding to his caress by revealing the deepest hue of their red color. The casual way he tossed them into the pot, a man completely at ease with what he was doing. Scents of preparing food filled her kitchen, adding to the warmth already surrounding them. She placed her wine glass on the counter and turned to hitch herself up on it, and found him there, his hands at her waist.

"Allow me, Mistress."

She nodded and he lifted her, placing her on the counter with the same care with which he had laid out his eggs on a towel. She splayed her knees, inviting him in, and he obliged, coming close enough that she could glide her hands over his beautiful furred chest, enjoying the touch of his mouth, scented with wine, cruising under her ear.

"Are you going to burn my supper?" she asked, a smile on her lips.

Mac turned his head, nuzzled her cheek with his nose. "If my Mistress desires me to do so."

She laughed, pushed him away. "Not a chance. You bragged about your cooking prowess, you're going to have to live up to it."

He returned to the stove. He didn't initiate further conversation, and she knew he was waiting. Maybe he thought it would be rude for him to bring it up, that she should initiate the discussion as Mistress, though the topic itself lay outside the bounds of their sexual roles. It was hard to tell where the roles ended and began between the two of them, though, so she took a breath and took the first step.

"You can talk about it, if you like," she said, taking up her wine and crossing her legs, bracing herself with a hand. "After all, I opened up the can of worms. Since you're here, I'm assuming you're willing for us to get more personal. But you may also…have problems with it."

His greeting had greatly reassured her, but she knew that it could still go south for them. She didn't want to wait. She wanted to make sure he could accept what she was, and that she knew what he was, and still go forward. If he couldn't…well, she supposed she could figure out a way to tie him to her bed and sexually torment him until he got over it, but there were laws against that route, and she controlled Mac physically only with her mind. If he chose to resist her, he'd have her outmatched. Unless she had a stun gun with the capacity to take down an elephant.

He turned and saw the worry in her eyes before she could mask it with a light smile. "You didn't think I'd come tonight," he said.

"I wasn't sure." She lifted a shoulder. "Cops can be funny about dating other cops to begin with. It was something I needed to know about you before I got too deep."

Too late on that, he thought. For both of them. He saw the unspoken truth of it reflected in her expression. He measured a blend of fresh herbs into a bowl, mixed them with his fingers. "Officer Violet Siemanski, Florida State Highway Patrol. A state trooper." He brushed off his hand, extended it to her. "Mackenzie Nighthorse, Homicide Squad. Though you seem to know that."

"I just suspected you were a cop. I didn't know where, or what level." She set down her wine, reached out and clasped his hand. He took it to his lips, brushed them over her knuckles, caressed her fingers.

"My pleasure, Officer. How long have you been on the force?"

"About four years. You?"

"Rookie." He grinned at her narrow look. "About twenty now. What did you do before you went into law enforcement?"

He returned to his cooking, watched her out of the corner of his eye. She hesitated, then took up her wine, that hand he'd just touched curled loosely in her lap, signs that he'd reassured her somewhat. No doubt about it, she'd completely knocked him out with the knowledge she was a cop. But what he felt for her couldn't be shaken that easily, nor was he going to let her worry for a moment that it would.

"I went into the Marines on their scholarship program. I never got posted anywhere very hot, just Germany, Japan."

"Scholarship program then, and a Stealth now?" He gave her a sidelong glance. "You on the take, Officer?"

She chuckled. "Hardly. My aunt was a bit on the eccentric side. Lived in a small house in a neighborhood backed up to the interstate. Never bought a car, bitched about every cent she had to spend on us for Christmas or birthdays. I took care of her when she got sick, because she couldn't tolerate anyone else. When she died, we were all stunned to find out she was a really shrewd investor, and she left it all to me. I've kept most of it in investments, using her portfolio manager. But I paid off my college loans, some of my family's debts, despite my dad's protests, and then a year ago, treated myself to the Stealth. I bought it from a guy who had treated it like a baby, who liked looking at it more than driving it, so it barely had any mileage." She crossed her legs and gave him a thorough appraisal, lingering over his bare chest and the prominent display of his groin area in the tight jeans. "I don't indulge often, but when I do, I go for quality. Goes from zero to fifty-five in under six seconds."

She could make his blood temperature do the same with those sultry eyes, but Mac managed to stay in neutral, gave her an arch look. "And how about zero to a hundred?"

"Fourteen point three seconds." She examined her nails. "According to the factory specifications."

"Of course." He chuckled. "So what else did you do in the Marines?"

"I trained to be an MP and served most of my stint in that. I liked it, and it dovetailed well when I went for my criminal law minor."

"What gave away that I was a cop?" Mac inserted it as a casual question, but it was bothering him. He needed to know.

She shrugged. "I just knew. You didn't give it away the way a rookie would, with the constant ready stance, but you had that air about you that...well, you know. We just know sometimes."

He nodded, understanding perfectly, though it disturbed him that he hadn't been able to out her in the same way. But then, she'd thrown him off stride from the first.

"What's the frown about?"

"Just thinking if I put in the right amount of oregano," he lied. There was male pride to be preserved, after all.

"So, do you always wear black jeans?"

He shrugged. "They don't show dirt, and they can all go in the wash together."

She chuckled. "Mackenzie, you just without a doubt told me you're a bachelor."

"I already told you I wasn't married."

"Yes, but now I know I can believe you."

He looked at her. "You can trust me, Violet."

"Not yet. Not until you know you can completely trust me." She gave him an even look in return that told him she'd seen the change in his expression, knew his frown meant something different.

But she didn't push it. Just gave him that face that said he wasn't fooling her, and took another sip of her wine.

"What's in there?" She nodded to the plastic container he'd left on the counter.

"That's dessert. A chocolate torte."

Her eyes lit up in anticipation and he grinned. "I think I've found your weakness."

No, that's you. Though she thought it rather than said it, he saw it in her eyes as if he'd heard her thoughts. A flush heated his skin, the reaction of an adolescent, but for once he didn't fight it, didn't try to remain cool. He let her see how much she was affecting him.

"The fanciest chocolate dessert I've had is a Sara Lee fudge cake from Wal-Mart," she said. "And that was pretty darn good. What's a torte?"

"A torte is a thin layer of cake with a filling in between the layers. In this case a chocolate gnoche mousse, which is like a whipped chocolate cream. When you place it in your mouth, it should melt into your taste buds. You don't have to distract yourself with the energy of chewing."

"And you made it?" She leaned over, lounging her body across the counter like a decadent queen, and peeked into the container. "Wow," she said. "Mackenzie, I might have to marry you."

He raised his head and saw, though she was teasing him, there was a serious undercurrent to her words.

"I would never be good enough for you, Mistress."

"I think you should let me decide that. So, what are you making there?" She straightened up, reclaimed her wine and distracted him with the sight of her moist lips pressed against the clear glass. "It looks fairly simple, compared to this."

"Making perfectly cooked pasta is an art," he informed her. "And since the dessert is rich, I wanted to provide something simple for the entrée. Angel hair pasta tossed in a blend of garlic and oil, with a bit of herbal seasoning, and organic scrambled egg mixed in for protein. A side dish of steamed vegetables. I make the pasta myself."

He had the pleasure of seeing Violet's mouth very nearly drop open. She caught it with a snap. "This isn't a casual thing for you."

"Yes, and no. The job." He gestured vaguely with the knife. "I needed a variety of things to keep me human."

"No meat? Is that typical for you?"

He nodded. "I've been a vegetarian for about ten years. When I worked deep cover in the dog fighting rings, early in my career, they liked to warm the dogs up for the crowd with farm animals." He sampled the herb blend, nodded to himself before he continued. "I saw them tear apart a pig, chickens, a cow, then other, weaker dogs. Later, when I was in situations where I saw men fighting for their lives, knowing they weren't going to win, I saw them lose all their identity. They were nothing but their fear in those last moments. The faces of those animals were the same, and I can't eat a hamburger or anything like it anymore without seeing that in my head." He shrugged. "I don't have to cause them to die for me to live. And so I made my choice. I hope that's okay."

She nodded, let him work in silence for awhile. Mac found it a comfortable one, enjoyed the smell of her perfume, the tilt of her head, the sparkle of interest in her eyes at every step that went into the process of preparing food well. He also liked the way her eyes often wandered over his body, enjoying it as she said she would.

"How did you get into D/s?" she said at length, her tone a little distracted.

Mac gave a self-conscious chuckle before he could stop himself. What the hell, he might as well tell her. The worst she could do was laugh.

"I had this dream growing up, about this woman. She's no one I know, just a figment of my imagination. She'd come to me, and I couldn't lift my hands, couldn't touch her unless she said so, and she'd do incredible things to me. When I was about twenty-five, someone took me to a place like The Zone, only a lot more vanilla, as a joke. Sort of a cross S&M strip club where the girls wrapped around the poles wore leather and cracked whips. It did things to me, watching them, and I couldn't get it out of my head. "

"So you investigated it some more."

He shook his head. "Not at first, but I wanted to. Told myself I was crazy, that it was crazy for a cop to be looking into something like that. We both know what a dangerous line D/s is to walk, what places it can take you, but it lingered in my mind. It was always there whenever sex was an issue.

"Then I got an undercover assignment where the suspect liked to frequent places like The Zone. I saw the less seedy side of it, started realizing it might not be up there with kiddie porn. On a lark, the suspect talked me into playing Dom one night to one of the willing staff. I sucked at it, but fortunately that helped my cover. When it was over, a Mistress came over to me, whispered into my ear. 'You're not a Dom, love. You're a sub. You ever want to find out what that means, give me a call.'

"I thought she was putting me down because I'd been so bad at it, yanking my chain. But something about the way she looked at me, trailed her hand down my arm like she had the right to touch me, and the way I felt, like I should stand still and let her do anything to me she wanted to do. That really got everything churned up inside. I couldn't get her out of my head. When the case was over, I called her. Lisbeth. And here I am."

"I liked her," Violet admitted. "And yet I'm jealous, regardless."

"No need. She liked breaking me into it, but once that novelty was over, she moved on. She didn't…there wasn't a true emotional attachment. Not…"

Like with us. The words hung between them, too potent and soon to be voiced.

"You're a complete enigma, Mac." She shook her head. "Most cops couldn't do it, even if they had the urge. It's like you've got this split personality thing going, where you crave a Mistress but you're terrified to let go of the control. You of all people know how much is outside of your control."

"I had bad panic attacks the first few times I was tied up. It still…I still have to fight them off. But I've learned to control my reaction. The…desire is stronger."

"Mac, look at me." When he did, he saw the stunned amazement in her gaze at his admission. "But you do it anyway."

He lifted a shoulder. "As I said, it doesn't really make sense. Guess it's not supposed to. With you…it's different."

Standing in her kitchen, cooking, the air full of scents and of her, he felt like he could tell her things he had not told anyone, had not had it within him to tell anyone, until he met her. But he returned his attention to preparing their salad, before he said what else he felt he needed to say.

"You scared me more than anyone, but now I don't know what I was so afraid of. There was a wall. I'm not sure I even knew it was there, though you tried to tell me it was there from the first. Every time a Mistress pushed on it, I felt like I had to keep her away from it, but at the same time I wanted her to try and shove past it, fight me for it. I didn't understand it, still don't maybe. I just know you did it, and I feel like you're inside me now, in a place where I've always wanted…a woman to be. Fuck me, I can't explain it right."

"You don't have to. I don't think there are any words for the 'why' of it, any more than there are for why I knew that's where I needed to go."

He nodded and opened a small covered dish, laid it out on the counter. "Appetizers. Marinated mushrooms." He picked one up, took it to her lips, offering it to her.

She could tell the raw sincerity of his admission had unsettled him. It was time to move it back into comfortable territory. Violet opened her mouth, closed her lips on the mushroom, watched his face as he brushed his fingers over her lips, carefully taking the oil away and then putting them in his own mouth, a quick lick to clean the oil off his fingertips and take her into him. The warmth of the gesture mingled with the effect of the wine, and spread through her.

"What I can't figure out is how a four-year rookie made me for a cop and I never once suspected you of being on the job," he said, shaking his head in disgust.

She tilted her head, managed a smile. "What did you think I was?"

"I thought maybe some type of company executive, but that seemed clichéd. I'd about decided you were a construction equipment operator. You know, bulldozers and such. Since you're so good at pushing around people bigger than you are."

"You're picking on me now."

"Yes." He gave her a wicked grin. "I am."

"There's only one reason I made you for a cop and you didn't make me," she observed, watching his delightful ass as he moved around the kitchen. How pants could be that tight and still be legal, she didn't know, but she thanked the fashion experts for all their blessings. So tight they creased the tops of his thighs and his ass as he moved, shifted, the cleft well-defined for her gaze.

"And what was that?"

"I'll tell you later. Come here."

Mac put down his knife, brushed his hands on the dishtowel and came to her, until he stood between her knees again. He braced a hand on either side of her hips, bringing all his overwhelming presence within her grasp. She moved a hand around his hip, over the curve of one cheek, squeezed, closed her eyes, enjoyed how the muscles tightened under her touch. She felt him begin to lean in, but shook her head, a bare movement. He stopped in mid-motion.

Her thighs dampened anew. She had spoken the truth. She didn't know what made her the way she was, why she so enjoyed a man willing to submit to her, why his obedience to the most subtle command, so subtle it was like he'd read her mind, could overwhelm her.

The man between her legs was high-powered, well-trained, but had never been broken. Until her. Until he became hers.

"Take the wine." She lifted it. "And drink. Drink it all, until the last swallow, and then give me that last swallow from your mouth."

He lifted the glass, his silver gaze now liquid heat, and put it to his lips. She slid both hands along his waistband and to the back of his jeans, firmly grasping his ass in both hands, kneading, stroking, easily imagining what it would be like to feel them flexing, tightening as he drove into her in a slow, pumping rhythm. She watched the glass tilt up, his head back as he downed the wine in slow, measured swallows, his throat working. She brought her hands back around front, palmed the tightly bound package of his erection and testicles, tightened her grasp.

He lowered the glass, holding his mouth closed to contain the wine she'd requested of him.

Violet released him, hooked one hand in the waistband of his jeans, and used her other to bring his head down to her. The wine flooded her mouth with his tongue, and she savored both, swirling them around, tasting their potency, consuming them.

"Perhaps next time I have wine in my mouth," he murmured against her lips, "you'll let me put your legs on my shoulders, and I'll put my mouth on your pussy, slip my tongue in your cunt and let all that warm, red wine run down inside. Mix with your sweet taste and drink from that."

"I like that image," she breathed against him. She felt his other arm slide around her, pull her closer to his hips, and she let him, rubbing herself against him before she eased off the counter at last, down his hard length. Her bare feet came to rest on top of his and she smiled up at him. "But I want dinner first."

Chapter 15

She couldn't help but feel pleasure just in looking at him. Sitting relaxed across from her, leaned back in the chair, knees splayed in the tight jeans. That powerful bare upper torso bathed by the light of the two lavender candles he'd brought with the lavender roses to decorate her table. He'd taken time, care, to make sure the setting was lovely, romantic. He wasn't just here for sex. He was wooing her as well. It was…flustering. The way he kept gazing at her wasn't staring. It was a physical caress over every part of her, and she was certain he was far too aware of the effect the attention had on her.

They left the more controversial topics alone at dinner, and talked about the things they wanted to know about each other. Usually, the first date outside of a dungeon was cautious, information warily given, but Violet found she could talk about anything with him, and he was generous with his responses to her questions as well. She learned where his family was from, what kind of upbringing he had, what made him want to be a cop. He was a good listener, and attentive to her in a way that kept her blood on slow simmer. Mixing their casual conversation with intimate reminders that he intended to serve her needs, he brought her more wine before she asked, retrieved her napkin when she dropped it on the floor, placing a light kiss on her calf when he was down there. And of course doing it all in nothing but a pair of jeans, so his naked chest and shoulders were accessible to her gaze and touch at all times.

She had eaten four bites of the most incredible pasta she'd ever tasted before she realized he wasn't eating.

"What's wrong?" she asked.

"Nothing. Do you like it?"

The corner of her mouth lifted. "It's wonderful. Did you poison it? Is that why you're not having any?"

He smiled, did not touch his fork. "I would not presume to eat until my Mistress permits it, and until I'm certain the meal is to her satisfaction."

She nodded. She put another bite to her lips, her body roiling at the sight of him, waiting on her will, his food untouched, capable hands lying flat on either side of the plate, his chest moving with even breaths. His eyes watched her every movement, lingered on her lips as they became glossed with the light oil on the pasta.

"God, you are too much," she said softly. "Eat." *Before I leap over the table and eat you alive.*

"So, can you tell me why you aren't married now?" She covered his hand when she asked and he turned it over, lacing his fingers with hers. "Is it the job?"

He picked up his fork, so he wasn't looking at her when he shook his head. "It's hard for someone like me to make a go of it with a woman without her knowing what I want, the sub angle. I've tried to have relationships without it and it doesn't work. Whether it's an unhealthy craving, or an obsession, I don't know. I guess you'd have the same trouble finding men out there who want you to tie them up and slap them around."

"Why do you think I went into law enforcement?" she said with a smile that didn't quite reach her eyes. "You're not giving me the total truth, Mac."

He raised his gaze and she held it, steady, unwavering, waiting him out. She saw the annoyance rise, then recede, become rueful resignation. She could almost see him weigh every option to evade the question, discard it. She decided to push a little. "I figured it was primarily the job that's kept you closed off from women. It's obvious there's a lot of anger in you."

He shrugged, lifted his wineglass. "Only when the Buccaneers piss away a game."

"Hmm. From everything you've told me, it sounds like you did a pretty good stint in undercover work, before you went public and then made Detective. I've read the articles. Undercover cops have difficulty reintegrating into life. It takes some of them years. They develop paranoia. Control issues. They avoid committed relationships, because they spin so fast from marriage to divorce it's not worth the effort. They can't share everything they've experienced, so it poisons them from the inside, unless they find a way to deal with it, share it. Just like soldiers." She didn't play with the stem of her wineglass or pick up her fork, kept him pinned under her relentless gaze. "Now you've chosen to go undercover again."

"I cook. I have hobbies. I enjoy trawling places like True Blue and The Zone, getting a couple nights of release here and there." His eyes glinted. "That's how I get the shit out of my system that collects from the job. I'm not a stereotype, sugar."

"Don't get mean with me, Mackenzie," she said mildly, but she put a warning in her tone that was unmistakable. "You know, I went online. Couldn't find anything about you, but I scoured a lot of stuff about police activity in Tampa, hoping to find a mention of you. I found an interesting photograph from a crime scene. It was a cop coming out of a sewer, one arm broken, dragging a body by the other. You couldn't really see his face, except for this one eye, because it just so happened his head was turned halfway toward the camera. They didn't name the officer."

Mac changed position again. "Well, that day sucked."

"You darken out the rest of that picture, that guy with all that deadly fury in his face could have been a Viking raider from centuries ago."

"Now you're romanticizing."

"I'm a woman." She smiled. "I'm allowed. But I'm also a cop, and I could tell that if you ever seriously pissed that guy off, there would be nothing, not an AK-47, not a tank, that would stop him from rolling right over you. I've seen some of that fury come out in you, when I've pushed your buttons. But you know how to hold it back."

She cocked her head. "You're not what I expected, in a lot of ways."

"Being violent is easy, too easy." He brushed it off. "Holding back, being gentle, restraining your strength when it's not needed, that takes—"

"Character," she said. "Loads of it."

The tension lessened between them somewhat, especially when she reached out, covered his hand with both of hers.

"A good Mistress has to know how to do the same," he returned. "So you should know."

"Mackenzie." She wanted more than that from him, so she waited him out.

He blew out a breath. "Jesus, you're like a terrier. I've seen a lot of things." He moved restlessly. "It's difficult to open up when you see what we see. Too many cops like me do the double life thing with spouses, and it tears them apart. I couldn't do it. Didn't want it. Especially if kids got involved."

He paused. "This is hard to talk about, Violet…Mistress. Can we…what was it that kept you from being married?"

She toyed with his fingers, felt his tension vibrating through his touch and made the decision to ease back for the moment, since he'd made the effort. "Okay. Why I'm not married." She lifted a shoulder. "Most guys think you're asking them to turn into, what did you call it? A pony? And I guess some Mistresses are looking for that, a Mother-son fetish thing. But I wanted a man, not a boy. I wanted the hardest bronc to ride." She leaned forward, her gaze covering his gleaming shoulders, the flat nipples, the tight line of hair down his sectioned stomach to the waistband of the jeans. Her hand reached out, traced a scar on his collarbone. "Not because someone had a cruel strap tightened on his balls or was digging into him with spurs to make him buck, torturing him into ferocity. I wanted the horse that was going to make me earn the right to the ride. I wanted to tame my slave, not have him come housebroken."

He met her halfway, captured her face in a hand that was a little too strong, too forceful in its grip. "Well sugar, you don't get much less housebroken than the 'pit bull who runs the yard'."

Her blood ran hot at the look in his eyes, the challenge, the invitation to play. With him, she sensed it would always be this way, the periodic reminder that she hadn't taken on a groomed pet, but a volatile, complicated man with alpha stamped all over him. And that was part of the excitement she hadn't known she craved.

"Arrogant stud," she agreed. She pulled her face from his grasp, put her hand on his chest, applied pressure. "Lean back in your chair. Spread open your legs so I can see that impressive package of yours."

He grinned, a show of teeth. "Make me, sugar."

The first night, it had been a challenge, a proving of her worth. It was still that, but tonight there was a playfulness to it that stirred her blood almost as much, mainly because she knew beneath it he was still testing her. She had rattled him, shoved him off his foundation at Tyler's, and she'd unbalanced him further, by making him as a cop when he hadn't had a clue that she was one. And now, forcing a partial confession of what had held him from opening up for a woman. The alpha in him was still trying to figure out where he could one-up her.

She sat back in the chair and smoothly crossed her legs, raised her fingers to the tiny row of buttons at the top of the modest neckline.

"You know why you didn't make me as a cop, Mackenzie?" One button flicked open.

"Why?" He had picked up his wine glass again, but she noticed he didn't drink. She took two more buttons through their eyelets, spread the fabric so the valley between the rise of her breasts was visible. Ran her fingers lightly over the visible curve. He swallowed.

"You're a male, chauvinist…pig." Three more buttons and she caressed the full breast, tracing one finger down the milky crescent, playing with the nipple beneath the fabric. He adjusted his seat and she tilted her head, deliberately studying the swelling going on beneath that zipper, the straining inseam where his testicles were fighting for room in diminishing capacity.

"You support women being cops, judges, but when the bullets are flying, you're wishing like hell there were no women around. It drives you crazy that you can't order them all back. You want a woman to dominate you in the bedroom, but you feel it's a man's responsibility to protect a woman, keep her safe from harm. It's a paradox only a Mistress could understand. A woman who understands you. You want to see how hard my nipples are now, aching for your touch, your mouth?"

"Yes," he rasped.

"Then sit back, spread your knees open, and stroke that long hard ridge in your pants for me. Masturbate yourself through your jeans. I want to see your hips move, thrust into your hand, slow, like you want to fuck me."

"Let me fuck you now."

"Not the way it works, Mackenzie. Obey me." She sharpened her tone, and he leaned back, watching the play of her hand over herself the whole time as he opened his knees, stretching the fabric tight over himself so she saw the long length of him testing it further. His hand moved over his crotch, hesitated, then he began to stroke himself as she'd commanded.

"Yes," she purred. "That's it." She opened the dress to her waist, giving her more room, allowing him see the shape of her fingers kneading her breast, tightening on the nipple beneath the thin cloth. She arched, letting out a breath as she kept her gaze on his hand, sliding down over himself and back up, the way a man did it, his eyes hot for her. His long legs were stretched out on either side of hers, one beneath the table, one out by her chair, and with her other hand, she reached down, slid a hand up his thigh, tightened her grip on it.

"Unzip your pants," she murmured. "Take them to your knees, so I can see you hold your cock in your hand. Jerk off for me."

"Let me please you with it, instead."

"Do what I tell you and it might get to bury itself in my pussy. But I want you close to exploding, Mackenzie. Show me how much you want me."

His hands went to his waist and he slipped the button, slowly took down the zipper. He had to rise out of the chair to obey, for the pants were that tight, and she enjoyed watching the undulation of his hips, the careful maneuverings necessary to wriggle out of them, push them to his knees. He sat back down, his cock ramrod straight between his thighs, and his hand went back to it. She could almost feel the heat emanating off of it, and her pussy wept for it.

You'll just have to wait, girl. Waiting is part of the fun.

"Good," she said. "Very good. Keep fucking yourself."

She removed her hand, slowly did the buttons back up to her throat. Her nipples remained high and taut against the shirt of the dress, holding his attention. With deliberate, casual movements, she cut herself a slice of the chocolate torte waiting in the center of the table. Laid down the knife. Licked one finger. Glanced casually over him to make sure he was obeying her.

Lifting the saucer, she settled back with it and her fork, and took off a small bite, all the while watching him perform for her.

"Tell me what you want, Mackenzie. No posturings. Tell me what's going through that male chauvinist mind of yours. Keep it going."

His hips pumped forward with his motions, and she could hear the faint slap of his ass against the slick surface of the chair as he thrust up through his fist. She knew her feigned indifference was increasing his desire and his frustration. She was lightly perspiring herself. He slipped his grip down, the loose skin stretching over that long, tall organ. She held the bite of chocolate up to her nose, deeply inhaling the scent of it, and getting that peculiar, heady musk of the male erection with the aroma.

"I want to ram myself into your wet pussy," he said, low, so she almost couldn't make out the words, just the guttural threat. "I want to bend you over this table, ruck up your skirt and fuck your ass for making me do this in front of you. I want you under me. I want to feel your body squirming beneath me, your legs locked around my hips. I want you wet and begging me to make you come. I want to own you, body and soul, the way you own me."

Violet blinked. A slow, controlled opening and closing of her lids. It took her a moment to remember she had cake on her fork. She opened her mouth, took it in, and knew this was the most incredible feast her senses had ever been offered, the light chocolate cream in her mouth, the scent in her nose, and the visual feast he made before her.

She separated the remaining cake from the cream and used her fingers to collect it. "Stop," she ordered. "Put your hands behind you and cup them under. Hold your ass, one hand on each cheek, hard and tight, the way I'd hold it. And don't let go, no matter what."

It took him a moment to obey, his expression heavy and dangerous, hungry. Well, she was hungry, too.

When he finally obeyed, she leaned forward and began to smear the gnoche on his cock. The tip, the sides, the area of his clean-shaven balls. He had obeyed her to the letter, his scrotum and pubic area clean except for one neatly trimmed triangle just above his cock.

He groaned as she put methodical care into it, going back to the plate to get more of the gnoche until his cock was slathered in it. Then she rose, took up her cloth napkin, and blindfolded him with it. The muscles in his shoulders twitched, nervous and impatient, but he did not resist her or disobey, keeping his hands cupping his ass.

"A slave should never see his Mistress with her head below his, even when her actions are to serve her own pleasure," she said. "That's why I wouldn't let you look down at me at our picnic, made you close your eyes." She went to one knee and took his chocolate-coated cock deep into her mouth.

It took all she had not to bite down on it, take in his taste, mix the pleasure and decadence of the dessert with the decadence of enjoying him. She licked, consumed the chocolate cream, tasted his cream in the mix, took him firmly in her hand at the base. His breath rasped hard as he struggled to obey her mandate and not move as she cleaned every impressive inch of him, her eyes noting the flex of his powerful thighs, the ripple across his abdomen, the tightening of his balls under the caress of her fingers. Her own reaction was sliding her thighs wetly against one another, and she made noises of enjoyment in the back of her throat, telling him what he could not see. How much she wanted him, was ravenous for him in fact, to the point that she wanted to keep him with her always, never let him further from her than a short cock leash would allow. Now she no longer wondered why some Doms were fond of keeping their subs in The Zone on a collar and leash, to reinforce the servitude and the bond.

"I want you," she muttered, and he growled in response, a primal reaction that she saw him struggle to take to civilized English.

"Sugar, I'm more than ready for you."

She rose, took off his blindfold and found his eyes blazing in response. "I'm protected from pregnancy," she said, her own voice thick with desire. "Will you…I don't want anything between us."

"I trust you. And you can trust me, sugar. With anything."

His voice was ragged with male hunger and something else, something that roused her heart into her throat, and mixed sweet emotion with overpowering lust.

"My Mistress honors me," he said, low, urgent. "Let me serve you. I need you, Violet."

She swallowed, nodded. Undid the buttons again, and slid the dress off her shoulders. His eyes followed its slide to her feet, and she stood before him, clad in nothing but her skin and her equal need for him.

"You can move your hands," she whispered, and moved forward.

He caught her at the waist, lifted her effortlessly over him. Violet put her hands to his shoulders, gripped, dug in as he slowly, perfectly lowered her onto him, his silver eyes locking with hers as he took her down, inch by blissful inch. Her thighs trembled as they spread over his on the descent, making the sensation of his invasion that much more excruciatingly pleasurable. His fingers tightened on her waist and she savored that touch almost as much, every sensation he was offering her, including his hot breath on her neck.

She came to rest on him, just a blink after she wondered, as she had the first time, if she could take all of him. Knowing she would, no matter what. She had to have all of him deep inside of her, her cunt closed around him like a possessive fist, stroking him, working him. She raised her legs and he helped her, his hands sliding under her thighs so she was at the right angle, and the position seated him impossibly deeper so she cried out in reaction, digging her fingers into his back as his hands returned to her waist just above her hips. His eyes met hers, full of dangerous intent that shivered over her skin.

"Hang on, sugar," he advised.

He lifted her and brought her down, hard, letting her feel the full force of his primal need. She screamed as her pussy convulsed around him, but he was drawing her up again, making her feel the rush of all that hot hard length against her wet inner folds, and she knew she never again would settle for a lover who did not have the incredible upper body strength Mac possessed. In a mere handful of days, there were many other "never agains" that Mackenzie Nighthorse had injected into her life.

He kept his gaze on her face, not doing anything but watching her desire grow and reflecting it in his own expression. That made her even more helpless and hot, his total absorption in building her response by controlling the rate of rise and descent on his cock.

"Come for me, Mistress," he said, rough. "Come like you've never come for anyone else."

That wasn't going to be difficult, considering the sensation he was coaxing from her now was more intense than anything she'd ever experienced. But he was begging her to lose control, lose control for him.

"I already have," she whispered. Her body arched as he plunged her onto him again, then lifted her high so she felt the ridge of that broad head at the lips of her opening, then down again. Like the rush of a roller coaster, the exhilarating pitch, a well-oiled machine working at the perfect speed to achieve explosive combustion. He didn't let her use any of her own strength, kept her moving in sync with the press and lift of his large hands at her waist. He would not let her hips thrust and move at the ferocious rate she might have chosen. He was giving her a slow, torturous build, a climax that would shatter her, leave her spent and weak in his arms, and she…she just wanted. She was all want now, a creation of formless, overwhelming desire. The shuddering reached through her, a ripple that quickly grew to a tidal wave shooting out from all directions from the well of her subconscious. She called out his name, part fear, part wonder, as the orgasm slammed down on her.

He was there, making her ride him still, keeping her at a pace that drew it out even longer, and the flashes behind her lids were like watching a never-ending ribbon of stained glass shatter before the power of a blinding sun. He increased the pace, brought her down hard on him now, and brought his hips into it, so all she felt was that thud of impact, over and over, merging with her heartbeat, pulling everything loose in her. She shrieked as he leaned forward, caught one quivering breast in his teeth, bit down on the nipple and suckled hard. Sliding his hands around her waist and hips, seating his cock in her firmly and deep, he changed the angle so he was rubbing against that incredible spot. The orgasm she thought was on its descent gained a new power that snatched her up and roared her over another pinnacle. She screamed with the pleasurable agony of it, only able to move in incremental amounts on his hard length, still pulsing, unspent within her. She milked him with her convulsing muscles, tugged on his hair, dug her nails in and used her teeth on his neck, just below his ear. It was excruciating to move upon him now, every motion like touching the most sensitive of harps, her body making plaintive notes for him, wanting something from him to give the song its meaning.

"Mistress," he growled. "May I come for you?"

She was enough of a Mistress that she waited a full minute as he kept up the rhythm, and his breath grew clogged and desperate, their gazes holding, sweat slick on both of their bodies.

"Mackenzie," she whispered. "On my command. This pussy is yours and it demands your seed."

She tightened her muscles on him and worked him in those tiny movements. One, two, three…

"Obey your Mistress, Mackenzie. Come for me. Now."

Though the stimulus of everything else could do it, she knew that it was her words that pulled him over, more than her head, mouth or pussy did. He stiffened in shock, his hands digging into her waist in a moment of delicious, bruising lack of control. Then his hips were lifting her off the chair as he drove her up, making her hold on as he bucked beneath her, groaning and then growling, shouting his release. He was unable to maintain control any longer before the power of the whispered command, proof of her hold over him. Violet felt his warm juices spurt into her, and she cried out at the renewed sensation, held his head close, his rough jaw scraping her breasts as he clung to her, rammed into her until the last drop was gone. Until their desires were, for the moment, sated.

When she regained some sense of her surroundings, everything around her looked hazy, surreal. She had to blink to bring it all back into focus. She was wrapped around him, arms and legs tight around his body, her head resting on his shoulder, lips pressed to that round curve that led to the hard biceps. He held her close, his arms all the way around her so his fingertips were at her ribs, just below her breasts, putting her in a cocoon of his strength, his heart thundering against hers.

"Are we dead?" She managed at last, and his chuckle trembled through her body, shook them both.

"If that's dying, sugar, everyone would line up to self-terminate." His hand touched her face, her hair, seeking, and she managed to lift her head, though she was grateful to lean the weight of her cheek into his palm. "God, you're the most gorgeous thing I've ever seen," he muttered. His lips pressed against her cheek, and when she closed her eyes, his voice resonated through her head, her heart. "You're so small," he said softly. "And yet, you're the most formidable woman I've ever met."

There was a pause, his voice dropping even lower, and she kept her eyes closed, willing him to open to her, say what was inside his soul.

"I want to hide you somewhere safe, and at the very same time I would give anything to just kneel at your feet, brush my mouth along your thighs, remind you I'm there to service you however you want me." His voice was wondering. "Mouth, tongue, cock." He touched her face, parting them so their eyes were able to meet. "Heart, soul, mind. It seems I've wanted that for such a long time." He swallowed. "And you're right. It was the job. Sometimes you get so dirty, you don't believe you can have something so fine. I really didn't believe I'd ever find it, a woman who could get past all of that. I didn't even know I'd given up on it." He shook his head. "I can't go further than that. I don't know how to say what I'm trying to say."

Beautiful, she thought. He was perfectly beautiful. Perfect and beautiful.

She kept rolling it through her mind as she laid her head back down on his shoulder, until she was murmuring it like a quiet lullaby. It took her into a post-coital doze she could not stave off with his hand stroking her head, his body rocking her to sleep.

* * * * *

When she woke, she was in her bed, still naked, and he was spooned behind her, keeping her warm. His even breathing told her he slept. She was glad for it. For the time to slowly turn over in his embrace, look into his face, etched by the dim buffet lamp light spilling in from the hallway, and lay her palm over his chest.

Everything moved too fast, and this should seem so, but every moment with him felt dipped in molasses. Something outside of time, and something she could call back and savor at length whenever, however long she chose to do so.

"Mackenzie Nighthorse," she murmured.

His eyes opened, that beautiful color that was not gray or pale blue, but simply silver. She'd always preferred silver to gold, the clean purity of it, the lack of ostentatious pretension that clung to gold. He lifted his hand to trace her cheek, rub his thumb against her full bottom lip. She bit him gently and he smiled, a slow, sleepy expression that made her heart do a slow roll in her chest.

She settled her cheek on his chest, listening to the slow thud of his heart beneath her ear while he stroked her hair from her temple, smoothing it down the side of her skull, curling it over her ear, rubbing her ear between his fingertips as he did so. It was an incredible feeling, that gentle stroking and fondling together, a non-sexual touch that was as intimate as a sexual one. She felt herself drifting, her weight melting into him, as if she were a snake lying on a sun-baked rock, absorbing the sensations to the point that all of her became liquid, formless, so relaxed were all her muscles.

"You don't like men touching you, do you?" she said softly. "That's a boundary. When Mark had you in his mouth, your cock was responding, but every other part of you was resisting. It helped break you down as fast as anything else."

There was a long pause, but at last he nodded against the crown of her head.

"Say it for me, Mackenzie," she whispered. "Trust me to want you, no matter what."

"I prefer not to have men touch me, Mistress. If that doesn't offend or displease you."

"Manners. I like that. It doesn't. And I'll let you in on a little secret." She tipped her head up, tapped his chin. "I'm not wild about having other women touch you, either."

"I'm willing to make the most monumental of sacrifices to keep you happy."

She was beginning to adore the many versions of that smile he possessed. This one had a rakish, teasing quality to it.

"I want something, Mac," she said.

"Anything, Mistress."

"No. I'm…I'm not asking it that way." She hesitated. "It's been a long, long time since I've asked this of anyone. It's like you said. You learn to let the club scene be enough, but even when you get the guts to take it out of the club, it's still…the focus. I want…" She stopped, shook her head. "I'm afraid to tell you what I want."

"Then let me take the risk," he said, lifting up on one elbow and turning her onto her back so she was looking up into his face. "I want to see you, Violet. Enjoy your company. Not just for sex, not just for D/s play. I want to go out to dinner. I want to see movies with you that we'll both like or hate, or argue about it afterwards over coffee. I want to have you over with my friends to watch a football game, and I want to take you and your beagle out for walks on the beach."

"How did you…how'd you know I have a dog?"

His eyes twinkled at her. "The pictures on the bureau. Water bowl and leash in the laundry room gave it away, too, though I had a bad moment thinking they were for me."

She snorted. "Detective. Forgot."

"Shield, real gun and everything."

The smile died from her eyes, and she reached up to cup his jaw. "You're sure."

He pressed a kiss into her palm. "I'm sure. I like you, Violet. You turn me on in a million different ways, but I want more. Every time I'm around you, I want more. If you're offering the chance of all, I'm game. Let's go for it." He gave a half chuckle. "Though it's a scarier thought than anything I've ever faced on the job."

She didn't have to ask him why. Because the job couldn't break your heart, not if you learned how to detach yourself at the right moments. There was no detachment to this, not if they wanted the full prize.

"Nevertheless." His eyes glowed in the dark, making her tingle in warm places. "You've invited me in, and the only way to shut me back out is to tell me to get out. And I might need to remind you, I'm not the type of sub who always obeys his Mistress."

But he was hers. For the time being, he was hers.

She slid out of bed for a minute, went and switched off the light in the hallway. She came back into his arms in the protective anonymity of darkness.

"You said," she paused, searching for the right words, "you didn't know you'd given up on finding it. There was more than that. Tell me what else was in your heart. I know you said you couldn't, but I want you to try. For me."

His face was a quiet silhouette for several moments, his hand lying on her stomach, the fingers moving in an absent caress. "I don't know," he said at last. "I've tried all sorts of rationalizations, but I just have two things in my gut that I know for sure. That I have to be a cop, and that I've been looking for something in a woman all my life… I didn't figure out the submissive part of it until about ten years ago. Didn't accept it at first, but even after I did, I knew there was something more. Sort of like it was the means, but not the end. There was something about it just out of reach, like that climax that goes only so high, so that you know something's missing. Something I didn't know…"

Her breath clogged in her throat. He chuckled, but it was a strangled, nervous sound. "Forget it, I—"

She reached up, touched him with insistent urgency. "Mackenzie, I order you to say what you were about to say. Now. I mean it."

His body moved into hers, a man so large he filled her bed, his eyes burning with desire. "It was something I didn't know, didn't understand. Not until I met you. I was looking for you. My Mistress. Mine," he said fiercely. "It's you. You're the beginning and the end of it all for me. The reason for it. I know it doesn't make sense after less than a week. But I know it. I just do."

After several long moments, she twisted away from him in the darkness, and with sure fingers opened the nightstand drawer. Lifting the lid of the carved wooden box, she pulled the bracelet out.

"What are you doing?"

"Sshh." She found his arm. When the cool metal touched his skin, she felt him go still, recognizing what she was doing. What she had in her hand. Violet's fingers trembled as she guided the bracelet around his strong wrist, found the clasp to lock the two ends together with a soft click.

She slid her hand to his neck, drew him down to her. He could have closed the distance himself, but in this moment she knew he would wait for her to do it, to show that she accepted him. Because it was his nature to wait for her bidding. Not any woman's bidding. Hers.

But once she gave him that acceptance, the rebellious sub she knew took over. He yanked her up to him, brought his mouth hard down on hers, his other hand cradling the back of her head, holding her tight against him, letting her feel his need and strength, what he could offer her, what he was offering. Her body gave up its own strength, let him hold her, consume her, and it wasn't until she felt his lips move to her cheeks that she realized that they were wet with her tears.

Her eyes had adjusted so she could see his startled expression in the dim light from the window, and she smiled at him. "Did you think you were the only one affected by what's between us?" she asked thickly, reaching up to touch his face with trembling fingers. "I've never been as terrified or happy or…anything, as I've been since I met you."

"You broke me down. I told myself that I couldn't afford you."

"So leave." She smiled as he snorted.

"I can't." There was a long pause, but she could feel him gathering his thoughts, so she stayed still against him, waiting.

"It was never supposed to be about…what's between you and me. You were right. I knew what I was, but I didn't believe it, not all the way down to my soul. I was afraid to, because I thought it was about strength and power."

"It isn't."

"I know. I just don't know what it's about now, but I guess it doesn't matter."

"It matters. And I know what it's about, Mac." She brought her lips to his. "It's about surrender. For both of us."

Chapter 16

He stayed to make her breakfast. And to give her information. While she watched him make muffins from the scratch materials in her kitchen, he told her about his case. She had heard about the two murdered men, but he gave her a high level of detail so she could offer her opinion, complimenting her instincts in a way she could not miss or deny being flattered by.

"You're moving in the same circles as the murderess," he explained, "and you're trained. The more you know, the more likely you'll remember something you saw, or you'll see something that will help." He hesitated. "I brought pictures of the victims. I thought you might want to take a closer look, see if you remembered them."

She examined them, the family-provided photos next to the gruesome remains of those smiling portraits. "They must have come on different nights from me." She tapped Rodriguez's face. "This one is familiar, but I didn't know him at The Zone. Most of us have a regular schedule when we go, and those of us with day jobs can't come as often or stay as late. Did they have memberships in other clubs?"

"None in common except The Zone."

"Well, why even have that commonality?"

"She wants the top of the line, the ones who are obsessively careful and well-established. She's saying something by killing them."

"Well, if that's the case, and she's as smart as you say, I'm willing to bet she finds her mark at The Zone, but she approaches them and picks them up elsewhere, so she's never seen with them at the place that they had in common." Violet slid the photos back in the envelope.

"Possible," he agreed, rising to put the case file away. "It's an angle we're investigating now."

Violet rubbed her stomach, eyed the steaming blueberry muffins. Her brow drew down over her forehead.

"I don't have fresh blueberries."

"No, you don't. You do have some raisins that look about two years old. I pitched them before you poison yourself."

"Did you bring a toothbrush in one of those grocery bags, too?" she asked sweetly.

Mac grinned, bent down and kissed her cheek, didn't appear at all surprised when she turned and bit his throat. "A good slave is always well-prepared."

"Smooth talker."

When he went back to the sink, she indulged herself in breaking off a piece. "You're dangerous to have around, Nighthorse. I'm going to have to spend all my time in the gym."

"You can work out with me, sugar. I'll keep you in shape."

She rolled her eyes at him, then abruptly sat up straight in her chair. "Mac, that's it. The gym. That's where I saw Rodriguez. The guys who visit the clubs like The Zone, particularly subs, they're workout-aholics. Maybe…what if your perp scopes them out at The Zone, notes the bag they carry in and out of the club? It's what most of us use to bring our change of clothes. Most of them have the logo of whatever the fitness club is. All she'd have to do is notice that, get herself a guest membership to that gym, stake out the parking lot a few days, show up on a night he's there.

"A guest membership is just a slip of paper, with no name on it," she continued, thinking hard. "So it gives her an excellent cover. She initiates a contact, gets to know him, lets him know by the vibes she's a Dom, wires into that part of him, wins his trust and—"

"Bingo," Mac said softly. "She has her victim, without ever having been seen together at The Zone, where she first selected him. Possibly not even the same place as the other vics, if they all had different workout memberships. And a gym is a meat market. Defenses are down, open to physical contact and stimulation."

He pursed his lips, nodded, pulled out his cell phone, dialed. "Consuela. Mac. Do me a favor, sugar. See if the workout clubs of our bondage vics keep any kind of guest membership rosters, and if there's any record of our victims visiting there with a guest in the past couple months. I've got a good tip. I think it will pan out." His eyes shifted to Violet, who picked up her orange juice, set it back down. "Just leave what you find on my voice mail. Appreciate it."

He disconnected, studied Violet who was staring moodily now at her plate. "What's bothering you, sugar?" He reached out, covered her hand on the table.

"Her." She shook her head. "I'm sorry. I'm going to sound stupid and naïve, and I'm not."

"No, you're not," he agreed. "So nothing you say is going to sound that way. Tell me."

Violet rose, went to her window, stared out through the sheer panel. "It offends me," she said at last. "Deeply. I… To be given the trust of a sub… Every Mistress, every Master longs for that. It's a gift beyond comprehension to the vanilla world. Maybe even to subs. From what you told me, this isn't a random one-night fuck, two people just living on the edge. She chooses a careful sub, a person who lives his life in a moral, responsible way. She wins his trust, builds that bond. She likely achieves that gift. And I think that's when she does it. That horrifies me." She turned to face him, raised her chin. "Now you can tell me I'm being too sensitive, too green."

He shook his head. "I've worked on this case for almost two months. When I leave you, I go to the station, stare at the pictures, try to connect the dots and sack out in the break room. I'm pouring my soul into this one. For the same reason you feel as you do now. I understand the deep breach, the line she's crossed, and it hits very close to home. It was a bond of trust, and that trust should never be betrayed."

Icy fear touched her abruptly at the flash of anger in his tone. "Mac, you aren't…I'm the only Dom you're involved with right now."

"I told you, I don't—"

"I wasn't questioning your fidelity. I meant for your job." She came to him. With him sitting, she had a slight height advantage to stare hard into his face, try to impose her will on him through sheer determination. "Your undercover work."

"Yes, right now. There hasn't been a need to branch out, because I felt hooking up with a well-connected Dom in the scene would be enough. I've been just trawling through on my off nights, watching the rooms and the action, trying to make connections. And see some connection I've missed," he added quickly, at her narrowed eyes.

"You won't go there alone anymore."

"Violet." He scraped back the chair, stood. "This is my job."

"And the ass you're carrying around belongs to me."

She was riding on fear, because she could see clearly what he did not seem to. *No safe words, no boundaries.*

His silver eyes became steel, reminding her of the expression on his face when he had wanted to go after Jonathan, that first night. And the picture in the paper. The unbridled fury wasn't there, but the icy edge of danger was.

"Careful, sugar. There's a big difference between a sexual submissive and a lap dog. I don't take orders from anyone but the sergeant when it comes to my job."

"No." She shook her head, staving off his annoyed response. "She knows what she's doing, and as a sub, you could be vulnerable to that."

"Violet, I've been on the force for twenty years—"

"But you're too close to it—"

"And I'm with you," he finished, startling her into silence with the forceful statement. "I'm with you," he said, more softly, touching her face.

"I know." She put her forehead on his chest, closed her eyes, listened to his heartbeat. "I had to try. I care about you, Mac. I care a lot. Let me help you."

"You are."

"Why are you the undercover person for this? They don't usually put in an established detective. You'd be too easily made."

"Because it's plausible that a cop who is really a sexual submissive would choose to indulge it in a heavy security place like The Zone."

"Then why is your sergeant letting you go in there without back up?" she demanded, frustrated. "This isn't my area of expertise, but shouldn't somebody be watching your back?"

"Somebody is," he said. "She just wasn't aware of it until this moment."

"Not if you're going in there when I'm not around," she said, not mollified. "Don't try charm, Mackenzie. It will only piss me off more."

Patiently he explained the call-in contact arrangement he had with Darla. Violet's eyes widened as he briefly touched on their conversation.

"You told your boss." She shook her head. "I knew you had impressive balls, but they're even larger than they look."

"It wasn't easy." He shifted, obviously uncomfortable with the flattery. "It just had to be done."

She nodded. "I get that. So you're going to do two things for me."

"What?" he asked warily.

She went to her phone table, came back with another card like she'd given him, scrawled her cell phone, pager and home phone on the back. "You give that to your sergeant. Tell her I'll be the inside person watching your back."

"Violet, that means she'll know. I don't want to risk you or your reputation in your department. It was hard enough for me to do it. You know cops work on the streets, close to the hookers and peep shows, and they don't see a big difference between what we do and the criminal side of it."

"You trusted your sergeant enough to tell her. Now I will, too. We both want the same thing. You, alive. If you trust her, I trust her." She held his gaze. "I won't crowd you, I'll defer to your experience, but I won't let you be in there unprotected. This is a smart, smart Dom, Mac. If she figures out you're there for her, I'm willing to bet she won't run. She'll want to stand and fight. And because she's a woman, she'll fight dirty. She'll try to take you down when you're not looking."

"I'm hoping not. I'd like the chance to take her down."

"Then we can do it together. Though I expect to get my department a stroke if I'm right about the gym bag."

"A full month's worth of Krispy Kremes, I promise."

"Arrogant creep," she retorted, but some of the stress eased out of her as he raised his hand, threaded it through her hair and stroked.

"What was the second thing?"

"What—oh." Her eyes crinkled. "You ever call another woman 'sugar' again, other than me, and you won't sit down for a week."

He grinned, the tension leaving his shoulders as well. "Yes, Mistress."

Chapter 17

Mac swore, viciously, as he knelt over the body.

Suarez stared down at the victim. "Might as well get a cookie cutter, the way she picks out exactly the same type of guy."

"Yeah." Only Edward Turner hadn't been a cookie cutout to his family, Mac thought.

"She moved on this one fast," Suarez observed. "They must have broken through that trust barrier fast."

It could happen that way. It was something about which Mac couldn't have claimed firsthand knowledge only a handful of days before. But he knew he would trust Violet with his life.

"Which may mean they had a prior association, or a mutual friend. Someone will remember her. She's getting bloodthirsty, and that means she's getting careless. Or she's playing more than one at a time."

"She's also getting bolder." Consuela squatted next to him. "She wanted to see the parent arrive on the scene this time. Body was still warm when we got here."

"You seal off the block?"

"Instantly, but you know she's too smart for that. We're doing a door-to-door, but my guess and my gut tell me she slipped out right between arrivals. Laughing her ass off, probably." She made a disgusted face.

"No, not laughing." Mac studied the body, his eyes marking every detail, evaluating its significance or lack of import to the crime. "This one snapped quickly. I think she's been carrying around her psychosis for quite a while. But something happened a couple months ago that manifested it. Suddenly, it was all clear to her. She could ease the ache with the kill. And now she's like a junkie needing the fix, it's rushing up so hard and fast in her. She's got a lifetime of pain to get rid of. Killing them wasn't enough. Seeing the parent find him tonight, she thought that might help, but it won't. She was in the house when he was discovered, I'd bet on it. Probably left out the back door while they were still standing over him in shock. She's going to keep varying her MO until she figures out what works for her, and nothing's going to work. She's starting not to care about being smart. Getting rid of the pain is what matters."

"Turner's on The Zone member list." Connie noted. "She's sticking to that, at least."

Suarez shook his head, looked like he would have spit if they hadn't been where they were. "She's got a pool to choose from. Seems like there's a rash of guys lining up to have a woman beat on them these days. Got dealers in school yards handing out coke patches to six-year-olds, and we're wasting time with this freak who was begging to get iced."

Mac used his pen to lift the chin of Edward Turner, looked into the lifeless gray eyes. "Suarez, that was your daughter that came through the station the other day, wasn't it? The Britney Spears wannabe in hip-huggers and crop top?"

"Yeah. She's into that stuff now. You know how teenagers are. Smart about some things, but hormones get in the way of good sense."

Mac nodded. "Even so, I guess if someone jumped her on the way home, raped her and left her dead in a ditch, we'd probably bend over her and say the same thing. I mean, with that outfit, she's got to be asking for it, a twelve-year-old dressed up in an outfit a hooker'd blush to wear?"

"Crime scene," Consuela snapped as Suarez surged forward a step, into her slapped palm. "Crime scene," she repeated. "Don't do this, guys."

"Look around the room, Suarez," Mac said, his voice deadly and low. "What is it that says freak to you? The picture of his family on the dresser? The TV Guide with his favorite sports shows circled? The suit he laid out in the bathroom to wear to work tomorrow?

"Did you notice the display cabinet in the front hallway? This guy was the United Way fundraiser chair at his office, raised fucking fifty thousand this year. In the laundry room there's a dry-cleaned and wrapped set of suits he was planning to have the men's shelter pick up to help some down-on-their-luck guys get jobs." Mac's voice was raised now, and he was vaguely aware of the uniforms just outside the door, frozen in shock at the outburst, but there was something boiling inside him, a fire he had to unleash or it would consume him.

"But you know what? That doesn't matter. Even if he'd been a selfish yuppie prick who'd made less of a mark on the world than a twelve-year-old not old enough to make her mark on anything yet except her daddy's heart, he'd deserve our help. Less than twelve hours ago, someone stood in this room and played God. I don't need a repeat performance from an asshole like you. Get out of my crime scene and go find another one that you feel deserves your special touch more."

"C'mon, Suarez." Consuela tugged on his arm, giving Mac a quelling look. "Let's take it outside. Walk it off."

It took a full moment for him to recall himself, take a deep breath, realize with grim amusement that the cops on the scene were tiptoeing around outside the door, unsettled by the outburst from their usually stoic Oak.

Tensions were high. This many murders in such a short time frame meant a lot of pressure on the squad to solve it, and Mac could feel it, see it in the face of every uniform present. He felt it crawling in his own gut as he stared down at another dead kid. He'd spent the past two days at The Zone without Violet, risking the wrath of his pixie, but she was on a twelve-hour shift for the next several days and he wasn't going to wear her out. He'd turned down several offers to play, evaluating those who offered and knowing they weren't whom he sought, knowing he was out of the age range anyway. Three FemDoms had brought in twenty-somethings, and he'd had them tailed, but he suspected Violet was right, that whoever their killer was kept them away from The Zone, so the connection was never made. So he watched the FemDoms that trawled, or sat in the shadows watching, and came up with nothing.

"The neighbor remembers a gray Grand Am in the driveway." Consuela had returned. "Lost plate tag. My guess is we'll get a stolen vehicle report later from one of the downtown neighborhoods, find it stripped and the inside trashed, just like the last two times. I've also got some info on the gym connection, a list for you down at the station, if you think you can pull that railroad tie out of your ass long enough to listen to another cop."

"Don't start, Connie. He was out of line."

"Suarez'll do his best on this case, like he does all of them. We're all frustrated, Mac. He was just blowing it off. He didn't want this kid to die. I don't understand this lifestyle choice anymore than he does. Most people don't. It doesn't mean we won't do our jobs."

"I know." Mac ran a hand over his face, the back of his neck. "I'll say I'm sorry. Even buy his daughter the latest Britney CD."

"Well, let's not go crazy." Consuela allowed him a small smile, her sharp eyes studying him. "You may need a vacation after this one yourself. That wasn't like you, you know. You're looking a little ragged around the edges."

"He's looking worse." He nodded at Edward Turner. "Are the parents still here?"

"The father. Mother died when Turner was in his teens. The dad is with the victim's sister, in the next door neighbor's kitchen."

Ten or fifteen minutes of wading through the initial flurry of questions and confused anger of the father, patiently probing through that for anything that might have unconsciously been knowledge of his son's killer, resulted in very little. Just like the two victims before him, Turner had kept this an aspect of his life his family never suspected existed.

"Why…what kind of person…she didn't just kill him, she humiliated him." Mr. Turner was a spare man, tall and lean. Mac suspected his leanness came not from an ascetic appetite, but as a permanent physical brand left from the death of his wife. He'd seen enough death and the way it affected those left behind to know some always carried it visibly, either through irreparable stress lines around their eyes, a nervous twitch, or gauntness like this man had. His son had been a strapping kid with wide shoulders, and he didn't think Edward had gotten that from his mother.

Mac nodded. "Mr. Turner, I need you to think carefully about any friends your son has, and give that contact information to the officer I'll leave you with when you and I are done talking. That includes any names he might have just mentioned in passing, his regular hangouts, that type of thing. Any very close friends of his will be important, any confidantes to whom he might have told something about more private details of his sexual life."

"You think…someone he knew did this? That wasn't Edward in there. He wasn't…like that."

This was the hard part, and Mac kept his eyes steady, his voice calm. "If it fits with the pattern of the two prior murders we're investigating, he would have been having a relationship with this woman. It's not likely he would have brought her to meet you, even mentioned her. Your son was a sexual submissive, a very discreet one."

Mr. Turner flushed red. "That's a lie."

"I have no reason to lie to you, sir. He had an active membership at several fetish clubs in Tampa, high-priced, very discreet. He was very careful not to mix this part of his life with the rest of it. To protect his family and career, I'm sure, but I'm thinking there might have been someone to whom he told—"

Mac had lost him, he could tell from the panicked movement of Mr. Turner's eyes, as a vicious flood of possibilities scattered like bowling pins what little composure the man had been able to collect.

He had to shatter their fragile illusion that the submissive posture and props were the act of only one mind. It was the worst aspect of this case, but it had to be done, to be sure his murderess had not been a peripheral part of Edward Turner's life that had come in contact with the family. The sister sat pale and silent, her hand on her father's arm, that touch staying with him even as he jerked with impatient, grief-ravaged movements. She was so still that Mac was afraid she might be in shock, and made a mental note to have the EMTs look at her as soon as he and Mr. Turner were done.

"You aren't going to rub filthy accusations all over my son's name. My lawyer—"

"Mr. Turner." Mac deliberately lowered his voice, made sure the man met his gaze, saw the patience and understanding, the lack of threat. "No one is accusing your son of anything. He's the victim, a very good man, his life taken away long before it should have happened. We're trying to find and stop his killer."

"But he didn't ask for this."

"No more than any man who takes a lover home to his bed does," Mac agreed. "Mr. Turner, I know this is very difficult, but your understanding of your son's lifestyle may make you remember things that can help us."

"Lifestyle." Turner surged up from his chair, knocking it over. The sister flinched, but her fingers had curled into his sweater sleeve and clung to her father's arm, even as his movements half-yanked her out of the chair. "My son was not some twisted weak pervert who liked having a woman...beat on him. He was a junior varsity quarterback, and a wrestler. He took care of his sister for four years when my wife died and I had to work two shifts, put off college when he was an honor student with scholarships to go anywhere he wanted to go." The man had tears running down his face now. Mac was sure he wasn't aware of it. "Saved her from a mugger one night, when there were no cops to be found. Knocked the bastard's lights out. He wasn't weak."

"No, he wasn't." Mac ignored the lead weight that had settled in his stomach, effectively compressing all his vital organs. "He was a conscientious man who lived a good life and kept his sexual preferences in the bedroom, a place he thought was safe."

"You're supposed to help. I'm calling my attorney, and if one word of this preposterous story gets out, I swear to God—"

"You do what you have to do, Mr. Turner." Mac took out a card, laid it on the table. "But remember I'm out there looking for the killer, before she does it to somebody else's son. If you think of something, you call me."

After the shocked numbness and the furious denials died away, if the man loved his son, Mac knew he would think it through, try to skirt around the edge of what he couldn't accept to find a killer's footsteps.

The man swept up the card, flung it at Mac's face. It was a distraction that he should have seen coming. Turner's knuckles slammed into his jaw, and then Mac was trying to fend off the man, trying not to strike back and cause him more pain. Several uniforms came to assist, along with the police counselor. The sister sat at the table, her head bowed, her chin pressed to her chest, her shoulders shaking with a grief hard enough to shatter. Mac stood back from the uniforms trying to calm Turner down. As if Turner's sister was on a separate stage, he watched her fight the pain that, up until this moment, could have been assuaged in the arms of her father or brother.

Every sub thought of this scenario, or something like it. That's why most never took the play outside of a club, not ever. To have one's sexual preference exposed, one that ninety-five percent of the world considered deviant, to embarrass one's family, a spouse…it was unthinkable.

But when it was a part of a person that couldn't be denied, it manifested itself one way or another. For most of them, the desire eventually overrode caution. Like most, Mac just hoped never to do anything stupid enough to have something like this happen. But Edward Turner had not been a stupid man.

The police counselor gestured, the subtle movement clear. Mac left the room, knowing his value to the family lay elsewhere, out of their sight. Even if he caught the killer, delivered her head to Mr. Turner and his daughter, they would never welcome the sight of him again, a man associated not just with their son's death, but a truth they never wanted to know.

He stepped outside onto the front porch and found his sergeant waiting for him there, leaning against a column.

"Good punch for a guy twice your age." Darla straightened, reached up, touched his face. "I've got a pissed-off Suarez in the dining room of the murder scene, Detective. You going to take care of that?"

"I clean up my messes. Is that why you're here on my crime scene, Sarge? To play daycare manager?"

Her eyes narrowed. "Careful, Detective. Maybe if the primary could keep his temper under control he wouldn't be thinking that's why I'm here. And I'll remind you," her countenance was hard and aloof, telling him he'd definitely stepped over her line, "that every crime scene that falls in our jurisdiction is *my* crime scene, as much as yours."

"I know. Jesus, Sergeant, I'm sorry." And he meant it.

Her anger defused as rapidly as his own, and she inclined her head. "You're pushing this one too hard, Mac. It's getting under your skin. But I'm not telling you anything you don't know. I should have given you some down time. You brought down that serial killer less than a handful of months ago and you haven't had a vacation since—"

"I'm fine." He waved that away. "I'm old enough to baby-sit myself, Sarge, don't worry. When we close this case, I'll cheerfully abandon the lot of you for a couple weeks in the Keys. Even if there's a major prison break and the streets of Tampa are swarming with death row inmates."

"I'll hold you to it," she responded. "I guess this one hits pretty close to home, hmm? Hearing everyone say he asked for it."

From her expression, he could tell she wondered the same thing herself, and what his position on it was. If it had been someone else, someone like Consuela or Suarez, he would have brushed it off, changed the topic. He'd never had any interest in being a salesman for his personal life, but she had gone out on a limb for him, and he owed her at least the answer to her curiosity. "It gets tedious," he admitted. "He asked for it as much as anyone who opens himself up to another person, hoping to find a connection, asks for it."

Mac glanced back at the door, behind which Mr. Turner and his recriminations lay. "But my father would have felt the same as him. I was varsity, myself. Was offered a scholarship based on my football skills. I went into law enforcement instead. Most people I know feel like this about D/s. That's why you always hope to find someone with whom you can finally be who you are. Isn't that what we all want?" He said it lightly, wanting to shrug it off, but her eyes told him she wasn't buying it. Cops never did, but they also knew when to respect the boundaries and back off. He didn't want to do this now, not with the stench of blood in his nostrils.

"Why *are* you here, Sarge?"

"Connie called me before we located you. She felt I needed to see one of the pieces of evidence on the body and talk about it with you directly. She pulled it off before you arrived on scene, handed it over to me when I got here just now."

Her face unreadable, she lifted the plastic evidence bag that she'd been holding under her arm.

It was a folded sheet of paper, standard ruled notebook stock. His murderess was smart enough not to personalize herself with perfumed stationary. In small block letters, only taking up one line in the center of the page, was her message.

You're next.

Mac's brow furrowed. When he shifted, he could see through the kitchen window, where Mr. Turner sat at the table, alone now, face hidden by his hands, shoulders shaking in that harsh way that men who rarely cried did, as if each tear had jagged edges. "The killer wanted to threaten whoever found the body? That's new."

"No, Mac." Darla's hands closed over his, made him turn the bag over to read the back of the page, the name of the person to whom the message had been addressed.

Detective Mac Nighthorse.

"She's made you, Mac. She knows you're looking for her, and she's made it personal." Darla Rowe was one hundred percent business now, and Mac knew that look on her face.

"Damn right she has, and she's going to be sorry for it."

"You want to know what our shrink says about her leaving you a note?"

"I have a feeling you're going to tell me."

"Says she's gunning for you specifically now. She doesn't care about being caught. In fact she's probably hoping it's going to happen soon, because with this many kills under her belt so quickly, she's got the pain of a rabid dog driving her. So she doesn't care if she takes you down right under our noses. In short, Psych says she's at her most dangerous now. You've drawn her out, and she's pissed as well as challenged. We need to put a man in on the inside with the security team. I know you said you didn't want that, that you have privacy issues, but now I'm more concerned about keeping you alive."

He faced her. "I told you, that wouldn't work."

"She knows who you are now, Mac. You could bring the whole squad in there, and it wouldn't matter."

"Yes, it would. Because she still has sense, and it might make her back off me and take another couple of victims to distract us for awhile. It's a double-edged sword. If she knows me this well, she knows I'm the genuine article, even if I am a cop. It's male subs that get her off, rouse the bloodlust. I'm a double treasure to her." He waved the bag. "With this, she's looking for a one-on-one gunfight."

"And we're supposed to give her that gunfight?"

"We're supposed to make her think we're giving her that."

Mac hesitated, then made the decision he hadn't wanted to make. He had to accept Violet's offer, and overcome his desire to protect her. He didn't like her being involved, but she was a cop, had taken the oath just as he had, to protect and serve. It would be an insult to her not to allow her to help. Even more important, it would be a disservice to the three dead men. Whatever resources offered to him, he had to use them. For them.

Even so, it was an effort to hand over the card, not snatch it back when Darla reached for it. "She's my back up."

You're a male chauvinist pig, Mackenzie.

"Yeah, yeah, yeah. Buzz off, sugar," he muttered.

Darla gave him an odd look, took the card, looked it over. Did a double take. "You going outside the squad now, Mac?"

She's already on the inside with me," he said, keeping his gaze level with hers. "She'll watch my back and she wanted you to have that as an alternate contact. I hope..." He cleared his throat. "You've respected my privacy, gone above and beyond, but this is my case, my job. She's volunteering for the duty. I'd hate to see it come back and bite her in the ass."

"She got the experience to cover you in something like this?"

"Four years with state, a couple years before that as a Marine MP. I think she'll do well enough. What she lacks in direct experience, she's got in grit."

"All right, then." She pointed to the bag. "But this makes me real itchy, Mac. Let's close this one. At the rate she's piling up a body count, we're going to have to move fast to keep the S&M angle out of the news. And the families have enough to deal with as it is."

"No argument there."

"Detective?"

Mac turned, cursed inwardly as he saw the young woman standing in the doorway. The sister, pale but determined-looking.

"I'm Mara Turner, Edward's sister." She hesitated, then the words tumbled out of her, as if she were forcing them from herself rapidly so she'd get them all out at once before she could rethink the decision. "I needed to tell you...I knew about...Edward's preferences. When I was staying at his place once, I found a magazine. We talked and I was open to hearing about it." She colored at Mac's lifted brow. "No, I'm not into it or anything, not at all, but he was my brother, and I mean, it's the twenty-first century, you know? He was a good person with a good heart, and I trusted his judgment. He seemed glad to have someone...he trusted, to talk with it about, an open mind that linked him between that world and the one we knew him in. I just...I wanted to tell you that about three weeks ago he told me he'd been seeing someone really special. I think he was even a little in love with her. I told him he should introduce her to Dad, that this was just one aspect of his life. He didn't, I mean...I take boyfriends home to meet Dad, and we sure as hell don't talk about our sex life." She managed a ghost of a smile that trembled around the edges.

"He said no." Her attention drifted over to the house, to the bedroom window behind which her brother lay murdered. "He said she'd asked him herself, recently, if he was going to introduce her to Dad. Edward told me that he had said no, that he didn't want to mix that part of his life...he couldn't take the risk of integrating the two. He was worried he'd hurt her, which is why I guess he called and talked to me about it, because it was bothering him. He cared. He didn't like hurting people. Then a couple days later when we talked he said she was fine with it, that they were going out this weekend."

"Did he describe her? Give a name?"

She shook her head, brushing away the tears that wouldn't stop running. With a nod of thanks, she accepted the tissue Darla handed her from her purse.

"No," she sniffled. "He never told me that. He said he had to respect her privacy as carefully as he'd guarded his own. I wish..." Her voice hitched and she turned away. "I wish that hadn't mattered so much to him. I wish he were alive."

Darla moved to put an arm around the girl as she broke down completely again, sobbing. The sergeant murmured to her, cast Mac a quick glance before she guided her back into the house.

Mac turned and faced Edward Turner's home, his eyes hard and hot as fired steel.

"Your little bloodbath is over, sweetheart," he said between his teeth. "You come after me this time. You may take me down, but if I go, you're going down with me. So help me God, this is your last one."

He crushed the plastic evidence bag in his hand and headed back down the walkway, to start the painstaking process of going over the room one more time.

"Mac, Mac!" Darla was hurrying after him, holding her radio.

"Sister okay?"

"Fine, fine. It's not that." She stopped at his side, taking a breath. "When you handed that card to me, I glossed over the name, just focused on the fact she was a trooper. But I know her name. You've been here, what? An hour?"

He nodded, his brow furrowed. "What is it, Sarge?"

The radio beeped and she raised a finger, responded. "I'm here, Roscoe."

"Yeah, Sergeant." The radio crackled in her hand. "I got it for you. The name of that trooper that got shot about a half hour ago."

Mac stared at Darla. Everything in him stopped. Blood, breath, heart. Darla's hand reached out, closed on his wrist as they waited three tense seconds for Roscoe to complete his message.

"Violet Siemanski. They've got her at Tampa General."

Chapter 18

As he had told Violet, his vehicle of choice was the Honda VTX motorcycle, and he was thankful that was what he had used to get him to the crime scene.

For the most part, he obeyed the law and practiced safe driving, except when he could find back roads where he could really cut loose and enjoy all the power the Honda had to offer. Now, he weaved in and out of Tampa traffic, went up on shoulders, barely stopped to check before he roared through intersections, cut the wrong way down one-way streets, and reached Tampa General's emergency room nearly nine minutes after he had bolted from the Turner house.

It was breaking all the rules, and he didn't care. He flashed his badge as he went past the emergency staff. "The officer that was shot."

"Exam One," the nurse responded automatically, and Mac was around the corner and striding away before she could say anything further.

The curtain was pulled back about a third of the way, and so he saw her right away, sitting on an exam table.

She was wearing a hospital gown, her hair in a loose ponytail on her shoulders, her makeup gone. She looked tired, vulnerable, young. Doing her best to mask it, she was carrying on a half-hearted banter with the two troopers standing in the room, but he could feel her fragility. It wasn't just a resonance of his own fear. Where they couldn't see it but he could, her hand clutched the edge of the table. The rest of her was perfectly still, except for the slight alterations of her facial expression, as if she was concentrating all physical manifestations of what was going on inside her in that one hand, that one tiny tremor. The top tie of the gown was loose, so he could see the bandage. The bullet had taken a chunk out of the surface area between her collarbone and neck. An inch to the left, the slug would have torn through her throat. A few inches higher, it would have been her face. Few inches lower, through the chest.

It filled him with a fury for her, a fury he wanted to expel by breaking something, someone. But from Roscoe's report, there was no one to expend his violence upon. Violet had shot and killed her assailant, a junkie who panicked when she stopped him for an expired tag, who had fired at her point-blank out the driver's window.

He stepped through the curtain, and her head turned. The first thing he saw in her face was panic. Then her expression altered, and what he saw there made his heart squeeze up hard in his throat.

Relief. Overwhelming relief.

Tears welled up in her eyes, but she blinked rapidly to try and hide the reaction that Mac had a feeling had stunned her as much as it did him.

He reached her in two steps, taking that shaking hand in his, zoning in immediately on where she was holding in her fear. He squeezed it, reinforcing the message that he was here. *He was here.* He wanted to pick her up, cradle her, but she was a cop, and he understood what she could and couldn't do. But he wouldn't keep it out of his face, his anger, his fear, his desire to shake her and hold her both.

He tuned in enough to realize an awkward silence had fallen as he and Violet stared at one another. One of the troopers cleared his throat.

"I don't believe we've met."

Violet opened her mouth, something to deflect questions, protect his identity, he was sure, but Mac turned, still holding her hand, and extended his other. "Mac Nighthorse. Homicide Squad, Major Crimes Bureau."

"Well, goddamn. Rick Martinez." The man took his hand, some of his wariness receding. "Didn't know Violet had a guy. Didn't know anyone was brave enough to take her on toe-to-toe."

"Someone was brave enough today," Mac said shortly.

Why couldn't they see how shook up she was? Why was he the only one seeing it?

Another uncomfortable pause. "Well," the other man said, sizing up the situation with an even look. "Hank Ramm. We were talking about who was going to take Officer Siemanski home."

"I'll take care of her," Mac said.

Hank, older than Rick, old enough to be Violet's father, looked toward her for confirmation. Mac wanted to be insulted, but he wasn't. He was irritated with the delay, but glad that Violet had men who watched out for her, though he wondered where the hell they'd been earlier today. It was an unfair question, since he knew troopers patrolled alone, but what was rational didn't mean a good goddamn to him at the moment.

He waited a heart-thudding ten seconds.

"He'll take care of me," she said softly.

The men nodded, and a few minutes later made their goodbyes. Hank pressed her opposite shoulder as he moved past her. "You call if you need anything, Violet. You did real good today. You remember that. You'll be back on the job in no time. Consider it a well-deserved vacation."

Mac waited until they left, then turned to her. "They're putting you on desk duty until they close the file?"

She nodded. "I know it's standard procedure, but I can't help thinking it's also because I'm young, less experienced, and I could have..."

"Don't. You're alive. No matter what happens, that's never something to regret, because if he'd do a cop, he'd do anyone."

She nodded, held up a warding hand as he took another step forward. "Mac..." Her voice broke and she sucked it in, shuddered. "I can't—"

"Just let me hold you," he said. His arms went around her and she held rigid for a second, fighting it. Then she pressed her face against his chest to muffle her sobs, her hands clutched in his shirt, clinging hard to the skin and muscle beneath, digging in painfully as she shook.

Mac looked over her head and saw Hank at the curtain. The man nodded, gave him a thumbs up. He turned, and really left them this time, apparently satisfied Mac would do as he said. Take care of her.

"It's okay, baby." He held her as close as he could, bending his head down over hers, brushing his lips over the bandage. Just a graze, a glancing shot that could so easily have hit its mark. "You're all right. You're alive."

"I was so scared, Mac," she said, mumbling against his shirt. "I've never been so scared. I've never had to pull my gun, then he was there, reaching beneath the seat, faster than I thought anyone could move, and training kicked in. I was telling him to stop, but he wasn't, and he jerked it up at the same moment I got mine out and there was this single moment when he shot, everything in slow motion."

He'd gotten off the first shot while she was still shouting at him to stop. Mac's jaw tightened. *Jesus Christ.* It was as much prayer as expletive.

"And then, it was all so slow, I knew he was going to fire again. There we were, a foot away from each other, his finger tightening, and I fired. Right in his face. He's gone. I killed him. I took everything away."

"*He* took everything away." Mac caught her chin, made her look up at him, caught her tears on his thumb. "He made his choice the moment he made the decision to draw that gun. I'm taking you home. Let's get you dressed."

"I know what a lot of guys think, that women have no business on the force. And it's because of things like this. Look at me, I'm falling apart."

"No," he said firmly. "No, you're not." He lowered his voice, brought his face even closer to hers, so their foreheads were pressed together and she closed her eyes. "You said that I was a male chauvinist, that I didn't want my Mistress to be a cop. That's true, but it's not because I think you can't do the job. It's because I know you *can*, because you're brave enough to do what you did today. Keep your wits about you and do the job, and I don't want to lose my Mistress. You're a hell of a cop, Violet, and to the man who loves you, that's a terrifying thing."

* * * * *

She wanted to ride his bike rather than take a car home. She got on behind him and he gave her his helmet. When she slid her arms around his waist, and her body up against his, she was holding him a little tighter than necessary. He didn't mind. She could squeeze him like a python if she needed to do so. Before the painkiller wore off, he wanted to hurry and get her home. It was a flesh wound, but he knew she'd be sore all over tomorrow anyway. The first time you were in a gunfight, you tightened up every muscle, and your body stayed that way unconsciously for hours. He needed to get her into a hot bath, give her a massage.

"I want to go to your place," she murmured. "Please."

He put his hand over her clasped ones on his chest. "We can be there in fifteen minutes."

He lived in a small bungalow on the marsh, one of Florida's prime pieces of real estate with the run down look of a fishing shack on the outside, a rambling, cozy interior and a breathless view of the marsh from the large screened back porch.

He parked the bike in a crofter on the side and took her hand to help her off. It wasn't a highly athletic maneuver, but he could tell she was still shaky, and the muscles were starting to stiffen, as he predicted. On a surge of emotion, he simply bent and scooped her up to carry her up the small path to his back porch door.

"Mac, I can walk," she protested. "It was just a graze, after all."

"I know. Humor me. I need to take care of you."

That quieted her down, and she placed her hands on his neck, those fingers little bigger than a child's. Those tiny hands had held a service revolver steady today and blown away a man determined to kill her. He pushed it away, held her tighter as she rested her head against his shoulder, settling in with a little sigh.

Violet knew that not all male submissives were nurturers. She'd gotten a hint and a hope when Mac made her dinner. But a nurturing, straight male submissive cop with powerful alpha tendencies? It broke all the preconceived molds.

When he took her to the bathroom first thing to run her a bath, she could all but hear the plaster shatter and fall away. The thought almost coaxed a weary smile to her lips, pressed against his shirtfront.

The bathroom was clean and had a deep, old-fashioned claw foot tub. He set her on the commode and knelt beside her, one arm braced on the outside of her hip as he kept his other beneath the water flow. After it warmed, he took her hand in his, placed it beneath the stream, and she almost wept at the comforting heat of his touch combined with that of the water.

"Too hot?"

She shook her head. "Perfect."

"Okay." He dumped in some mineral salts from a vial on the shelf and tossed in a couple of green bath beads. "The salts worked so good at Tyler's, I went out and got myself some for daily use," he explained at her curious look, managing a smile that didn't quite reach his eyes. "The beads have got aloe, one of my Mom's remedies for scrapes and cuts. They've also got somewhat of a male aftershave smell, but nothing too overpowering. Do you have to keep the bandage dry?"

She shook her head. "I can take it off. There's no stitches or anything."

"I'll do it." He took his hand out of the tub, released her, dried his fingers on a towel. "With your permission," he said quietly, and then began to slip the buttons of her ripped and bloodstained uniform shirt. As he took it off her shoulders, she watched his face when he ran light fingers over the bandage taped over the curve that joined her throat to her shoulder. He put gentle pressure on it. "Why they always use this goddamned hair-pulling tape… Take a deep breath, sugar."

She did and he pulled it off so quickly, there was just a faint tingling burn.

"You could get a job doing bikini waxes," she said, trying for humor.

"Lucky me," he responded, laying his fingers over the welt that showed the track of the bullet. There was murder in his eyes, and she felt something rise up, threaten to choke her.

"Mac…"

"Sshh, it's all right." He shook it off, visibly. Gently taking the shirt all the way off her arms, he reached around her to unhook her bra. She pressed her cheek to that wide bicep a moment, letting herself feel her connection to him, the connection he had underscored with a deep black marker by showing up at the hospital to take her home.

He didn't have to do this, didn't have to be part of her life in this way, but after less than a week of having one another, he had chosen to do so. Had as much as said that's what he wanted when they made love after dinner less than three nights ago. This was one of the worst days of her life, or her best, depending on the perspective, and he had jumped in with both feet to be part of it, no holding back.

Pressing a kiss to the top of her head, he brought the garment forward and off her body. He unlaced her boots, took them off, his hands sure and strong on her ankle, the arch of her foot, and then gently raised her to her feet, removing her trousers and the practical underwear beneath. She stood before him only in her delicate cross and her own fragile, mortal skin. He turned, took a washcloth off the counter, dampened it and turned back to her. Bemused, she felt him raise the cross from her skin, touch it and her sternum with the cloth.

"Gun powder," he explained. "We'll take some silver polish later, give it a good cleaning, but that'll do for now." Then he tossed the cloth in the sink, bent, slid his arms around her, and lifted her again. The hard thighs, the buckle of his belt and the buttons of his shirt pressed against her. She welcomed them, the heat of his skin through the fabric. Though she didn't think she was cold, she was shivering.

"Shock," he said, as if reading her thoughts. He lowered her into the water, shut off the spigots. When the heat of the water enveloped her, she moaned in pleasure, and he smiled, kissed her fingers. He arranged a cushion beneath her head with his other free hand when she wouldn't let go of him.

"I'm going to scare you up some food. I'll keep checking in on you, so don't you worry about falling asleep. I'll take care of you tonight."

"I know," she said, her eyes falling half shut. Her nose recognized the smell of the bath beads, and the smells that had clung to his skin from the first night she had met him.

They comforted her, surrounded her, so she could find it in her to be an adult, let his hand go, but something in her chest tightened painfully as his fingers slipped from hers. She listened to his feet recede, was absurdly comforted when she realized the kitchen was close enough that she could hear the sounds of him moving around, finding her dinner.

The proximity worked for Mac as well, because he was able to see the profile of her head on the edge of the tub. Keeping his peripheral eye on her as he set some tea to brew, he pulled one of his Mundial cooking knives from the maple wood block knife holder and quickly and quietly chopped up some fresh asparagus and set it in a soup stock to cook. When a tremor ran through his hand, he stopped a moment, taking a steadying breath, tearing his thoughts away from the sudden image of a bullet fired at Violet's face, tearing through that pale, delicate flesh and ending her life.

He prepared the soup with extra care and precision, put some fresh baked bread in the warmer, keeping his mind in a culinary net so it couldn't go where he wasn't ready to let it go yet. He could have his mental breakdown later. She needed him to be the strong one right now.

A soft cry and a splash from the bathroom, and he was at the door before the knife hit the counter. She blinked wildly, and he knelt by her, drawing her to him.

"It's okay, sugar. Flashback. They happen a bit at first, whenever you doze off. You're okay."

"God." She pushed her hands through her hair. "I am so pathetic."

"No, you're not," he said, tightening his hands on her. "You want to know what I did the first time I took a life?"

She nodded, her arms folded against her front. It was an unconscious gesture of someone trying to shield herself from pain that was attacking her from the inside. He rubbed his hands over her wet, bare back, fingers marking each bump of her spine, trying to soothe.

"At first, I tried to blow it off like it was any other day. You think, when you're a rookie, you're supposed to be as tough about it as the older guys. I pretended like I was fine, even got a little snappish when the vets tried to bolster me up, like Hank did for you. Later, I remembered the way they looked at me, not snapping back like they normally would. They knew I was going to break. They tried to get me to go for drinks with them. No way, I was fine. I went home because you know, that was standard, I didn't have any choice. They let me go for the rest of the day."

He nudged his chin against her forehead, and she burrowed her head deeper into the crevice between his head and chest.

"I woke up at two in the morning in a sweat," he continued. "The perp's face, those shots, roaring in my head. I put on my clothes, drove a hundred and twenty miles and knocked on my mother's door at four in the morning. Not a smart thing for a guy to do when the woman in question has two sons who are cops. I probably took ten years off her life, making her think one of us had been killed.

"But she knew. She looked at my face and knew. I was too manly and old to let her undress me and put me in a tub of course." He smiled against her temple. "But she ran me a bath, fed me, sat with me, and held my hand when I finally fell asleep on her couch next to her. I know she didn't let go. Not until I woke up and felt I could face it, because I'd managed to get through the first night, thanks to her."

"You're not making that up." She lifted her head, looked hard at him.

"No, I'm not." He smoothed back her hair, kissed her brow.

"How many times…?"

"Seven times in twenty years," he said. "Once it was a woman. Once it was a fourteen-year-old kid." He framed her face in his hands. "Just some advice. Give yourself time to accept it, mourn it. Let it run around in your head awhile, wait a few days to analyze. In our line of work, there's no walking away. Sometimes the choice has to be made, and sometimes it's made for us. I can tell you from experience, the first way is a lot harder to live with than the second. It's that simple. Okay?"

She nodded, thinking, and he brushed his thumb over her lips. "Let me get you something to wear, if you're ready to get out."

Violet was, and she waited in the tub until he brought her one of his T-shirts. He didn't let her dry herself. He had her step out onto a soft floor mat, and then rubbed her gently with a thick terry cloth towel. A dark heavy cotton that had his musky smell, the T-shirt was so large it fell to mid-thigh and slipped off one shoulder. When he had it on her, he picked her up, carried her out onto the back porch where the sun was setting on the marsh in a glory of rose and gold, a confirmation of life, and miracles. She looked at him as he settled her, his face intent, and knew it was a confirmation of something else, something too clearly present in this past hour to be anything else.

Love.

Chapter 19

After they ate, he curled up behind her on the bed in his room, stroking her hair until she fell asleep watching out the window as the moon rose over the marsh. When she woke, its light was streaming in. She held her hand up to it, watched the play of silver on her pale skin.

I'm alive.

A large hand lifted into her vision, entwined its fingers with her own, and she felt Mac's broad chest pressed into her shoulder blades.

And I'm not alone.

In that quiet moment she saw what she was and could be to him – Mistress, lover, woman. What she already might be to him. Everything. A humbling, terrifying and exhilarating thought all at once.

"Okay?" he murmured, his voice like a soothing stroke over every raw nerve, drawing a curtain over the things she could not bear to face right now, that her consciousness would have to accept a small piece at a time. A bullet firing, a man's face turning into meat, the stop of a heartbeat.

"Let it go for tonight, sugar." His hand whispered down over her back, the curve of her waist, her hip, his fingertips smoothing over her skin like raindrops sliding down, the touch of something natural, expected, known. Something that sustained life. Hope.

"Do you know what I thought when he lifted the gun, and I knew it was going to fire?" She kept her eyes on the movement of the waters through the marsh grass, stirred from the movement of some creature who dwelled there, she expected.

She could have chosen not to tell him, knew it probably was not wise to tell him, but in the loneliest hour of the night, there was only truth, and a trust that she could tell him anything.

"What, baby?"

Her lips curved at the endearment, one a Mistress didn't often get to hear. Her alpha male.

"I thought, 'What if I never see Mac again?'"

She looked up at him then and found him leaning over her, those silver eyes so close and alive, silver filled with moonlight. "That was the last thought I had before that gun fired."

His arms closed around her and he lifted her up against his chest, enclosing her in his heat and strength. Warmth. Life. He was pure, pulsing life. She kept her arms tucked into her body, letting him hold her completely, surround her, her forehead and lips pressed to his chest.

"Make love to me, Mackenzie," she whispered. "Please. Nothing but you and me."

He eased her back, looked into her face. He didn't ask if she was sure, but he gave her that moment. She reached up, touched his jaw.

The kiss took her under, into a warm, languid world of pleasant dreams and slow thoughts that drifted into waters that turned her, spun her in a dizzying eddy of light and sensation. She opened her mouth and tasted him, the moist heat of responsive flesh, and his arms increased their hold upon her, so she felt the beat of his heart and the arousing stir of his cock against her hip and stomach.

He eased her to her back, his silhouette over her, and the moonlight gave her another glimpse of his expression, intent, devoted to her, worshipping her, cozening her, desiring her. He could have held back, let her only see the gentleness, but as if he knew instinctively what she needed, he revealed that flare of male desire, the impatient lust to take, and her blood stirred, suddenly eager for his passion, the brutal strength of a taking.

She brought his head down to her breast and then took her hands beneath the covers to find the hem of the T-shirt she wore, get it out of the way. Before she could, he had bracketed her breasts in his larger hands, stretching the soft fabric tight over the taut points, and brought his mouth down on one to torture her through the cloth. Dampen it with his mouth, lick and suckle her through the rub and caress of the cotton.

"Mac." Her voice was a breath of sound in the quiet bedroom. His knee pressed between her thighs, and she spread open for him, cradling him, gasping as he seated his cock against her sensitive clit and pubic bone. She was naked beneath the shirt. And he had come to bed naked, making himself available to her in any way she needed him.

He didn't crush her, but he used his weight to advantage, keeping her helplessly pinned as he nursed her breasts, one then the other, then back to the first. She didn't know how he'd act as an equal partner in the bedroom, had wondered if he'd rush it like most men to get the pussy he craved, but he was paying ardent homage to her breasts. The fluid arousal in her lower body emanated through her like a cyclone of energy, through her belly, widening to encompass her breasts. From the anchor point between her legs to the flare of her arched upper torso, she became a tornado, undulating, twisting the small amount allowed by his grip. He stopped suckling and started flicking her nipples with his tongue. A firm flick, several rapid flicks, one slow, then over to the other for the same treatment and back again. The quick tweak of friction made her jerk and her heels dig down into the mattress helplessly. Her pubic bone ground insistently against him, her cunt slick against his hard abdomen as she mewled in ecstatic distress.

"Mackenzie," she gasped.

"No orders, sugar. Just take it. Let me make you crazy." He pressed his hips firmly against hers and she screamed at the rocket of sensation that spun through her pussy and up to each nipple tip that he continued to torment with that firmly flicking tongue. Left. Right, back again. Flick.

She felt the shudder start in her thighs. At the exact moment he raised his head, shifted his grip to her upper arms and shoved hard into her, her climaxing pussy clamped down on him, making him ram through the tight clutch of her muscles. He lifted his hips, slammed into her again, and kept to it, bucking her light frame like a doll on the bed. He was giving her full strength, holding nothing back, and it was frightening, bruising her. Yet she wanted it, his loss of control, this savage hunger in his eyes that could consume the image of gunfire and hatred, sweep that away and leave nothing but a helpless surrender to this.

She was strong enough to match him emotionally on any field, but she knew he was making it clear he had the strength to shelter her whenever she needed it. Protect her not only from whatever life threw her way, but from herself. Like now. Under that was his anger, irrational as they both knew it was, for risking her life, for making him worry, and so she opened wider, let him give it all to her, all of himself, the anger with the desire.

She had no choice, regardless. All she could do was hold on, cry his name and let the pounding waves of the orgasm take her once…twice…three times. Each time she thought she was done, he changed his angle in that skillful way he had, and she shot into the storm again, until she was sure she could bear no more, that his hard, relentless cock would be the instrument of blissful destruction for her.

She came off the third wave like a surfer who had been tossed into the embrace of the ocean and rolled over and over, landing on the sun-kissed beach in a state of limp, exhilarated exhaustion. Her pussy was like a small fist, opening and closing in spasmodic vibrations on his cock, and it took more than a few moments to realize he was still hard within her, his body held still and waiting against her.

Though she had not commanded it, he had offered it as a gift to her, which made the gesture all the more potent. Her body quivered in renewed response as she touched his face without opening her eyes, traced the firm lips, the tense jaw, the trembling body.

"Come for me, Mackenzie," she whispered. "You have my permission. Come for me now. But do it while stroking inside me very…very…slowly."

His hands went to her thighs, raised them so her ankles rested on his shoulders. He levered her up higher, his face close to hers, and then he began to stroke her, slow and even.

"All the way to the head of your cock," she whispered. "Then back in, so slow, so gradual, feel every kiss of my pussy upon you. Ah, God." He was hung like a horse in truth, filling her completely. "Out…slow now…slow."

"Mistress…" His hips jerked, his shoulders shuddered.

"Stop," she said abruptly, sharply, and he froze, his expression conveying how close he was.

"Mistress—"

"Obey me, Mackenzie."

He stopped, fully deep inside her, and her muscles contracted, squeezing him, stroking him. He had a skylight to let in the sun across the bed during the day, and here in the night it cast a reflection, so she could see the outline of her legs as she lowered them, curled over his hips and taut buttocks. She could see the powerful ridges of muscle standing out on his back. She ran her palms over them, caressing the breadth of those massive shoulders, sliding down, down, cupping her hands over him, feeling the heat gather, no matter where she touched him. She reached his ass and traced her fingers in the crease, dug her nails into the muscular crescents.

"God, I'd want you for your ass alone," she muttered.

"And here I was, thinking it was my mind." He gave a weak chuckle. "Mistress, you're destroying me."

Her lashes rose, so she looked into the passionate silver eyes, registered the tremendous struggle for control and his overwhelming need. For her.

"That's the point, Mackenzie," she whispered. Then she closed her eyes, took him in through her other senses, skin touching skin, her fingertips whispering slowly down the smooth, firm body, the muscles earned, the occasional change of texture from a scar.

"It's like going into a temple and seeing the sacred relic there," she said, her voice still no louder than his held breath. "Wanting to touch it. Not because someone told you not to, though there is that." Her lips curved slightly. "But because you can sense a living presence in it, just beneath the surface of the elements. And you know, if you can just touch it, really feel it, feel what it means, what its soul is made of, then you can be part of it. Forever connected, never alone."

She lifted her gaze, and in his she saw the truth of her words reflected back to her. She saw that gateway open and beckoning, her words having opened it within him. Break the body, and the soul must defend itself. Her body had been broken today, and her soul had turned to him to be her champion. Now his hands touched her face, as she was touching his body, with a hesitant reverence, trying to absorb the meaning of every inch, take it into him, the way she was taking him into her.

"I'm all yours, sugar," he said. "My soul is yours."

"Now," she breathed. "Without moving, without any friction, start to come for me, Mackenzie. Just from my command. Feel my voice on you like my warm, wet pussy, every syllable caressing you…"

He groaned, shuddered, and the climax burst from him, took him in the imposed paralytic state. Violet's words clogged in her throat, overcome by watching him battle his nature to obey her, allowing the climax to crash through his body, his cock pulsing but not moving within her as it shot hot seed. He quivered, staring at her, his face rigid with restraint, his hips moving just a little, quick jerks that could not be helped because of the force of the sensation.

It was the sexiest thing she'd ever seen, a man fighting to climax almost motionlessly, his entire being centered on the woman beneath him. Which made the energy from him even more powerful.

She lifted her hips, unable to resist the temptation herself anymore. He surged forward, knowing he'd been released, and they came together like the explosive collision of two planets, shattering into a million pieces to form a whole new universe.

Chapter 20

"You're going to work," she snapped. "I will be *fine.* You said you need to investigate a couple of leads at the gym and at the office. I can handle myself today, Mac."

He made a noncommittal noise and slid a stack of buttermilk pancakes in front of her.

Violet looked down. He had put fresh strawberries along the side of the pancakes, and cut them so they looked like rosebuds, using their green tops as a frame of greenery. Humor struggled with her attempt to make a serious point. "You are seriously cute," she informed him.

He smiled. "Same goes, sugar." He feathered his hand across her cheek, and she pressed into his touch.

Mac didn't have the heart, or perhaps the bravery, to tell her he'd never seen her look so appealing, sitting there at his table in just his shirt, looking ill as a hornet. But he could see in her face she needed him to back off. And though he didn't want to be more than ten feet from her today, he understood how important it was not to crowd at a time like this. "Can't blame a big male chauvinist pig for wanting to protect you."

She snorted. "It wouldn't matter if I was a female bodybuilder, you'd want to protect me, keep me out of danger. You were seething with it when you walked into the emergency room yesterday, like you wanted to shake me for daring to have a job that took me out of the kitchen and the bedroom."

His jaw flexed, and some of that anger swelled to the surface. "Well, I did want to shake you. I don't want you in danger, ever." His hand closed over hers. "Look at you. You weigh nothing, you're like a miniature doll."

"A doll that can bring you to your knees and make you beg," she reminded him with a challenging fire in her eyes.

"Want to try arm wrestling?"

"I'd win, because I'd order you to let me win."

His grin was quick. "That's what you think, sugar. And you don't strike me as the cheating kind."

"I'll stay right here," she promised. "I'll even make you dinner, use my formidable culinary skills. Popcorn and peanut butter and jelly sandwiches. We can rent a movie, and I can moan occasionally to get sympathy from you. And I have Boscoe."

He had gotten up early and retrieved her beagle, so now the short-legged hound was beneath the table, responding to her ear fondling with a happy grin.

He hesitated, and she saw the truth of it. "You're going out tonight, on assignment. I'll meet you at The Zone, then."

"This isn't your case, Violet."

"You said yourself, being with a Mistress will get you better access to the other players there. Now that I know that, we can do better mixing and mingling, give you that choice." She caught her fingers in his shirt, drew him close. "Besides which, you're mine, and I don't want anyone else touching what's mine. Understand?"

He brushed his lips over hers. Pleased to see the spark back in her eyes, he cursed the fact he had to get back to work, especially since his cock responded as eagerly as Boscoe to the sharp command.

"Yes, Mistress." He gave her a deeper kiss, enjoyed the way her hand curled into his shirt, dug in. It was difficult to break the contact, raise his head. "But you can take the night off. I *am* scoping out the gym angle today. That's why I may be late. I'm going to hit a couple of them this evening, during the prime times. Why don't you go see your Mom for a few hours? You talked to her last night, but I'm sure she'd want to see you, and you said she's only an hour away."

She looked at him, hard. "You're not lying to me."

"No, I'm not," he said firmly. "And I never will."

Though if he told the total truth, he didn't want her even the short distance away at her mother's. He wanted her tucked safe and sound into his house tonight, watching old movies and waiting for him to come home. Ruefully, he realized she was right about him. When it came to *his* woman, his Mistress, he *was* a sexist pig.

* * * * *

"Top Form is a workout club owned and run by two of your Mistresses, Tamara and Kiera Whitmeyer. Five of the female Doms from The Zone have memberships there." Consuela handed him the printout. "Two more, Lisbeth Holmes and Marguerite Perruquet, had a temporary guest membership. One of the male Doms, Tyler Winterman, also has a membership there, if that's relevant. However, only one of your vics had a membership, and it was a guest membership he used once. The hunch's got a good feel to it, but there's not a strong evidence connection."

Mac studied the paper. "She could have staked out the parking lot at the workout clubs of the others rather than getting a membership. Even followed them to a bar to make the contact. It's going to be one of these. I can feel it."

"Well, make it come together soon," Consuela glanced over at the pin-up board. "I'm getting real tired of the visuals around this place.

"Now this is of particular interest," she pulled out a sheet. "This Marguerite Perruquet had a brother kill himself at age fourteen. The investigating officer said he picked up some serious undercurrents at the house. If he had to guess, he would have said the boy had been sexually molested by the father. Never could prove anything, though. From what we got from The Zone staff, Marguerite prefers younger men."

"She's symbolically punishing the brother?" Suarez raised a brow. "That seems fucked up."

"Unless she blames him for leaving her alone with the father, because maybe he turned to her after the boy died. I'm going to go sign up for a guest pass at Top Form this afternoon," Mac said. "I'm with Connie. I'd sure like to nail whoever our murderess is before I'm standing over more of her work. Here's another interesting coincidence." Mac pointed to the timeline. "Marguerite's guest membership coincides with the time frame in which Rodriguez was murdered, the one vic who *did* have a membership to Top Form."

"But no correlation on the others, though admittedly the gym that Turner belonged to doesn't keep any type of records on guest memberships."

Consuela ran a hand over her tired features, reminding Mac that she'd been busting her ass on the research end of this case as many nights as he'd worked the field angle.

"You okay, Con?"

"Yeah." She studied the murder pictures. "You know, Mac, they didn't deserve to die like this, but I got to admit, I don't totally disagree with Suarez. It's a dangerous thing to give someone this much control over you. A guy has to have something wrong with him. It's like some type of weird Mommie Dearest complex. And don't even get me started on the women who like to be tied up. Hundreds of years to get men not to treat us like house pets, and you've got a bunch of idiot bitches begging to be tied up and beaten."

"I don't know, Connie." Suarez flashed her a grin from his desk. "I kind of like the idea of you in thigh-high boots with a whip."

She shook her head. "Dominatrixes, my ass. Probably just feminists who get off on beating men the way we've been beaten down all these years. Still sick, but at least I can understand that better. It's the subs I don't understand."

Because she was trying to understand the politics of it, and there were no politics to it, Mac knew. It was about trust and power exchanges, not political correctness. Submission was the offered gift. In a way, it was not much different from marriage, two people submitting to one another's will, open to the give and take that led to unity, a complete opening of the heart to one another. Pain and relinquishing control could break down the walls even faster, make a person realize what it was he really needed, without all the fog that political baggage could bring into a relationship.

Consuela cocked a brow. "Mac, you with us?"

"Mmm."

"I think you've been immersed in this stuff way too much. Go out, go see a ball game. Hit on some gorgeous woman and have her blow you off."

"Classy." Mac chuckled, shaking his head. "How about you do the same, Con? Go home, have your husband go down on you a few times, if you can keep the kids out of the room long enough."

Suarez hooted with laughter. Mac snatched up his files and narrowly dodged the stapler Consuela slung his way. Grinning, he retreated to the conference room, enjoying the stream of creative Cuban epithets following him, and the more relaxed expression on his co-worker's face. A few moments later, he heard them return to debating the pros and cons of the S&M lifestyle and blocked it out, focusing on the information in front of him.

An hour later, he looked up to see Darla leaning in the doorway.

"I hear you're headed for the gym. You think you should take some backup?"

He shook his head. "I'm just scoping it out, see if I pick up a scent. I'll check in with you at nine, let you know if I'm hitting The Zone tonight, though I doubt it. Violet will be incommunicado today, but she should be back in the game in a day or so."

"Is she doing okay?"

He nodded. He wanted to say more, extract some further promises from Sergeant Rowe to keep Violet's identity secret, even if it cost him his life. No matter how he had accepted it, he could not tolerate the idea of her being exposed to the type of thinking he'd just heard, though rationally he knew she was an adult and likely had heard it before. As he had, countless times. Like kids hidden in a closet, hearing what other kids really thought of them.

"You okay, Mac?" Darla studied him. Mac deliberately relaxed his body, stood up and snagged his coat off the back of his chair.

"Yeah. I'm off to get a workout."

* * * * *

He had come at a busy time, as he intended, and he took some turns on the different machines, circulating, exchanging idle chatter, looking for familiar faces. One face he didn't particularly care to see was that of Jonathan Powell, but after making initial eye contact, the tall blond turned his back on Mac, ignoring his presence with an expression of disdain.

Fine by Mac. As much as it would delight him if the cold-blooded prick was involved so he could cuff and incarcerate him, nothing about Jonathan matched their murderess's profile. There was no law against being an asshole.

"Well, well, look who's wandered into my den."

Mac turned to see Kiera or Tamara, he wasn't sure which, working the weight bench.

"Tamara," she supplied, with a knowing look. "Will you spot me, honey? I usually call one of those trainers over, preferably the one with the tightest ass, but since I have someone so willing to serve," she ran an appraising look over him, "with an absolutely superior ass, I'll take you."

"Sure," he said agreeably, moving behind her as she lay back on the bench. The position of course put her where she had a prime view of the bulge of his genitals in the tight exercise shorts and her gaze went pointedly to his face. "If we were somewhere else, say the locker area, I think I could make that come to attention. Interested in another round?"

"Flattered," he said, with an easy grin, though his insides were tight at her intense regard. Not necessarily with desire, though she was adept at stirring a man's lust, whether his mind was interested or not. Quite frankly, he found the pair of them terrifying. Violet would be amused at the thought, he knew, but a man had to be honest with himself.

"I see someone's got your heart as well as your cock on a short rein these days." She smiled herself, and it was a surprisingly pleasant and kind expression. It was an abrupt reminder that Kiera and Tamara, as scary as they could be, kept their intimidation within the rules. They didn't force their attentions where they were not requested, and they did not coerce any sub who said "no". They respected boundaries, and for the first time he understood why Violet was so interested in making him accept that idea.

"Well, good for you both, honey. You and Violet suit. Still, Kiera will be disappointed. Your display at Tyler's was…memorable. Eighty pounds, if you will."

He loaded up the barbell, appreciating that was a good amount of weight for a woman to lift over her head. He stood at careful attention as she took it off the rack and began her reps. She was a finely made woman, and now that they'd established the lines, he felt at ease appreciating the ripe breasts, the soft brown skin, the tight concentration of the full lips, the light sheen of sweat on her working muscles. He found himself gravitating toward the mental image of a smaller, more delicate form in the same position, that small mouth less than a foot from his aching balls. Amazingly, that image tightened his loins in a way that standing right over Tamara's lithe form and hearing her open invitation did not.

Regardless, he suspected Violet would be hard-pressed to believe he was thinking of her if he got a hard-on right now. In fact, he figured she'd probably pistol whip him until his head caved in before he managed an explanation. He grinned at the thought and changed the direction of his thoughts, just to be safe.

"So where is your sister today?"

"Oh, she just went off shift. She was supposed to meet Marguerite for lunch at the Tea Room. Marguerite runs the place, and we're thinking of integrating a classy coffee room here at the club. You know, for clients to enjoy after they have their workout, socialize some more. A kind of franchise of the Tea Room inside of our club. She left a few minutes ago."

"You both work here?"

"She does. I'm actually the owner, she's the manager, so I can pretty much just show up, work out and handle the stockholders. She handles day-to-day stuff in the club. She likes to do that versus any of the aggressive sales stuff, and I hate being bogged down in maintenance and repair details and breaking people into the machines. That's why she's going to see Marguerite. She's working out the details with her now that I've closed the deal."

"You're a good complement to each other, then."

"The joy of being twins." She nodded, and he helped her take it back up to the rack. She sat up, considered him, gave him another sultry smile and a perusal so blatant it had some of the surrounding customers raising a brow or grinning.

"If you ever change your mind, hon, my sister and I'd love to sink our teeth into you. I suspect you're the meal of a lifetime."

"Again, I'm flattered." He inclined his head. "But I think it's fair to say…I'm off the market as long as my—"

He stumbled to a halt. He'd forgotten, and he never forgot. But he'd almost said it aloud, called Violet what his mind had accepted her as. His Mistress. Of heart, mind and soul. Just as she'd said from the very first she would become to him.

"…I'm otherwise involved."

Tamara rose, running her hand familiarly up his thigh, over his hip bone and to his waist. "Our loss, hon. Maybe Violet will share you with us again sometime." Then she left him, drawing the attention of every patron with her African queen looks and the lithe body displayed in the shimmering spandex.

"I hope not," he muttered.

It was getting easier to admit that now. He wanted to be committed to one Mistress, and her to him. While some interactive play was fine, he wanted the main event, the focus, just to be with her. As long as he had Violet, he wouldn't care if he never saw the inside of a BDSM club again.

However, he had other issues to deal with at the moment. Kiera and Tamara worked as a team. Nothing about the crime scene suggested more than one player in the room with the vic at the time of death. He had written off Lisbeth right away. The woman was as frank and honest about herself as she was with her subs. She didn't have any demons in her closet and seemed to have little interest in a man young enough to be her son. There were the five female Doms with permanent memberships, but he was particularly interested in Marguerite Perruquet.

He'd watched her pick up a twenty-something at The Zone the last night he was there. She'd kept the young man at her foot like a pet dog, lapping sparkling tonic water out of a bowl while she talked to other Doms, occasionally slapping him on the ass with a sharp quirt she carried, tucked into a metal band on her forearm. But when she took him down to play in one of the rooms, that cruelty turned to dangerous gentility. She'd put him on a turnstile, raised it vertical, spun him upside down so he could eat her clit, then strapped a cock to his head and made him coordinate fucking her with it while he licked at the base of her pussy, nibbled her thighs. All the while she teased his cock, positioned at her eye level, with her mouth, her teeth, working him and threatening him, telling him he could not come until she did. By the end of two hours, she had made him come for her several times, in a variety of ways where she was alternately playful and vicious, loving and cruel, until Mac understood why she was a Mistress of great popularity at The Zone. A sub's only regret with her would be that she rarely chose the same man for more than one night.

Or maybe she did, but her pickups for longer term relationships didn't occur at The Zone, and those she hooked up with weren't ever going to be able to talk about it.

The early evening crowd thinned, and he went to the locker room before his lingering became suspicious. Police investigative work was ninety percent tedium, two percent clues and eight percent hunches. Of course, this case had been a little less tedious because of Violet. He'd cook her up a quiche tonight. He'd seen what was in her fridge and knew she lived on frozen food. Not anymore.

Once in street clothes and headed for his bike, he was annoyed to see he was parked diagonally from Powell's Lexus, and the arrogant dickhead was in the process of putting a gym bag in his trunk.

Mac passed him with a cold nod and the blond shot him a baleful look as Mac picked up his helmet to straddle the Honda.

"You know what I don't get about you, Mac? You play the game all wrong."

"Not interested, Powell," he said briefly, fitting his key into the ignition.

"You don't get it, Mac. And I thought you would. It's obvious you don't like to give up power, but you resist it out front. I play the game in reverse. They think I'm all theirs, I give them everything they want until the end, indulge every whim, and then when they lose their hearts, I cut them loose. It's a power rush like you wouldn't believe. These Mistresses, they salivate all over you. You could choose any of them, but you get yourself tied up emotionally over a little inexperienced cunt like Violet. All you're really looking for is a ring in your nose. You're not fooling anyone."

"Powell, I'm not going to brawl with you like two kids in a school yard. Skip the goading insults and tell me what you want."

Powell stepped forward and, sensing trouble coming, Mac got off the bike to face him.

"You got me kicked out of The Zone. You're welcome to your opinion but not the right to interfere in my personal dealings."

"Wrong. Protecting a woman, even if she's not his own, is every man's business."

Jonathan sneered. "If she'd chosen me, she'd be so twisted around my dick by now she might as well be on her knees sucking on it."

"You're an asshole, and what burns you is that Violet didn't choose you. She's beautiful, she has taste, and she knows trouble when she sees it. You don't need a Mistress. You need to be neutered."

He knew how to handle an idiot like Powell, so he was ready for the lunge, the swipe of Powell's fist, his keys clutched in them. But Mac was angry as well. Not enough to let it control him, but enough for him to take a split second to consider and then take great satisfaction in following up his block with a clip to Jonathan's jaw. Powell sagged forward and Mac caught him. The sharp jab in his neck spun him around, and he was vaguely aware of Jonathan regaining his balance at his back as Kiera pulled the syringe out.

There was no time for anything. The helmet dropped from his fingers and his body fell into their hands. They effectively used his momentum to roll him into the open door of the van next to his bike. All over in five seconds, and likely not a person around to see it. Jesus Christ, he was in trouble.

* * * * *

"Wake up, sweet thing. Wake up."

The soft crooning of the gentle voice was as melodious as a Motown lullaby, but it brought Mac back to consciousness like a cold spike shoved into his vitals. It took his mind a moment to catch up with the reaction, but the abrupt attempt to lunge to his feet got him nowhere.

He was in Tyler's dungeon, secured over the large spanking bench, stripped naked. Bolted securely to the floor, the bench didn't even quiver when he yanked against his bonds. His waist was on the edge of the bench, his knees pressed into the cold floor. An iron bar attached to a strap around his legs just above each knee held his thighs apart, wide enough that the position caused painful tension in his lower back, buttocks and thighs. He was hyperaware that the position made his cock and balls hang out free and accessible to anything anyone wanted to do to them.

Close to the juncture between testicle and leg, another strap had been buckled around each thigh. His wrists were cuffed and the rings on those cuffs clipped to the straps, so his arms were held immobile at his sides. He had no way to protect his skull from the single bullet he was sure the woman somewhere beyond his field of vision intended to put into it. His head was unsupported over the edge of the bench, his neck muscles groaning in protest.

"Would you like to hear my secrets, Mac? The ones you've been trying so hard to figure out?"

Her voice stayed whisper soft. He knew that type of voice, knew the ice that climbed up his spine from hearing it was not an overreaction.

"I'd rather have you turn me loose," he said mildly, "but since I suspect that's out of the question, go for it."

Blab all you want. Give me some time to think, figure out what chance I've got not to be vic number four.

"You try to play it down," she observed, "But I know how miserable you are. How miserable all of us are. But a Dom cannot escape the pain. She must face it, help her slaves find a release to it, ironically through the experience of physical pain. Do you know what the source of all of it is?"

Mac shook his head. "No."

Abruptly his back was on fire, as a lash came down on it from somewhere behind him. Hooked with barbed tips, it took his flesh with it when it was yanked away.

"No, *Mistress*," she snapped.

Swearing through a haze of pain, Mac bared his teeth. "You're not my Mistress, bitch, so beat me to death, you won't hear it from my lips."

He heard the movement of air as an arm was drawn back for another strike, but the blow did not come. Ten tense seconds passed before she spoke again, and this time her voice was laced with amusement.

"As we told Violet, you're a treasure. Jonathan, please put down the cat and go get the other item I wanted to use."

As Jonathan's footsteps retreated, Kiera's came closer, and then she was in his field of vision, standing before him. She wore a black unitard, no jewelry, her hair slicked back from her face, her boots laced securely to her thighs. Latex black gloves covered her hands up to her elbows. She took a seat on the couch, crossed her legs and laid an arm along the back, as if she had nothing but time, but her eyes had a singular intensity that felt like she was drilling holes in his head already.

"So where is your sister? Is she part of this unholy trinity?"

"Mac," she said, "you don't need to worry about being a cop. You're going to be dead shortly, and all that matters is you'll be free of pain, of having to hide who you are."

"I admit, Jonathan surprises me. *You're* not a tremendous surprise, all in all, but he is."

"Oh, there are even more startling things than that." Powell's footsteps returned. Mac jerked away at the rough touch on his jaw, but it was a futile gesture. Jonathan merely wrenched back his head with enough force to sprain muscles and shoved the ball gag into Mac's mouth, strapping it tightly around his head.

Kiera watched them impassively, then waved Jonathan back. "Give him ten lashes, love, to focus him on what I'm about to tell him, and then I want you to go cuff your left hand and left foot on the St. Andrew's cross. I'll come finish binding you in a moment. We want to be all ready to play when Mistress Violet gets here."

That cold hand around his intestines tightened exponentially and Mac's lips lifted in a snarl he could not voice around the gag.

"Ten, Mistress? With the barb?"

"Yes. Don't worry, love. I told you, he likes pain. Violet will be fine with it."

She looked down at Mac, the corner of her mouth curving. Those large dark eyes were trapped somewhere between lust and pain. Both characteristics obviously dwelled within her in such phenomenal quantities that it was like looking at a person with a demon inside her. The monster was far larger than the body housing it, so that it made every word she said seem distorted, every facial expression an obscene aberration. It was something Mac was sure Powell could not see. He could, because in his line of work, he had seen it up close and personal. A person so far gone in death, blood and their own pain that there was nothing that could save them.

"I told Jonathan how you and I used to play together, and that you enjoyed kidnap scenarios," she said evenly. "I asked Tyler to leave Violet a message this morning, before he went out of town on his book tour, asking her to meet me here this evening for a very special surprise for her. Tyler's very generous with his dungeon for those he trusts, and Tamara and I have used it often. Jonathan rather hates you, so he wasn't keen on helping fulfill one of your fantasies at first. Then I told him you didn't really have any set boundaries, though I'd discovered there are certain things you truly dislike. So my gift to Jonathan for helping was going to be letting him fuck you in the ass. Jonathan's not really into men, but he does have an appreciation for the things that can cut someone's ego down to size, and I personally will enjoy seeing you suffer a bit. He really is like a Dom in sub clothing, a sort of twisted one, but an interesting specimen altogether." A fond look came into her eyes at something Mac was glad he could not see. "Look at him. He's getting hard, just thinking about it. Jonathan, do my bidding."

"With pleasure, Mistress."

Mac sunk his teeth into the heavy rubber of the gag as the metal barb tips struck his back, jerked off more flesh.

Kiera watched him, her face detached. She was in a place where she was seeing things that weren't visible to the rest of them, Mac knew, and it did not seem to bring her any joy, just a grim purpose that boded ill for all of them.

"I can lash you so you'll feel the pain, but it won't draw blood. Jonathan has less experience at that. You'll just have to live with the scarring, at least for a short time." She blinked once.

A second and third strike fell, and Mac felt the pain jolt through his body like electrical current. His shoulder began to itch, as blood made its way down his back over his biceps, getting slowed in the hair on his arms.

"Very few can take it without screaming, but I know you can. Violet is going to be so impressed with your stamina."

The last stroke fell a few moments later, when all of them had merged into one vibrating field of pain on his back. Just as he released his breath, an eleventh came, striking across his ass, a barb catching his scrotum. His incisors sank down, slicing through the hard rubber, the reaction singing up through his gums and jaw.

"Jonathan, that was very naughty. Go cuff yourself."

"Yes, Mistress. My apologies, Mistress." Jonathan snickered.

The pain was unbelievable, worse than being shot, and for this there was no adrenaline kick in, nothing but throbbing, tearing agony.

"Now that you're paying attention, I'm going to tell you my secrets," she said, rising. She squatted down next to Mac and stroked her hand over his hair with her long fingers, following his cheekbone with her nail, pressing down a little hard, watching him as she traced the soft skin just below the vulnerable right eye. Mac kept his gaze steady on hers.

There was no fear now, only fury. He wouldn't give her fear, which meant he couldn't think about Violet getting here. He had to resolve this before then, one way or another.

"You know I like to mix potions. That cat was tipped in a very special mixture I make to punish my baddest boys. It's an alcohol base, mixed with a derivative of crushed nettle juice. Highly irritating, isn't it? It will keep hurting this badly all the way up to the last moment."

She brought her head down closer, so she could speak softly, where Jonathan could not hear. "I don't like to make my subs suffer just for the sake of pain. I draw their pain from them and then I release them with that one shot to the head. You're going to know it's coming, but I didn't want it that way. I don't want to hurt you except in ways that will give you release, focus you on what's important." She glanced toward Jonathan, now cuffed and waiting for her to finish restraining him, making him as helpless as Mac. "But him I intend to shoot between the eyes. Give him a full minute to see it coming, because he's a heartless bastard. Justice can be almost as invigorating as mercy killings, hmm?"

She smiled, feathering his hair off his forehead, as if she were stroking a puppy. "Lord, you are magnificent, you know that? I don't know what it is about you. I suppose you're thinking, Tyler will know who did this. Yes. Yes, he will. So I suppose I'll have to wait for him to come home and take care of that, just as I'll take care of Violet. I'm thinking I'll make it look like one of those 'sad, perverted life' stories. Erotica writer, living on the fringe of society, of reality, plays sick sex games with friends, offs them before he offs himself. And oh..." She put her fingers to her lips, her eyes widening. "One of them is Tampa's finest, a homicide detective who was working undercover to find the S&M killer, and got too close because, he too, sadly, was part of that sick S&M scene. I'm sure that will result in a full departmental investigation, because how could we allow our fine police force to be infiltrated by such a sexual deviant?"

She stroked her finger down the line of his throat, her voice softening. "For you see, that's the problem. We all know what we are, but the world will never accept us. Would you like to hear a sad story?"

I'd like to put you out of your misery before Violet gets here, he thought grimly. How long did he have? Ten minutes? Five? An hour? If Violet had gone downstate to visit her mother, she might not get back until late afternoon, early evening, and then it was ninety minutes to Tyler's from Tampa. He tried not to think what Kiera could do to him in that amount of time, since she'd managed to inflict some serious damage in less than thirty seconds, but it would give him more time to plot a way to stop her before Violet got here. Or maybe Violet wouldn't come. Maybe she'd left a message on his machine that she'd decided to stay overnight at her mom's, or was running late.

Christ, Nighthorse. Focus. Powell's out of the picture, so figure out a way to overpower her. While hogtied to a bench bolted to the floor. Good trick.

"Tamara tried to tell me from the beginning. You see, she knew when we were twelve what she was. I was her first submissive. I delighted in pleasing her, whether it was eating her pussy under the sheets at night, or doing her homework, or giving her my share of Halloween candy. I could sit at her feet for hours just for the pleasure of her touch on my hair. But she trained me to be a

Mistress with her, to understand what it was to release people's emotions through pain, enjoy the sensuality of that, the give and take. When to hold the reins tight, when to let a sub have his head and when to put it to good use." Her lips curved. "One of them came to be quite dear to me. Long after Tamara was bored with him. She didn't really approve of us playing separately, so I had to hide my times with him. It made it even more exciting." Her eyes grew darker and Mac watched the changes in inflection, learning everything he could about her changes in mood and what they meant.

"But I wanted more. For the first time in my life. I wanted to wake up with a man around me in the morning. Silly, wasn't it? Totally impossible for people like us. T told me, over and over, but sometimes the heart just doesn't listen, does it?

"I told him what I wanted, and he said he couldn't. That he loved me, but eventually he was going to have to give up the scene and settle down with someone vanilla, that there was no way he could live his life like this forever and get where he wanted in his career. I lost my pride. I told him I could do that, would do that for him. He cried, told me that 'together we'd always want to play the game.' I could see how much it hurt him, what we could never have but wanted so much. It tore me to pieces.

"It was inevitable that she found out about him, of course. I'm a Mistress, but I'm her sub, and your Mistress always knows everything you're thinking. You and Violet aren't there yet, but you would have been, you already sensed it coming. I broke down and told Tamara everything, the pain was so awful, his rejection.

"She loves me, has always looked after me, so she pretended she was me, went to his parents, told them what he was. Of course, it was his worst nightmare. Or so he always said it would be."

Her expression shifted, became dreamy, the closest to tranquility Mac had yet seen reflected in her face. "Tamara called me, told me to come over to his apartment, that she needed to show me something." She turned those soft brown eyes to him again. "You remember *Bambi,* the original book by Felix Salten, not the Disney whitewashed version? When the stag comes to get Bambi, to show him Man, with a capital 'M', lying dead on the forest floor, shot in a hunting accident? And Bambi is so afraid to get close, because the idea of Man was larger than life to him, something beyond his understanding. I was afraid like that when I walked into the room, smelled the blood. I was so afraid, because he was an extension of who I am, and if it had become too much for him, it would become too much for me. I was doomed. But Tamara made me come look at him, look at his face.

"He had shot himself, and was lying on the bed, curled up as if sleeping. There were thin tracks dried on his cheeks, and the side of his head was all blood. But the amazing thing was his face. His expression. It was so peaceful, so…released at last. It was then I understood, something I don't think even Tamara understood as much as I did at that moment. All of them are looking for that release, all of them who are dedicating so much energy to hiding what they are, keeping it separate from the vanilla world. I can help. What is a sub but a person who wants to return to the bosom of an All-Powerful Mistress or Master, be watched over and cared for? Sometimes, I wish it was me. I imagine it is me, and I can be like them, at peace. But I'm a Mistress, and it's up to me to take care of a sub, help them find pleasure through pain, release through death. It follows and fits, don't you see?

"'There is Another who is over us all, over us and over Him.' Just as Bambi said. I am the 'Other' who can make things right for people like my love, my Thomas. We're all afraid to embrace death, even when we know it's the best thing for us. I could have helped him, so he never had to experience that awful moment with his parents. I could have released him and revealed his truth to them, so they would at last know, as he always wanted them to, but not be around to see their rejection or pain from it. He didn't have to suffer, none of you do.

"Struggle all you want, love," she noted the tensing of his muscles. "Those are lag bolts, holding that into an oak floor with solid sub-flooring beneath. Tyler entertains all sorts of guests here, drives them near insane, so he's made it strong. You'd have to be Superman to get that loose."

She rose, went to Jonathan. Mac shouted around the gag, tried in some way to communicate to Powell the fatal mistake he was about to make, fought the chains, the bench, shoving off with his knees, his thigh muscles straining. Powell glanced over at him, then his attention was caught by his Mistress as she fondled him. He had stripped down, so now he was as naked as Mac. Being naked in the same room with Powell was a nauseating experience all by itself, but as Mac strained at his bonds, the lingering after-effects of the drug they had given him only made him dizzier.

Kiera cuffed Jonathan's right hand, locking it to the cross, bent and did the same to his right foot, completing the process of making him helpless.

She came back to Mac, freed his gag with a rough jerk. "You can tell Jonathan what it is you wanted to say, now that I've gotten you all nicely trussed."

"You might as well kill us both and be done with it," Mac spat out blood, regretting that he just missed her boot. "Violet isn't coming."

"Of course she's coming. I expected her here already."

"Violet was involved in a car accident early in the week. She went to visit her mother today."

Kiera stared at him a long moment and Mac pulled his lips back in a feral grin. "Really messes up your plans, doesn't it?"

"You're lying," she said flatly, though there was a seed of doubt in her eyes. "If that was true, you wouldn't have told me, to buy you more time."

"Unless I'm just sick of listening to your babbling rationalizations of why it's okay to murder people in cold blood." Mac weighed his options and made his choice. Kiera wasn't going to believe anything except what would take her by surprise. "Violet is a cop, like me, Kiera. She shot someone in the line of duty this week. You'd have heard about it on the news. Remember, the highway driver killed by a state trooper? That trooper was Violet. She got a flesh wound and she's on desk duty all week. Tyler probably didn't know she wasn't back at work yet."

"Liar!" She seized the cat and Mac ducked his face automatically, protecting himself as she brought it down. It caught his ear, shoulder, the back of his neck, one cheekbone. The smell of his own blood, the burning pain of his back, all of it was adding to the nausea. *If I'm going to die, let's get on with it before I have to throw up on myself.*

"Why won't you understand that I'm trying to help you, release you from your pain? The hiding?"

"Because I accept who I am, Kiera," Mac snapped. "Unlike you and your dead boyfriend, I realized a long time ago that being a sub is just part of who I am. An important part, but not all of it. I enjoy serving a Mistress's pleasure, as much as I enjoy being a cop, or watching a Buccaneers game, or spending a day out in the Gulf on my boat. Being a sub doesn't make me less of a man. And to Violet, it makes me more of one, more of what she wants.

"All you're doing is making excuses. You're killing because you can't stand your own pain. Your sister fucked up your head early and you're acting out. It's not about you playing God, it's about the kill. Just seeing my blood is starting to make you shake. I can see it."

"What the hell is going on?" Jonathan demanded.

"Well, welcome to the party at last," Mac said derisively. "She's going to shoot us both in the head and make it look like Tyler did it. I'm a homicide cop and I've been tracking her. She's killed three other guys this past six weeks the same way. She'll call your parents after she does it, to make sure your nearest and dearest know what you are." He raised a brow, blinked against the blood running down into his eye. "Do you want my mother's phone number? Oh, sorry, that will mess you up further, because my mother died some time ago."

Thank God, because this would kill her.

"Shut up!" Kiera struck out again. This time her aim was wild, hitting him a glancing blow on the shoulder. She dropped it, turned to a cabinet and pulled out her gun, a polished nine millimeter, a Walther P99. A neat little gun to make a neat hole in his head. Mac forced himself to keep his eyes open as she jammed the barrel against his temple, her trembling finger on the trigger.

"Jesus Christ." Powell yanked against his bonds. "Jesus. I don't want any part of this. Kiera, Mistress..."

"Oh, do shut up." Kiera turned the pistol toward him.

"No," Mac snapped, with enough thunderous force to snatch her attention back to him. "Why kill him first? He's not going to tell anyone about you, a self-centered bastard like him. You want him to suffer, remember? Then he should live."

She hesitated, uncertain, and the gun turned back toward Mac. "I should just kill you," she said slowly. "You're the one who needs release. You're too angry. I can feel how much pain you're in."

Most of it from that damn cat, he thought dryly. "Do it," he urged, his eyes glittering, focused on her, focused on the gun. "Do it and let him go."

"Mackenzie." A voice came down to them from the top of the stairs. "You know better than to give a Mistress orders. I've taught you better than that."

Chapter 21

Son of a bitch, son of a bitch, son of a bitch. Mac would have said it out loud if he thought it would help.

He turned his head over, fighting the sick waves of pain rolling over him. Violet stood at the entrance to the dungeon in street clothes.

"You're not dressed for the occasion," Kiera said, her gaze and the gun swinging toward Violet as his pixie made her way, one casual step at a time, down the stairs.

"I had thought to change upstairs, but I wanted to come down here and see what I was missing. Apparently, quite a lot."

"You stop right at the bottom, and you keep your hands where I can see them. You ruined it, Mac," Kiera said, though she never took her eyes off of Violet. "If you hadn't made me pull the gun, we could have had some fun first.

"I want you to take off your clothes," she told Violet. "Strip down to your underwear, so I can be sure you're not carrying anything, and move slowly. I hate to order a Mistress, but I've got to see this through, you see?"

She backed up as Violet reached the bottom of the stairs, keeping the gun trained on the smaller woman at chest level. That fragile network of curves, flesh and muscle, the vital organs beneath. Panic gripped Mac, caught him up as it hadn't since he was an unarmed rookie in the middle of a domestic fight, a baby in a crib two feet away while the drunk father waved a loaded .38 at the teenaged mother. He had managed that. He would manage this. He would not let Kiera kill Violet. It wasn't going to happen. He made it so in his mind, made it so in his resolve, let it coat him like armor.

"There are only the dungeons for us, Violet." Kiera's eyes were expressive, appealing. "We're like medieval torturers who can only live with the prisoners, dispensing pain and release, never letting the world above see who we all really are because they can't bear our truth."

"Wrong." Violet took the final step down. "I want Mac. In The Zone, out of The Zone. I want to eat dinner with him, watch him shave in the morning, listen to him yell at the political pundits on TV. I want to nag him to mow the yard, and wake up curled up next to him in the early morning." Her glance went to Mac, lingered on his back, the hot fury of her reaction piercing through him, though she kept her voice admirably even. "I want that as much as I want to have him chained for my pleasure in a bedroom. I want him to be there for me, with me. I want him to take care of me, and I want to take care of him. Don't you want that, Mac?"

He locked gazes with her. "Absolutely, sugar."

For a remarkable second, it was just the two of them in the room, all the danger, blood and restraints gone. Then they came back, as Violet shifted her attention to Kiera. "The dungeon is only one part of it, Kiera, as Mac told you. You had one situation that went bad. You could have found someone else if you hadn't given up."

"He won't accept you that way. He's a cop. He can't take you out into the light of a normal relationship."

"Wrong," Mac said. "I can, and I have."

"Your shirt," Kiera snapped. "Now."

"You don't have to do this," Violet said, slowly toeing off her shoes, pulling her shirt out of the waistband of her jeans. "This can't end well, Kiera. It's gotten out of your control."

"Oh, please," Kiera chuckled. "If there's anyone who understands the presence or absence of control, it's Mistresses like us. I've been neck-deep in the practice of it since I was a teenager. You're a rank amateur."

"A Mistress is born, not made," Violet returned. "You're not a Mistress, Kiera. You never were. You're your sister's sub, which makes me the one in the room with the true control. If you give me the gun, it will be over and there won't be any more hurting."

"This is the last time I'm going to tell you. Take off your shirt," Kiera snapped. "And save your pathetic two-hour class in police psychology."

Her finger had moved off the guard back to the trigger. Mac heaved against the bench, heard wood groan.

Kiera shot him a glance. "Give it up, Mac. This is over. If she hadn't been a cop, if she hadn't known, we could have had so much fun with you gagged. I was going to let her play, let her get you and her off one more time. We might even have let Jonathan do you like I promised. You don't understand. But you will. You'll understand when I shoot. I'll see it in your eyes, and we'll all know I've done the right thing. Now, Violet," she snarled.

"Fine." Violet yanked the shirt over her head, pulled it off her arms and flung it into the air between them, a projectile of cloth aimed for Kiera's face.

Kiera's trigger finger jerked, and the gun went off. Eyes locked on the muzzle, Mac saw the gun kick high.

She was going to miss. Violet rammed into the taller woman, sending them crashing over a heavy wooden chair, taking it with them in a tangle of arms and legs. The bullet hit the wall as the gun spun away out of Kiera's hands.

Violet had police training, but Kiera worked out in a gym regularly and had her in strength and weight. When she rolled to her feet and took a martial arts stance, leaped forward and tackled Violet before she could go for the gun, she demonstrated she'd had contact training as well. The two women made it to their feet. Violet landed a punch, but Kiera knocked her back with a hard kick. Undeterred, his fiery Mistress rolled, rammed forward, slamming them against Jonathan's cross. Powell grabbed a generous handful of Kiera's hair, and she screamed, turning on him as Violet yanked a gun out of an ankle holster.

Kiera shoved her elbow into Powell's stomach, gaining her release, and flung herself on Violet before she could get the gun up. She rolled Violet over with another hard kick to her mid-section, taking her wind and making her drop the gun. Violet spun and grabbed her, and they went over Mac, tumbling to the other side of him. Violet landed on the bottom, her head hitting the wall. Kiera struck her, rolled off and scrambled away.

When they rolled over, the bench groaned, and the significance of that exploded in Mac's mind. As Kiera went for the gun and Violet tried to orient herself, he heaved against the bench. Not up and back this time. Left, then right, left, then right.

The anchoring had been designed for the pull of an aroused sub, resistance anticipated forward and back. He snarled, heaved again, side to side, fast as the pumping of a piston, every muscle screaming, demanding release, despite the awkward positioning of his legs. The floorboard cracked, twisted.

He roared, using the sound to galvanize him to further action. The floor ripped in response. The right side of the bench came loose abruptly, unbalancing him. Mac rolled with it, using the momentum to tear the bench free and coming to his feet, face to face with Kiera, who had just claimed the gun and leveled it at Violet. The roll put him squarely in the middle of them. He kept going, a forward charge, the bench anchored to his front like a Roman wooden shield.

Violet screamed his name. The gun fired. Kiera shrieked as he took her down under him. One wooden leg drove into her left breast, the other under her right arm. The impact to the breast caused a scream of pain. Still manacled to the bench, he had no mobility in his hands, and she still had the gun, but then Violet was there, stomping on her wrist, knocking it away, while Kiera abandoned all training and went after his face with teeth and nails.

"Roll off," Violet shouted. Mac obeyed slowly, fighting through a haze of pain roaring through his body as if his insides were on fire, but his sense of self-preservation galvanized him to get him away from those wicked nails. Violet swung down with the P99 and clipped Kiera's temple, stunning her, but the woman lunged forward nevertheless.

"Watch your feet," he managed hoarsely, but it was too late.

Kiera caught Violet's ankle, yanked, making her land with a heavy thud on her back. Violet's foot caught her squarely in the mouth, snapping her head back, and then

Mac was back on her, adrenaline filling in as his body weakened. He aimed better this time. When he landed, the four-by-four solid polished leg of the bench went directly into Kiera's face, caving in her skull with a sickening crunch.

There was no finesse to it, nothing but clear, brute strength, messy and final. Kiera's body went slack. Mac closed his eyes as the burning in his back merged with the burning in his gut. God, he was going to throw up after all.

"Let me out of here!" Powell screamed.

"Shut up," Violet snarled, not bothering to look at him while she freed Mac from his restraints and moved him off the mangled bench onto his back. Onto blissfully cool tile that gave him a second's respite from the fire in his gut.

"Mac. Oh, Mac."

Fuck. He hurt. His hands automatically went to his abdomen, where the bullet had punched through the board and into his body.

He heard a heavy thud above them and started up, but she slid her arms around him. "That will be the local police. We're here!" she shouted as the footsteps continued above them.

"Likely… soundproof," he reminded her.

She bounced up, loosed Jonathan with quick jerks, threw a robe at him. He caught it automatically, but before he could bolt, she caught his cock barehanded and twisted hard enough to turn him white, a maneuver Mac remembered had been very effective on him.

"You go up and show them how to get down here. Tell them we have an officer down and we need EMTs. Right now, you're just an idiot on a questionable kidnapping charge. You run, and I'll have you marked on the attempted murder of two cops, you got me? I'll make sure you get a prison cell with the meanest son of a bitch Master you've ever met in your life, whose idea of a bedtime lullaby each night is making you scream in pain."

Powell bolted for the stairs, but she was already kneeling by Mac again. He was covered in something wet. His own sweat, he realized, though he was trembling uncontrollably. The pain was enormous, sick waves of it.

"Afraid you're not seeing me at my best," he said, through clenched teeth.

Her eyes darkened, "Jesus, Mac, if this isn't your best, I'll be overwhelmed when I finally do see it. You took a bullet for me, you jerk."

"Can't...couldn't...have to protect you. Keep you." Her hands were light, like the touch of angel wings on his flesh. "Sorry I involved you...but you did it."

"We did it, Mac. Mac...Mackenzie," she snapped sharply.

He pulled himself out of the pleasant white haze enveloping him.

"Mackenzie." She was very close to him now, her lips just above his. She had the most beautiful eyes, even when they narrowed as they did now, telling him she meant business, and there'd be hell to pay if she wasn't obeyed. "I absolutely forbid you to die. Do you hear me?"

"Yes...Mistress."

"So all that sappy stuff you agreed to, about wanting to be with me forever, letting me nag you, you just said that to buy us time and save your ass, right?"

He managed a smile. "You bet."

She eased her hand under his shoulder, trying to avoid the torn flesh from the scourging, but Violet could tell all his focus was on the lethal agony in his midsection. He didn't even flinch when her fingernails accidentally caught in a welt, reopened a half-clotted wound on his shoulder.

"Oh, Mac."

"You shouldn't…have come. Could have killed you."

"Don't make me slap you around in your current condition," she said, trying to keep her voice steady, though fury and fear were pumping through her in equal measures. "You'd be dead, she'd be gone and we'd have had to run her down before she got someone else. I was at my mother's late, didn't start here until about 7:30 because I couldn't raise Tyler on the phone."

Had almost not checked her messages, God help her. She kept talking, knowing he wasn't hearing half of it, but hoping he could hold onto her voice like a lifeline. "I knew he had left for his tour, so I figured T&K were in the dungeons with you, waiting on me like he said. Though I couldn't understand for the life of me why you would have agreed to go alone with them without waiting for me, unless…" Her voice caught. "I thought you set it up as some sort of surprise for me. To make me feel better."

"Not brave enough…for that. They…twins…always scared the shit out of me."

She fought tears with the smile. "I was pulling up the driveway at about five after nine when your sergeant called me, said you hadn't reported in. I figured something was up. Mac. Mac!"

"Wh-What?" He blinked his eyes back open, but the pupils were dilated, no focus.

Where the hell were the EMTs? She put her hand over his, over the wound, let him feel her touch over the source of his pain. "Mackenzie, I mean it. You're going to obey me, because you've told me over and over there's nothing you'll refuse me. You understand? I don't care how much you hurt, you will not wimp out on me. You hear me? Mac?" She shouted it, and he jerked.

His silver eyes focused on her for the barest fraction of a moment, enough that she saw he acknowledged her words, lingered on her face in a way that made the tears win, roll down her cheeks. His hand brushed her leg, rested on her thigh. "Yes, Mistress," he repeated. Then he lost consciousness.

*****

They airlifted him to Tampa General. When the copter touched down on the pad, Violet jumped down, a step ahead of the gurney. She stayed out of the way, but refused to be pushed back as the EMTs ran Mac across the ground to the ER doors. Nurses and a doctor burst out, sprinted to meet them, falling in with the rapid procession headed through the double doors to the prep area.

The doctor was young, reminding her this was one of Tampa's teaching hospitals, but she was reassured by his quick fire of orders to place an emergency call for the surgeon on duty. He tapped the bracelet on Mac's wrist. "Get this off of him and get him ready for Dr. Hilaman."

"We'll need to cut it off," the EMT responded. "It's got a key lock."

"No," Violet shouldered forward, yanked the key from the thin silver chain around her neck, snapping it. "I've got it."

They gave her room, and she didn't waste time, lifting his wrist and fitting the key to the discreet locking mechanism. Mac twisted his hand away, bringing up the other hand to fend her off. Even unconscious, he didn't want her to take it.

The emotional reaction overwhelmed her, made her vision gray around the edges, the fear of losing him rushing into that vulnerable opening he'd torn in her heart. But she kept it together, leaned over him, shoving the nurse off her. "I've got it, baby," she whispered. "It's me. Let me take care of it."

She felt the speculative looks of the medical personnel around her, but then Mac's grip slackened and she had the bracelet in her hand.

"You're going to have to stay out here, sugar." The big black nurse was nudging her back with kind but determined intent. "Go give his information to the ER desk. That's how you can help now."

"*Don't* call me that," Violet said, her voice trembling. But the nurse was already gone, behind swinging gray doors that sealed Mac away from her.

* * * * *

"I need to speak to a member of Detective Nighthorse's family."

With his thinning hair and unfashionably plain black frame glasses, Dr. Hilaman looked more like a computer nerd than a surgeon, unless one looked through the lenses of those glasses and saw the hard, direct look to his eyes. They swept the waiting room, took stock of all the police waiting there.

"You're looking at them," Darla said quietly. "Mac doesn't have any living family, doctor. I'm Sergeant Darla Rowe, his boss. I signed the surgical waiver. And this is Violet Siemanski. She's his…" She looked toward Violet, standing next to her.

"I'm his," Violet said simply. "Is he…has he…" She couldn't force herself to finish it, not without a hint of hope visible in Dr. Hilaman's countenance.

It had been eight hours since Mac had disappeared into the surgery. She felt Darla's frozen stillness beside her, of those behind them. His immediate co-workers, Detectives Consuela "Connie" Ramsey and Martin Suarez, and a waiting room full of cops. It seemed like Mac's entire squad had emptied out to share the vigil. As if by being present, they could convince Fate to swing in the fallen man's favor.

"No," Dr. Hilaman said, but there was no easing of his expression, no reassurance of any kind to be found there. He studied them, his gaze shifting between Violet's face and Darla Rowe. "I'll talk to the two of you, then, privately, about his condition. If you'll follow me."

Violet walked at Darla's side, not looking at her, not doing anything but focusing on Dr. Hilaman's back and putting one foot in front of the other. She didn't want to hear his prognosis. She had a sudden, desperate and irrational thought that if she didn't hear it, her will alone could make him survive this night.

Stop it, Violet. He needs you. Don't lose it now.

She remembered the night Mac had held her in the tub, after the shooting. How he had kept the demons from taking her over. Well, she owed him the same. She'd hear Dr. Hilaman describe them, and then figure out how to put herself between Mac and whatever threatened him, drive them off and keep him with her.

Instead of taking them into one of the small anterooms, Dr. Hilaman took them down a hallway closer to the surgery, into an X-ray room, dim except for the series of films placed up on display on the lighted view screens. Dr. Hilaman stopped on the other side of them, leveled his somber eyes on Sergeant Rowe. "I know I don't have to tell you that Detective Nighthorse is in extremely serious condition."

"Violet is a police officer as well, Doctor. We both understand what kind of injury this is."

He nodded. "All right then." He directed their attention to an overlay chart of the human body, pinned up on the wall next to the X-rays. Violet had a difficult time shifting her gaze away from the stark black and white of those X-rays, the shadows and light of Mac's body, to the garish colors of a cartoon-like depiction.

"This is the entry point, through the small intestine. The bullet came in at an angle, and it did significant trauma to the pancreas. The spleen was completely compromised. We removed it. The pancreas is a difficult area to work on, because of the spongy quality of the organ, but we were able to stitch it back together. See this vein here?" He motioned with his pen. "This is the splenic vein. It's a tributary into which a number of veins flow from the spleen, pancreas and parts of the stomach. It, too, was badly damaged and had to be repaired, as well as a whole series of smaller arteries."

"He's not out of the woods yet." Darla spoke in a wooden voice.

"Not by a long shot." It was clear that Dr. Hilaman had a learned opinion of Mac's chances, and Violet watched, her tension building, as he measured their capacity to hear it.

"You don't think he'll make it," she said. Her voice wasn't her own. It was hollow, as if it echoed out of the aching chambers of her heart.

"He's tough, and in good condition, but the overall health of the body has little to do with the prognosis for this kind of injury. The bullet and the debris that it forced into his body—wood splinters, fiber stuffing—they made a mess of one of the most closely knit areas of the human anatomy. The next several days will be critical. If he comes through them, there will still be a long and difficult recovery period. A dangerous one. With this type of injury, late complications could arise. Complications that could cause a serious setback, even death.

"If he makes it through post-surgery period," Dr. Hilaman said steadily, "he will need home care, a nurse. A long period of recuperation, likely six months or more, time for his body to heal from the trauma."

"He'll have whatever he needs," Violet said. "Can I see him? I want to see him."

Need to see him. Touch him.

The doctor looked toward Violet. She put everything she could into her expression to convince him. To make him understand that Mac needed her near, that the connection between them, her strength, her presence, was vital.

"You may sit with him," he said at last. "And you—" He turned to Sergeant Rowe. "You may look in and satisfy yourself that he's alive and getting the best of care.

Ordinarily I'd allow no visitors, but I suspect you both would be in there the moment I turn my back."

"And we are armed," Rowe pointed out, without a trace of a smile.

"There is that."

* * * * *

Violet sat in the ICU, watching lights blink, listening to machines beep, to soft-soled shoes slap with varying levels of urgency up and down the hall. The stench of antiseptic filled her nostrils. She hated it. Hated the wait.

Her hand stayed on Mac's, her fingers tight on his wrist, so every thready pulse beat was answered by the sure sound of her own. Though she didn't trust the beeps from the machines, she marked every tone of them as well, jumping at the slightest variation.

The nurse came in as she did every half-hour, laid a hand on her shoulder. "I'm going to need you to give me a few minutes with him this time, Officer. We need to take some readings. And you need a few minutes' break. Go get some coffee."

Violet knew by the tone of the nurse's voice she would brook no resistance. Since she was allowed here only as long as the nurses passed on good behavior reports to Dr. Hilaman, she knew she had to obey.

Still, she had to set her jaw and firm her resolve for several moments before she could release his hand. The power and virility was leeched from his skin, making him look like he belonged in a coffin. "I'll be right back," she whispered to him, pressing a quick kiss to his forehead, savoring the taste of his skin, still living.

At the end of the hallway there was a cramped nook with a couple of chairs and a side table with old magazines. Violet assumed it was provided for those, like her, who were temporarily ousted from their loved one's side for tests or procedures. Darla Rowe sat in one of the chairs. Violet didn't want coffee, didn't want to be any farther from Mac than she had to be, so she walked the twenty steps down the tiled hallway and took a seat across from her. "Are they all still here?"

"Some of them had to go back to work, or home to their families, but they're taking shifts in the cafeteria on the third floor. I've been getting the reports when the nurse comes out, taking that down to them. How's he look?"

Violet met her gaze. "He's still here."

Rowe nodded.

The two women said very little, but as the moments passed, Violet felt the other woman's regard become more intent upon her, and the weight of unspoken words building between them. She liked the look of Mac's boss, and under normal circumstances would have gone out of her way to be nice, but she wasn't really feeling nice at the moment. Perhaps it was that hostility emanating off of her adding to the rising tension, as much as something similar coming off of Darla Rowe.

"I've been fortunate," the police sergeant said at last, her voice a quiet murmur. "I haven't had to do this that often. But when I have, I've always wondered how platoon leaders do it in war zones. Watch their men go down, knowing that if they'd done one thing or another, it wouldn't have happened. Even when you send them out in the line of duty, you still did the sending."

Violet lifted her head. The early afternoon light was coming through the window in the nook, throwing Rowe's profile into relief. She was hearing a tone of voice she was sure the woman rarely used, because a sergeant couldn't afford to second guess herself, not with a squad of men and women depending on her confidence. But the quiet of this out-of-the-way part of the ICU against the boiling activity just outside it, the strain of keeping watch here in separate solitude for hour upon hour, left time only for contemplation and bitter hindsight, apparently for both of them. Violet was glad for the distraction, she realized, because her own thoughts were eating her alive.

"There were other ways he could have conducted this case," Darla mused. "He was pushing himself to the forefront from the beginning. He said he wasn't her target victim, but I think he expected to be made by her, so he could *make* himself her target. He didn't seem at all surprised when she left a note on the last body, telling him he was next."

"She…what?"

"The bitch addressed it to him."

"And you didn't pull him off the case, then?"

"No, I didn't." Darla leaned forward in the chair, propping her elbows on her knees, looked steadily at Violet. "I trust my people's judgment, Officer." Violet saw her high regard for Mac in her face, heard the pride. "What I didn't see, however, was that he was pushing too hard, and he was already tired. He was way overdue for vacation time. I trusted his instincts, but in this case, you're right, I should have pulled him off the case. He knew what he was doing the whole time, and knew this could happen. It had become too personal."

"Yes, it had," Violet said abruptly. "He was determined not to have another person's trust betrayed, their life taken. And you couldn't have stopped him from trying, exactly because it *was* so personal."

She was furious, knowing Mac had taken the risk, but she understood him enough to know he wouldn't have let it go down any other way. He was that damn stubborn. "Well, I expect he'll get that vacation now." Her voice cracked slightly. She tightened her jaw, looked toward the window.

"Yes, he will." Darla leaned back in her chair, studying Violet in that way that was starting to get on her nerves, so she turned her head, met the sergeant's look head on.

"Is there a problem?"

"My niece has converted to the Wiccan faith."

Violet blinked. "Excuse me?"

Darla shifted, uncrossed her legs, re-crossed them with the right leg on top this time. "I'm fond of her, and so of course I did some reading on it. It's a very alternative type religion, if you're familiar with it at all?"

Violet nodded, drawing her brow together in confusion.

"It attracts some nasty fringe elements, as the road less traveled often will. But at its core, it's a lovely faith, with principles that draw from…" A smile touched her lips that Violet did not understand. "…from natural law. People live in a very unnatural world, Violet. Those who walk outside the lines of that unnatural world, seeking their natural place, the way their instincts call them to be, they often walk a road of high risks for themselves. Doesn't make them wrong, just a bit braver, or perhaps more foolish, than most of us." She let her gaze travel down the hall, toward the open door to Mac's room. "I don't claim to understand the path that calls to the two of you, but I do know it's a hell of a risky lifestyle for two cops."

"All relationships have risks, Sergeant Rowe," Violet said at last, not sure what the woman was after, but giving her the simplest, most honest answer she had.

"So they do." Darla rose, her expression unreadable. "I'm going to go make my rounds, see who's still around, give them a status. What should I tell them?"

"Tell him he's an oak. And oaks survive what no one else can."

Darla reached out, closed her hand on Violet's. Turning her hand over so their palms met, Violet laced her fingers with the sergeant's, gripped hard. She closed her eyes, unable to bear the emotional connection and eye contact as well. She just squeezed, and Darla squeezed back, a silent communication of what the man twenty feet away meant to both of them.

Then she pulled away. Violet waited until Darla's footsteps retreated to raise her lids, which she suspected gave both of them the necessary time to compose themselves. Her timing was good, for as she opened her eyes, the nurse came out of the room, nodded at her. No change, a good thing at this point.

Violet rose, went back to the room. She paused in the doorway a moment, looking at him there. He was such a big man, his feet all the way at the end of the bed, those long arms lying pale and unmoving on the covers. That beautiful chest, the hair she loved completely shaved from it for surgery. But that didn't matter. Sinking down by his side, gripping his hand again, she imagined that the strength and love she'd felt in Darla Rowe's touch would soak into him with her own, reinforce the fight going on inside to keep him with them all.

In the raw clarity that the strain of the past hours had brought to her, Violet knew why she'd been so determined to have him the first time she'd seen him, when she'd sensed he was a cop. A part of her had believed it was a sign, that she'd found the fairy tale, someone who would share her life as well as her bed, someone who understood what she was, who she was. All the corners and rooms. Now, denied his strength, she still wanted him with all her heart, wanted him to live, to be with her, to see if they could make a go of it.

The mother who had held her son through the night when he first had to take a life had died several years ago. The brother had been killed in the line of duty a decade past. She knew they were here, sitting in this room, helping Mac find his way back to her. His living family was right here. Her fingers tightened on him.

She was so tired, but she couldn't close her eyes. Each time she did, she saw it in slow motion, Kiera knocking her on her ass, her head hitting the wall. The struggle to stagger to her feet, her head ringing from the impact. The squeezing panic in her chest, knowing she was going to be too late. She'd thought the terrifying roaring had been in her head, but then Mac had ripped the bench loose by throwing his body to the side and rolled, coming to his feet. That gorgeous mangled broad back shielding her as he charged forward. She'd heard the scream tear from her throat, knew it was not going to stop him. The jerk of his body was the only pause he made, and she saw the bullet punch out of his back, no more than an inch away from his spine, and thud into the wall by her head.

At the time her mind had shut down, refusing to acknowledge it, because she'd needed all her adrenaline to focus on taking down Kiera. But in the helicopter she had seen it replay over and over in her mind, and waves of terror came with every rewind, until she was praying silently over and over for a miracle, praying for the copter to go faster. Praying to go back in time so she could be faster and make it not happen.

There was no worse place to be shot. Dr. Hilaman knew it. Every cop knew it. But she believed in Mac more than in medical science. She believed in his indomitable will, which had resisted her so strongly from the first and yet kept him fused to her, despite his fears of accepting his true nature. Knowing the alternative was unthinkable, she had to believe he would survive.

She knew now that he wanted her as much as she wanted him. At that moment when she had answered Kiera, when her eyes had locked with his, there had been nothing but the truth of their hearts. No time, no shields, nothing but the simple honesty of two lives stripped down to the last breathing moment together.

"Mackenzie." She laid her cheek on his large hand, rubbing against the coarse hair, the rough knuckles. "Wake up. I need you so much."

The tone of the monitor stumbled, made her heart jump three beats. She straightened to glance at the machine. In her peripheral vision, she saw the nurse in her blue scrubs standing in the doorway.

"I think it was just a skip," Violet said. "Damn thing keeps scaring the shit out of me, every time it goes irregular."

"Well, let's see if we can't make it a bit more flatline."

Violet spun.

It was Tamara, not a nurse, standing in the doorway. Kiera's sister, composed as a cold statue, leveled a .38 directly at Mac's chest. Her finger squeezed the trigger.

It was ten feet to the door. There wasn't time for Violet to reach for her ankle piece or do anything but throw her body over Mac's upper torso, curling herself over his chest and head, her own skull an obstacle the bullet would have to shoot through to get to his.

The first bullet ripped through her shirt at the waist, burning her. Violet flinched at the staccato sounds of shots, her heart hammering so loudly against her chest she couldn't tell whether it was her own heart making her jerk, or slugs tearing through her flesh. Mac's hands moved, confused, scrabbling, his subconscious responding to shots the way any conscious cop did, even if he didn't have the physical ability to protect himself. He found her body, gripped, and she held onto him, kept him covered, unable to move even as she heard shouting, running feet, thuds.

"Officer Siemanski! Violet! Violet! Get off him, move off! He's gone flatline."

She heard the horrible whine of the monitor, would have wanted to cease living herself at the sound if her hand hadn't been curled around his throat, feeling his pulse pounding against her fingertips.

"No, the unit's been hit," a nurse called out above the din. "Get a new one in here, stat. Get a cuff on him. Officer, you *have* to move."

A variety of voices, calling at her from different directions, the hands of the nurse, then Suarez and Connie, prying her tight fingers off him.

Pull it together, Siemanski.

Letting go of Mac was the hardest thing she'd ever done in her life, but she managed it, rolled away, let the doctors and nurses swarm over him.

Falling back to the wall, she assessed the scene. Sergeant Rowe was checking her weapon, returning her service pistol to her shoulder holster. She stood just beyond Tamara's body, which was collapsed in the doorway, a macabre sight with nurses and medical personnel stepping hastily back and forth over her while a doctor checked her vitals, confirming that she was dead. Uniforms hovered just behind him, waiting to lift the corpse out of the way. There'd been no time to wound. The sergeant had taken Tamara straight through the chest cavity, twice, and dropped her. Two Styrofoam cups floated in a pool of brown liquid running across the hospital floor, on a direct course to intercept the trail of blood that leaked from Tamara.

Darla's gaze met Violet's. "Thought you could use some coffee," the sergeant said.

Violet nodded, a jerk of her head. The shock and terror were wearing off, leaving anger. Deep, tear-the-ass-off-the-nearest-fool-willing-to-get-close-enough-to-her anger.

"Why wasn't she being watched?"

Consuela Ramsey, standing at Rowe's side, stiffened at the tone. "Early this morning, a uniform informed her that her sister had been killed. She told him that she was going to their parents' place to break the news. She wasn't a suspect, Officer Siemanski."

"So someone was careless enough to let her know Mac was here? Did they just pull their heads out of their asses yesterday? And how the hell did a woman who was a dead ringer for the woman who put Mac in this bed walk through a hospital of cops without a single fucking one of them noticing?"

"Officer," Rowe said sharply. "They were in—"

"Why didn't anyone recognize that she didn't belong on this floor?" Violet snarled. "What, Charles Manson could throw on blue scrubs and waltz right through the children's ward here?"

She had started low, vicious, her teeth gritting over the words, but when she finished, she was one step below an enraged scream, bringing a momentary stunned silence to the room, the hallway, and likely to everyone on the entire floor. The doctor on call opened his mouth to snap at her, order her to get the hell out, she was sure, but before he could, someone else spoke.

"Singing... Beautiful sound."

She whirled on her heel. Past the arm of the nurse checking his blood pressure, Mac's eyes were half-open, looking at her through a haze of pain and drugs. In them she saw a hint of that frightening distance that people teetering on the edge of life and death had. But they were open.

Violet circled the nurse, barely managing not to knock her out of the way, and put her hand against his face. "Mackenzie, you hear singing?" She groped to change gears, had a terrifying, hysterical thought. "Do you hear angels?" She looked around wildly to see if they had him hooked up to a new unit yet, so they could be sure that great heart wasn't grinding to a halt.

He made a noise, bringing her attention back to his face. There was something else in his expression, something it took a moment for her to recognize. Amusement. Amusement with her. His voice was a broken rumble.

"Just one, sugar."

She closed her eyes, put her forehead to his, both hands to his face. She felt his arm move weakly to the edge of the bed, brush against her leg.

"What…happened? Shots."

"Don't worry about it." She stroked his cheek, bent close so all he could see was her. She felt the press of the medical personnel against her, wanting to get her out of there. But this was important, as important to his survival as anything they were doing. "You just have to rest, and get better, because there's a lot I want from you, Mackenzie Nighthorse. I'm not going to let you keep your ass in this bed forever."

"You could…come put your ass in it with me."

Violet brushed her lips lightly over his, nearly broke into tears at the slight pressure of response. The nurse's touch on her arm had become an insistent clamp. "Soon, baby. But let them take care of you. I'll be right here."

He nodded, already slipping off again, but his finger caressed her leg once more. A promise that he'd be back. A promise he would keep, or she'd go yank him out of hell itself.

Violet moved back to the door as the new monitoring unit was brought in with several more nurses to get him hooked back up. Tamara's body was being lifted onto a gurney. A clean-up crew was moving in to handle the rest, the coffee and blood, as other staff members shooed the cops who had responded to the shots back toward the elevators. She thought to look down at herself, and discovered the bullet that had passed so close to her side and through the mattress had only burned the upper layer of skin, nothing serious. Glancing back into the room at the wall, she verified that Tamara had only gotten off two shots. The one that had nearly hit them, and then the one that had gone wild, hitting the unit, when apparently Rowe had put the first shot into her back.

Violet stepped outside of the room, looked down at the bloodstained floor. "I don't know whether to scream at you some more or thank you," she said at last to Mac's boss and Connie, both standing on the other side of the grisly puddle.

Darla put a restraining hand on Consuela's arm when Mac's co-worker curled back her lip to snap. "Easy. We've all had a tough day. Detective Ramsey, please go with the body to the morgue, make sure everything is handled by the book."

Consuela blew out a breath, nodded, giving Violet a curt look that Violet returned with venom. She knew Darla was right. It didn't make her any less pissed.

"I'll put a man on the door," Sergeant Rowe said mildly, though Violet noticed the fingers of her gun hand were quivering slightly, held close to her leg. "I assume Mac's in no further danger, but the hell with it. I don't know about you, but I'd just feel better knowing the protection's there."

Violet looked at that shaking hand, lifted her eyes to Darla's face. "Have you ever—"

"Not in over twenty years on the force. This is my first." Darla gave a shaky laugh. "My nerves are shot to shit. But I'm glad as hell, if I had to finally do it, that it was to protect one of my own. I'm going to go for that coffee and then deal with this mess. Want to come?"

"I'd suggest decaf," Violet said, casting a pointed look at her fingers. "But I'll stick here. Maybe you could bring me back a cup, though. When you're done." She hesitated, brought a couple of dollars out of her back jeans pocket, reached over and put them in Darla's hand, met her gaze. "My treat."

Darla closed her fingers over Violet's, held there a moment. Nodded and turned toward the elevators.

"Oh." She stopped halfway there, turned back. "You know, that was an amazing and selfless thing you did. You better have a good pair of running shoes."

"How's that?"

The sergeant cocked a brow. "Knowing Mac, when he gets out of that bed and finds out what you did to protect him, he's going to chase you down and have your hide."

"He won't have far to go," Violet said, managing a tired smile. "I'll be right here."

Epilogue

Nine months later

Paperwork had kept her late, so the flicker of relaxing candlelight on the back screened porch should have been a welcome sight as Violet took the Stealth over the marsh bridge to their street. Instead, for just a moment, she was torn between wanting to go in and bury herself in his arms, and turning the car around and driving it as fast and far as she could, to outrun the ache that had been growing in her chest ever since he'd returned to active duty a couple weeks ago.

"Damn it, get over it," she snapped.

She pulled up next to his bike and noted that the Aztec lilies she had planted were coming into their second blooming of the summer. Bright, vibrant, passionate red. She had a sudden urge to rip them out of the ground. Instead, she worked her fingertips into the tightness in her temples, staving off the headache, taking a deep breath before she got out of the car.

Once in the house, she tossed her keys on the kitchen table and gave Boscoe his required ear scratching before she blocked out the jumble of emotions, composed herself the same way she did right before she went to work, and headed for the back porch.

Mac rose from his hammock chair, his smile easy but his eyes showing his concern, and she knew she wasn't masking her feelings well enough. He touched her face, curling a loose auburn strand back behind her ear, brushed his lips across hers. She fought back the urge to devour that firm mouth, to press her nose against him and just inhale all of him into her.

"Good day?" he asked, pulling off his wire-framed reading glasses. A very sexy accessory she hadn't even known he used until she had moved in here six months ago to oversee every halting and occasionally harrowing step of his return to health.

During that period, Violet learned that time could be slowed down and valued, one tick of the minute hand after another. Insurance and the same family trust fund that had paid for her Stealth paid for a home nurse when he was allowed to leave the hospital, but she took over the evening shifts, effectively moving into his home.

Boscoe staked out a spot on the sofa and became Mackenzie's watchdog when she wasn't around. She planted mums by his door in the fall, set a poinsettia on the kitchen table at Christmas and held Mac's head in her lap when he fell asleep on the sofa at nine-thirty on New Year's Eve night.

There were many times that the powerful man she loved had been filled with rage at the weakness that barely got him to the bathroom on his own. When it got to be too much, he took out that anger on her, the nearest target. In return, her fear would goad her to tear his ass apart verbally when he did too much and wore himself out.

But then one day the tide turned, and she saw him start to grow stronger. He began to do desk work for his job, investigative work, and returned to working out with weights to build up a body that had gone lean and gaunt from the months of recovery. She would come home and find him sweating and tired, but with a triumphant gleam in his eyes that told her he was getting better.

They made love several times then, carefully, gently. But she was afraid to do more, demand more. Over the nine months it took him to recuperate, D/s was an area they did not touch. He had reclaimed the bracelet, asked for it the moment they would let him wear jewelry in the hospital again, but she had not moved to reclaim the rights that went with it.

She couldn't initiate it. She didn't know why, because she knew the longing was still there in her, but she had no emotional strength to face what it was that was keeping her from going there with him. When they made love, she sensed a hesitance in him, as if he was waiting for something from her, but she turned away from it, squelched it with the passion of vanilla lovemaking, and stopped the topic from coming up.

"Good enough," she responded, taking a seat across the side table from him, close enough that they could link hands as they always did, establishing a loose connection. He poured her a glass of wine, and then he surprised her by bending over, untying the canvas sneakers she'd changed into before she came home, and taking them off, his hands gently taking her feet up to his lap to massage them.

"Mmmm." She made the casual noise of pleasure, but her gaze was riveted on the way those long-fingered hands moved over her arches, caressed her toes. The way his T-shirt stretched over his shoulders as he bent to remove her shoes. "We stopped a car carrying a kilo of coke this afternoon, but they're trying to get off on a technicality. You heard about that?"

"On the radio." He nodded at the police issue he kept just inside the door of the house. "Caught the tail end of it when I got home. George was an idiot, searching the car the way he did."

"So do you think we have a chance of making the bust stick?"

As he gave her his opinion, she put her lips to the glass, let her eyes fall shut. That deep, melodic voice, the joy of being able to listen to every syllable, set off an odd trembling deep in her stomach, a need so strong it spread through her limbs.

She didn't know when the words disappeared. His voice just became the music her soul yearned to embrace, to compose the right notes to make their songs come together again, as easily and beautifully as they had before.

His hands touched her face, and her eyes jerked open. She stared at him, leaning over her, and he lifted his hand, showing her the tears from her eyes wetting his fingers. He studied her, and she saw something in his expression, something that made the ache spread.

"I'll go check on—"

"No, you won't. Come here, sugar," he murmured.

Before she could object, he had his arms around her and he pulled her over onto his lap, cradling her. She knew he had built up his strength again, but it was surprising to feel how much, because she hadn't availed herself of it. For so long, she had been focused on the areas of his health that needed bolstering. Her body tightened in need and want in a way she had not permitted it to do for some time.

"Let it go, Violet," he said softly against her hair. "I swear to God, if you don't, I'm going to slap you around."

She shoved against him, trying to get away, and he simply yanked her back. She struck at him and he blocked her, capturing her arms, proving without a doubt he'd regained his physical supremacy over her. She punched and pummeled, shouted at him, and he hung on grimly, until words became curses and curses became tears.

At last, when Mac thought he was going to have to shake it from her, great racking sobs tore out of her chest. She collapsed against him, too exhausted to fight anymore. *Thank God.*

It was the hardest she'd ever cried in her life, Mac was sure. What was more, he knew the cause of every single tear that dampened his shirt front.

For nine months, he had watched her suppress every tear, every complaint, every worry for him behind an inhuman level of energy focused on making him better. Now, at last, she cried for each awful moment since that terrible night in the dungeon. For every time she'd been vicious to him to make him take his medications. Every countless instance she'd bullied, coaxed or teased him into resting so he wouldn't kill himself with the frustration of inactivity. All the times he'd felt her lie awake for hours next to him, barely breathing herself as she'd kept a hand on his chest. Her terror that he would leave her in the night had been a palpable thing. Too weak to hold her or comfort her, at times he'd wished he could die, just so he wouldn't cause her such pain.

But she wouldn't let him, and he learned that a person could love too much. She had shut down her own emotional and physical needs so effectively that she didn't know how to get them started up again. His going back to active duty had been the catalyst for her deteriorating temperament, the reason as obvious to him as it was incomprehensible to her. Well, he was better now, and he wasn't having any more of this bullshit.

She had soaked his T-shirt. When she ran out, ran down to hiccupping sobs, he removed the garment so her cheek wouldn't be against the wet. He used a dry portion of the cloth to wipe her running nose, dab at her eyes. She watched him as he did it, her beloved face confused and young. Pushing her head back beneath his chin, he coaxed her into nestling her cheek against his bare skin.

They quietly watched the sun go down. He didn't say anything, simply stroked her back, her neck, her hair. Her hand crept over the scar on his belly, her other palm around his back, on the marks of the lash that would always be there.

He lifted his head, brought his hand to her jaw and made her look into his eyes. "It's over, Violet," he said, and his voice was rough. "Don't let it take any part of what we were from us." He caught her hand from his stomach and bit her fingers, not gently. "I'm yours. I never stopped being yours." He kissed her lips, hard, willed her to nip at him as she had done once. When she would have turned her head away, shielding her reaction, he caught her chin in a hard grip, yanked her face back to his. Saw a flash of temper.

"I didn't die, because you ordered me not to. You don't get more 'yours' than that. I wear your collar." He raised his arm, showed the bracelet to her. "Because I want you more than I've ever wanted any fucking thing on earth. So don't deny me any part of yourself, and goddamn it, accept me again. Let me please you, Mistress. Tell me what you want."

Her throat worked, but he didn't see tears. He saw a glimmer of something, something he had hoped to see for nine of the longest months of his life.

"I love you, Mackenzie," she said at last.

"I know that."

She smiled, a tentative gesture, but genuine. "Arrogant jerk."

His hand slid down her shoulder, grazed the side of her breast. During the summer, she always changed out of her uniform before she came home from work, so she wore thin cotton drawstring trousers and a cropped halter top. He placed his palm on the bare expanse of her stomach and moved up, taking up the hem of her loose shirt, sliding it until her left breast was uncovered, displaying the lace of her bra cup. His fingers traced the nipple beneath, and then he pushed the cup down and lowered his head to suckle her. His hand came around to her ribcage, to hold her firmly to his mouth, and she laid her hand on his head, tugging on those curls as his head moved.

"Mackenzie…" she murmured, her thighs loosening, wanting him, aching for what she felt going on beneath her squirming buttocks. She wanted him so much, she was just so afraid…

"Damn it, Violet. I'm yours. I'm *yours*." And in his frustration, he scored her with his teeth, caught the side of her breast, goading her.

Something cracked within her, something that was pain and joy both, a bright, excruciating light, merciless in its heat and power. It felt like a granite wall breaking up inside her body, pummeling the softest, most vulnerable parts of her.

She caught his face, pulled it away from her, met flashing silver with her own determined gaze. "Then fuck me, Mackenzie. Take me. Make me as much yours as you are mine. Leave your mark on me, be as rough as you've wanted to be all these months. Let me feel the animal in you I've always known is in there."

They stared at each other for a long moment. The sun was melting on the horizon, a flood of orange fire that glinted off the light in his eyes and matched what was rolling through her blood, flame hot as the purifying depths of hell.

There was a moment of hesitation, but only a moment. Abruptly he was out of the chair, taking her with him, and he spun her, shoving her down onto her belly on the mosaic table. "Spread open for me then, sugar," he whispered. She gasped as he ripped the seam of her loose pants and the panties beneath in one tear, exposing her to the humid air, relieved only by the lazy turns of the ceiling fan above them. She had a moment to adjust her knees before his foot was against her instep, knocking her feet out wider, a cop move that made her instantly, gloriously wet. His arm snaked around her waist and he yanked her back against him, her hips in the air, her feet leaving the floor, toes not even brushing. She caught hold of the rough grooves in the table surface, the pads of her fingers holding on, looking for an anchor, but there was none but him.

He sheathed himself in her. Hard, brutal, shoving home into her like the slamming of a magazine into the stock of an automatic. She screamed at the combination of pain and pleasure, and knew how much she had missed this, the desperate urgency of a powerful man. Her powerful man. He pulled all the way out, stroking her clit with his broad head, then slammed into her again, jerking her body forward on the table.

"That's your cock, Mistress," he gasped. "Take every goddamned inch of it and scream for mercy, because I'm not feeling merciful. All I want is to feel that sweet pussy of yours sucking on me until eternity crashes down on us."

It was absolution. Because she felt it from him, all of a sudden she understood it, understood why she hadn't been able to let go, embrace him again as she'd wanted to do. It was so absurdly obvious.

She'd blamed herself. She thought she should have been faster, better. She was supposed to keep him safe. He was giving her the punishment she wanted, stroking away the pain while offering her the gift of himself, a complex give and take she was helpless to explain. With every stroke, she knew he was telling her that, come hell or high water, she was his Mistress.

His hands cupped her breasts, gripped them in his long palms, used that grip to increase the impact of each hard thrust into her, squeezing her nipples between the fingers of both hands.

"You've got a beautiful ass, Mistress," he muttered. He lifted her up higher so it was arched high in the air as his cock continued to pound into her relentlessly, her feet dangling. She was leaving nail marks on the table.

"You'd rather sink those little claws into me, I know." His breath was hot over her ear. "And you will. Again and again, until I carry your scars on my back and I'll be proud as hell of them. But tonight you'll wear my mark."

She sucked in a gasp as his teeth sank into her shoulder, quick, precise, deep, and the pain surged through her blood like a sweet drug. He held on, like a stallion holding a mare in place with his strength. God, she couldn't believe how much she'd missed his strength, that strength that could mesmerize her, but was also all hers to command.

The climax built higher and hotter than the hottest Florida sun, and she was whimpering with each stroke, unable to get a purchase on the table, not wanting one, but feeling out of control, rushing at breakneck speed to where they were going. All her fear and guilt were being swept away before physical response, and her breath was harsh and loud as the slap of his thighs against the backs of hers. His fingers dipped, caught her clit and began to manipulate it.

"Oh, no..." She went over the crest like a rocket, her hand clinging to his other arm, now anchored firmly just above her breasts. Her body strained forward, unable to do anything but convulse in the throes of the strong climax as he brought her down on him again and again. His thighs quivered, his breath rasped, and she cried out with him again as he shouted out his release. His cock worked inside her like the power of life itself, virile and potent, creating mysteries beyond the desire for knowledge, taking them into the realm of blind faith.

She clung to him, let him make her serve his cock until he chose to slow, until her cries became soft, mewling whimpers. At length, he eased her forward so she was flat on the table, his knuckles rubbing a soft caress between her shoulder blades as her deep pants slowed into soft sobs, quiet hitching breaths.

He leaned down and placed a soft kiss in the center of her back, dwelling there, a tender, rubbing caress.

"My Mistress is generous, and kind," he said softly. "But she's done nothing to deserve a punishment from her slave."

"It's not a rational thing," she whispered. "I just needed to know…I needed to give you that."

"As I said, my Mistress is generous," he responded simply. She was limp in his arms as he turned her, lifted her into a sitting position so they were facing each other. His cock was glistening with her come and his, and the beauty of his slightly damp, living breathing body overwhelmed her. He fastened his jeans and then lifted her in his arms.

"Should you—"

"Ssshh…" He took her inside, to the bathroom, set her down on the lid of the commode. "You worry too much."

"What are you doing?" He took out a bottle of peroxide, several cotton balls.

"I want to make sure I don't cause you any infection."

She turned her glance to the teethmarks. "I wasn't expecting that."

He went to one knee, dabbed the cotton at her shoulder.

"You wanted the animal. You can call him when you want him." Something in his voice turned her to him, made her lift his chin so she could see his face.

Mac closed his hand over hers, held her gaze. "I've seen it enough to know it lives in all of us, and it's not always a bad thing. You bring it out in me, and only you can harness it. Don't stop being my Mistress."

"It's not a choice I have." She smiled. She placed her forehead against his, closed her eyes. "Oh, Mac."

"I know, sugar." His hand cupped the back of her head. "We made it, and you did it. I love you with all I've got. Let me take care of you again, as I've wanted to, for nine fucking months. Don't be afraid."

Everything inside her loosened inside at his low, fervent tone. "I want to spend my life being your Mistress." She raised her head, looked at him kneeling at her feet. "I want to make you beg for my pussy, see your fine ass every day and know it's mine to do with as I wish."

He arched a brow. "Pretty unorthodox marital vows."

"Was I proposing marriage?"

"Sounded a bit like it. Sounded a lot like it."

"Okay, then. Let's say I am." She tried for a teasing note, but her voice shook. "What do *I* get, if you accept?"

He put down the cotton balls, took both her hands in his. "I'll make you feel so loved and desired, sugar, you won't know where one ends and the other begins. What's more, it won't matter. You won't need to separate them."

"Okay," she said, only a little terrified. "So, how will this go, then? You promise to love, cherish and…"

"Obey," he murmured, a whisper from her lips.

The kiss was hungry and powerful, and she gave herself over to it. To have his tongue inside of her mouth, her own curling deliciously into its grasp, feeling his flesh give way under the not-so-gentle bite of her teeth. To be as rough as she wished, to hear him growl against her with need. When she pulled back, she saw he was fully erect again against the crotch of the jeans.

"I think you have a little trouble with that last vow," she gasped. "We'll have to work on it. In fact, I'm thinking

I might need to take you to bed and remind you who your Mistress is. Right now."

Lord, please, now.

"There's no one I'd rather have set me straight. Though I expect it will take a lifetime." He smiled that smile that melted her heart, started to get to his feet.

"We'll see," she sniffed. "I'm giving you sixty or seventy years to shape up, Mackenzie Nighthorse. After that, I'm dumping your ass."

He grinned, caught her lips in a kiss again, swung her up in his arms. "Try it, sugar. Just try it."

About the author:

Joey W. Hill lives on the Carolina coast with her wonderful husband and a houseful of animals. She is published in two genres, contemporary/epic fantasy and women's erotica, and has won awards for both.

Joey welcomes mail from readers. You can write to her c/o Ellora's Cave Publishing at 1337 Commerce Drive, Suite 13, Stow OH 44224.

Why an electronic book?

We live in the Information Age—an exciting time in the history of human civilization in which technology rules supreme and continues to progress in leaps and bounds every minute of every hour of every day. For a multitude of reasons, more and more avid literary fans are opting to purchase e-books instead of paperbacks. The question to those not yet initiated to the world of electronic reading is simply: *why?*

1. *Price.* An electronic title at Ellora's Cave Publishing runs anywhere from 40-75% less than the cover price of the exact same title in paperback format. Why? Cold mathematics. It is less expensive to publish an e-book than it is to publish a paperback, so the savings are passed along to the consumer.
2. *Space.* Running out of room to house your paperback books? That is one worry you will never have with electronic novels. For a low one-time cost, you can purchase a handheld computer designed specifically for e-reading purposes. Many e-readers are larger than the average handheld, giving you plenty of screen room. Better yet, hundreds of titles can be stored within your new library—a single microchip. (Please note that Ellora's Cave does not endorse any specific brands. You can check our website at www.ellorascave.com for customer recommendations we make available to new consumers.)

3. *Mobility*. Because your new library now consists of only a microchip, your entire cache of books can be taken with you wherever you go.
4. *Personal preferences are accounted for*. Are the words you are currently reading too small? Too large? Too...**ANNOYING**? Paperback books cannot be modified according to personal preferences, but e-books can.
5. *Innovation*. The way you read a book is not the only advancement the Information Age has gifted the literary community with. There is also the factor of what you can read. Ellora's Cave Publishing will be introducing a new line of interactive titles that are available in e-book format only.
6. *Instant gratification*. Is it the middle of the night and all the bookstores are closed? Are you tired of waiting days—sometimes weeks—for online and offline bookstores to ship the novels you bought? Ellora's Cave Publishing sells instantaneous downloads 24 hours a day, 7 days a week, 365 days a year. Our e-book delivery system is 100% automated, meaning your order is filled as soon as you pay for it.

Those are a few of the top reasons why electronic novels are displacing paperbacks for many an avid reader. As always, Ellora's Cave Publishing welcomes your questions and comments. We invite you to email us at service@ellorascave.com or write to us directly at: 1337 Commerce Drive, Suite 13, Stow OH 44224.

ELLORA'S CAVE
ROMANTICA PUBLISHING

Printed in the United States
79341LV00009B/5

9 781419 951657